HUNTERS OF THE COLUMBIAN MAMMOTH

adrian del valle

© 2017 adrian del valle
All rights reserved.

ISBN: 197960603X
ISBN 13: 9781979606035

For my brothers and sisters

Lucy Peter Valentine Efrain Charlie Victor
Augustina Francis Danny Rosie Alphonso

Other novels by
Adrian Del Valle

Curby

Diego's Brooklyn

Emanuel

Searching for the Sun

Short shorts

The Piano Player from Greenwich Village

I would like to express my deepest appreciation to
Arthur Cintron for designing and illustrating the cover.

CHAPTERS
(It is recommended that the reader book mark the appendix section)

Chapter 1	Pronghorn Plateau	1
Chapter 2	Matwau's Valley	24
Chapter 3	Ayashe	44
Chapter 4	Saber Tooth Tiger	85
Chapter 5	The Falling River	115
Chapter 6	Otaktay's Village	125
Chapter 7	Aleeka	148
Chapter 8	Nakoma's Tribe	180
Chapter 9	The Thunderfoot Trail	230
Chapter 10	The Scavenger's Wrath	242
Chapter 11	Mantotohpa's Tribe	256
Chapter 12	The Path To First Hunter	281
Chapter 13	Otaktay's Tribe	313
Appendix		341
Wyoming Paleo Indian Glossary		344

CHAPTER 1
PRONGHORN PLATEAU

Paleoanthropological dig site, Central Wyoming
August, 09, 2017

Following an urgent phone call, Dr. Halstrom flew back to Casper-Nanona International Airport and returned to the dig site at Pronghorn Plateau. After parking the loaned Land Rover next to the field tent, he stepped inside. As he had done earlier that week, he reviewed the rest of the paper work he had started, shuffling them around in order of importance.

"Dr. Halstrom! You must come quickly!" Without a welcoming greeting or waiting for an answer, Dr. Petak Singh headed back up the hill to the current face of the team's dig.

"Yes, give me a minute." Busy with paper work and the ever present drive for funding the project, Dr. Halstrom barely looked up. "I'll be right there, Petak."

Meticulous to a fault, he stacked the papers he was going over according to the donors with the most money potential, weighing them down with rock paper weights. He then left the tent, making sure to zip up the screened opening to keep out flies.

Standing before the current dig site, he put his hands on his hips. "So, what exactly did you guys call me back for? Good heavens!"

Singh's smile stretched wide. "It is too exciting, Dr. Halstrom, is it not?"

"Careful with that!" said Dr. Halstrom. Get those students out of there. I don't want anyone inside that grid except for you and Dr. Anderson."

Dr. Barbara Anderson, in jeans and a plaid cotton shirt, the long sleeves, rolled up, wiped sweat from her hazel eyes with the back of her hands. Underneath the dirt and grime, her face was pretty, her petit frame, strong from athletics during her college years.

"This is unbelievable. I think we have two perfectly preserved skeletons from the Paleolithic Period," she said. "Apparently, this soft clay material kept everything intact. We knew we had something important, but didn't want to get ahead of ourselves when we called you in New York."

"Yes, it was surprising to everyone involved that anything like this could have been discovered here," said Dr. Singh. "Especially with the remoteness of this plateau. This has certainly been a lucky find."

Nodding, Dr. Anderson agreed. "It was fortunate for us that Jesse Thompson, the owner of the ranch called us after they took away that old, crumbling barn. Who would have thought such a find could have been buried underneath all of that rubble. And here we thought it was only going to be about the Paleolithic Indian tools the workers found here."

"Like the Clovis points? I was hoping for another toe bone from Denisovan," said Dr. Petak Singh.

"Giant Neanderthals?" She frowned. That DNA evidence was from Spain."

"You're forgetting about the two teeth and the toe bone from Siberia."

"Um...so I did...for the moment. It's just not enough to convince me that large populations of huge Neanderthals were in Europe...or here in the Americas, for that matter. As you already know, humans didn't cross the Bering Strait until after the major ice ages were over. That was long after Neanderthals went extinct."

"Or absorbed into the European and Asian populace. I believe their genes range around two or three percent in those groups, Dr. Anderson."

"Yes, and that would mean you and me," she replied. "Beringia and the subsequent migration of game animals that crossed that land bridge is what brought humans to the Americas at least twelve thousand years ago and possibly as much as sixteen thousand. It was the beginning of the spread of humans that would eventually reach all the way to Tierra del Fuego at the tip of South America."

"Hold on and stop arguing for a minute." Dr. Halstrom climbed down a short aluminum ladder into the hole in the ground. He squatted before the partially exposed bones, took out a magnifying glass from a deep pocket in his cargo shorts and scanned the skull nearest him. He then picked up a four inch long spear blade lying next to one of the buried bodies, well-honed and made of quartz. "This fellow under here was definitely well built."

"And at least six feet tall, according to our measurements," said Anderson.

"Fourteen thousand years before the present, according to our preliminary measurements, Dr. Halstrom," Singh blurted out, still reeling from the excitement of the find.

"Yes, we'll send out a sample for carbon dating to verify that. Hey, Petak, look at this spear blade! This is amazing! It's perfectly honed."

Barbara Anderson stared at it and then looked down at the bones. "Obviously it's some kind of ritualistic burial. I'm starting to see what appears to be saber tooth tiger claws on the male's chest."

"Smilodon!" Said Dr. Singh.

"We'll have to first meticulously clear out all of this clay material to be sure." Halstrom turned the blade over. "I love this quartz blade."

"Perfectly honed and fluted," Said Singh.

"Right, typical for a Clovis point," Halstrom agreed.

"These claws, Dr. Halstrom…I'm inclined to believe that they may have been part of a necklace."

Dr. Halstrom stared at it. "Obviously, you're right, Singh, each one has a hole in it. The sinew that held the necklace together decayed into nothing, leaving only the claws. Okay, let's get busy. Tell the students they're not to say a word to anybody."

Noon: next Day

Anderson, sitting inside the grid, leaned back against the dirt wall. "Phew! I'm exhausted."

"How come? Me and Petak did most of the work this morning!" Halstrom teased.

Anderson laughed. "Very funny! At least we can see almost all of it. This female skeleton next to the male is beautiful!"

"Strong, too! Look at those leg bones," he said.

She peered at him, pensively. "If she was alive today, my guess would be that she was into gymnastics. From the thickness of the bones she appears to have been quite muscular."

"And old. These two lived to a ripe old age."

"Certainly not like the rest of the ones we find from this time period."

"Forty years! That was the average life span," said Singh.

Barbara scratched the bridge of her nose with a dirty finger. Her blond hair, straggly and full of dust, reached to her shoulders. Turning the brim of her Seattle Mariners cap backwards, she perused the skeleton from head to toe.

"What's this?" She reached across the male's chest and picked up a finger bone nestled on top of the female's ribs. "How do you suppose this finger bone got here? They have all twenty of theirs, so where do you think this one came from?"

"Maybe it was part of the ritual," Halstrom said.

"Maybe!"

"Or a necklace," Petak surmised. "Someone important to her, like a long lost relative. That's why there's a hole in it for the sinew to go through---like the claws."

"Let me see that!" Doctor Halstrom examined the finger bone closely. "This is from an adult male and cut from his hand with a sharp instrument."

"That isn't something you would do to a family member," said, Barbara.

"I wouldn't think so, but let's not jump to conclusions. It could also have been a keepsake for a lost loved one...like you said before, Petak. In the meantime, it may take the rest of the year before all of the studies come back."

The three paleoanthropologists sat resting in the grid, elated at the find of the decade. Dr. Halstrom admired the condition of the two specimens and the attention to detail in the conjoined burial.

These two may have been a mating pair. Why else would they be buried together like this?

Halstrom could easily imagine the life they must have lived. It pleasured him to entertain thoughts of that pristine existence—a time before civilization and all of the modern, so called progress of today's times.

He glanced back at the two recent doctoral graduates. "I wonder what kind of lives these two had. I can't help but believe that they lived in a world of beauty."

Barbara Anderson shrugged, "I'd like to believe that, myself. In a lot of ways, I wish I could have lived back then. Just think, the world was so uncomplicated, so uncluttered, so...so..."

"Unpolluted," Singh interjected.

"Yes...definitely," she agreed. "Just, man against the elements."

Petak sighed. "If only we could go back to see what these two saw when there were mammoths and giant sloths to hunt."

Halstrom shook his head. "Don't forget about short faced bears. They stood as high as ten feet and weighed up to two thousand pounds. And what about dire wolves? The males could get as big as one hundred and seventy five pounds, as big as a modern day Saint Bernard, except that they ran in packs. You better sharpen your spear, Petak."

"I'm thinking I should do that, Doctor Halstrom. Maybe I can find a pretty Indian girl like this one, yes?"

"Actually, you wouldn't have had to worry about predators or even those giants. You would have been a member of a clan; a tribe. You had their protection. The biggest threat to injury and death, in my opinion, would be when hunting the Columbian Mammoth. We're talking about an animal twice the size of Jumbo. He was the record breaking elephant in the Barnum and Bailey Circus. In comparison, a bull Columbian mammoth could get as heavy as twenty two thousand pounds and we're not even talking about the occasional specimen that can grow larger than the average. Like you, Petak, I wish there was a way we could go back and see the lives these two had. That would be amazing."

Spring, 11,980 BC

A thin line of smoke lifted feather light and grey before the distant cliffs. Far below, a black raven soared in a wide circle, 'rose upward with a thermal and then screeched as it flew over the lone tribesman's head.

Man That Runs Too Fast stood alone and awestruck at the immense valley before him, pristine and untouched he had thought by any tribe he knew of. That was until he saw the smoke and it made him uneasy. It had been a long while since he had seen signs of another human and that was well before the cold of winter.

Spring---a time of new life. The air settled warmly over a valley full of game, berries and grubs. The highest peaks lie far behind, the long walk across the forest and mountains, a hardship.

Overhead, white clouds drifted in a sky as calm as a sky in the aftermath of a storm. The new sun spirit shined brightly, the fragrance of the valley, filled with ripe growth. Nearby, a stream splashed noisily as it rolled over moss covered rocks. It twisted and turned, splashing its way through dense groves of horsetails that grew wherever level flood plains spurred out. Disturbed beds of duck weed, cast off by the current, floated along with it toward the valley floor.

The heavy seal skins the lone Bandu wore had served well in the frigid mountains. Here, they were too cumbersome and no longer needed. He loosened the sinew from around his waist and let the garments fall where he stood. Foot coverings, simple wraps made of deer hide that had to be replaced often, were dropped alongside. A wolf-skin vest and firm fitting leggings, also made of deer hide, were left on top.

Man That Runs Too Fast, or Lan as his fellow tribesmen called him, stood tall, his torso, long and hard---his muscularity, honed to perfection from countless hunts. He untied the sinew from a snake skin bandana, the ends of which held two of his deceased father's molars in deference to the elder's life spirit. The braid that everyone in his tribe wore was untwisted and left to fall dark and wavy over his shoulders, partially obscuring the tribal scars decorating his skin.

Of most importance was the forewarning of the raven that flew high and saw dangers before-hand. Made up of curvilinear lines and webbed scrawls, the scarred wings covered most of his back, fanning out to the shoulders. Tattoos of vipers encircled veined biceps, spitting poison at their own tails.

From his neck hung saber tooth tiger claws, their dagger like points, resting against his chest. His pectorals stretched tautly and were well defined---the outlines deep---the skin---hairless. His face was naturally hairless as well, clear and wind burned with masculine creases between the lips and cheeks. Strong jaws held a set of even teeth as white as sunlit snow---his neck, thick and well-muscled. To his ankles were fastened bear claw necklaces, a bear he once killed with blood-letting arrows.

Lan stepped up to his waist into cold, clear water and faced the valley, tall, naked and resplendent in his tribal wares. Before him the wind brother lifted his arms and blew a long breath that bent the horsetails back---sent seeds by the hundreds to scatter like snowflakes into the distance. Above, in the full glare of the new sun brother, two orioles sky danced with dips and curves, their colors masked black against the brightness of the sun. A light wind fell warmly onto his skin, the only sound, the running stream and the orioles overhead.

Before this long journey over the mountains had ever begun, he had spent the winter by the ocean in a limestone cave. The cave had proved to be a safe one and far from the dangers of warring tribes. Along the coast, shell fish and seal were plentiful. The maritime air, although often windy, was warmer than it would have been further inland. Here in this valley, during the mid-days of spring, it was pleasant.

Inside of the depths below, smoke from a single campfire sifted into the clear radiant sky. A number of smoke plumes would have pointed to a settlement. One could judge the size of a tribe by the number of their fires.

Crouching low, the Bandu leader watched the smoke and thought out the risk of approaching the camp in full view.

Hunters!

High above, a black shadow began to cover the ground. The distant sounds of honking grew louder as an abundance of migrating geese and a myriad number of different species of ducks had begun to fill the skies. This was a new, yet, welcomed sound that had not been heard since the birds flew south before the cold time. Layer upon layer of flapping wings were filling the overhead sky. Indeed, when the anticipated full strength of the migration arrived, the birds would surely blacken these very same skies.

It is too long that I do not see my people. There will be a time when they will see what I am seeing now.

Lowering himself into the stream, the Bandu chief sat in the water's chill, closed his eyes and thought back to the tragedy that had led him here. It was well before the long walk he had made across the high mountains, and well before the cold time when he and Fast Eagle, along with Distant Cloud, were gutting a horse they had killed.

Woodland Forest off the coast of Oregon
Seven months earlier

"I remember a hunt before many more hunts that would come," said Fast Eagle, probing a developing fire with a stick to add height to the flames.

Looking up from a deer carcass, Lan listened to a story he heard before. Distant Cloud had already removed one of the hind legs and was busy cutting away the skin. The men had chanced upon the lame doe late during the day, alone and drinking at a fast running stream. The sound had muffled their approach.

"Ten hot times passed when this happened," said Fast Eagle. "I was with my mother's brother, the one we called Sits by the Setting Sun. I followed behind him when he tracked a large grass eater. It was then that we could hear the bear and smell it close by. It made the sound the bears make when they are alone. We heard it somewhere in the trees. The sound was low. I still could not see the bear, but I could hear it when it started to run along the ground."

To better animate the story, Fast Eagle stood next to the fire, his calloused fingers spread wide, the nails, broken and black with dirt under their edges. The tracks in his palms were creased deep from gripping spears during a lifetime of hunts.

"We waited there and did not make a sound. The bear stopped when we stopped. I did not see when the bear started to run. I only saw the bear when he saw it. He lifted his kill stick and called out to it with slow words. 'You must leave this place and not kill a brave hunter like I am. You and I, we are brother hunters.'

"But the bear would not listen. It kept coming to us with his eyes looking at Sits by the Setting Sun. It was then that he started to run at the bear. He ran fast, and when he was almost one with the bear…he…ugh…"

Fast Eagle suddenly stopped telling the story. His eyes widened with surprise and then he began to choke and make gurgling sounds with a trickle of blood running down the corner of his mouth. His eyes closed and he fell forward, hitting his head on the burning logs.

Startled, Lan and Distant Cloud jumped back from the sparks that flashed into the black night like a thousand windblown fire flies.

Lan jerked his head up in time to see Man Walking, the Dinga tribe leader where Fast Eagle was just standing. Like the rest of his men, he went to war naked, his head shaved except for the hair that draped down from around both ears to his shoulders. Fastened to the ends were ten thumb sized snake skulls, five to each side. Deep scar-drawn animals embellished the skin of the Dinga chief's body. On each of his big toes were rings with the beaks of owls sticking out like hooks. Around both biceps, a thin band of human flesh held white and black eagle feathers to his upper forearms, the tips of which pointed toward his wrist. Bear claws were strapped to the back of his hands and laced with poison. The curved points extended beyond the knuckles and were there to rake deep wounds into his enemy's skin; or to preferably render them blind.

Man Walking pressed his foot against Fast Eagle's back and calmly pulled his spear out. At the same time, an ax split into Distant Cloud's temple from another Dinga tribesman. The Bandu fell sideways on top of Fast Eagle, limp and shaking until his entire body relaxed and slid off of him.

Wide eyed, Lan froze at the sight of the ax, the chiseled edge dripping with Distant Cloud's blood. It had all happened so fast. He was both horrified and stunned by the suddenness of the attack. He hated the Dinga, but the odds were overwhelming. He could have easily chosen to fight until they killed him, kill as many Dinga as he could before they struck him with a final blow. But his love for his tribe and their need for his leadership overshadowed all of those wanton desires. It was not fear. Hatred shielded him from that.

Seizing the chance, he ran out of the camp, narrowly avoiding an arrow that whined past his ear and hit solidly into the tree next to him. The Bandu chief, an exceptionally fast runner, ran like a deer into the black of night.

The Bandu Village

Sleeps by the Fire, stood in the open ground before the village huts, horrified by what he saw. Both young and old lay frozen in death throws throughout the Bandu Village. He was left to live out his life; for even the Dingas feared the shaman elder. He was a keeper of spirits. He had power.

High above the trees, a swarm of black specks silently approached the huts. It grew in size by the moment, and soon, amidst the telling drift of decaying odors, a flock of black vultures floated down from the sky. Alighting on the low branches of the surrounding trees, the birds impatiently bumped one another in a scuffle of slapping wings. Beaks twitched back and forth with the bickering that followed, bringing with it a touch of whimsy to the forced association. They soon settled in, leaning featherless heads angularly toward the still bodies below them.

The better part of the day had been spent by the shaman dragging bodies into two huts left unburned. Gray haired and stooped, he had seen violence in his lifetime, but never anything like this. The entire village had been emptied and was all too much to bare. Leaning on a walking stick, he took a few painful steps toward the death birds.

A brazen vulture glided silently to the ground on outstretched wings. Its long neck snaked into an S, then straightened as the bird lifted its head to stare with blinking red eyes at the unmoving bodies. There, the vulture waited for a movement or gasp for air that would scurry it back to the trees. It edged closer, hopping deviously from one foot to the other, then stopped a few short steps from the opened head of the nearest victim.

One foot was left barely touching the ground with the heel, the claws opening and closing like a pulsing spider. Nervously, the vulture slunk its head between its shoulders and eyed the flock's next meal. With restrained anticipation, it shifted its weight to the other foot and then hopped lightly forward in the well-trodden soil. Stopping short of the body, it stretched and noticed for the first time, the gray haired human, unmoving and standing there watching.

The vulture turned toward the woman and then suddenly jerked its head back around to eye the man once more, the string of saliva hanging from its beak, whipping around with it. Satisfied the man was of no threat, the bird turned slowly back to the corpse---a heavy woman with blood dripping to the ground from an ax wound to the skull. The vulture stepped into the warm, reddish-brown puddle. It took a long look behind itself for a last check before dipping its beak into the wound. Pulling out the soft, white tissue inside, it fidgeted around nervously, stabbed into the open wound, pulled its head out and stabbed back inside. Again and again, it stabbed at the moist tissue.

A noise made it check the huts, the man and the rest of the flock, 'though without earnest this time, the taste of blood soaked brains, too overwhelming for any wariness it may have had left. Reentering the head with its own head, it buried it up to its neck.

Sleeps by the Fire felt exhausted. He had very little strength left and now he would have to chase after death birds. He leaned on a walking stick and hobbled toward the inattentive vulture. Halfway there, he picked up a few stones.

The bird naively watched with blank expressionless eyes as the first stone bounced nearby and did not associate it with the gray haired man.

"Go spirit killer," yelled the old shaman.

A second stone bounced underneath the bird, causing it to spread its wings and to lift one of its legs out of the way. It jumped and squawked, following the stone with red empty eyes until it stopped in front of a bush.

The vulture snapped its head around and looked at the old man with a knowing, grievous stare---facetious and full of contempt. It lowered its head, thrashed its wings and quickly flew to its place on a crowded branch. As if on cue, the entire flock turned their gaze from the vulture to the corpse as each awaited its chance to grab a portion for themselves.

One by one the shaman struggled to get as many of the bodies into the huts as he could. As soon as he pulled one inside, the vultures dropped down and yanked at the woman's open wound. It was not long before the skins of other bodies were broken into, ensuing a frenzy of eating as much as the birds could in the short time it took for the shaman to return. They would then scramble beneath the bushes, no longer troubling themselves with flying up to the trees.

Sleep by the Fire waved the walking stick at them, but he could only do so much. He threw stones and cursed, dragged partially eaten bodies into the huts, tried to hurry, but it was all of no use. He was spent and the vultures in a frenzy and way too numerous.

The life spirits of the bodies had to be saved. To be eaten by a scavenger would be the ultimate tragedy. Death birds were not hunters like saber tooth tigers and wolves. A person's life spirit would be lost forever, never to rejoin their ancestors in the sky.

"My People, I cannot save you all. The death birds now own you."

Just saying those words made him shudder. Sighing, he shook his head. Branches, dry grass, baskets, anything that would burn were thrown into both huts. He stepped back to watch from a safe distance, the roar of the burning fires.

"Go fast to the clouds my people. Soon you will thank me for putting your bodies into the fire and saving your life spirits from the death birds. It is then that I will be strong with you and you will be strong with me. In the dark times to come you will light your fires and look down from the black sky. Know that what I have done is what my father would have done and what his father would have done before him."

Lowering his arms, the shaman could do no more. He collapsed to the ground, withdrew into a ball and tearfully trembled.

All of that was now in the past. Lan looked away from the thin line of smoke rising from the valley below. Rubbing his eyes, he paused from the awful memories while searching the distance for signs of game. He had not tasted meat since leaving the winter cave and was famished. He needed to hunt, but the memories would not go away no matter how much he tried. He missed the old shaman as well as Fast Eagle and Distant Cloud and many of the others like Deer Eyes, Morning Thunder, Quiet Spring and Leaping Frog.

And the others? They are now with the Dinga. It is their way...as it is our way. Take your enemies men, women and children. A tribe grows strong with more hunters and woman to bare young.

One day I will take my people back and bring them here...but how?

Though it seemed so long ago, he remembered it all clearly as if it happened only yesterday. After the Dingas attacked him at the campsite and killed Fast Eagle and Distant Cloud, he recalled returning to the burning village. Among the dead bodies and burning huts, Sleeps by the Fire was the only one he had found there left alive.

The air was windless with thick plumes from the fires fusing into the night sky. Like scattered embers, stars were thrown about the blackness; a forgotten moon, hidden somewhere on the other side of a cloud.

Standing silently next to the shaman's crouching form, Lan stared at the smoldering ashes. Neither man looked at the other.

Lan spoke first. "Go with me to the big water. There we will be safe from this place."

Sleeps by the Fire frowned. "No...I must stay here with our dead. Man Walking will not touch me. He fears my spirits. You, Lan...you must leave. Save yourself from Man Walking's ax. There is nothing you can do here. They will soon come to me for my power to heal. It is then that I will go to them and they will be my people."

The shaman grabbed Lan's helping hand and pulled himself up. "The Dinga will see your tracks and hunt you like they hunt the grass eaters. They will put you in their fire and eat your flesh so you can never seek your revenge. If you go past the big water, the Wadu will find you and swallow your eyes. They will then take your head and carry on top of a long stick so all that watch will laugh at you.

"If you walk with the sun on your left to the hunting place of the Manama, they will put you in their fire...alive. Sharp Knife's people will then wound you and feed your crippled body to their coyotes. It is the reason they keep them, to take the life spirits of their enemies. So, it is only you yourself that must find a place where the Dinga and the others cannot find you."

"There is no place like you speak?" said Lan. "There is no place for me to walk where they will not follow."

"Find a place where the Dinga do not go." The shaman's voice sounded full of worry.

Breathing deeply, Lan squatted and grabbed a handful of dirt. As he spoke, he slowly emptied it onto the ground. "All we know is this place where we now stand. This…this is our hunting place."

Despite the pain in his limbs, the shaman stood as tall as he could, looked to the mountains and pointed stiffly at them. "That is the new hunting place. That is where you must go. Cross that high place to the other side to where you will find the new hunting place for our people."

"I have seen the high place you talk since my head was here," Lan said, measuring the appropriate distance from the ground to his knee. "It is the place on the other side that I cannot see that leaves me here. This…where I now stand is all we know. Your new hunting land is on the other side of the high place. That is a sacred place we do not go. None of our fathers has ever made that walk. If I listened to your words and took this walk would Man Walking not follow my tracks?"

The shaman put his hands together, his voice, softening like a caring father. "Man Walking will not follow you."

"You believe this like you know the sun will not fall. He will track me, will he not?"

"He will not track you through the sacred lands. No one will. The spirits there are too strong. Wait for the end of the cold time that nears. The high place will be too cold to cross now. Go to the big water. That is where you must wait for the cold time to pass. This is when the Wadu leave that place to live with the forest. Man Walking fears the Wadu. He will not follow you there. He will not take that chance.

"Go to the caves by the big water. There the winds of the cold time will not touch you. Mark your new land on the cave wall. Mark with the red dirt and the black of your fire the animals you wish to live in your new land. Mark it with flowers and trees. Mark on your wall everything you want that is good. When the cold time is over and the time of new life begins, that will be your time to cross the place of water and trees. That will be the time for your words. Talk to the tree spirits to let you pass. Tell them you will not make fire and that you want only to cross to the other side. It is then that the tree spirits will welcome you. It is they who will talk to the high place that touches the sky."

"How do you know their eyes will see what you see?"

"They will see what I see, because they are brothers."

Lan smiled as though a great weight lifted off of his shoulders.

"Sleeps by the Fire is like the eagle, he sees far. When the time to walk to this high place is now, I will follow your words and find this new hunting place you say is there. One day I will return, and the same way the two knife hunts the white light of the dark time, that is how I will return for our people."

"They will wait for you as I will, Lan. Go now before the Dinga hunt your tracks with the first light."

Without waiting for an answer, the shaman got up and limped to a clump of bushes. He reached behind them and struggled with something heavy, stopped to get a better grip, then dragged out a very large, half-filled sack made from three complete elk skins sewn together. After spreading the opening wide, he crawled inside.

The Bandu Chief waited with curiosity while the shaman fumbled around until worming his way out with a few baskets and bone implements. The tribal elder looked at them with mild interest as though remembering something about each one. Shaking his head, he placed them gently to the side and crawled back in to look for something else; something he knew was in the very far end of the sack.

"Mph!...eh! In back...it...it is here...I put it in here myself."

Sleeps by the Fire's words came back muffled and garbled, his head bumping inside the sack and waving around underneath the skin as he moved about. The outlines of his arms rippled underneath the elk skin first one way and then the other. The sound of bones and wooden sticks hitting one another were soon followed by a rattling noise that stopped when it hit the ground. Something else made a crackling sound as if a string of stone beads dropped onto a hollow skull.

"This is the one. This is… no! That is not the one!"

(More fumbling and shifting about)

"It is this one…"

The shaman turned completely around and stuck his head out along with his find to look at it in the sparse light coming from the burning huts. As he looked, he shook his head again, said something under his breath, and then tossed a wooden shaft on top of a pile of baskets.

"No…that is not the one!" Digging back inside, he moved in deeper, scattering a few things out of the way until he grew silent.

"I think I found it."

With that, he struggled to back out of the sack, shoving things to the side, mumbling the whole time until it became clear what he was saying.

"This is the one…I know it is. It must be." He held the object outside for a better look. "Yes! This is the one." With a lot of huffing and puffing, he emerged from the sack. "It is still here!"

The shaman grinned with admiration as he eyed a spear honed as perfectly as any he held in the past.

"This kill stick has a strong spirit," he said, as he ran shaking, arthritic fingers along the edge of the blade. "It belonged to Wandering Wolf. He was a good hunter when he used it."

Lan could see that the spear was a strong one, the elder holding it and smiling broadly as if he had been the one who had made it. The blade's reflective luster, honed from quartz, was chiseled to a fine Clovis point. Through the thin scalloped cutting edge, where its pink colored opaqueness was absent, it was so translucent he could see the shaman's fingers when he ran them along the other side of the blade. At the back end of the spear, red and yellow tail feathers, plucked from a hawk, fanned out to the sides.

In a rough manner and in the same way he would have grabbed his own spear when rushing off to a hunt, Lan snatched it from him, lifted it shoulder high and jostled it around for balance. Made from the strong hardwood of an ash tree, it was neither too heavy nor too light. He clamped down on it, jerked the spear as if to throw it, then pointed the quartz blade at the glowing fire to check along the shaft. Rolling it around, he sighted down the length of it to the blade at the far end. It was perfectly straight.

"I remember Wandering Wolf." He lowered the spear and traced his fingers along the wood to feel how smooth it had been shaved. "He was one of our best hunters and now he hunts the sky."

A quiver followed along with an assortment of arrows of all sizes, every one of them with black obsidian blades. Some had thin shafts for small game like hares and fowl. Others were longer and thicker with bloodletting grooves, used to take down large game such as moose or elk. If a vital organ was missed, the animal could be tracked or die from blood loss. Extremely long arrows were for hunting at a distance where the dangers of confronting an animal such as a bear was best avoided. It was these arrows that were used to thin the enemy's ranks.

Lan's lower lip pushed upwards, his hazel eyes, focused and glaring. "These arrows are strong."

The shaman's arms folded across his chest. "They are only strong for the hunter that knows how to use them. Your arrows always go where you look…better than any of others. I put more of the black rocks on the bottom. If you lose an arrow, you can make another."

Reaching into the quiver, he pulled one out with a red ring imprinted around the shaft. "This arrow is the strongest. It is the only one that I said the hunting words for. The stone was sharp and the wood dry when it was made. Save it for a time when you must use it. When that time is now, use it with much thought. It can only be used once. It is then that you must break the arrow and bury it under a stone so that it can never be used again."

Sleeps by the Fire raised the arrow to the sky, mumbled a chant and then put it back into the quiver.

Lan put his arm through the strap and swung the quiver over his shoulder.

"I need water skins."

"I will get them."

Before leaving, the shaman handed him a palm sized, deer skin pouch with a length of sinew attached so it could be tied around his neck.

As if the shaman forgot something, Lan stared at him, but said nothing. As soon as the elder re-entered the sack, he opened the pouch. Inside were stone chips for cutting, two flints and dandelion cotton for starting a fire, three long strips of sinew to make traps for small game, willow bark for headaches and treating cuts, crushed cattail… "I still have my bone knife…and my ax," he mumbled as he continued to move things around inside the pouch to see what else was in there. "The bear claws I wear on my ankles, I have that power as well."

"Yes, you own the bear's spirit," said the shaman, returning with two water skins. He looped both over the leader's shoulder. "The bear runs next to your side as does the black bird that follows you in the sky."

"I wear the black bird on my back. The spirit of the two knife and that of my father, they are there to protect me like the others." Lan's voice a mere undertone as he poked around inside the pouch, but there did not seem to be anything else.

"Yes, those spirits run strong inside your blood." The shaman secured the straps from the water skins.

"There is one more thing I need."

Bewildered, Sleeps by the Fire checked his demeanor but it gave no hint of what he had forgotten. "This is not tight enough. You will lose your water skins that way." He tugged at the straps and checked the string from the pouch.

"The tree!"

He had hidden it from the Dinga in the event that they found the sack. "It is up there!" He pointed to the lower branch of the cedar behind them. "The bow that belonged to your father... Hunting Wolf."

Now that he knew where to look, Lan could see it clearly. The bow had been made from a composite of flat strips cut from buffalo horn, birch and oak. The wood pieces were bent into arc shapes by bending them slowly over a fire. Glue from melted fish bladder was then applied between the layers and finally a wrapping of sinew to bind it all together.

Retrieving it from the branch, Lan held it towards the fire. Decorations garnished the flat strips of buffalo horn on the outside of the bow. Two wolves, etched in relief and in full stride, seemed to jump out as if alive. At the opposite end, a deer leapt over a bush below a radiant sun. Shadows and fur were enhanced with finely scratched lines. Snarling fangs and antlers stood out in bold relief. Beneath that, an array of colorful pebbles and bits of iridescent shells lay imbedded in the horn.

"My father made many kills with this bow," said Lan, "as I have with my own, and now Man Walking has taken my bow."

"Yes, your father was a good hunter. These bows were taught to us from tribes to the north. No other tribe we know of has this power. Our arrows fly much farther than the old Atlatls."

"Yes, when word of the bow's power reached us, it was you that told my father to take that journey to our brother tribes in the north. They caught many of their hunting animals with it. It was a gift that brought them much wealth and now that gift is ours.

There are other tribes like the Wadu and the Manama that also want to learn of this power."

"Only you can make others the same way, Lan. Those tribes do not have this knowledge and only Man Walking knows of it now that he owns your bow."

"He cannot make others," Lan said. "He, like the rest, know nothing of its secret. If he tries, he will fail."

"If the Wadu find you, you must keep this secret. It will make your tribe stronger when the day comes that you return for your people."

Sighing, Lan looked all around at the burning devastation. "I am ready now to leave this place."

"Run with our spirits my young brother."

The tribe's leader firmly gripped the elder's shoulders. "I run with our spirits and you in my thoughts."

Sleeps by the Fire smiled. "And you in mine."

A last and final look around the village was hurtful. It could never be home to his tribe again. Then, as in so many times in the past, the Bandu leader left the huts and entered the same game trail he walked down so many times in the past.

The shaman raised his arm up in farewell even though the tribe's leader was out of view. He kept it high until the sound of footsteps dissipated into the darkness.

Oregon Coast

After a night of continuous light running, Lan made his way to the coast. Following the water's edge, it took the entire rest of the day and the next night before reaching the safety of limestone cliffs. From a high vantage point early that next morning, he scrutinized the rugged land along the bordering surf. Pocked with a multitude of caves, the cliff's utmost reaches scraped jagged fingers at passing clouds---so high; he had to lean back to see them. In audience, lay the vast and open sea—"the big water," a place without end.

Shadows from clouds, swept silent vigils across the open mouths of the caves---these, the countless, easily imagined faces with eyes that stared back. Theirs, was a foreboding lot, a profusion of vexatious spirits. For, this, like the mountains, was a place filled with the lore of rumored evil, a taboo certain to give Lan the protection he would need. It was as untouchable as the mountains that he would one day have to cross. Here, he would be lost to the anonymity of one cave among many.

Time moved quickly through the cold of winter. Lan filled his days with the likenesses of elk and buffalo he painted on the walls. Yellow illumination from grass and seal oil torches shook heartbeats into the images he marked on the stone. More than the artful drawings of prey, these symbolized the real animals that would live in his new land, a place beyond the land that touches the sky. Stone walls became vibrant with color as he instilled life into deer, bears and moose, filling the barren spaces between with birds, flowers and trees. At the forefront, with their heads thrust high, a stag and his mate thunder across Lan's imagined world.

Red ochre cloaks the stag within charcoal outlines. Magnificent and regal, he pursues his estrous half, lusting to insure immortality through promised offspring. Legs are bent high in mid stride as together they drive towards the cavern's dark---the virgin womb within the cave's depths. There, they will re-emerge into a new world, the world Lan paints on the walls with charcoal and ochre strokes.

CHAPTER 2

MATWAU'S VALLEY

Opening his eyes, Lan did not want to think about the past anymore. He had crossed the place of trees and high mountains and it had been easy. Once he found the pass, the mountains, though difficult, proved achievable. He arrived in this pristine valley and it was everything he had hoped for.

He waded out of the stream, returned to his belongings and got dressed. The berries he had saved, he put into his mouth. It was all that had sustained him on the high alpine slopes, 'though did little to satisfy his need for meat. Far below, he could see the valley floor. Here in the foothills the ground lay treeless, the grass and wild flowers, growing in abundance.

With the rest of his things gathered together, he followed the stream. Partway down, near a crowd of trees, a heron stood at the water's edge. Her drab grey plumage, striated in a variety of browns, blended invisibly with the flat rock she stood on. Stiff-legged, her head slunk between her shoulders as she glared into the clear, cold water that mirrored her image. Attentively, she cocked her head to the side and suddenly jerked it downward. The yellow flash of her beak darted below the surface and immediately lifted back out. Pointing the beak upward, she shook a spotted salamander until it faced head first toward her throat. With short gulping movements, she swallowed the salamander whole.

At the edge, Lan lay down and attempted to snatch one of the many salamanders submerged with their heads just breaking the surface. They were slippery, but he soon caught one. He bit off the head, spit it out and chewed into the amphibian's bland, fish-like flavor. He liked its taste and tried for another. The spotted brown wrigglers were plentiful and enough to cut the hunger pains rumbling in his stomach.

A storm-felled tree, the weathered bark covered with fluorescent, teal colored lichen, lay across the stream. Pulling the bark apart exposed a nest of larvae that tumbled to the bottom into a pile of writhing, plump bodies. He reached in and picked out the fattest among them, as large as his thumb, put it between his teeth and pulled. The elastic body stretched until the insect snapped in two. He sucked out the green insides that had the consistency of drying cream, an acquired taste he was used to. Hungry for more, he stuffed the rest into his mouth and reached in for the fat one trying to dig its way into a crack.

Ahead were unforeseen dangers and uncertainties. Excitement, tinged with fear raced inside as he looked out onto the valley, although it seemed to beckon with a view that appeared vast and crisp with new growth. In their heights the sky spirits smiled. He could see that in the clarity of the clouds and the shear walls of sunlight streaming through gaps in the whiteness. The Wind Brother blew strongly and nudged him with a gentle push---coaxing him toward the green slopes below.

Dusk

Emerging from a tall stand of trees, Lan entered a clearing. At the other end of the valley, the sun had descended beyond the far side of the cliffs. Soon it would bury itself at the end of the world, leaving everything below in shadow. Cool air began to sweep off of the mountains. It felt damp and presaged the colder air of the coming dark time.

Dry branches were gathered to build a fire. Next, he removed dandelion cotton and two pieces of flint from the pouch around his neck. Striking the flints would take time, but it was a well-rehearsed routine practiced over a lifetime.

Aside from the cold, there were other needs for building a fire. Inside the bleak darkness that was soon to come, stalked the strange and unfamiliar world of the dark time. Filled with predators, familiar as well as imagined, it belonged to saber tooth tigers, bears and the dire wolf packs that hunted the valley.

The dark was also a haunt for Death Spirits. Feared more than anything living, they took on the illusionary forms that linger in expectant worry. They were the cause for mistrust and fear, for within that dark time was the overpowering embodiment of an unknown world---a black world---a world where a man ceases to exists, but rather, falls into dreams of an awake world already lived.

The dark made grown men huddle close to a fire that comforted yet at the same time lent betrayal in its warmth. For, from that fire was drawn an awareness that man tended the fire. It was this which roving bands looked for---these lights, where the number of fires could estimate the number of men.

The flints were put back into the pouch and the flame from the tuft of dandelion snuffed out with his fingertips. There would be no fire tonight. After digging out a hollow depression beneath a fallen log lying deep inside low foliage, he squeezed inside. Dry leaves along with the dirt he had just dug out were pulled back in until he wedged himself in like a frightened rodent.

It would be the best he could do to warm himself against the nights chill, and all he could do to protect himself from the evils of the dark time.

The short faced bear

Morning was welcomed with newborn enthusiasm. Lan set out to follow the stream, purposely avoiding the game trails. Slowly and quietly, he moved through stone bramble and black brush until the bank of a lake came into view. In the mud were the prints of deer and a fox. Crisscrossing those, a rabbit had scampered excitedly, leaving a trail of droppings behind.

Prints of bears were here as well, including a female with two cubs. New visitors to the lake, the female's prints were light from a winter of fasting. Between hers were those of her cubs as they scampered playfully in the delight of new and exciting sights.

From the pouch hanging from his neck, Lan removed a long strip of sinew. At one end, he fashioned it into a loop so that it could trap a small animal once it stepped inside. Two more of these loops were made and set on the ground. From a nearby tree, three branches were broken off where they started to split into a fork. He left the bulges from the forks intact. After stripping away the leaves and side stems from each one, he pushed them deep into the ground in front of young saplings. The opposite end of the noose was then tied to the top of the sapling. To set the three traps, he hooked the stems under the bulges. Each noose was adjusted so that they lay flat on the ground with berries left inside as bait.

Ahead, elk tracks were dug deep into the mud and heading away from the lake toward dense woods. Lan followed them to a depression in the leaf bed where a fawn had waited for its mother. He continued to track them, finding signs everywhere, like the occasional print between the leaves, their droppings, or fur caught on bushes.

The tracks led to a meadow rich with new grass where morning dew still wet the shadows. Butterfly wings fluttered in the sunlight among beds of aposeris. In the midst of white pedaled daisy wheels, bluebells and nightshades scattered themselves generously about. At the far edge of the meadow, beneath a crush of pines, white beams covered the trunks of mountain ash. The white flowers and red berries bloomed with extravagance, splashing the virtuousness with interruptions of color.

Crawling forward, Lan stopped whenever the doe raised her head. He moved easily through the tall grass with unhurried patience until he could get close enough to use the bow. Any noise or movement on his part could ruin the hunt.

An enduring wind bent the meadow. The doe lifted her head to face it. Her eyes went shallow, but she saw nothing, so she buried her head back into the sweet vegetation.

Somewhere within a nearby cluster of trees, a flutter of wings broke the silence. The doe raised her head again as well as the fawn. The newborn, only days old, did not look in the same direction as its mother. Instead, it watched the small clump of grass that moved against the way the rest of the grass was moving. It appeared only as something different to the fawn's unpracticed eyes to see it wave around that way, but it was only that. It was only something odd, like a lot of the new things it was seeing for the first time.

With a thick arrow notched into the bow, Lan drew it back to his shoulder. Standing up slowly, he sighted down the arrow at the fawn---now bumping its head underneath its mother for milk. Holding the aim, he paused to gauge the exact moment for release. With a sense of certainty, he whipped the arrow forward, hitting the fawn hard with an arrow that was longer than the animal's body. The fawn fell onto its back and kicked at the sky in an effort to dislodge the arrow from its side.

Bounding from the expendable fawn, the doe stopped a distance away to look back in confusion. Upon seeing Lan running up to her newborn, she darted into the cover of trees.

As he stood next to the fawn, it made him think back to when he was a boy. It was during a kill with his father, Hunting Wolf, that they found a newborn like this lying in deep woods. Frozen in fear, it blended perfectly in the dappled light, with ears that were laid back and oval eyes that looked hopeful. Hunting Wolf nudged him to make the kill, but had Lan been alone that day, he never would have.

Shortly after, while the fawn lay bleeding at his feet, he felt sadness as he held back his feelings with feigned pride. He looked down at the fawn through a beginning of tears and his father's strong hand firmly caressing his shoulder. He could still remember the compassion in his voice. "The forest keeps count of **ALL** of her children."

Hunting no longer emitted those feelings. The young elk was a source of meat---nothing more. In a less than maximum effort, he cracked open the skull with his ax. He scooped out a piece of the brain and checked that he was alone. The white flesh was delicious. Had he been out hunting with his fellow tribesmen, he would have been the first to be offered the delicacy. Finishing that, he cut out the liver and ate that as well, though it would have been given to the hunter who had made the kill.

He gutted the fawn where it lay, removed the head and carried the carcass to a rocky outcropping. After collecting dry wood to minimize smoke, he chanced a daylight fire.

Meat soon crackled and sputtered in the flames. Lan nervously watched the smoke drift upward and across the valley towards the far off cliffs.

Behind him, a jumble of rocks covered a rocky hillside high enough to afford a clear view. He climbed to the top of it and looked in the direction of where he had last seen the hunter's campfire. There, a sizzling bright sun mirrored off of the cliffs like white fire. Along the length of it, various shades of coral pinks fingered into brilliant vermillion. Between those, lighter shades of sulfur hues melded into one another.

They have no smoke. They could be here...near where I stand...an outsider in their hunting place.

He grabbed the claws hanging from his neck and looked anxiously in all directions. He had only to chant the words and then wait for the saber tooth's power to fill him. The cat's eyes would be in his eyes. Its teeth would be in his ax. He would have the saber tooth's courage, its cunning, its celerity.

And Hunting Wolf, did he not have his father's power as well? Was he not there to guide him, to join him on the hunts, to sit by the night fire, to offer companionship? Even now, was he not here to protect him from the men out there, men he did not know?

Sighing deeply, Lan looked back from the distance and returned to the fire. With a serrated bone knife, he cut easily into the side of the roasting fawn. He removed a large piece of bubbling hot flesh and left it hanging from the blade to wait for it to cool. It would be a welcomed meal after the humble existence he had to rely on in the high place. And had the doe been chosen instead, the bulk of the meat would have been wasted and left behind, along with a helpless fawn.

After eating his fill, he cut as much from the carcass as he could consume in three days. The rest would have to be left to vultures and coyotes. He licked his hands clean of lingering scent and returned to the same log where he had spent the previous night. The meat, he left high in an upper branch of a pine tree. Everything else was left on the ground except for the water skins which he took to the lake to refill. While there, he checked the traps.

Two ground squirrels chattered and tugged against the choking knots. With enough meat to last a few days, they could be freed and hunted another time.

As soon as he stepped from behind a bush, a noise sent him abruptly back to cover. The scent in the air was unmistakable. He knew instantly what it was, the pungent odor hanging over the bank as if the animal stood before him. Terror filled memories of the beast sent surges of fear down his spine. It was one of the biggest of the predators and ferocious, one a lone hunter would never want to encounter---a short faced bear---a two thousand pound predator twice the height of the tallest man. It had the strength of ten men, ten strong men, ten youthful men, ten men without fear and armed with spears and axes.

Here was a beast that could outrun a man. It left him with no place to hide and had a sense of smell so powerful it could track him on odor alone. With one swipe of a paw, it could dismember a limb or worse still, behead him.

CRACK!

Somewhere behind Lan, back about thirty paces, in a place deep in the tangle of brush, a solitary sound echoed off of the surrounding trees like a rock thrown against a stone wall. The noise sounded crisp and clear; not unlike the sound of a huge paw stepping on a twig, breaking it in two. Petrified, Lan squatted low, his stomach tightening when he realized that all he brought with him was an ax. He carefully parted leaves from in front of his face, looked to where he thought the noise had come from and was startled to hear the sound of another splitting twig coming from a totally different direction.

CRACK!

That one was closer, having amplified from within the density of trees, and in the midst of a forest without so much as a light wind to break the silence. A light wind that only now began to gently lift the leaves---so ever gently---a sigh of a breeze---a warm scent carrying breeze.

The huge bear nosed the ground as if caution preoccupied all else. It stopped short to turn a wet, pulsing nose towards a scent---a familiar scent, one the bear seldom encountered. It sniffed again, its head like a pendulum as it swayed back and forth, the long tongue, licking its black snout with long tasting strokes. Lifting its head higher, the bear looked to where the odor was strong and pervasive and where the sound of short gasping breaths was tellingly apparent.

Lan became aware of his running sweat and the scent that it would give. He thought of the fawn and any trace amount of that scent that could still be on his body. Gradually, he eased his hand over to the ax, held fast inside of a netting tied to his waist. He inhaled deeply and silently and then pulled on the cold feel of the stone. Half way out, he stopped to listen to a new sound. Just the leaves rustling, nothing more, but it did not stop his heart from beating out of control like the hooves of a charging buffalo.

He pulled on the ax handle. His fingers were shaking so much, he was sure to drop the heavy obsidian blade back into the netting. The sudden sound of that, though faint, would certainly alert the bear. With both hands this time, he carefully pulled the ax out.

There would be only one chance to kill the bear, a hard blow to the thin facial bone in front of the ears. If he missed, the bear would be upon him in an instant of butchering claws and bone snapping fangs. If the bear stood on its hind legs, its head would be out of reach. His only choice then would be to climb the nearest tree, but with the bear in close pursuit there would be little chance of that.

My bone knife will break in the bear's thick skin. This ax is all I have.

Lan's head snapped around. The bear was moving again.

In its search for the source of the smell, the bear took a step and sniffed the air on both sides. Gradually, it closed in on the field of black brush that separated it from where the human had crouched down. Its nostrils flexed in and out while its head bobbed up and down. Jutting from the bears open, salivating jaws were large canines the size of a man's fist.

Sure that the beast could hear, Lan's heart beat strongly from the terror. With every heartfelt breath, he breathed in the bear's stench, and with every exhalation, breathed out his own disclosed fear. For a long while neither one moved, but became part of the serenity of the surrounding forest.

Suddenly---explosively, a shattering of splitting branches and scattering leaves made him stiffen---jolted his heart beat three times faster. He could hear the bear charging. Although he wanted to, he could not make himself stand. All he could do was listen to the tremendous power of the beast as it tore through the forest.

His grip white-knuckled around the ax handle. His whole body shook with what he was going to do, what he had to do if he could only get up enough courage to be accurate enough to make the first blow count. He was going to rise up on his feet and slam the ax into the bear's skull---get up now and yell out his courage, not stop until the frenzied nightmare was over and either he or the bear lay dead.

The bear was half way through the underbrush. Lan's eyes widened. He remained perfectly still. The only thing he could not stop from moving was his jugular vein. It pounded inside his neck like tribal drums. Out there, the bear growled so loud it sounded like a million reverberating locust as the beast ripped out everything in its path.

Lan forced himself to slowly stand to face the bear with the ax held high and behind his shoulder. He was ready to scream out, scream at the charging bear and slam the ax down with all of his strength. His whole body kept shaking and he could not make it stop. If his legs gave out now he would never get up again, and certainly not with the bear in pursuit of him.

He fought a strong urge to shrink to his knees and cover his head from the animal's gnawing teeth. It was an urge he had to fight, because to do that would mean he would be giving up his life spirit. All he could do then would be to chant to the bear to plead for a quick and painless death. That would be easy, frighteningly easy. He could close his eyes right now and be in the dark time once again. Only this time it would be forever.

Another roar

He forced his eyes open to the throaty growls that totally encompassed the forest. The fur on the back of the bear's neck stood straight up, its ears flat to the skull. But it was the teeth, those horrible fangs and that explosive, heart wrenching growl that frightened him the most.

And although Lan kept looking at the charging animal, he in some strange way did not see it anymore. He heard it, he smelled it---he trembled from it and now became blinded behind the wall of terror, a wall made up of fangs and shaking muscles and that awful, ghastly roar. What he had to do, he was going to have to do now.

With the claws in his grip he began to chant.

"I have the power of the two knife, you cannot kill me."

"I have the power of the two knife, you cannot kill me."

"I have the power of the two knife, you cannot kill me."

Lan's voice sounded low and indiscernible behind the thunderous roars of the short faced bear. Fear and anticipation would soon come to an end, because the beast was almost there. He tried to chant louder, but nothing came out. All he could do was mouth the words. And no matter what the bear did, he was going to have to fight as if the saber tooth tiger was there with him---as if his father was standing alongside. He believed that as strongly as he felt his own heart beats.

He squeezed his father's teeth inside his right fist. In the other were the claws and now he could feel the sudden rush of energy racing through him. The power of the spirits was coming. He was sure of that, because the surge made him stand straight like his father would. The blood of the saber tooth broiled beneath his skin. He was ready to kill. He was going to kill the bear, kill without hesitation, kill without the hindrance of any more fear.

His back slammed against the tree nearest him as he held the ax up and what he saw next astonished him. While standing there frozen, the bear ran right past. He could hardly catch his breath as he watched the plodding beast continue along the bank. Unbelievably, the wind had been in his favor all that time. The bear, so focused on the traps, never saw him standing rigidly against the tree.

The tree runners. That is what it wanted.

At the sight of the bear, the squirrels jumped and pulled at their bindings. They screeched in panic as the bear slapped its paws down in an instant of easy kill. It chewed the first squirrel until it was no more than a flat piece of fur, swallowing it whole. After finishing the second, it sat on its haunches with its legs outstretched. Cast off pieces of flesh from the squirrels insides were licked up along with blood drops from between the bear's legs. Hungry for more, it licked its snout and then sniffed the ground.

Cold leaves stuck to the sweat on Lan's face, masking him from the brute that slowly ambled to a steep entry at the water's edge. There, it entered the shallows. His legs cramped, Lan lowered his body inside the brush and waited hopefully, but the beast's thirst was extreme. Its massive head dipped underneath the surface and then high out of the water. Liquid poured extravagantly from the jutting fangs and water soaked fur. When its thirst was finally satisfied, the bear ripped into the steep sides of the bank and pulled itself out. For the opportunistic bear, the small meal was only that, a small addition to berries, carcasses and the kills it made. Slow moving giant sloths were its prime prey as were the wounded and dying. It shook itself dry and lazily traced the edge of the lake until it was well out of sight.

Satisfied the bear was gone, Lan filled both water skins. He then returned to the log where he prepared for another cool night. Lying with his eyes open, he could not think of anything other than the huge bear and the close encounter he had with death. It would be a long while before he would forget that bear. And tomorrow? Tomorrow he would see about the men who tended the fire.

The hidden encampment

A faint mist lay low and damp between the trees of the valley floor. A high ridge of cluttered stones afforded a clear view of the cliffs, which evidenced smoke lifting from the same campsite as it had a few days earlier.

Spring camp, not hunters. Their fire burns in the same place.

After a steep and rocky descent, Lan walked out onto easy ground until he reached the base of the nearest cliff. Sheer rock walls climbed high and vertically towards a plateau at their summit with the full length of the cliffs stretching across the entire valley. A scan of the profile showed only one way to the top. Once there, a day's walk would take him to where he could look down at the men's camp in safety.

Morning shadows from the rising new sun allowed the crags and protrusions in the cliff-face visibility. One erratic crevice had eroded along the stone wall in a diagonally upwards direction. After years of freezing and thawing, it had split into a wide enough space to get two hands inside. The rest of the wall appeared smooth in every direction.

He put the spear down and laid the quiver and water skins next to it. The deer skin leggings were loosened, removed and laid flat on the ground. Except for the water skins and bow, everything he owned was placed on top of the leg skins with the legs folded over them. The same strap of hide that had held them tight to his waist was now used to bind it all together. He put his arm through the strap and lifted the bundle onto his back. To make the water skins lighter to carry, they were emptied half way and looped around his neck. He put his other arm through the bow. The last thing he did was to put a short stick in his mouth.

Morning shadows went deep inside the crevice, a dangerous place to put ones hands without first checking to see what was there. Snakes liked to curl up in places like this to get out of the blistering sun. Scorpions and poisonous spiders made webs inside, spiders like the brown ones with bristly hairs all over their bodies; spiders with a nasty bite. That and the subsequent dizziness from the poison would surely cause him to fall to his death. With both hands inside the crevice, he felt for a footing and then moved diagonally upwards, checking the opening with the stick as he went along. The climb so far went along easily.

Half way up the cliff face, the crevice started to narrow. The difference was gradual at first, but soon it got harder to get a finger inside. At this height, it was a long way to the ground. Looking down at the tops of the trees and the collection of sharp edged, skull cracking boulders gave him a sickening feeling. He could easily visualize his body slipping off of the cliff-wall and slamming into the rocks below, splitting his head open. He also imagined the night creatures that would come to lick his blood and eat the flesh off the rocks.

The next handhold dislodged a shower of pebbles. They took time to fall as they skipped and cracked down the steep sides, and then the silence when they settled to the ground---a silence that belied the grasping wind. It kept whining inside his ear, made the height bring with it a terrible feeling of fragility and the threat of being yanked off of the cliff at any moment. This was no brother wind. Those were gentler. These howled like tundra wolves and blew in from the north in collaboration with Death Spirits; the kind that at times pre-shadowed violent storms.

Far below, the ground swirled around and around in a dizzying blur. Lan's head snapped back as he fixed his eyes on the grain textured wall---a vertical wall, one that had become smoother, flatter, foreign in its height and from all that was familiar. There no longer appeared to be a top to it anymore. It was as though the summit pierced the clouds, making the rest of the cliff seem insurmountable. He thought to climb back, but it would be best to go on. At least that way he could see where the next handhold would be, although by now, the crack had become as thin as a knife blade.

He spit the stick out. Snakes and spiders were the last of his worries now. Any hand hold would be welcomed. He listened to the stick and the time it was taking to fall. He could hear it hitting the side of the stone wall on the way down and finally when it cracked against a boulder at the bottom.

A few arm lengths farther along, he stopped to feel for a larger opening, or stone projection, or anything he could take advantage of. Spread out like a flattened lizard, he held himself in that awkward pose unable to advance any further.

If I stay here like this, I will lose my strength.

The stone felt cold on his face, pressed there for balance as he pasted his body to the side of the cliff. He wanted to rest, but to hold on with nothing more than finger tips and toes took energy. Leaning back to look for the next handhold would only throw off his balance. Even taking a deep breath---that could cause him to lean too far back and lose his grip. It was frightening to think that so little kept him there and that a fall awaited the slightest of errors.

He carefully stretched into emptiness, rising up on his toes to reach to the right where he slid his hand as far as it would go. He felt along the sandy texture of the cliff-wall just above his head and toward the left. One of his fingers bumped over a small bulge which he grabbed between a thumb and forefinger. Wet with sweat, he wiped them on the cliff and quickly grabbed back on. He needed another foothold or this would be as far as he could go. Scraping his right leg along the wall, he felt for something---anything, but the effort proved fruitless.

His right arm burned from fatigue and the bulge the only sure thing that kept him from falling, a danger he could not stop thinking about. The veins in his arms seemed ready to burst through the skin…and the sweat…sweat was lubricating his fingertips. He was sure to lose his grip on the bulge. He could not possibly hold on for too much longer, he thought. There had to be something---soon---anything to grab onto. He stretched toward his left for a grab hold that might only be a finger's length away, or a fingertip out from that. Looking to the right with his head flat against the wall prevented him from stretching his left hand any further. He blindly covered every bit of stone within the range of his reach---nothing---not so much as a knob or crack, or protrusion of any kind.

It was all becoming hopeless...and so soon. With one last hope, he held fast to the cliff and started to turn his head ever so slowly the other way around. Taking short, shallow breaths, he kept as close as possible to the cliff until he faced the left side. The three points holding him there were marginal at best. Clamped to the bulge with the two fingers of his right hand and his toes in the crack, he swept his free hand across the flat stone as far as reach would allow. Surprised and with partial relief, his fingers bumped over a shell shaped projection. He grabbed onto it and with the shallow grip, shifted his entire body closer to that side. With extreme care, he scraped his right leg upwards and away from the crack for something else to put a toe into.

Nothing here but a flat wall. I must pull myself up with nothing but my hands.

The shell shaped projection was now the best grip he had. If he did not pull himself up now and away from a reliance on the crack, he would never have the strength to remain where he was, nor climb back down and find the same hand-holds he had used to climb up. He pulled his body upwards as far as he could and let go of the bulge, relying solely on the grip he had on the shell shaped projection. With his feet dangling in mid-air and all of his weight supported by his left hand, he slid his right above his head and flat along the wall. His arm tingled from the strain as though a hundred pricking needles were piercing his flesh, stabbing deep into his shoulder muscles.

And then it was there---an indentation. He put both hands inside and pulled himself upwards. Holding on to it, he was able to anchor his left foot onto the shell shaped projection below. The other foot, he placed on the bulge.

Sand and pebbles filled the inside of the indentation, making it unstable. Holding on with one hand, he swept some of it out with the other, then quickly grabbed back on. With the good grip he had, he was able to sweep out more. Loose particles and dust came raining down on his face. Shaking his head, he squinted from the grating dust in his eyes.

Despite the stabbing stings, this was his only hope, there was nothing else---just this---this marginal hand hold; a last and final crack in the wall that was either going to become a link to the top or a link to his death.

Squeezing both eyelids shut and shaking his head from the pain, he dug out more loose particles, but was not ready to rely on it. There was still some loose rock that had to be cleared out. A large, flat piece broke away. He cast it off and suddenly his whole body jolted downward, crying out when he looked over his shoulder at the ground below.

An overwhelming feeling of terror shook inside as he scraped his feet along the gritty wall to find the footholds again. The bundle on his back weighed him down, while the blinding dust stung unbearably.

Thoughts of thirsty rats, should he fall, breaking through his eye balls to drink up the liquid, and the worms that would track through the wetness of his flesh was all too horrible to even imagine. He tried to stay focused, but no matter how much he tried, he could not stop the awful visions from haunting him.

And now the flying death spirits in the guise of large black vultures---those were beginning to haunt him as well. He could see his own body dropping in a free fall while the birds silently swarmed in and circled as he flailed about. One by one the vultures in the vision swooped in and began to pick at his skin in a fall that seemed to last forever. Amongst them, and twice Lan's size, the most aggressive of the lot flew in. Suspended in mid-air, both he and the vulture hovered facing one another. The death bird was so close, he could see hordes of fleas jumping between its feathers and onto their new found host...him! Sitting in wait and crawling around the rim of the bird's eyes were red mites the size of cranberries. Like a column of ants, each made their way along the top of the bird's beak to the hooked point at the end where their red forelegs then reached out to jump onto the fresh meat.

At the same time the hooked beak opened wide, immensely wide, and inside, the vulture's pink glistening throat. Pieces from Lan's body were being swallowed up before him; ears, fingers, chunks of meat---all of it going down the vultures gullet with undulating neck movements, one piece at a time.

Shaking his head from the awful vision, Lan searched for the next hand-hold. Thinking of death birds would never get him to the top. He had to think about the climb and nothing else.

From a distance high above his head, something green stuck out like shrubbery.

I can see the top. It must be.

One indentation led to another and finally to a sharp edged, shelf shaped stone. After that, a rougher surface in the cliff-face was far easier to follow until he finally reached the top. He grabbed onto the flat ledge of the surface and pulled the rest of his body up and over it. Rolling onto his stomach, he gasped and coughed along with a glorious feeling of relief.

He rose up on his knees, removed the bundle from his back and threw it to the side. He thanked the attending spirits; his father, the saber tooth, the mother sky---the sun brother. He thanked them over and over again, individually, one at a time, any spirit that even remotely had anything to do with the climb. He included the snake demon for not grabbing his legs and yanking him downward to certain death. He thanked the tundra winds for not blowing too strongly, and lastly, he thanked the death spirits for not sucking him in and swallowing him whole.

He dropped to the ground and rolled onto his back. For now he did not want to move. He wanted only to breathe in deeply and feel the cool mountain breezes blowing across his body. He would have lapsed into a deep sleep right then and there if it was not for the soreness in his eyes. Blindly, he clumsily tore at one of the water skins and felt for the knot. Pulling it apart, he lifted the skin over his head and poured what little remained onto his face. Opening his eyes wide, he blinked them clear, rubbed them and then opened them again into reddened slits.

The ground before him was flat with little growth. He lifted his gaze to boulders strewn about like legless carcasses, and the dwarf trees that struggled to survive under the less than favorable conditions. Beyond the cliff edge, an expansive view spread out in all directions. He sat crossed legged to face it while loosening the snake skin bandana. Unraveling the braid, he ran his fingers through the wetness of his scalp. Cool air swept from across the valley with winds that were constant and at times strong, unimpeded by the lack of growth here on the high plateau. The facing sun shined intensely, the air, sterile and pure; the running edges of far off cliffs, distinct and precise in their clarity.

Below, the forest seemed endless and heavily wooded. Conifers and deciduous trees, their leaves fresh and new, waved across a repetition of hills to far off mountains. Through the center of the valley, a narrow river looped in and out of the forest with mud banks lying at frequent bends in the river. Off to the right were the mountains he had crossed. From their foothills a gorge cut into the valley floor, the trench, dug deep with stone embankments on either side. Nearby, he could see the open meadow where he had hunted the fawn and the lake where he encountered the short faced bear.

To the East and beyond the cliffs, another mountain range staged the rising suns. There, too, was another pass, easily seen from this high vantage point. And beyond that? The flat place, he supposed, the grasslands and plentiful game that the shaman said would be there.

"Cross that high place to the other side. That is where you will find the new hunting place for our people."

This seemed a spiritual place borne of natural beauty. Lan wanted to learn its knowledge, its soul---its magic. Indeed, this was the land he believed he drew on the walls of the cavern. With his father's molars in hand, he stood and raised them towards the mother sky. Squeezing them inside his fist, he stood at the edge of the plateau and faced the valley. The words that he shouted echoed into the far distance.

"I am Man That Runs Too Fast. It is the other side of the high place that I walked from. This is the place that I asked for in the cave. It is the place that Sleeps by the Fire told me to find and now I am here. Know that I will return with my people and bring them to this new hunting place."

Lowering his arm down, he stretched his hand open where the impressions of teeth reddened the skin. He looked again at the plateau where all around, it was blown clean by the winds.

Very little grows here. It is only a sitting place---a place where a hunter sees everything the sky mother sees.

Ahead, the cliff made a gradual curve and then straightened across the valley. There, the whispered veil of a dying fire lifted white and vertically before dissipating into a flat parallel mist.

I can walk with the light of the sun and reach it before the dark time.

He stretched the tightness from his arms and legs. It was not very far at all.

CHAPTER 3
AYASHE

Ayashe (little one) sat as though uninterested in Matwua's (enemy) shuffling about camp. She stood shorter than most of the woman in her father, Akule's (looks up), tribe. Deep brown, almond shaped eyes gave her an exotic beauty, accentuated by long, dark lashes. Despite a petit stature, Ayashe was strong for her size. She was also quick to learn new things.

Well before she was born and when her father was still in adolescence, a high death rate from sickness left a shortage of women in the camps of the plain's tribes. Akule reached maturity with little chance for a mate. Frustrated, he and another male, unburdened by superstitions and taboo for the mountains, made the long journey to steal women from the Wadu, a coastal tribe.

Back then, Alawa (pea) and three other Wadu women had been too occupied in conversation while bathing children in a river to have noticed the tall men approaching from behind.

Stealing, as well as trading women was an accepted practice Alawa understood and a way for tribes to exchange new blood. In time, she learned to accept the tall people of the plains as her own. She bore Akule just this one child, although compared to his own people, Ayashe was considered of little value because of her small stature.

Alawa often told her daughter stories of how she had grown up with the Wadu and how much she loved them. Her glowing descriptions captured Ayashe's imagination and pride. It was the reason she continued to wear the finger bone necklace her mother gave to her as a child, a finger bone that had once been given to Alawa by her father, (fire walker) a brave leader. Ayashe embraced her grandfather as well as the Wadu Tribe, despite having never met them.

Wadus removed the right forefinger of enemies they killed. The more finger bones a warrior possessed, the braver he was perceived to be by the rest of the tribe as well as by their enemies. A full ring of finger bones around a warrior's neck would cower most men. Revered as their greatest fighter ever, Fire Walker wore three rings, representing over three hundred kills, more than anyone else in the Wadu Tribe.

Because she was considered of little value to her father's tribe, Ayashe was traded during her fourteenth summer to Matwua. The dowry consisted of a flint ax, a few furs and a handful of ornamental necklaces. Since then, seven more summers have passed.

A fine specimen, Matwua's thick body, muscular limbs and tall height were typical of the men of the plains tribes. Taller than the tribesmen from the coast, his arms were crushingly strong. His hair spread outwardly in tangled misdirection before fanning out to round, well-padded shoulders. Evolved from a colder climate when his ancestors first migrated from Siberia, the thickness of his head hair, barrel chest as well as light skin were all adaptations to the white-out of winter. There were other adaptations to the cold as well, like a large nose with an increased amount of membranes to warm cold air. Now, having settled in the flat grasslands for thousands of years along with a high protein diet of mammoth and other grassland ungulates, the plains Indians evolved into a massive size.

Around each wrist Matwua wore badger claw bracelets. On occasions when it suited him, he liked to wear the sun-dried carcass of an eagle on his head with the beak resting over his forehead. He wore nothing else during the hot time, except for a triangular groin patch---a tough piece of hide to hold everything in and to protect his vitals from barbs and bushes.

Matwua had at one time followed Nakoma (great spirit), the tribe's leader. Now an outcast, he was no longer a member of that tribe. Unlike the other tribesmen who coexisted with one another, Matwua had been troublesome and often quarreled with his fellow hunters, settling disputes with gut reasoning and heavy hands. Excluded from hunts, he was stripped of the prestigious position of "First Hunter", a title of high merit earned after completing a physically grueling ritual. Seeking revenge, he was thought to have raped and killed Una, Achak's woman.

Killing a member of one's own tribe was against tribal law. Despite Matwua's prowess and need as a hunter, his demeaning character and lack of concern for the welfare of the tribe left Nakoma no other choice. In a final decision, along with that of the elders, Matwua was taken to Mantotohpa's people and offered to Akule as a mate for his daughter, Ayashe.

However, Matwua's reputation preceded him. Like Nakoma, Mantotohpa expressed no desire to include him as one of his own. That left no choice for Matwua, but to take his newly acquired mate to the mountains, alone.

"Bring that," he snapped, pointing at two water skins.

Tied at both ends, Ayashe threw the sealed wolf stomachs, heavy with water, over her shoulder. Hunts thrilled her. After a final check around camp she hurried off to catch up to him.

Lan leaned forward and peered over the cliff edge into an empty campsite far below. An ideal location, it lay set back against the face of the cliff within a concave formation. Strewn with bits of bone and rock debris was a level dirt floor. To the immediate left, what he saw there made him flinch.

"No!" he blurted out loud.

A talus of jagged rocks sloped downward from the top of the cliff to within steps of the stranger's camp. It was an easy descent and nothing like the perilous climb he had made earlier that day.

Immediately above the encampment, a stone ledge extended outward from the cliff wall which allowed protection from rock-falls and driving rainstorms. In the middle of the floor and propped against a boulder, an aged spear with the color of hardwood appeared as though it would be too short to throw any great distance.

Off to the side, the fresh rib cage of an elk, the meat left untouched, hung from a dead tree growing out of a crack in the wall. Long leather straps held the ribs high above an expended fire where it had been left to smoke.

Around the encircling perimeter of the camp, and clear of foliage, discarded bones and hides of old hunts lay thrown about. At its forefront, a row of tall posts stood as pedestals for the skulls sitting ominously on top of them. A saber tooth tiger, a grizzly bear and several dyer wolf heads stared out from deep eye sockets along with their foreboding spirits. Facing toward a wall of trees at the far end of the clearing, they forewarned all who might trespass.

There will be a time when I will bring my people to this place. If these men follow me I will have no reason to kill them. It is by their fire that I must now walk to fill my water skins.

Biting off a mouthful of fawn meat, he checked the woods for movement while listening for voices. There was nothing left to do now but to wait for whatever tribe presented itself.

The hated Dinga went to war naked. Here, he would know them by the dotted scar lines depicting the animals they hunted.

Wadu, by far the most feared of all tribes and with the greatest numbers, spared no captives lives. Lan shook from the thought of them. Lying on his back, he blocked the sun with his arm.

If these are Manama, they will try to kill me. They will then cook me in their fire...as would the Wadu and the Dinga. I cannot go back the way I came. The only way off this cliff is here, through these men.

<hr />

An echo of slapping flints startled Lan awake. He rolled over and peered over the edge with nervous anticipation. Startled, he slunk back. "Big Man!" He mumbled.

This one comes from the flat land beyond this high place where I now stand. It is the place where new suns are born. He is from the tall people that hunt the long tooth. That is what our elders tell us.

Columbian mammoths grew larger than any known animal and never seen on Lan's side of the mountains. The high, rugged terrain, as well as valleys like this, were thick with trees and rocky outcroppings---far too impassable for so cumbersome a beast. It was an animal that had two horns longer than the length of a man. Carrying its tremendous weight were five legs, one of which could lift a hunter and throw him to his death. It was an animal that had become more myth than truth, one that had grown out of proportion to its true size in the light of many a night fire---a beast as big as a mountain.

The man's size impressed Lan. There were no tattoos, no tribal scars, only his naked skin covered with what appeared to be dirt, tree sap and dried blood.

How many are like this one. This huge hunter could easily crush me with little trouble.

Matwua's wide back concealed a rekindled fire when he bent over to place a log onto the flames. He walked heavily to a corner where he picked up something round. Lan could not see what it was, only that the man began to tap on it. He turned it around, hesitated as though thinking and then picked up a small stone from the floor and twisted it into the round thing he was holding.

After what appeared to be an unsuccessful attempt at drilling the stone into it, he held it up to get a better look.

The upward glance startled Lan. He quickly darted away from the edge, but interest soon lured him back and what he saw next, took him by surprise. From beneath the overhang stepped a youthful woman who casually sauntered over to where the man stood.

"Binatsu te keya. Mo bukanik gah botchka…est mo taksinay bot Matwua tuksta est latzo, (Your stone is dull. That is why Matwua cannot make the hole in the turtle)," she said.

Matwua's voice returned basso and fully resonant, the strange tongue they spoke, foreign to any Lan had heard before.

"Agh!… Tste keya." He threw it back into a corner.

Taking the stone from him, the woman sharpened it on the large boulder. Next, she picked up the turtle shell and began to drill a hole into it. Every time she pressed down, the silky strands of her hair bounced across her chest and brushed across her large, pink nipples. Odd how she did not have the look of his kind either, her being much smaller…and cleaner.

Their words are not mine.

Puzzled, Lan could not relate the woman to any tribe he knew of. And there was something else besides perfect breast that jostled underneath all of that hair. It was something white and hanging from her neck. It was flipping around from one breast to the other; distracting to follow between the interrupting flashes of pink. It had the look of bone…white bone…white finger bone.

"Wadu!" Lan spat on the ground.

The woman weaved a strip of hide through the hole and knotted it at the end to finish the necklace.

"Keya na labo. (Here is your turtle)."

The results pleased the man who impatiently snatched it from her and looped it around his neck.

Lan's attention turned to the woman when she bent over to pick up something small, a tool perhaps. He could not see what it was, nor did he care, more interested in observing her full buttocks twitching their naked curves to the sides when she walked to the other end of the camp. Silk brown hair hung delicate waves down the sculpture of her back. Her legs were well muscled, the skin, smooth and youthful with a tan that graduated from light to medium. The back of her knees dimpled evenly above well-formed calves.

For the rest of the day, Lan watched everything she did until the arrival of nightfall. Naked in the chilling air, she grabbed one of the wolf furs and stood by the fire, wrapped it around herself and faced the forest.

Matwua walked up from behind, slid the small piece of elk hide that covered his groin area to the side and stroked his thick erection.

"My need is to sleep," she meekly said.

Reaching for the end of her wolf fur, he wrenched it from her and tossed it to the side. He squatted before her, grabbed her by the arms and pulled her to the ground before she had a chance to say anything else.

It was not her place to choose otherwise. Knowing she had to give in, she clamped her jaws down tight, spread her legs out to the sides and stared blankly at the stone wall.

Matwua entered her forcefully, grunting as he continued to violate her.

Flush with hate, Lan moved away from the edge and chose a place alongside one of the boulders in which to sleep.

He drifted into a preconceived dream. It was a dream where he looked into the woman's eyes and ran fingers through her hair. He said sweet things to her, wrapped his arms around her, pulled her closer to him---listened to those soft words she whispered into his ear---into his dream. He touched her cheek with his cheek, traced finger tips down the run of her back, then lightly over her hips and around to her soft, yet firm buttocks. He said soft words to her and returned to the front to touch below her stomach where his fingers spread to fully envelope her mound. Lustfully warm, he pressed his hardness against her side and smelled the sweetness of her neck. His lips touched her lips as he looked into the gaze that returned his through wanting eyes---eyes that were long lashed and lustful and blinking back softly---like flower petals flexing in the rain.

She moaned as soon as he caressed her nipples. She wanted him now and he knew and picked her up and laid her on wolf fur that was pure white with long hairs that glistened in the moon light. The soft fur outlined her body as she lay back sensually perfect with a look that beckoned and lavish breasts pulling at his desires. Her heavy breathing became controlled yet delicately quivered as she parted her thighs, the hairs from her mound, long and unfolding from a compressed, wet state. She was speaking to him in whispered words that sounded teasingly sultry and so full of coaxing.

Motioning for him to lower himself down, she closed her eyes, the smile no longer there. She was too full of emotion for that. Instead, she immersed herself into the full anticipated ecstasy of what she knew was to come. She grabbed his manhood and guided it inside of her, raising her hips to receive him further.

Lan opened his eyes to a black sky filled from end to end with a crush of stars---his breathing, heavy, the smell of smoke, slight in the cool air.

Unable to put the woman out of his mind, he turned and squeezed himself into the depression underneath a boulder. He thought about the man, the scars on his skin, his huge head---the scraggly hair. He tried to remember everything ugly about him. That way, he would not have to think about the woman anymore.

Awakening to the sun on his face, Lan slept more than he had wanted to. Wasting no time, he rubbed sleep laden eyes and leaned over the edge. Eager to see the woman, he was disappointed at the sight of an empty camp. No sign of either of them.

Gone hunting! A good time to go down.

Loading everything onto his back, he took a long hard look at the forest below him before descending the talus. It was an easy climb down. When he reached the overhang, he stepped carefully to the end of it and looked below his feet to the floor of the camp. The odors were strong with a smell of urine and sweat---fermented sweat, and the smell of rancid meat.

Large rain drops started to bounce and form small craters in the loose soil. He had not noticed before that it had started to rain, only now feeling the drops in his hair. And somewhere out past the forest, somewhere beneath the horizon's still, an explosion cracked the dull, quiescent sky.

He scanned the forest for signs of movement before jumping down the rest of the way.

The animals hide from the rain. With nothing to hunt they will soon be back.

In the dampness, the man's odor strongly permeated the camp. Strange, how their presence still lingered as though they never left. To stand in the silence and see their personal belongings, the place where they ate, where they slept, their footprints in the dirt, or even to stand next to their fire, felt eerily personal.

Lined with stones, the fire pit still smoldered from its center. In among the ashes, a blackened buffalo skull lay half buried. Cracked opened for the brain inside, it lay where it was tossed along with an array of broken bits of bone.

Lan stared at the open ground on the other side of the outer post and to the far end of the clearing where the trunks of the trees melded into the black shadows of the forest. It all remained unchanged, the birds as active now as they had been all morning. It was a sure sign no one was approaching, unless the birds had grown accustomed to the man being around. Would they then not carry on whether or not he was there?

Facing the horizon, he lifted his hand to it so that the first finger lay across the base line of the distant trees. Between that and the rising sun, he counted three fingers. Had they made a kill in the early hours of dawn they would have been back by now.

He kills nothing and now the animals hide from the rain. He will soon return.

In camp, sunlight worked its way into the back-most corner of the encampment. In the center of the drizzle darkened floor and just outside of the fire pit, stood the boulder with the spear leaning against it. He wanted to touch the kill stick, appraise it, but caution made him hesitate---a fleeting thought of caution that he soon dismissed. Worried for its guarding spirit, he carefully approached the oaken spear.

This kill stick has seen many hunts.

Setting the bundle down next to the boulder, he gently picked it up by the middle of the shaft and held it away from himself. His grip spread wide. He could only close his hand halfway around it. Taupe in color, the spear was roughly honed and dark where it was held. Turning the shaft in a continuous circle showed the point at the end to be evenly carved. Burned black in a fire and chipped from use, it was hardly a design to fit the butt end of a stone blade into. It was so unlike his own spear made from strong ash, the quartz blade, honed to a triangular shape and sharpened, the balance even, the flight straight and distant.

Yet, there was something plausible about this spear, something time-proven, a conjectured strength---an inner power. Just the look of it, the intentional burning, its age, the weight of it, showed it to have once been a strong killing tool.

What of its spirit, does it still own this kill stick?

Lan raised the spear above his shoulder and stabbed at imaginary prey. Tossing it into his other hand he stabbed and...

The clearing!
He looked anxiously across the open field toward the forest.
The birds no longer make their sound in the trees.
Engrossed in the spear, he had forgotten to recheck the clearing. He leaned it against the boulder, careful to leave it in the exact same position where it was before.

In the corner beneath the overhang, a tool made from an antler lay half buried in soft dirt. Next to it were two wolf furs rolled into tight bundles. On the other side, a skin from a juvenile bear had been neatly folded and wedged into a corner among the winter furs.

At the back wall, sheltered by the overhang, lay a log dragged in for sitting, and on top, the turtle shell he had seen earlier.

Hanging from the dead tree, the rib cage from the elk smoked above the fire. He reached for his bone knife, climbed up and cut into the leather straps.

Light rain continued to fall with persistence. Strange, how the air felt so still with not a hint of wind---the woods---silent...and where were the birds? He cut through the rest of the straps and braced for the noise.

With a cloud of dust, the ribs came crashing to the ground amidst a horde of fleeing, green headed flies. The sound echoed loudly, especially so in the confines of the concave depression. It had amplified to such an extent, it made everything inside seem twice as loud than it actually was; made the sound of ribs hitting the ground split the silence. Another check---no one there.

He broke off a leafy branch from a nearby bush and set it on top of the boulder. Hastily, he lifted the bundle onto his back along with the elk ribs. Not wanting to delay any further, he backed away, scratched out all of the remaining footprints with the branch and then jogged past the line of skull laden posts and into the forest. Leaf litter underfoot hid his tracks as he made his way through thick brush to avoid the game trails.

The rest of the day was spent by the river bank where he readied everything for the climb to the pass. He was satisfied with the valley. It had plenty of game and water and would serve his tribe well. Fruit trees grew abundantly as well as berries and he recognized the leaves of edible tubers below ground. Mountains on every side protected the valley from winter's winds. It was perfect in every way. The only obstacle was the man, and Lan and his tribesmen would one day take care of him.

There was only one other thing that could alter those plans. It was not about the valley. He was sure he had settled on that. And it was not about moving on to the next valley, which he needed to do for the future safety of his tribe. He had to know what dangers lie on the other side and the tribes he would find there.

No, this was about the woman. He could not get her out of his mind. His abstinence had been long and she was by far more beautiful than any woman he knew of. He could leave now. He had plenty of meat, enough to last through the next pass. But that was not what he really wanted. He wanted her. He wanted her more than anything and he was willing to kill to satisfy that wanton lust.

The elk ribs, he left hanging high from the branch of a maple. Having been dried over a fire, the meat would last without spoiling. He finished the rest of the fawn, and although it filled him, fresh meat would have been far tastier.

Traps were set underneath the cover of flowering bitter vetch. The purple petals, veined in violet, made good camouflage for the sinew used. In the morning they would be checked for small game.

Rain kept the animals away. Without a kill, Matwua and Ayashe returned to camp. Believing smoked elk ribs awaited their return, they were surprised to find it missing.

Matwua looked with disgust at the empty straps hanging down. "Mas tet! (bear) A mas tet has taken the bondo (elk)." He checked for prints. *Why are there no tracks?*

Angry, he looked along the ground like the well-seasoned hunter he was. The foot trail was searched all the way to the forest, including any open ground that could hold a print. Troubled, he rechecked the trail again.

"I know it was a mas tet!" He said.

She joined him and rechecked the same places where Matwua had already searched, but found nothing new.

"Here!" He finally shouted.

She ran up with raised brows. "Mowatchi! (man from the high place)."

He wears skins on his feet," said Matwua, looking up toward the mountains.

Indeed, it had to be a Mowatchi. The prints were too small to be one of his own kind. And there was something else about the prints, something Matwua readily saw in the dirt and it did not take an experienced hunter to be able to see it. It was not about size, or shape, or how deep the prints were pressed into the soil, nor how long they had been there, or even the skins the man wore on his feet. The Mowatchi was alone.

Day break

Moisture steamed the valley as a strong sun sucked the wetness back to the clouds. Matwua returned to the forest determined to find something to eat. Ayashe, frightened of the new man's presence, who might even now be lurking nearby, did not want to remain in camp alone.

After checking the usual places, they traveled farther than most of their hunts. Eventually, they surprised a female coyote that had backed herself into a den full of newborn pups. The shallow burrow made the kill almost effortless for Matwua as he plunged a sharpened spear into the coyote's throat.

Ayashe screamed with laughter.

The animal shrieked loudly. In an effort to breathe, it choked on its own blood. Air was forced out through the wound in its neck, followed by large, red bubbles and the hissing sound of escaping air. Once again, Matwua lunged the spear into the coyote's neck and waited for the gurgling to stop. Grabbing it by the front paws, he pulled it out of the burrow.

"You killed a jonga!" Ayashe jumped up and down excitedly. She dropped to the ground and sat crossed legged with a frozen grin on her face, her head resting on her fist as she watched him clean the kill.

From the open wound in the jonga's neck, Matwua sliced through the tough hide, lengthening the cut and pulling it apart as he went along. Using the ax, he chopped through the spine, severing the head with one blow. It caused it to roll away on the sloped ground with the tongue sticking out of the animal's mouth. He quickly caught it and slammed it down hard.

He wanted the fangs for their trophy value. After several blows with the ax, he wrenched them both free.

"Take this and wear the jonga."

The other fang, he kept for himself.

With a laugh in her voice, Ayashe caressed the bloody fang to her face. "Now I own the jonga's spirit."

A cut into the belly of the animal was begun below the ribs and continued to the animal's anus. Reaching in, Matwua pulled out the intestines and stomach. He stuck his hand inside the chest cavity and grabbed the esophagus, entwined it around his fingers and yanked downward until it snapped away. The heart and lungs were ripped free the same way. By grabbing the coyote by the front paws and lifting it high, everything inside spilled onto the ground with the heart falling on top. After licking his arms and hands clean of blood, along with mired, ill-fated flies, he picked out the heart from the rest and ate it in two bites.

All this time Ayashe waited patiently while Matwua ignored her stares even though he knew she was as hungry as he was. She smiled when he dropped a piece of liver onto her lap, quickly ate it and silently waited for the scrap of kidney he threw to her.

"Bring the head," he snapped.

"The little jongas, should we not bring them with us?"

"Let the nahgoes take them. Their meat is not enough."

Lifting the carcass to his shoulder, Matwua returned to camp with Ayashe close behind.

⊱⊰

Back in camp at the fire pit, she stirred ashes up from the bottom, exposing burning cinders from the morning fire. She placed dry leaves over them and blew on it until she got it burning. Sticks were thrown in and lastly, logs placed inside.

After the coyote was skinned, Matwua laid the carcass on top of the logs. Before long, the roast permeated the camp with an appetizing aroma. The huge man was famished and would not wait for the animal to fully cook. Tearing into hot blistering flesh, he ripped off a foreleg from the shoulder. Scalding rivulets of grease and blood fizzled from the tear, but the man's calloused hands seemed to be unaffected by the heat. He blew on it and when it was cool enough, he bit off an impossibly large mouthful, barely chewing before swallowing the large chunk whole. He continued to engorge himself until he was overstuffed.

From beneath the shade at the back end of camp, he laid his heavy bulk down and called out to Ayashe.

"I will find this Mowatchi and with the new sun I will hunt him. It is now that I must rest."

Indifferent, Ayashe waited for her turn at the meat---waited for him to close his eyes and snore contentedly.

⊱⊰

The traps Lan set were empty when he last looked. He put the spear and quiver down and began an inspection of his hunting tools. The arrows were checked by examining the tail feathers adhesion to the shafts and combing them straight. The ax proved flawless with no chips or any other imperfections. While examining the spear, feelings of anticipation emanated from his gut as he thought about the man. He could not get him or the woman out of his mind.

By nightfall it was time to check the traps again. Upon arrival, he found a fat rabbit kicking at the knot around its leg. He picked it up and slammed it to the ground, breaking the animal's neck. Filled on elk ribs, he saved the fresh meat for the next day, hanging it high in a pine tree before settling in for the night.

Bright squints of morning sun streaked awakening rays between the branches of the trees, scattering highlights of windblown leaves onto the forest floor. Along the bank, the usual tracks pocked meandering trails into the mud. Off in the distance, through the openings in the forest, the cliff Lan had climbed stood imposing and radiant in the sun's full cast.

At the water's edge, he squatted on his knees, opened the rabbits belly and dipped it under. Blood spread outwardly like red smoke along the mirrored sky in ever widening ripples. As it floated away, Lan's own distorted image began to stabilize across the water's wavering surface. Behind the image, a shimmering shadow began to hover over it and soon cleared into a mosaic of colors until morphing into a large man standing over him. Believing it to be a bear, Lan dove into the river. Long hard strokes quickly brought him to the middle where he turned to look at the shore. From his distance he stared at the man that was staring back at him.

In Matwua, a nurtured hate broiled inside. For his entire life, tales had passed down from the elders of the tumultuous conflicts among the Mowatchi tribes that lived beyond the high place. The stories spread around many a night fire, instilling fear and resentment at the very thought of them.

For Lan, however, the man staring back, controlled all of his treasured possessions and now created an obstacle. Without kill sticks, he could go no further.

Looking at the woman convinced him of what he really wanted. Deep feelings of lust tempered the flame of anger. Her returning gaze, however, held trivial interest. It was a gaze with a lack of emotion, empty and no more than a curious gaze at a mountain, or a river, or the dream-filled look into ones night fire. Yet…those same long lashed brown eyes, without any intention on her part, could draw into them a man's virile spirit. They were sultry and erotic and full of sensuality, like those of a woman in the throes of passion.

He could hear the big one talking in their strange language.

"Let the nahgos (wolves) finish him. I will leave him nothing."

Matwua was upset at losing his ax in the river when he had thrown it at the Mowatchi. It was a lost opportunity and all for nothing. He barked out a series of orders to Ayashe. "Grab his kill sticks…and the bo bo (rabbit). The nahgos will soon take him. I will leave him nothing."

"The bondo (elk) he took from us is not here," she said.

"Take his ax and the rest," Matwua snapped, pointing annoyingly at them.

"These water skins are full," she stated.

"Bring them!"

"It is good that the mas tet and nahgos eat him," she sullenly muttered, adding the quiver and bow in with the rest.

They then turned for the trail that led toward camp, stopping short as soon as they heard the sound of the Mowatchi's angry voice.

"I am Man That Runs Too Fast! I lead the Bandu and I will show you no fear. You mean nothing to me."

⟞╬⟝

Skewered on a stick, Ayashe held the skinned rabbit over the fire until the pink flesh turned brown, leaving it on the logs to cook.

"This is a good ax." Matwua turned the Mowatchi's ax around to examine it. Dropping it next to the fire, he then picked up the man's spear. "This spear will not hold this sharp rock when it is inside an animal. It will break if it goes past the ribs when I try to pull it out…and it is too light in my hands. It has no power."

Tossed to the side, the spear rolled along the floor and stopped at the cliff wall. The arrows were unlike any kill sticks he knew of. He never saw anything like them. He pulled one out of the quiver. "These arrows are many times too weak. Look how it does not know how to kill the nahgo (wolf) or the mas tet. (bear)

Dumbfounded, he shook his head while mumbling softly, "No…it cannot kill the mas tet."

Ayashe agreed. "The mas tet is too big for those kill sticks."

Matwua stared at the miniature spears and tried to imagine killing a bear with them. "Maybe it kills the bo bo."

He stepped to where the rabbit lay cooking and turned it over with one of the arrows. The inspection was thorough and other than the jumper's lack of skin, the missing head and disemboweled cavity, he could not find the wound that actually killed it. "The Mowatchi killed the bo bo with a rock."

Proud at having solved the dilemma, he threw the arrow into the fire and kicked the quiver into a back corner.

"You can make me something with the rest of these small black rocks so I can wear them around my neck."

The bow perplexed him even more. Sitting on the log, he admired the etched wolves that seemed so real, and the deer they chased in the light of a sun. His brows crunched together as he slid slowly to the ground to study the scene with utmost scrutiny.

Eying the flat pieces of buffalo horn embedded into the bow, he muttered under his breath. "Pretty bone."

The artwork was far better than anything he could do, and nothing he would have thought of himself. It was so perfect…so exact. The way the nahgos were running and all of those pretty pebbles and iridescent bits of shells; he liked those best.

"What is this stick? Does this Mowatchi use it to call his spirits before a hunt? …So pretty!"

He held the bow so that it hung straight down, then raised it up high and turned it around, his lips left slightly parted, his legs sprawled out from beneath his large belly.

Ayashe liked the thing, too. She wanted to hold it so she could look closely at the nahgos and the bondo. No longer feeling threatened by the outsider, she felt relieved that he had been left defenseless.

"The Mowatchi is many times brave or he did not see his own death."

Matwua answered her in an angry tone. "He will soon see that death in my hands."

Nodding, she added, "When he had these kill sticks, that was the time for his long walk from this place."

She moved to the log to sit next to him. The first thing she remembered about the stranger was the way he had stared back. She recalled the mad look on his face, but mostly, she remembered the irritation in his voice. Warmly, she wriggled into her man's strong shoulder and placed her hand on the thickness of his thigh.

Late day passed into evening with a fire that no longer raged. Matwua finished tying the coyote and what was left of the rabbit high onto the overhanging branch of the dead tree. He licked his fingers while walking to the back corner and returned wearing the dried out carcass of an eagle. Adjusted so that it fit squarely on his head, he made his way to the clearing in front of the line of post where he stood and glared at the forest. Furious for not having been able to kill the Mowatchi, he grinned deceitfully. His body and pupils remained unmoving while stiffly turning his head to stare sideways at the line of trees. He seemed crazed, the lasting grin, stretching and bearing a full set of oversized teeth. One of the lower canines was missing, another chipped, the rest crowded in like boulders that had tumbled into a pit too small for them.

The grin turned into a sneer. Facing the forest, he furiously shouted in its direction. "I will soon hunt you, Mowatchi. If you still live after I wound you, I will bring you to my fire and give you great pain."

Torture was fun, Matwua loved it. Wounded animals suffered from his need to see that pain. He cut off paws and ears while the animals were still alive. Their stomachs were sliced open and the intestines pulled out. He liked that almost as much as he liked seeing the animal's squeal and kick when what remained of them burned in the fire.

He pulled one of the burning logs out; causing sparks and flames to raise high into the night air. Yellow light flashed across the walls, stretching the man's shadow into an eerie being with monstrous proportions. Reentering the clearing, he worked himself into a frenzy.

"I do not have to give the mas tet raw meat. **You will burn like the jonga I cooked in my fire."**

Flames from the log nearly touched the ground as he carried it low and deeper into the clearing. There he stood like a wild ape, half bent with his head turned sideways and slunk between his shoulders. Perusing the forest, his eyes narrowed as he held the eagle carcass tight to his head while waving the burning log before him.

"You cannot take what belongs to Matwua. Now you wait with the bondo you took from me. You wait with no kill sticks, because they are here with me."

Nightfall

Within the concave formation, the camp long settled into a quiet pall. A cloud filled sky filtered out the stars and partial moon, leaving everything below in total darkness. A strong breeze blew through the encampment. Above the fire, the sound of dry leather rubbing against rough bark creaked from the weight of the carcass as it swung back and forth from the overhead branch. The rhythmical sound, along with accompanying crickets was all that disturbed the silence.

Matwua dragged one of the wolf furs next to the fire and rolled it out so that it lay fur side up.

Out there, beyond camp, sitting unseen beyond where the light of the fire could reach him, Lan squatted low and continued to watch and wait. Though he could not see his things, he knew the quiver and water skins were where the man had thrown them—somewhere around the back wall of the camp.

My spear rolled to the side. And my ax...that is by the fire next to him. The bow is near the log where my arrows were left.

Ayashe edged a few steps past the crackling fire and looked hard into the blackness. She could feel the Mowatchi's presence. It was not something she knew for sure. It was only a feeling. He was out there...somewhere close by. He had to be.

He has fear for Matwua. He will not come to our fire...not with nothing in his hands.

Stepping back inside, she grabbed her wolf skin fur and spread it out next to Matwua. Laying on her back, she closed her eyes and fitfully fell into a light sleep.

Concealed within the bleak darkness, Lan took in a deep breath, eased himself up and stood tall. For an enduring moment he stood there, silent before pressing his foot down onto loose pebbles. The sound seemed loud---so loud, it was as if they echoed across the valley. He stiffened and waited with a held breath.

His steps could surely wake them from a deep sleep, make the man look up and see him approaching. Once inside, where could he go, he thought. The cliff would enclose him from both sides as well as from behind.

When I am inside, I will have no chance to run if he wakes...and I will have nothing in my hands.

Wary and more cautious, he removed the foot coverings and set them on the ground. With a predetermined placement of the next step, he pressed his heel down and then rolled the well calloused sole forward to muffle the sound of the loose pebbles underneath. Like a saber tooth's stalk, he stealthily took one step at a time. Only three more, he guessed; slower, quieter...two more...stop! That sound---he held his breath and turned toward the noise.

It was easy to make plans from the outside, but to engage in those very same plans with real and tangible actions and the heavy breathing man slobbering his every breath and voluminous snorting and wheezing within a step of where Lan now stood was heart stopping.

He waited while the man rolled into a more comfortable position. Even the crickets stopped their repetitive scratching—the scorched and headless carcass hanging from the over-head bough, now settled in the stilled wind. The silence all around seemed eerie and portentous.

As Lan stepped into the light, the moving image of fiery flames played across his skin. On the other side, the two sleeping forms lay contented within the warmth of the fire.

Then, the fall of a lone pebble as its teetering hold gave way from high up on the cliff-face, its precarious brace of one or two grains of sand loosened by some undetectable, subtle vibration; like a shrew scurrying about or a beetle in its nightly quest for food.

Lan's head snapped around toward the sound of the pebble that rolled and tumbled. No! It crashed and slammed, like a liberated boulder as it banged its way into an ear shattering clamor down the wall of the cliff. It then shot across the floor and finally ended its short but tumultuous freedom inside the abrupt silence once again.

Knowing the man must have heard, he faced the penetrating eyes of his open stare. He looked straight at him, the firelight reflecting red in his eyes. All around, the cliff enclosed Lan with its high density of stone as if in aid of the big man lying there. Straining through the shadowy light, he looked for a sign in the huge face for the coming anger. He could see the whites of his eyes, could feel the animal behind them emerge, and that animal was looking through Lan as though he was merely a scrawled outline on the wall behind him. He waited for an attack, but the charge never came; only the quivering exhaled slumber from the man's open lips. For, though his eyes were open, they watched only his dream.

If I had my bow, I could easily wound him with my many arrows. I would then run in and finish him with the ax.

He let out the long breath he had been holding and edged cautiously through camp toward the back-most corner beneath the overhang. Underneath the gravel and loose dirt, he felt around for the quiver and quickly found the strap to it. He slid his arm quietly through so that the quiver hung behind his left shoulder. The water skins, he found in the same place and positioned them over the same shoulder. The bow still lay next to the log where the man had sat looking at it. Grabbing it, he looped it over his head. Finding the spear in the dark would be near impossible. It was somewhere by the wall to the right of the fire.

My ax is next to his head. I cannot leave it with him.

Six steps toward the fire put him back into its flickering glow. He eased fully into the light with the fire burning hot on his face. The sound of snapping embers and heavy breathing was now joined by the returning crickets that no longer felt his presence in the clearing.

Looking down at the man, he struggled with a new emotion building up inside. Fear changed to hate and he did not want to struggle with that if he was going to get out of there alive. That kind of thinking was foreboding, because it led to an urge to kill. He wanted those thoughts to go away. And he wanted the images of his persuading past human kills to go away as well. They kept replaying in his mind and only served to make killing again easy---a challenge that could get him killed instead.

Why can I not take my eyes from this woman?

He could leave now, run out with the things he had, but looking at her sleeping naked on the fur kept him hesitant to her allure. Her thighs were smooth and soft where they joined, the muscular line of her belly, leading to well-formed breast. The rest of her outlines stood defined by strong curves---so exquisite---so perfect.

His jaws flexed when he turned to face the man.

Matwua stirred, moved his head to the side and lowered it toward his chest. From the light of the embers, a reflection within the entanglement of hair flashed back at Lan.

My ax!

Macabre thoughts were all that filled his mind as Matwua's cavernous chest drew in the night air.

It would be nothing for me to lean my kill stick into his chest and run it through his heart. If only...

He thought to try and find the spear, 'though exactly where it was he did not know for sure. And that would take time...and noise.

Quietly, he removed the quiver, water skins and bow, placing them gently on the ground. Lying flat alongside them in the dirt, he reached up and pulled himself forward until his head was just two finger's width away from Matwua's. Lightly, cautiously, he extended his hand toward the ax handle. With torpid fingers stretching, he barely touched the wood and then ever so slowly, encircled the handle. Gently, he lifted it up and immediately stopped at the sound of scrapping. His body stiffened.

He hears...slower...I must do this slower.

He had not noticed until now that his hands were shaking. Pausing, he pressed his lips together as he lifted the ax slightly off the ground and then suddenly stopped and laid the ax back down.

This will not be easy. I cannot simply pick up my ax and walk quietly into the dark. The ax is entangled in his hair.

He took a slow breath, lifted and pulled ever so gently, but it caused the hairs at the other end to lift up and become taut.

I must find another way.

The huge man's thick chest expanded as the enormous cavity inside filled with air; the stench, overpowering, the murmurs, loud with basso vibrations.

From the deer skin pouch, he took out a stone chip and readied himself. His grip back on the ax handle, he gently lifted it and pulled until the hair lifted straight. One by one, the hairs were cut. There did not seem to be many. He cut a few more, waited for the man to exhale, then cut again, and then another until the chip got caught in a snag.

Nothing left to do now but to…

"Huh?" Matwua grunted.

Lan watched in fear as the huge man's head lifted off the ground with the last of the strands ripping from his scalp. From deep within his cavernous chest came a low pitched groan that rumbled loudly and full of vibrating resonance. The fluttering tremors rolled along the ground and into every bone in Lan's body. In total disbelief, he let go of the ax and bolted upright. Unbalanced, he fell to the side and stumbled into smoldering ashes. Sparks shot into the ebony night, flashing the entire wall with an instant of light and the huge shadow of the man lifting his monstrous bulk into a towering stance. Before Lan, stood the biggest man he had ever encountered, two heads taller and twice his girth.

His booming vociferous roar vibrated with ear splitting ferocity. Hot animal breath engulfed Lan like vipers venom, paralyzing him with fear as he stood to face him.

Wide eyed, Matwua screamed, **"Why are you here, Mowatchi?"**

The ax, somewhere near Lan's feet, was useless where it lay. He could not move, much less reach for it. It was as if his legs drove their length into the ground beneath him and anchored themselves deep inside the valley floor.

Matwua took two steps between them---so close, the hair on his stomach touched Lan's chin. The moment seemed unending, Lan's body becoming totally acquiescent since he was sure the spirits had abandoned him. It was as though the outcome was irreversibly settled. Nothing felt important anymore, his tribe, the hunts, not even the woman, now sitting up with her mouth left agape. All he could do was stare blindly into the darkness at the massive human that he could smell as much as he could see. The closeness was both violating and intimidating---the odor, strong and invading. And somewhere from up above, the breath that came down was coming down through wheezing nostrils. Lan could hear it grow louder and the breathing stronger as the man lowered his huge face directly in front of his.

Glowering, sunken eyes, red from reflecting embers, stared from beneath heavy brows. Floating in a lecherous soup of virulent hate, they penetrated Lan's mind and took from him his thoughts and sense of reasoning. A sickening feeling filled Lan as energy flowed out of his body.

Matwua lifted his fist over his head, though to Lan it was as though the instant was prolonged, and he, powerless to stop it. It was as if the giant's fist weighed a ton, the arms bulk rising higher, now higher still, beyond his shoulders and reaching up, the knuckles, tight, jaws clenched, teeth barred, eyes leering and wide and as cold as ice, the whites---red. And to stage his killing fist, he shouted again with an explosion that shook Lan's insides.

Lan stepped back and onto his ax. As soon as he did, Matwua's arm came crashing down. Ducking to his left, the blow grazed Lan's right side, knocking him to the ground. He scrambled for the ax and sprang to his feet with it, but found himself trapped at the back of the concave wall. He grabbed the saber tooth claws and squeezed the dagger like tips. The more he squeezed, the more he felt the spirit of the saber tooth pulse inside his veins as it rode the rivers of adrenaline, breaching every nerve, every cell in his body. It raced on with immediacy, filling his mind, his heart, his limbs and finally his loud scream of conviction.

With a raised fist, Matwua took three steps towards him. At the same time, the full swing of Lan's ax broke suddenly into a wide slicing arc. The obsidian edge sliced through the tension, the fear, the hate and then violently slammed into the huge man's forehead.

Cowered into a corner, Ayashe screamed at the horrible sight before her.

Matwua grabbed onto the ax handle and staggered into the embers. Embedded deep between his brows, the blade had wedged fast. He struggled toward the double vision of the stone wall in front of him and slid downward along the side of it. To keep from falling, he rested half bent over and leaning against the wall.

At the opposite wall, Lan dove to where he knew the spear had been thrown. He plowed through loose dirt and gravel in a frantic effort to feel for the wood shaft that was buried somewhere underneath it. Finding it, he darted to the outside of the fire. Without hesitation, he threw the spear hard into Matwua's stomach.

Matwua screamed as he grabbed the spear and fell to his knees. He tried to pull it back out, but the blade stopped when it reached the skin, pushing it outward like a tent.

Within the confines, the man's cry magnified as if it came from a beast twice his size. His eyes closed tight and then he turned the shaft so that the blade aligned with the slot it made when it first went in. He pulled it out the rest of the way along with coiled intestines and a flow of blood and yellowish bile. Not a man to vocalize his pain, he held in the urge to cry out. He dropped the spear as he fell to the ground, clutched his stomach and curled into a fetal position.

Blood pumped wildly through his veins. His heart raced for the first time in a long time. He felt fear and it panicked him;

his labored breaths, compromised by mucous and blood dripping from his nose.

In disbelief, Lan stepped clumsily out of camp. Upon reaching the line of posts, he wrapped his arms around the nearest one and collapsed at the foot of it.

Too frightened to move, Ayashe could not stop from crying, though she tried, muffling those cries in her hands. Now unsure of the man's purpose for her, she cringed in fear for her own life. Despite that fear, she had to go to her man. No longer hesitant, she got up and ran to his pain wracked body and placed both hands on his chest. As she rocked back and forth, she wept with tears that gave little comfort.

She reached out and touched the ax, but was too afraid to try and remove it. Seeing the large hole in his stomach for the first time, she instinctively covered it with her hand, pushing parts of him back inside. Body fluids oozed between her fingers. She finished stuffing the intestines back into the wound, but could not stop the warm liquid that kept dripping out and onto the ground into an expanding, muddy puddle.

Nervous thoughts of running to the clearing to get a clump of grass came to mind, anything to stick inside the hole to stop everything from coming out of Matwua. The Mowatchi was out there waiting to kill her, she was sure of that, but she had to do something…anything. If he was going to do it, she thought, did it really matter when?

She stood and swallowed, then crossed her arms out front as if to protect herself as she forced the shaking steps she took. She could barely make out a form---black---she could not see, but knew it had to be the Mowatchi. Ignoring the weakness in her legs, she kept them moving, but could not stop her lips from quivering until she was almost at the first line of grass.

What is it that he waits for?

A sudden breeze made her cower. He could be here behind her, ready to smash the ax down like he did her Matwua, forgetting the ax was still lodged in her man's head.

Somehow she got to where she could feel grass underneath her feet, but could not remember getting there. She bent to pull out clumps of it along with the roots and then boldly hurried past the dark shape to Matwua's side.

The grass, she stuffed inside the wound along with dirt which she wet and packed all around. It seemed to work except for a small trickle seeping from the bottom. Packing in more dirt, she sat next to him while holding everything in.

Tears returned as soon as she laid her head on his chest. Below her face, his deep, comforting voice, vibrated softly.

"You know the death words. I…I want you to say them when the death spirits take me."

Ayashe wiped her eyes. "I…(sniff)…yes, I will say them for you." She lifted her head up for the rest of what he was trying to say.

"I…uh…I…" Matwua coughed and took a deep breath.

She put her ear closer to his lips.

"I want the keya. The one…you put…the hole in."

No longer caring about the Mowatchi or where he was, Ayashe got up and ran to the back of the camp for the turtle shell. On her return, she snatched a bear skin along with both wolf furs. The wolf furs, she draped around Matwua. The bear skin, she enclosed around herself.

In a feeble voice, he said, "What are the words…the words you will say to our spirits?"

Ayashe tried to say them, but it only started a new wave of tears. After they subsided, she tried again. "I…I Ayashe leave your hunting sticks so you can hunt. I give you water and….oh…" (Sniff)

"You must say you will give my spirit to the sky."

"I…give your spirit to the sky."

"Remember to cover me. I do not want the death birds to find me."

"Yes…and I will give you some of the jonga you cooked in the fire. You will need to eat on your long walk."

"That is good. I can say no more. I…rest…must rest."

A flash of light burst from the fire pit. Ayashe, startled, turned to see the Mowatchi stirring the ashes and throwing kindling into it. It didn't take long for the fire to grow warm.

Matwua awoke to a cold sunrise. He labored for every breath, his hands over his chest and clutched into fist. Before long they slipped off and fell limply to the sides. As if to say something, his lips parted, but all he managed was a faint whisper. Forcing air into his lungs, he tried again, but it was a shallow breath and too meager to lead to another. His eyes opened wide and though he tried, that last breath was the last he would take.

For a long while, Ayashe rocked and cried as she sat alongside Matwua's body. She did not want to believe all that had happened and now would be vulnerable to the man's impulsive vagaries. She tried not to think about that, not until she heard footsteps approaching from behind.

"It is good that it is over. I will not take what is his. Your man is a man of many strengths. I will give him the words of my spirits."

Although she did not understand the meaning of what he just said, his voice sounded kind and unthreatening. At least, for the moment. She looked back at the ax embedded in Matwua's forehead that still disclosed within the stone a deadly finality. When the Mowatchi finally pulled it out, she looked away, the gaping wound left, leaving a crescent shaped gash in Matwua's skull.

Looking down at the wound reminded Lan of the Wadu and how they would have scooped out the brains and eaten it to deny the man's ancestors his life spirit. He wondered, too, if the woman would have been a part of that feast had she still been with that band.

He gathered stones and placed them in the blood and excrement around Matwua. It was built up further until the entire body was nearly enclosed, leaving a large opening on top.

Ayashe waited quietly watching while the Mowatchi filled the cavity with Matwua's spear, a water skin, and then for the kindling and flint that he put inside. When he seemed satisfied, she left to retrieve what was left of the cooked coyote. From the opposite side of the grave, she warily approached and stood with it in her arms. Her hopeful expression was returned with a nod, so she gently placed the carcass inside, left it there and stepped back into the shadows.

The bear claws Lan wore around his ankles, he removed and laid on top of the man's chest. "You are a good hunter. I give you the strength of the bear and your hunting sticks. I give you fire so you can make your light in the dark sky. One day we will hunt together. When that time is now, you can give the strength of the bear back to me. Run to the sky and be a brother to me."

The opening was then closed with more rocks and finally ashes from the fire spread over the grave.

"Do not hold me as your enemy. I will keep you from the death birds and those that would eat you. I covered you with these rocks and now you are hidden from them."

Inside camp and sitting on the log, Ayashe sat whimpering softly. Hearing the man moving about the enclosure, she kept her head down and peered through the tops of her eyes. Thankful for the thoughtful ritual, she followed his every move with a renewed hope of her own. As soon as he neared, she lowered her head even further.

He looks for the other water skins. Hurry and leave. It is then that I will feel safe.

Smirking critically, she took a full glimpse when he lifted the water skins to his shoulder. He then circled around somewhere behind her, somewhere she could not see.

Why does he take so long? I dare not look at him.
(Footsteps)

She flexed as soon as she heard them. Her heart beat three times faster as the footsteps went from the well-trodden soil to the gritty ground outside the fire. Either he was going to walk around the opposite end of it, or he was going to come to where she was sitting. She wanted to look, but was too afraid to, turning away and leaning to the side as if it would distance herself from him. She could chose to say something, but knew the words would only come out as an incoherent babble of stuttering nonsense. And what would she say, what could she say, how would he understand?

Mowatchi man...do not kill me? No...he does not know my words. How would he know what it is I talk? He sees my tears. He knows what I feel. There is nothing I can do. He knows I will not follow the way he will walk. Why would I...?

Lan's shuffling steps suddenly stopped directly in front of her. She instinctively slunk away, then immediately took hold of herself and did something she never thought she would ever have had the courage to do. She did it without thinking. Had she thought about doing it before hand, she never would have, because it was something you just do not do. Unless you have no fear or if for some inhuman reason you did not worry about the outcome. There was no undoing it now. She already committed herself. She just had to see...see if...

Her head tilted back so she could look straight into the eyes of the Mowatchi. A wanton killer was not however what she saw there. Nor was it distrust. His expression, instead, appeared humbling and imploring and reaching out for her.

Lan looked down at the eyes that bordered on the edge of tears. Glassy and with long wet lashes sticking to the skin of her eyelids, they were filled with both sorrow and suppressed hatred. And although a tinge of forlorn hope that one could only see after a long and examining study was also there, its hidden meaning was lost to her tears.

A strong breeze blew down off of the plateau. Ayashe, breaking her gaze, turned and squinted at the smell of damp leaves and pine. As it drifted in, it lifted her hair into upturned curls. She searched the distance and listened to the sounds of the forest that carried on with innocent dissociation. The Mowatchi's plans for her did not seem to matter anymore. She lived in the valley through seven cold times. Matwua hunted without incident, facing mas tets and nahghos. He had cared for her the only way he knew. His death had been so sudden, so final, and now she would be alone. She heard when the Mowatchi finally left and it pleased her.

A fresh gust of wind stirred the balmy air as well as the silence. High overhead, a raven chased its shadow along the walls of the cliff, screaming calls to a nesting mate. The shrieks returned lonely and hollow, disturbing the serenity of a forest still buried in morning mist.

The raven fluttered into the nest and alongside the playful beak of its mate. He gave her the cricket he held out and folded blue-black iridescent wings behind. Leaning to preen her feathers, he tucked in any that were misaligned, snapping at the fleas that darted about. He waited for her to settle herself into a more comfortable position before laying his head gently across her back.

Following a stream against the current, Lan made his way through a changing landscape. Maples and other deciduous trees gradually became displaced by tall conifers. The green pines were striking against the tan and coral-pink colors of the cliffs. Far beyond that, the seduction of formidable, snow covered monoliths drew a yearning for what lie to the other side.

He stopped to look down the gradual slope he just climbed to wait for the footsteps he so fervently wanted to hear. Shading his eyes from the late sunlight that was shining the mountains and stretching shadows inside the forest, he searched intensely into the unfamiliarity of it and listened. Having covered a long distance since his departure, he worried for the woman, but all that could be heard was the stream bubbling over the anchored stones in its path.

The elk ribs, along with everything else, Lan dropped to the ground. He removed the wolf skin vest and leggings, threw them over his shoulder and left for the stream. In shallow, turbulent water, he laid them on the bottom and held them down with rocks so the current could wash away the encrusted dirt. Farther in, he dipped his head under and quickly raised it back up to check the slope. A far off and barely audible wolf cry resounded from across the valley. Dire wolves were troubling and elusive.

Undermined by a storm and freshly fallen, a pine tree lay across the stream, the exposed roots, reaching out like an absurd looking animal. He collected the skins from the river bottom and hung them on one of the higher branches of a pine tree to dry. Halfheartedly, he expected to see the woman walking up at any moment since he was sure she had followed.

Along the ground, broken branches, the bark, blue-green from lichen, splayed twisted unrelenting fingers into the soil. It was as if they shared an intimated unwillingness to leave the parent tree, rather than to descend helplessly into the slopes void. He collected them for a fire and lifted his head to another howling wolf cry that was echoing off of the cliffs.

That wolf could be anywhere. His voice falls like a badly aimed arrow.

Another cry followed, almost too low to hear. More silence and then two more cries over-laid one another. Those were much closer, on top of a nearby cliff. He was sure of it, and this time it was not an echo. He looked up and checked along the cliff's utmost edge and stopped where two wolves leaned their heads toward the valley.

They will try to join the others. Those are lone males hunting for females.

———

Without Matwua, Ayashe stood in the clearing outside the encampment contemplating her future alone. She had none of his hunting skills and little chance of surviving the next cold time. Although tubers were plentiful along with other edible plants, once the ground froze, those food sources would be hard to find. Most certainly, Matwua had been crude and harsh, but he was also gentle at times. His hard face would express an endearing kindness, or perhaps she only wanted to believe that. Odd, how she felt a certain relief in his death.

From the clearing, she collected an armful of purple flowered sow thistle. She could see all that was theirs from where she stood and now it was all hers. At its distance it appeared so bare and lifeless even though everything remained the same. The skulls were mounted on the same post. The sitting log was where it always was, and surely the forest was without change. Still, it all seemed so different. At one time she loved this place—now, it meant nothing. She had enough of it. She now knew what she really wanted. She raced back to camp and hastily placed the flowers on the grave.

"I leave you your hunting stick so you can hunt. I leave you water and…and I give you the jonga…and…and water."

I already said water. What was the other thing? If I do not hurry, the Mowatchi will be too far to follow.

Oh…the sky…I must look to the sky.

"Sky spirits," she began, with her arms outstretched and rushing through the words, "I gave him all these things…now take him."

She ran to the center of the camp to get what she needed, thinking all the while about what else had to be done for Matwua.

It could not be more than just one thing since she was fairly sure that everything he needed for the journey was inside the grave. She tried to remember while filling the bear skin with the items she herself would need; flints to start a fire, she would certainly need those. The tooth from the jonga that Matwua gave her, she had to bring that as well.

Along the floor of the camp was left nothing of use, and no water skins. That was given to Matwua. As long as she caught up with the Mowatchi, it would not be needed. With no meat left to bring with her, she rolled up the fur.

"The bo bo!" She looked up at the dead tree. It was still there. She brought the cooked rabbit down and stuffed it inside the bear skin. *He forgot the bo bo...or did he leave that for me?*

Now she remembered what Matwua had said. *"You must cover me with dirt."* But...there was something else? *"You must say the rest of the words to the sky spirits."*

She ran back to the grave. Along the way she picked up a handful of dirt. Spreading it across the top of the stones, she looked up and blurted out loud. "Sky spirits...take Matwua fast to the clouds."

She flicked away the last of the loose dirt from her fingers and wiped them on her skirt. "That is good!" she mumbled, while hurrying back to the bear skin.

"The Mowatchi did not kill me. He does not want to kill me. Maybe Mowatchi man would like to keep me for himself?"

She used the rest of the straps that were hanging from the tree to wrap around the rolled up fur. When she got half way through tying it all together, she abruptly stopped, straddled the bundle and sat on it.

Then...why did he not make me carry his things like all men do? No... Mowatchi man does not want me with him. He runs to find another.

Despondent, she left the bundle there, scraped her feet through the dirt on the way to the log and sat on it.

He left me here for the mas tet and the nahgos. That is what he did.

She laid her head on her lap with her arms wrapped around her thighs and stared sideways at the bundle.

Why did he not kill me? Why did he leave me here for the mas tet? Maybe Mowatchi man did not make me carry his things, because he thinks I am many times too weak.

That made her mad. As soon as she thought about that her eyes opened wide and she jumped to her feet.

*Matwua knows I am strong. I can carry many things. I have strong feet. I will show that Mowatchi man that I **am** strong.*

"Oh! The wind!" *The wind will take away his tracks. I must follow them before the dark time comes.*

Out of the camp she ran with the bundle bouncing from side to side across her back. When she got to the nearest stake, she impulsively slapped it as she went by.

If the Mowatchi lets me follow him at least until we find a friendly tribe…that would make me many times too happy. He could leave me and not have to own me. I could find a man there. A man like…like…well… like the Mowatchi. One that is strong and brave and nice to look at. One like…like him, only more gentle. (Giggle)

She felt relieved to see that his tracks traced the side of a stream and were easy to follow. She stopped now and then to adjust the bundle or to take a drink. Afraid of losing the trail, she drove herself up the grades with a determined will.

Overhead, the sun burned with an intensity that seemed to magnify off of the cliffs or anything else it reflected off of; like the water, or even the stones along the ground. The only comfort was the cool pliable mud alongside the stream.

The bundle was getting too cumbersome to carry, the hills, steep and numerous. She kept the hope that the man would soon come into view. She searched from the next rise and the one after that, and the next and the next. Finally, after topping a high hill, she saw his skins far below, hanging from a tree.

Nervous, she approached cautiously and laid her rolled up fur a good distance away. Nearby, the man lay naked and so far, did not appear to be too unsettled by her being there.

She needed to drink. She waded into the stream through pink, trumpet oleander and tall pillwort grass, pushing quietly through the shallows to sit at the end of the fallen tree. Cupping the water, she drank her fill and then lifted a branch of pine needles out of the way. Ducking under, she stared at the man standing with his back to her.

His lean shape appeared hard and narrow, so unlike the men of her tribe. Oblivious to his nakedness, neither she nor anyone else she knew of felt shame for bare flesh. She herself wore no top as was the custom of her people. If she felt cold, she would simply wrap the bear skin around herself. Surprisingly, looking at the Mowatchi made her blush.

Cold water swirled between her toes. She kicked at the current and splashed water onto her legs.

This is a peaceful place.

Buoyant clouds drifted in an eggshell sky. Beneath the pines, dry needles, windblown and whist-full, drifted down in twos like rust colored wishbones. While holding onto the branch, she continued to kick at the water, splashing noisily as she wet her face and chest with her free hand.

"Cough, cough…ahem…mm mm!"

Checking the man again, she was mindful to stir the water from time to time.

He was still standing with his back to her, stretching his arms behind himself and inadvertently waving the muscles into clumps. The way his hair twisted down his back seemed an odd way to tie it. The snake skin around his head was different and pleasingly decorative. Even the scarred drawing on his back was something she had never seen before.

The men of her tribe, heavily built and full of bruises had ugly scars because of the closeness to their prey. They rarely washed and could not be bothered with something that they deemed had no purpose. Ayashe liked to bathe. As a little girl, her mother, Alawa, had always bathed her.

She carefully parted the branch to the side and looked through the fan of green bristles and pine cones. She stretched to see, but the man had left. She slipped into the stream and submerged herself under, wetting her hair thoroughly. As soon as she finished, she returned to sit on the log until the man appeared cresting a hill with an armful of sticks. Rather than to get caught staring, she quickly turned to the rippling water that was reflecting the setting sun. She thought of Matwua and could not help but feel for his loss. There were times they shared happy moments together and it made her eyes wet all over again. Covering her mouth, she began to weep softly

Crack! Crack! Crack!

While striking flints together, Lan thought of the land he would find beyond the pass, envisioning what it would be like.

He imagined a beautiful meadow with a herd of deer resting in grass. There is a river nearby teaming with fish and a moose wallowing in the shallows up to its knees. Behind them, a flock of geese alight onto a meadow with one honking and chasing another with its head low to the ground.

A friendly tribe runs up to greet them. They are all laughing and screaming with the children grabbing both the woman and his hands to lead them to a feast in their honor. Outside the leader's hut, he and the woman wait to be welcomed.

Piles of trout and catfish and a roasted deer are spread out on otter furs. Along the edges is a colorful mix of berries and flowers with an array of fruit at the corners.

When they finish eating, Lan is given an eagle claw necklace which included the feathers and the top beak of the bird. Brushed

wolf furs are placed over their backs as they listen to tribal drums sounding the together dance. Arm in arm they watch as everyone in the tribe dances around a fire well into the night. When it is over, he picks up the woman, carries her into an empty hut and closes the flap of hide that serves as a door behind them.

In the last of the fading light, Ayashe gathered dry sticks and branches. These were added to a small pile next to the bear skin where she began to strike two flints together.

A lone wolf cried out from the distance.

Mowatchi's fire is strong. He does not worry about nahgos. Look how he sits with his back to me and pushes at his fire with that stick.

He killed Matwua to save his own life spirit. So now it is he that lives. Now, it is I that must look to what happened through his eyes. When it is good for us to walk again, I will carry his things. That is the way of my people.

Starting a fire from nothing takes time---a long time. She kept striking the flints and waited for the sparks to light the kindling of cottony fibers. She turned to look at the man while striking the stones together, although hitting them a little harder than necessary.

CRACK CRACK CRACK

Why does he not give to me fire? That is easy for him...not for me to take this...and make all this...like this. Why does he not...

Thump!

Turning toward the sound, she was surprised by the sight of a burning stick next to her. She stuck it under her own pile, adding a few more sticks to it and arranging them on top. She turned around; only to see the backside of the man once again as he busily resumed poking his own fire.

With the bear skin covering her, she stared into the flames while holding the coyote tooth. She tucked it close to her face with thoughts of the kill and how she had laughed when Matwua dragged the animal out of the hole.

Thump!

Twisting around, she picked up the elk ribs Lan just threw to her, brushed the dirt off and ate ravenously. When she finished gnawing every last scrap of meat from the rib, she looked for the rabbit. After heating it in the fire, she consumed most of it except for a leg that she left lying in her lap, unsure as to whether or not she should save it for the next day.

Thump!

Lan picked up the rabbit leg thrown his way, glanced at her and then turned back around.

She quickly turned away, lifted the edge of the bear skin over her head and laid on her back with her nose sticking out into the night air.

More wolf cries

Dire wolf packs had always frightened her, especially during the night. They were there to run the perimeters of cold dark mountains, to seek out man's fire and from that darkness, return the light through watchful, yellow gazes. For, along with the awake dreams that sustain in near slumber, a deep sleep is denied for the fear of them.

Licking her hands clean of scent and the bones left to disintegrate inside the fire, she laid back quietly thinking----mostly about wolves and what an entire pack was capable of.

Wolf cries continue

That last howl made her shake with fear. Unsure of what to do next, she lay pensively thinking for a while longer. Unable to fall asleep and in fear of being dragged off into the night, she grabbed the bear skin and stood quietly next to the fire. She checked the surrounding forest for yellow eyes floating in the darkness or the sound of panting and trotting from an animal she could not see. The thought of them pulling her body apart and then gorging on her flesh made her shudder. She wrapped the fur tightly around herself, took a deep breath and edged warily over to the Mowatchi's fire.

CHAPTER 4
SABER TOOTH TIGER

Daybreak---Lan turned over and was quietly pleased to see that the woman was sitting there, ready and waiting.

Ayashe shyly looked away from him. With animated movements, she occupied herself with nothing important, since she already had everything for the coming day's walk next to her. She was prepared to carry everything of his, including the water skins and what was left of the elk.

With a slight hint of a smile, Lan started toward the pass while Ayashe carried everything except for his spear, ax and water skins. She struggled with the bow until she realized she could carry it across her back by using the bow string. In time, she lagged farther and farther behind at a considerable distance.

The mountain's incline proved steep and a struggle. Despite that, its charms distracted her from the hardships. Douglas pines were everywhere, cones scattered beneath them like faithful children. She picked them apart for the seeds inside. Jays darted in and out of branches, their wing-coverts banded with pretty blue color. Some squawked territorial alarms while others sang melodious arias to prospective mates.

A squirrel darted behind the trunk of a tree with its furry tail nervously flicking about.

(Giggle) "Run little bock tu."

Violet helleborine, white orchids and May lilies spread themselves thinly around a forest floor cushioned in pine needles. Between a stand of trees, she spotted something red growing a short walk away and was delighted to find that they were wild berries. Snapping off a deep red one, she could not help but wonder if the Mowatchi had seen them as well. None here had been picked. She wanted to call out to him, but felt it would be better if she did not draw attention to herself. She ate a handful, the rest she saved for later.

Except for the few times when she thought of Matwua, the days walk was pleasant. She repeatedly looked back until the last glimpse of the valley faded between the closing walls of the high cliffs on either side. The stream continued to subdivide until it became a mere trickle that eventually withdrew into an underground spring. Worrying she would be regarded as a burden, she quickened her steps. She wept softly, shedding tears for Matwua and the familiarity of their valley lost. She shed tears for her survival, for self-pity, for desperation and loneliness. Lastly, she shed tears for the unfairness of it all.

By now, the man was far ahead and out of sight.

Mowatchi man wants to lose me, that is why he walks many times too fast.

She thought to call out, but decided it would be seen as a sign of weakness. Determined to catch up, she had to show him she was strong and capable.

Is this his way of trying my strength?

The ground became hard and rock strewn. Fear of losing the trail was fast becoming a reality. She followed the general direction by keeping the sun in front of her.

This forest is covered with leaves. I cannot see his tracks or those of the nahgos that I know live here.

Thirsty, Lan stopped to rest. Water would be a precious essential from here until reaching the other side of the range of hills, so rationing was critical. Sitting crossed legged, he waited for the woman to catch up.

He knew he should not have allowed her to fall so far behind. On long excursions like this, it was his habit to cover as much ground as possible. Unused to a woman accompanying him, he had not realized he walked too fast for her. He saw that she was trailing behind for most of the day, but every time he had looked she was always there. He stood and waited, then moved to higher ground. At the top of the hill he noticed a fresh print.

Two knife!

Crouching low, he studied the print next to his feet.

This two knife was just here. The paw is large and it is an old male. When he walks he leans heavily on his paws and limps to one side.

He took a closer look.

One of the claws is bent. It causes the two knife much pain. This one does not want to lean on the broken claw, so it is too slow to make a kill. It hunts the shadows to look for easy kills or the kills of others.

He sprang to his feet and scuffed out the big cats prints. His pace on the way down the grade took on the hunting lope he and the men of his tribe often used during the hottest times of the year to run down their favorite prey, deer and elk. The men's strides were long and steady as they pursued a herd in the sweltering heat for as much as half a day if needed. The herd's skittishness never left them in range of the arrows. As soon as the men came within sight, the herd easily sprinted away until they felt safe to graze again. Not long after, the men would catch up, whooping and hollering and waving their arms which would set off another chase. The hot burning sun did its part in overheating the herd, and every time the deer tried to rest, the hunters would be upon them. Again and again, the terrorized herd drove themselves on until the men relentlessly ran them into exhaustion.

In time, the weakest, the old, or a lame individual would fall behind, giving the hunters the opportunity they were waiting for.

The chase ended with a hail of arrows and was well worth the effort with enough meat to last.

As Lan crested the hill, Ayashe looked up with relief. Her pulse quickened. She tried to appear relaxed, tried not to look too thirsty, or tired, or even pleased to see him. As the Mowatchi's steps pounded the ground before her she quickly looked down at the ground.

"Here…take this," he said, stopping in front of her. "You must be thirsty."

He says his words without anger. It cannot be that while we stand here, his wish is to harm me.

She drank uncontrollably, making loud gulping noises while keeping her eyes on the Mowatchi the entire time. Her arms kept shaking and it was not from the weight of the water. He was watching her the same way she was watching him and she no longer was paying attention.

"Oh!" Surprised at the sudden gush that splashed down, she stumbled backwards. She quickly squeezed the opening shut so she would not lose any more water. The embarrassment made her laugh nervously, in part because she was glad to get the water. She started to drink more, but was too conscious of the gulping noises and it was making her want to laugh. The man's look remained serious. She tried to hold it all back which only made her want to laugh even more. She squeezed her lips together, but that didn't stop the urge either because the whole thing was so silly, especially since she was supposed to be serious. She began to laugh uncontrollably and nothing was going to make it stop. She could see that the Mowatchi was smiling and that was encouraging her even more, so she covered her mouth, but could not stop giggling between her fingers.

"Here…sit with me," he said.

The humorous mood all but gone from the closeness to him, she sat nervously with her legs tucked to one side. In the silence that followed, thoughts of what had gotten her started came back to mind and she blurted out laughing all over again. She then looked away and tried her best to become serious, though giggling from time to time.

"I am called Lan," he said, his hands flat against his chest."

Ayashe turned to face him while covering her wide grin.

Pointing to the east, he said, "My people come from the big water."

He looks to the high place where I see nothing. His words are like the songs Alawa once sang from her Wadu people.

Your words are not mine Mowatchi, but I will listen and one day we will know each other's talk. You can tell me then what it is you are telling me now.

"Dasu Lan (You are Lan)?" she asked, touching his chest gently with a fingertip. "Tetzu Ayashe (I am called, little one)."

"Ay sha?"

"Ayashe!"

"Ay yashe."

"Toka (yes)," she said, energetically nodding her head.

"Toka," he repeated.

Wiggling ten fingers in front of her, he said, "Where are your people?"

"Pee poh?" She softly questioned with a blank expression on her face. *Why does he show me his fingers?*

"My people, the Bandu…were attacked. Many of them were killed."

As he spoke, he held his hands out in parallel and outlined her body to sign a person. He then outlined two more individuals next to her. After simulating blows to each of their heads with the ax, he stood and waved as if to summon the rest of his tribe.

She looked to where he was waving, shrugged and returned a questioning look. "Tetsu ulok shtup gixstoqui. (I do not understand your words)."

She did however know what the attack sign meant. She knew that one all too well.

Picking up the water skin, he pointed to it. "Water."

"Woo ta," she repeated.

"No more water," he said, shaking his head, no.

His woo ta word means water?

"Ba ba." She pointed back. "No ma woo ta," she tried repeating, shaking her head along with the strange sounding words. "Ba ba. Nik chukta…ki ba ba. (Save drink water. No water)."

Saying nothing else, Lan grabbed the water skin and quiver of arrows, as well as her bear skin bundle. He turned his back to her and left for the top of the hill where he had found the saber tooth tracks.

Following close behind, and with nothing left to carry, Ayashe admired the artful scar-lines on his back. She also liked the braid and the way it swayed from side to side across the muscles of his lower back.

Deep in thought, Lan's strides were long and quick. *There is no need for her to know of the two knife. She has already seen too much. Still, it gives me much worry.*

Ever since he was a boy, saber tooth tigers frightened him. He recalled back to his thirteenth summer when he awoke to an early morning from the screams of a woman being dragged from her hut by a man eater. It had happened so fast there was nothing anyone could do to stop it. By the time the men gathered outside, the saber tooth was far off and dragging its prey behind.

Lan was surprised when his father, Wolf Hunter, called to him to bring his spear and join the trackers. He never expected to be picked. Besides his being too young for such a dangerous hunt, it was only the bravest of the men that were chosen to go after a saber tooth. It was a test, an honor, an out of the ordinary initiation of sorts, and mostly because his father was the tribe's leader. Wolf Hunter had faith in his son, and Lan was not going to disappoint him.

It was exciting to leave the village with the men he had grown up with and looked up to. He was even allowed fourth place in line behind the trackers and his father. That way he could watch and learn the ways of a tracker and how every subtle clue was used to their advantage.

So as not to warn of their approach, the lead tracker, Owl That Sings, stayed well ahead of the rest. Lan saw how they found signs of the saber tooth even on hard stony ground. In the absence of prints, they searched for disturbances in the foliage and smelled the feces from the predator for freshness. They felt through its waste for human teeth or other recognizable parts like fingers and toes, because they were not looking for just any big cat. They wanted the predator that made the kill.

Any distinctive difference in the prints they did find were compared to the prints they were looking for; flaws in the heel like nicks and scratches, size, and the way each digit left their impression. Any one of these could serve as a guide for finding that specific animal. This time, they were able to easily follow fresh drag marks and the blood from the victim.

Ahead, in an open field, lay the saber tooth tiger swollen from eating the more meaty parts of the woman, like breasts and buttocks. It was both odd and gruesome to see someone from the tribe that you knew and loved in such a state. Her face, despite total body dismemberment and spilled bowels, looked totally bare of any trauma as though she was asleep.

Owl That Sings ran ahead to be the first to slay the saber tooth. Killing so large a predator, alone and with no one's help, was by far the greatest achievement and he wanted that all for himself.

The old tracker's spear slammed into the saber tooth tiger's shoulder. Startled, the cat sprang from the carcass and charged the aged hunter. Its roar sounded deafening. The attack proved vicious. The huge predator dug its oversized fangs into Owl That Sings, shaking its head viciously as it tore away the limbs. No one could get to the lead tracker before the saber tooth ripped the body apart. The man's screams were horrific, the whole attack so real and nothing Lan had ever witnessed in his short life.

And then the popping sound when the saber tooth dug its fangs into the man's skull. That was what he remembered most. Blood lay everywhere. The man's eyes had burst from his head with pieces of his brain scattered throughout the grass.

In a rage of defiance, the saber tooth faced the charging men with its razor sharp claws digging into the ground. Lan ran in with the rest of them, though he did not know what was moving his legs, he was so frightened. Throwing his spear along with the others, he watched with relief when the big cat collapsed and curled into a ball. And then the look of disappointment when his father looked back, followed by the trackers as they all glared at him with frowns on their faces. No one spoke, but stood still in the long drawn out silence that followed.

That silence, Lan remembered all too well. His spear was not in the saber tooth where it was supposed to be. It was not where all of the other spears were. Instead, it stuck out of the ground with its feathers blowing in the wind like a worn out killing tool. And this, not a killing tool you kept for memories of good hunts---a tool of merit. Those were tools of proud entitlement and certainly not the spear before him.

His father stooped down and removed the front claws from the animal's right paw. Handing them to his son, and with slow, spaced out words, he said, "Wear these and you will wear the spirit of the two knife. It is the two knife that has always walked with me. There will be a time that will come when you and the two knife will be brothers and you will not fear him like you fear him now."

It still hurt whenever Lan thought about that hunt for the man eater, wishing that he had not missed and that it was his spear that had been the one appraised to have killed it.

Though he went on to prove his courage, that day kept haunting him. It played on his insecurities, his pride and self-worth. It haunted him even now and when he had first looked at the tracks.

He turned to the woman. "The sun is hot. We can stay and rest until the shadows come."

A mature conifer offered shade nearby. He lay underneath it, put his hands behind his head and peeked through partially closed eyelids.

She still worries. I could force her and it would be easy. If she stays with me the way I want her to, she will always know of this time and I do not want that in her thoughts.

Lying on her back beneath thick boughs heavy with needles and pine cones, Ayashe leaned her head back on her hands. The fragrance lent that of a mix of the pine as well as the sweet smell of spoiling undergrowth. Above her, heavy branches swayed and hissed in a stiff wind. It felt warm on her face and was calming to listen to---an endearing soulful whisper, although with an erraticism that at times could rebel like a wayward child.

Nightfall
Ahead, a wall of boulders lay exposed within a wide clearing. The rocks made an excellent windbreak---a good place to start a fire.

"We can make traps," said Lan. "I saw many of the tree runners when we walked to this place." He picked up a handful of twigs and handed them to Ayashe. "Take these and follow me."

The sticks puzzled her. She stayed behind while he pushed aside a few beech ferns. *Is he not going to make a fire with these?*

"Watch." He pointed at his eye and then at the trap he was starting. "I use the stick to make a trap."

"Trop?"

When he showed her how to make a noose, Ayashe fumbled with her own knot, making it too tight.

"No...like this." He took her hands in his, holding her outstretched fingers while guiding them through the steps. His self-assurance and manly odor distracted her and she dropped the sinew. Patiently, he picked it up and finished the knot.

"See how the line closes?"

"O-o-o!" She shrieked, yanking her finger out just in time.

Ayashe liked the trick. After all, what else could it be? She looked down with interest at what the man was drawing in the dirt.

"This is a tree runner and this is his long tail."

Her face brightened. "Bock tu!" *They are many times too fast. He will never catch one.*

She followed along to a clump of greenery where he dug up an edible root. Slicing it into thin pieces, he placed a few inside the trap. Three more traps were made and finished with bait and then he left her there to build a fire.

In his absence, she added a few of the berries she had left to two of the traps. She then returned to her rolled up bear skin and cut a long, thin strip from one of the straps. Dividing that into three more pieces, she made her own traps. When they were finished, she stepped back to admire them.

My shtick trops are many times more good. If it is true that they will catch the bock tu, I will find many at first light.

With more traps than the probability of enough rodents to fill them, she ran to the fire and excitedly jumped the last step before sitting down.

Her wide grin made Lan smile. "I see your traps and they are made well."

Ayashe shook an agreeing nod with no idea of what was just said. All she did know was that the moment was a happy one and she could not wait to see if the traps would work. She rolled her fur out faster than usual and laid on it sideways with her head propped up so she could watch him stoke the fire. Her interest soon shifted from the stick he jabbed the fire with to his face where the yellow glow and diverging shadows sharpened his features. She dropped to the thick outline of his pectorals, left bare between the opened vest. Muscles flexed every time he pushed at the branches. Beads of sweat shimmered from his chest, dripping irregular tracks down his hard abs.

She parted her legs, leaving one bent at the knee. The other she laid flat to the side so she could expose herself to the fire. It felt good on her legs. The full subjection to that as well as to the preoccupied man enticed her, sent warm welcoming shudders up the insides of her thighs.

His manner pleased her and she liked the way he had touched her hands. If he took her, she would not resist. It would be easy to give herself to him; warm feelings tingling deep inside when she thought about that. She could try to dismiss those thoughts, but really did not want to. Not now, not with all of these new sensations, feelings she liked and wanted more of, an increasing warmth that filled her with want.

His smell, his sweat, his flexing muscles---the vigorous strapping brawn about him attracted her, as well as the killing instinct he so readily showed. The fear he wrought, somehow and in some way was making him so desirable a man. Everything he did seemed to be in a sexual way, like the way his jaws moved when he spoke, the kindness he showed her, his long, full strides---his gracefulness.

"Mowatchi man knows many things," she gently said, in the words of her people and a quiver in her voice.

Lan pretended not to notice her lying back with her legs parted, the softness of her inner thighs curving toward her dark shadow. She was so exposed---so inviting---so teasingly seductive. His desires made him yearn to break the constraint of worry he had for her fears. It was difficult not to go to her. He was not sure if she was still afraid, remembering the screams that now replayed in his mind. He wanted to give her more time. There was no rush. They were here together, alone, 'though he wanted her like no other woman. His abstinence had been long, her repose so beautiful.

She waits…it must be this way. That is why she lays there like that. The more I look, the more I can no longer wait. I can no longer think if she may want me or she does not want me. I will wait no more. I will get up and go to her side of the fire. I will look down and quietly lower myself and lay next to her and if she does not turn from me…then I will know that she is feeling what I am feeling.

His pulse beat wildly as he leaned back and slid the leg skins down to his ankles. Kicking off the foot coverings, he pulled the leg skins off the rest of the way, leaving them crumpled where they fell. With his gaze steadily on Ayashe, he stood and untied his braid.

She made no effort to divert her attention; impassioned as much by the looks he gave her as well as by the undressing he did in front of her. She examined every part of him, while he quietly removed the vest and tossed it on top of the skins. Watching him walk to her side of the fire, fully erect with a body leaving nothing from symmetry, flushed her cheeks---made her heart run. Her stomach quivered inside like feelings of fear, only these were so much more pleasurable.

Her warm, heavy breathing blew on his neck when Lan lowered himself down next to her. He grabbed the far side of her skirt and lifted it above her hips. Their gazes remained steadfast on each other as he lifted the near side up as well, leaving her hirsute mound fully exposed.

Opening her legs to the sides, Ayashe reached for him with her mound raised high to ease his entry, enveloping him fully with urging hips.

"Sh-h-h! Lan reluctantly slipped out of her, lifting his head for a noise that had come out of the forest.

The night suddenly emptied of all sound as they strained to listen. Disappointed, Ayashe also lifted her head to listen for the sound he heard...or thought he had heard. No crickets or hooting owls, even the wolves were quiet. It was all so strange and too unnatural. It was a night forest with an absolute vacancy, the unseen within, making everything inside seem as intangible as a dream. Both of them stood with the fire at their backs while waiting for another sound. Ayashe, realizing neither one of them had anything to protect themselves with, ran back for the spear. She quickly returned and handed it to Lan. Still no sound, no rustling of branches, no tiny paws scurrying about the underbrush, only their own labored breathing and the fire behind them.

They stared at the line of trees as if they knew something terrible, something big and terrible was going to jump out of there at any moment. It became more and more frightening to even think about, because then there would be a fury of biting and screaming as they all fought to save themselves, fought to keep from being stripped of their flesh and to stay alive from whatever was out there, whatever was so horrible it made every animal in the forest hide from it.

A low rumble stopped as soon as Ayashe heard it. She listened again with afore-trained concentration. There, again, the both of them heard it that time.

Rushing to the fire, Lan pulled out a burning branch and returned holding it out front. He passed by Ayashe, took three cautious steps toward the forest and waited. Hearing nothing he took another and then stopped abruptly for a low throated growl that rumbled from deep inside the blackness.

This is the two knife with the prints I saw on *the ground...and now it is here.*

Waving the torch at the trees, he checked for a recognizable outline or shadow. Seeing nothing, he stepped back to where Ayashe stood shaking with the ax in her grip.

"We have to make more fires. Take this branch and hold it up high."

With the extra branches already gathered, they stacked them into two piles and lit them.

"This will not be enough...stay here!"

With his spear raised high above his shoulder, Lan entered the forest knowing the densely packed timbers favored the big cat. Walking past the place where he had picked the ground clean of branches earlier, he penetrated deeper inside. As he crept forward, he turned around to look at the campfires that were fast becoming smaller and smaller specks of light. His head suddenly snapped to the front. A strong feeling, and not something he heard, or fast moving shadow, but a deep feeling made him become more wary. He waved the flaming branches out front.

This two knife makes me want to run back to the fires. What then would she think of me if I stood there and did nothing?

The spear seemed so flimsy now, the forest closing him in like one of the animals in his traps. It was unnerving to slip into the black silence between the trees and not know where the saber tooth tiger was, yet knowing that it knew with certainty where he stood at any given moment. He moved further through the undergrowth with thorns scraping his legs. Warm blood slowly began to seep from the cuts.

This two knife licks the air and taste my blood.

Each bush, each tree offered a possible hide. The saber tooth could be lying low nearby, behind a boulder in the diffused light. He looked hard into the murky blend of rocks and foliage, the flames lighting the trees overhead with silent moving shadows. Startled, he waved the torch at them, but there was nothing shaped anything like a saber tooth tiger, there or anywhere else.

I must remain strong. The two knife do not climb trees, so why do I look there? Fear is taking my thoughts. If it runs at me I must show it no fear. I will be ready and hold my spear high.

He could almost see the big cat's narrow lenses encased in yellow, envisioning the powerful limbs driving the animal forward. Its undulating strides were shaking the muscles of its limbs. And then he saw himself throw in his spear and watched as it slowly arched through the air...and then slam into the ground with the feathers blowing emptily in the wind. Once again, he stood before that same saber tooth from his past, only this time it was he who the predator cat was running toward and not Owl That Sings.

He covered his face and felt the huge fangs stab into his skull, followed by a loud popping sound as his head was being crushed by the saber tooth.

He left the spear leaning against the tree nearest him and quickly piled branches together. As soon as he bent to pick them up, he heard panting coming from the other side of a line of bushes. He stopped what he was doing and remained perfectly still to listen to the sound that seemed labored with an underlying hoarseness.

"You are old and tired. I am Man That Runs Too Fast. I am strong and have my spear."

He straightened tall and waved the flames in the direction of the panting and then to both sides and all around, but saw nothing.

"I am a strong hunter. I do not fear you."

Slowly and with deliberate steps, he edged backwards until he returned to the fires and Ayashe's side. As soon as he dropped the branches, she threw her arms around him.

"Tetzu matay (I am afraid)."

"Help me with the fires. We must make many."

They stacked branches into piles so that the fires formed an enclosing circle.

"This will not be enough. We need more."

"Nag boksta!" Trembling, she pleaded for him to stay there. "Lan, ja nag boksta din motzu."

Her arms in his, Lan pressed his face to hers and smelled the sweetness in her hair, his body shaking from her uncontrollable shivers.

Ayashe never questioned his bravery. She knew he would protect her, knew without a doubt that he would kill the nag boksta.

Lan said, "We must make more fires. My need is to go back into the forest."

With her face pressed against his chest, she whimpered softly. "Ayashe matay. (little one afraid)."

(Another roar)

Both jerked from the loud call that thundered from deep inside the cold dark night---so loud, it was if it had come from within the very bowels of the earth. Like an immortal soul with monstrous proportions, it rumbled out of the timbers as a solitary entity of subjugating power, illusive to the eye, yet deathly blood lusting.

"Chta niktu matay."

From the roaring flames, Ayashe pulled out a burning branch, "Sta te natza Dasu. Tay bok na. (I will go with you. I bring many sticks back.)"

"You must wait for me here."

He took the branch from her and threw it back into the fire.

"Dasu bawna! (Your spear!)" she urgently stated, making a throwing motion as if to throw it.

"My kill stick! I left it by the tree!"

Ayashe left to retrieve Lan's ax. She returned holding it out to him.

"That you must keep for yourself," he said.

She watched him leave empty handed and fade into the forest where the trees shook from the yellow torch light. The sound of dry pine needles crushing underfoot gradually lessened with distance until they could not be heard anymore.

"La-a-a-n!"

Ignoring her cries, Lan stole deep into the forest. He waved the flames out front until he saw the spear up ahead. Spreading bushes aside, he stepped cautiously through dry plant litter, the crunching sounds, the only noise until he stopped to listen.

Snap

That sound was from the big cat, and he saw a movement not far from where his spear lay. A movement he thought he had seen, but the next time he looked, it was not there anymore, and now he was not so sure he had seen it the first time.

SNAP

That was louder, much louder.

This was the saber tooth tiger's element, the night as clear as day. It saw all the human did, its head hanging low and bobbing from the heavy breaths it took. Its tongue pulsed in and out of twin shearing fangs while moving forward with its body slunk low to the ground. Snarling, the cat pushed out its claws and with deadly intention, sliced them into the earth.

Back at the camp and deep inside one of the fires, burned the largest branch. Ayashe pulled it out and faced the forest. It was unnerving to leave the safety of the fires and enter the darkness surrounded by trees. All around, the burning branch enlivened dancing, hoodoo shadows; the contorting figures, chasing across the rocks and trees with seeming indifference. She knew what lay out there and it remained with unwavering persistence, out in its bleak familiarity where the beast silently watched her every move---waited for its right moment.

She waved the flames out front the way Lan had done. "(Go nag boksta! Go from us)." she shouted.

I have so much fear, my need is to wet.

She squatted to take a pee.

Ready with the spear, Lan shouted, "Bring your fire closer."

"Ta dosh nayg boksta? (Where is the saber tooth tiger?)"

He handed her the spear to hold while he began to gather a pile of branches. They had to work quickly. The saber tooth was not going to stay behind the brush much longer. Darting back and forth, he finally collected enough to last until morning. Heavily burdened, they returned to the fires where they settled in for the night.

Replete with admiration, Ayashe sat up looking at Lan who kept tossing about while trying to fall asleep. Still naked, she covered him with the bear skin. With the nag boksta out there, she knew it would be hard to fall asleep as well. She lay between the front curl of his body and the warmth of the fire with no need to cover herself. Snuggled into him, she grabbed his hand as soon as he reached around to hold her and pressed it tightly to her breast. She tried her best to forget the horrible creature waiting inside the forest, or at the least, to try and dream of sweet pleasures with the Mowatchi. During the night, she got up occasionally to add branches to the fires. Whenever she listened, there was no sign of the big cat, only the comforting sounds of a natural forest.

Night gradually cooled into the dampness of early morning. Ayashe awoke to the sounds of hungry chicks chirping in their nest. A fog filled breeze worked its way through the pines and returned no odor of the saber tooth tiger. Sure that it was gone, she rechecked the fires.

Lan opened his eyes to Ayashe sitting with an ever stretching, toothy, smile. Seeing that he was finally awake, she giggled as she held high what she had been holding onto most of that morning. Between two fingers and held up by the tails were four voles and a field mouse.

"Ki bock tu! (No squirrel!)"

She excitedly explained how she had found the animals in the "shtick trop" and that it was her berries that caught most of them.

Pleased, Lan groggily rubbed his face and pointed. "Put them in the fire."

After removing the heads, the voles and mouse were placed on stones near the flames. Ayashe remained there and waited for them to cook while Lan left for the forest to find the saber tooth tracks.

To amuse herself, she lined up the dismembered heads in a semi-circle between her legs. Next, she touched each one with a twig to get their attention for an imagined meeting. It was an important engagement, the heads arranged according to size. The largest had to be their leader. That was only appropriate, and he had to sit on top of a mound. She built up a pile of dirt until it was just the right height.

The leader must sit on this.

"You…the big one. You are Lan, our leader and this is where you sit."

She placed the large head on top of the mound so it would face the rest. The mouse, she decided, would be her. She separated it from the four vole heads and hopped it off to the side. Addressing the large one sitting on the mound, she said, "You belong to Ayashe. Those women over there…they belong…**in here**!" The last two words she said out loud before jamming the four vole heads inside the mound and covering them up.

"I found the two knife tracks," Lan said, as he emerged from the forest.

The mound was hastily plowed flat and the heads swept away. She picked out the cooked field mouse from the fire, but could not hold onto it.

"O-o-o!" She cried, burning herself.

"Throw it up…like this," said Lan, grabbing and throwing a vole into the air and catching it. He did that several more times before blowing on it and brushing away the singed hairs. All of it was eaten, including the cooked innards and soft bones inside.

Throwing the mouse up into the air the same way, Ayashe caught it and continued doing that until it felt cooler. The singed hair, she brushed off the way he had done and then bit off the front half of the mouse. Chewing through crispy skin and bones, she found the mouse to be delicious.

Never before had she considered such small game to be worth the effort. Her tribe only hunted the biggest of animals. Now that she learned how to make traps, she embraced the idea. Before she finished chewing the front half, she put the back end of the rodent into her mouth, leaving it stuffed with hardly enough room to chew.

"Soon, we will leave the mountain. We will find your people."

"Pheeg foe," she tried?"

"People," he corrected.

"Phiful!" She was sure she got it right that time, the wiry, blackened tail of the mouse flipping between her lips as she continued to chew.

"People!" he said, shaking his head.

"Phee...foe!" She again tried, nodding her head up and down as if knowing she got it right that time. Her lips were left in a frozen pucker from saying the end of the word.

Lan looked at her affectionately, his words lost to her innocent smile. He grabbed her hands and brought them to his chest.

Still chewing, she tried hard not to laugh. *He is many times too pretty.*

"I am Bandu," he said, grabbing her hands and tapping his chest with them.

"Lam," she corrected, her mouth full and pointing a finger back.

"Yes, I am Lan. It is my people that are called Bandu."

"Phee…phoh!"

"No!"

"Pee-poh pampoo?" By now she was getting frustrated with the whole thing.

"People!" He loudly corrected.

She tried to swallow the mouse, but it needed more chewing.

"Lan grabbed the water skin and poured some into the palm of his hand. Holding it out to her, he said, "Big water. My people come from the big water."

She quickly swallowed, along with a serious expression. "Nah woo ta," she loudly assured, vigorously shaking a no sign with her head.

"Yes," he nodded. "We must save our water, but that is not what I now speak. My people come from the big water."

"Bg...pee poh...woo ta ban doo," she repeated, sticking a finger into his wet palm and examining it with a sideways tilt of the head as though it was something he treasured.

Her face in his hands, Lan grew quiet.

Ayashe looked dreamily at him.

Wanting her, he stroked her hair and laid her onto her back. He ran a finger across her brow and down the side of her face, and then lowered to explore her nipples with his tongue. He had wanted to do that all along. They were as perfect as she was, and gloriously pink. He caressed the whole of them and when he could not hold back any longer, he held her head up and entered her.

Ayashe urgently received him and succumbed to ecstasy so fast, it surprised even her. Again and again, his lust brought her to fruition until finally he cried out with pleasures of his own. Both lay intertwined in each other's embrace until Lan finally spoke.

"There is something I want to show you. Come, let us walk to the tracks."

"Too...niff?" She remembered that word from the night before.

"Two knife!"

"Nag boksta! She put two fingers to her lips to show her sign for the big cat. "Twoniff...nag boksta." Her voice trembled from just saying the words.

She lagged cautiously behind as Lan followed the tracks he found earlier.

"This mark is no longer strong. Dirt from the dark time winds covers it." He brushed away bits of dry leaf matter and pine needles from the print. "Here...look...one of the six legs crossed here." He showed her the beetle tracks superimposed over the paw print where the insect had scurried across it during the night while foraging for food.

Ayashe checked the forest for the huge predator before looking down and eying the drag marks of the beetle. "Rigbishtga!" (Many legs)

She hated many legs almost as much as she hated no legs, whether those were snakes, worms or slugs. She understood the long absence of the saber tooth. She followed as he tracked the last of the prints to the bottom of a hill where they became lost in the undergrowth.

Lan raised his spear and pointed it at a continuation of hills. "Two knife goes there. It does not go where I walk."

⁌ ⁋

Four fingers at the horizon. The sun seemed to be going down faster than usual. They had covered a lot of ground since the fires. Cupping his hand, he made a motion to Ayashe as if he was drinking. "Our need is to find water before the dark time comes."

She held up the water skins to show she understood. "Woo ta!"

This place was vaguely familiar to her. Somewhere beyond the green expanse of hills lay a trail that dropped through the last of the foothills. Below that were the flats, a vast and endless plain dominated by tall grasses, mammoths and the tribes of her people. In an elevated voice, she pointed toward a low lying ravine. "Woo ta!"

There were more ways to finding water than what was visible on the surface. Lan knew that as well as she did. During downpours, water will course through the shortest route possible to a low point in the terrain. The dried out drainage could be followed to where it would eventually lead to water.

"Stay here!" Holding the spear low at his side, he jogged toward the ravine where it cut deep between two hills. He followed it down and stepped carefully around loose rocks until reaching the bottom. There was no pond where he expected one to be, only a dried out bed. Hacking into the soft dirt with a stick, he dug through the surface layer and pushed it aside. Underneath was mud which he excavated further until water started to seep into the hole.

Slowly, steadily, the mountain gave up its fluid sustenance. Swirling, silvery-brown effervescence, percolated, then bubbled and foamed as it arose from below until swelling into a muddy puddle.

Lan waited for the suspension of soil to settle to the bottom. The rest, he pushed to the side. After satisfying a long thirst, he filled both water skins.

His head down, he retraced his own footsteps up the ravine. Upon reaching the crest, a fresh print that had not been there before made him stop short. A little farther along was another. The details were clear; the wide spread of the print, the cut in the pad---the impression of a bent claw. The tracks went in two directions. One set headed toward the top of the ravine where Lan had been busy at the bottom filling the water skins. From there they turned around and tracked in the other direction toward where Ayashe sat waiting.

She trembled when she saw the nag boksta slinking towards her, crouched low and holding its head down with ears laid back and flat to the sides.

The saber tooth tiger stalked forward, its claws digging into the passing ground. Gradually, it shortened the distance between them, holding its body low. The belly sagged and scraped in the dirt while the rest of its massive body swayed from side to side. A frightening beast, it stared straight ahead with eyes that were widely oval...and yellow---so deeply yellow, yellow like evil puss. They were menacing eyes and the kind with abhorrence and vengeance for this prey. And not any prey---only this---this, that was not the kind the big cat was accustomed to. It was not the kind it licked with adoration, the kind it had love for---prey like buffalo and deer and giant sloths. Those, it had a symbiotic relationship with by culling out the diseased from their ranks, brought a quick end to the old and relief to the dying. This prey was different. Its look was different, its smell unique and so unlike anything it had ever hunted.

Ayashe stumbled backwards. The beast was almost there, the muscles in its limbs shaking every time one of its paws hit the ground. She did not want to look anymore, it was too terrifying, but somehow she could not pull away from it. It was as though she was already being swallowed up by the beast and Lan was nowhere around.

"La-a-a-a-a-n!" she nervously mumbled, too low to be heard.

She tripped on an exposed root and braced herself for the fall. Landing on her back, the ground hit hard, knocking the wind from her. She lifted her head and sucked in at the sight of the huge predator that was closing in fast, the jaws opening wide and exposing long, slaying fangs that were longer than her hand. Strong shoulder muscles rippled under its fur. Just before reaching her the beast sprang into a final, lunging leap and landed with its legs straddling her. The saber tooth's belly pressed down onto her limp body. Yellow fangs scissored open for a deafening outcry with every intention to panic and numb its prey. Full of reverberating deepness, the sound rattled every bone in Ayashe's body.

Fear rushed weakening quivers down the length of her spine as she watched the sneer curl into a reveal of tarnished, yellow fangs. The saber tooth licked the drool from them and exuded a sour breath from deep within its gut, bringing with it low rumblings whenever the cat exhaled. Like a pre-digestion, its breath steamed into a consuming, engulfing cloud.

The sight of the jaws in front of her face made her shake uncontrollably. She turned away from the stench of its last meal, the musky odor---the festering urine. The throating, clunking, effortless growl rumbled deep inside her---so very deep---like rolling thunder, only here she could see into the demons face. This was bestial intimidation that served to weaken her will, Ayashe's seductive beauty no more than another meal to feed the saber tooth's persistent hunger. Relinquished to blissful indifference, she lost all hope. It was as though she lay reposed in some safe haven, no longer feeling the terror, but instead, complacency as she surrendered herself to the saber tooth.

From the crest of the hill, Lan ran toward them with his spear held high.

In a blur of spotted fury, the saber tooth whipped about, gripping the ground with its claws. Dust filled the air along with the cat's belligerence, its back limbs tucked underneath to ready itself for a lunge. There it waited for the human as though he intended to run right through its slashing claws and severing fangs---waited for him to reach the even ground at the bottom of the hill.

Lan stopped short of the saber tooth tiger that 'rose up on its haunches and whipped its claws through the air. It snarled at him with ribs pounding wildly, coughing and honking and catching its breath.

Turning with the spear pointing dangerously close to the cat's fangs, Lan shouted, "You are old and kill only woman and sleeping animals. Now you must fight me, Man That Runs Too Fast."

The saber tooth backed away with Lan stepping forward with it, prompting the cat to slash at his chest. It winced from the spear with suspicious caution and now casually began to circle the human slowly. The black tip of its tail twitched nervously while it looked back in judgment as though the human were merely a trivial hindrance. As it shuffled into a tighter circle, it gauged the human's strength through cold yellow slits. At times the big cat sneered at the nuisance, at others it simply panted heavily without looking at him and instead, kept its focus on Ayashe.

With deliberation, Lan raised the spear above his head and brought his arm back slowly. The other he held out front for balance, turning with the huge beast while aiming for its ribs.

Now is my time and my spear must not fall short.

But nothing could stop the events of that first hunt from plaguing him like it always did.

Once again he was there, running with the men that were all shouting and shaking spears over their heads---except for him. He was running without one, running without a spear in his hand and he did not understand why. All he did know was that he was back in that first hunt and that he had to kill the man eater no matter what the others did.

Ahead lay the uneaten remains of the woman and the dismembered corpse of Owl That Sings. Alongside, the huge predator waited defiantly. Before Lan and sticking out of the ground was his spear, but no matter how fast he ran, he could never reach it. He tried and tried, but every time he was about to grab it, the spear reappeared farther away.

Looking over his shoulder, he saw his father running alongside and smiling back, his spear held high while shouting for the joy of the hunt. Lan shouted with a renewed joy of his own and when he reached the spear, he yanked it out of the ground. Both yelled and raised spears in triumph and together continued to run toward the saber tooth tiger.

The next time Lan looked over his shoulder, his father was no longer there, 'though he knew he could never stop running. He had to keep on running at the predator as fast as he could, because he was never going to relive that first hunt the same way.

The next time he looked, he saw his father standing at a distance, tall with his spear at his side. Behind him, the rest of the men had lined up with their own spears standing straight up like his, the blades, pointing at the sky.

The wind brother pushed Lan on as he quickly closed in on the roaring beast. He lowered his spear and lunged forward and with the momentum he had, drove half its length into the big cat's chest.

A loud roar woke Lan from that first hunt. He was left dumbfounded with no awareness of where he was, only where he had been. In disbelief, he stared at the predator, now thrashing about with gurgling shrieks and the spear buried deep in its chest. The cat choked and turned its convulsing body around, kicking and twisting from the spear that was fulfilling its deadly intention. It spat and clawed, but the struggles proved futile. The thrashing only forced the blade to sever arteries and blood vessels and to slice into the lungs. The saber tooth collapsed to one side with its blood red tongue hanging loosely and flapping about. It tried a gurgling roar that altered into a cry of pain, which only made it choke even more.

In a frantic attempt to scream out in a last call of defiance, the saber tooth pumped its chest, the roar all but broken and blood spewing from its mouth. That final cry sounded pitiable and not the forceful thundering call it had always relied upon. It was not the loud roar that sent prey into their holes, shaking in terror.

After a few jerking convulsions, the claws withdrew into their sheathes, all save for one left leaning to the side. Along with the stillness that followed, glittering dust drifted downward and draped over the aftermath of solitude that so casually displaced the violence. It settled over the pounding hearts as well as the crumpled carcass that belied an existence of only moments ago. Lastly, the tailings softened the hard edges of conflict along the torn up ground.

Lan lifted Ayashe's head up. Her eyes opened slowly as she tried to focus. Recalling the horrible nightmare, she trembled when she saw the beast lying on its side.

"Nag Boksta!"

"Two knife is dead," he replied.

She did not understand the "dead" word. All she did know was that it was still there. Lifted to her feet, she grabbed the water he held out to her and swallowed desperately. She could not get enough.

He wiped her face and neck with more water.

"Matay nag boksta," she cried.

"There is nothing here that can hurt you," he replied, wetting his hands and wiping her face with them.

His gentle words sounded soothing. She wanted him to know that since he saved her from the nag boksta, she belonged to him, touching his chest and then her own to emphasize the point. "Lan pee poh…Ayashe pee poh."

Accomplished, and with a long held fear all but erased, Lan stood proud. He killed a saber tooth tiger with only a spear. No one hunter in his tribe had ever done that. He wanted something of the saber tooth to wear so that all who met him would respect him for killing so great an animal. First, there was something he had to do.

With his father's molars held toward the sky, he shouted out loud. "You ran with me to fight the two knife and now he runs with us. It is your time to hunt together, you, the two knife and the big man. One day I will join you and we will all hunt together."

He brought his arm down and stared at his father's teeth. "It was in your words that there would be a day when I would not fear the two knife."

Approaching the carcass, he lifted the massive head up. "See… no more life spirit." He pulled on the ears and slapped the top of its head.

"Ayashe matay! She cried out, shuddering as if the predator would wake from its deep sleep.

Lan laughed. "Come, I want to give you something from the two knife." He grabbed her by the hand and despite her protest, lifted her up to sit on top of the cat's huge chest.

"O-o-o," she moaned. She wanted to scream.

The skin is moving. Strange, how it slips back and forth over the ribs.

She wiggled around to feel it again, and then moved the skin of her own chest with her fingers to see if it did the same thing. She nearly slipped off, grabbing onto the fur to keep from falling.

Between her legs, she could see Lan below busily removing one of the fangs. Using a rock, he hit it hard on both sides until it loosened. After cutting away the connective tissue, he pulled it free, leaving the other chipped fang in the saber tooth's jaws. Next, all twenty claws were removed. Once the sheathes were slit open, they were easily pried from their roots.

Ayashe smiled back as soon as he looked up at her. She patted the carcass with approval, though careful not to pat it too hard.

By starting a cut along the outer edge of the ear, then around in a continuous circle until reaching the center, a long thin strip of skin was removed. He did the same thing to the other ear as well. Using the blade of one of his arrows, he drilled holes into all twenty claws and ran the strips through each one until two exact bracelets were completed. It took a while, but when it was finished, the bracelets were prettier than any Ayashe had ever owned.

Lan said, "Come, I want to give you the spirit of the two knife."

She slid to the ground. When he began to tie one of the bracelets to her wrist, she looked up with surprise. She had no idea that they were for her. It was all she could do to keep her arm steady and could not wait to hear it rattle. She eagerly lifted the other arm up so he could tie the second one on. When he finished, she shook both wrist.

Clackety, clack...clackety, clack

She loved the sound.

Clackety, clack...clackety, clack...clackety, clackety, clackety, clack.

She continued the steady rhythm and began to dance around an imaginary fire.

Clackety, clack...clackety, clack...clackety, clackety, clackety, clack

Laughing and dancing, it was wonderful and so much fun. Everything was perfect and right now it was all she wanted to do. Her energetic twist and turns eventually encouraged Lan to join in. Both circled one another with Lan copying her steps. He jumped when she did, twisting first one way and then the other. Following that, they swept their arms toward their feet and back over their heads. Around the imaginary fire they went, turning first one way and then back and then the other way again, until they were laughing so hard they had to stop to catch their breaths. It ended when she threw herself into his arms. He lifted her high into the air and turned her around until the world spun in an exhilaration of colors. Ayashe threw her head back, giggling until he finally put her down. Holding onto him, she could not remember a happier time. She wanted to remain in his arms forever. No longer was there any lingering fear left for him. She trusted him completely.

Lan grabbed her by the wrists and lifted them above her head. "Now you own the two knife's spirit. He will always be there to protect you."

It was late and a fire had to be started. She set it within the scent of the carcass, standing back to watch its magic and the smoke spiral into the sky. A partial moon along with a scarcity of clouds, revealed a countless spread of fires. There, the deceased looked down with a power to see into the corners of the dark time to watch over all who still lived.

At that very moment, three shooting stars streaked across the black horizon. "Look there! Do you see them," said Lan. "It is the new spirit of the two knife that runs there. He runs behind the man. My father is the one in front…the brightest one…see how he leads them?"

It had to be that way. He was sure of it. And the way they ran together, that would be the way they would run with them.

CHAPTER 5
THE FALLING RIVER

Warm winds blew through the pass, bringing with it a change in temperature. Air laden with moisture added to the humidity, making the day hot and unbearable. Despite the heat, there was a rekindled energy in Lan's steps. Far beyond the hills was a silvery reflection of a water fall. It meant a river of sizable breath, one that could be followed off of the mountain.

Ayashe had not noticed the falls and he was not going to tell her, at least not yet, wanting to wait until they got a little closer. After winding their way through low hills for most of that morning, they finally arrived at a particularly high one. Lan pulled her to the top so she could look out onto the expansive view.

"Look there…a falling river."

Ayashe touched the palm of her hand to sign for water the way he had. "Ba ba, saban. (Water, dark time)." They would be there by nightfall, she guessed.

They held one another and thrilled at the view. For Ayashe and her tribe, a river of any kind had always been a welcomed sight. She thought of the children and how they would run in and splash about while the woman filled water skins.

Bare hills gave way to tall evergreens. Walking within the cool enclosure offered relief from the heat. Ayashe played with Lan's braid, twirling the tip of it between her fingers. She drifted innocently to his lower back where she continued to walk them to his flexing buttocks. Palming it, she left her hand there to feel the strong muscles ripple as he walked. She looked to see if he was looking back, but his mind seemed to be preoccupied by something else, which only served to make the game that more tantalizing. She redirected her searching fingers to explore more of him, venturing further for the full sculpture of his round buttocks while softly giggling with mischievous pleasure. Her interest soon shifted to his face. She fumbled for his hand, grabbed it between hers and nestled it cozily between them. Her upturned gaze and silly grin finally caught his attention and it prompted her to squeeze his hand a little harder.

"I can hear the water. We will be there soon," he said.

Indeed, the sound of the falls was getting louder, its magnitude not realized until they pushed through thick layers of vegetation to reach a high vantage point. Awestruck, they looked to where the full height of the waterfall came crashing down from the top of a cliff. The rush shimmered past them, pouring its torrents as if from the clouds. Breathtaking to watch, it dropped between outlying pines and rocks to a distant depth where it exploded into a tumultuous agitation.

Along their side of the falls, trapped water formed numerous, saucer shaped pools. Spaced at varying heights, they were continuously being refilled by the swirling eddies above them. They looked on, mesmerized by the power of the falling water, ear shattering as it thundered past them. Scarlet iridescence, blazed across the falls from the setting sun. Soon, the coming darkness would disrobe the thin veils of bejeweled colors until they would become lost to the softer grays of evening.

"Hona ba ba," (Pretty water) she shouted. She moved closer to him so she could feel his body next to hers.

It does not matter if he does not know my words. He knows what it is that I see.

"We cannot go down when it gets dark," said Lan. "We must stay here until the dark time passes."

Ayashe stepped out of her skirt. She left for one of the shallower pools, eased herself in and laid across the flat surface. Most of her body remained above water, her chest lifting and falling from her heavy breathing.

Disrobing, Lan followed and squatted next to her. There, he playfully poured water over her erect nipples. He repeated that several times before going on to the rest of her breasts.

Orange peel bumps lifted from her skin. She laughed nervously as Lan encouraged the water to flow down the middle line of her abdomen and then on to the well of her belly. From there he swept it to the drier areas of her hips where it tracked around the outside of her mound and down the crease of her buttocks. He then stood and stepped back to admire her.

"You are many times more pretty than spring flowers."

He was making her so nervous she could not think. She shook warmly inside and had not realized she was staring at his fully erect manhood.

Her desire for him excited Lan, driven by the command he had of her. He wanted her in the water with her skin dripping wet, so he left for a splitting stream that was coming down from another pool farther up. His braid swung across his back as he waded away from her. Untying it as he walked, he let it flow freely behind. Beneath the stream, he sat and lifted his face to it, rolling his head from side to side, then tilting forward to let the water flow over his neck and shoulders.

As soon as he wiped the water from his eyes he saw Ayashe standing before him with one leg leaning fawningly to the side, the fine hairs, wet and lying flat. He followed the thighs upward to her dark temptress and on to the undersides of her full breasts.

Ayashe's mouth parted as she ran her finger tips along the side of his temple---an urge to press her mound to his lips coming to mind. Instead, she fingered his hair and lightly down the back of his neck. Her smile remained slight while tracing the side of his face.

Guiding her down until she straddled him, Lan palmed a rush of water so it would soak her hair. She squinted from it, her eyes aglow and looking back with expectancy. He pressed her hair flat against the sides and down along her back before pulling her closer. Cupping her breast, he tasted her tender nipples, absorbing their fullness and mouthing them before circling his tongue around each one.

Beneath the water, he entered her. His lips brushed hers then deliriously down her neck, brushed across her lips again and along her lower jaw. She was almost there, so he pulled her closer and moved to give her what he was feeling, what was totally encompassing him.

It was all she could do to keep from crying out, the feelings were so intense. She did not want any of it to stop---not now, not ever. She wanted it to go on and on and never end; lustful feelings that were fulfilling her desires and now heightening toward a passion filled ecstasy.

Like blossoming flowers, petals unfolded and shed in a forceful wind. Spiraling upwards, they drifted ever higher with the surging turbulence, higher than the storm clouds themselves; as high as the very door of the raging tempest where they were met with an explosive deluge that filled their floats. Twisting and turning, the petals tossed about with a denied control. The tempest door slammed again and again until the last of the raging storm subsided. With the final swells of euphoria, the clouds whirled away, taking with them the downpours, the flashing lights---the outcries.

Clearing into a serene vacancy, the sky emptied as the final remnants of the storm withdrew into a distancing tail of wind. Before it, the closing door of the tempest touched ever so slightly, then opened and closed, then opened. A trace of lingering gales slammed the door shut with a final and numbing intensity, leaving everything below in total silence.

Sailing downward, the petals swung pendulously---falling, falling, drifting, drifting, then hovering for a moment before alighting ever so gently onto the surface of the pool.

They both remained motionless and dreamed until the water's cold returned. Ayashe opened her eyes first, took a deep breath and tightened her arms around Lan. She gently nibbled his ear. She nipped his chin and took small bites along his neck. When he did not respond, she tickled him in the ribs.

Lan quickly wrestled her onto her back and tickled her the same way. She tried to pull away, but he had her by the leg and would not let go. Ayashe finally broke free and ran around the pool, splashing and pushing back until she had enough time to pull out a fern. Whipping around, she spanked him with it, then splashed toward the bank where he caught her and pulled her back in.

With the good lead he had, he ran out of the water in the direction of the trees, slowing down just long enough for her to catch up. He suddenly spun around, pulled her to the ground and held her by the wrist so she could not move. Trapped beneath him, he stuck his tongue inside her ear and then enveloped the whole of it entirely inside his mouth.

She could not stand it. She screamed from the vibrating noises he was making. Unable to take it anymore, she tried in vain to pull away from the tickling tongue he kept circling inside.

From there, Lan gently nipped the bridge of her nose, licked across her eyelids, her cheek, back across the bridge of her nose and then down the other cheek. No longer fighting back, she relaxed, raising any part to him that he wanted to lick. She turned her face to the side so he could lick there as well, then the other side, then back. She liked the way he brushed his lips back and forth over hers---liked what was growing between their bodies. She returned his gaze with long lashed brown eyes and ran her fingers through his hair. She gently held his head, waited for him to finish licking her nipples, then guided him farther downward so his tongue could travel below her belly and on to the creases between her mound and upper thighs. She enjoyed every tingling sensation he was giving her as well as the control she held in her hands.

The following morning

Shocked, Ayashe could not believe Lan wanted to climb down the side of the falls. She knew there was a far better way to reach the flat place, the route she and Matwua had taken when they first set out toward the hidden valley, though she could not remember how to get there.

I do not want him to leave me and climb down alone. When he sees he can no longer go this way, we will find another.

"Look there!" Lan said. "In the clearing....do you see what it is that I see?"

Far below, on the flat ground in the beginning of an expansive grassland, a cluster of huts neither Lan nor Ayashe had noticed before appeared as dark specks near a dividing river. It took a while to see what he was pointing at.

"Otaktay," (kills many Sioux) she finally said.

Otaktay's tribe was familiar to her and one her own people traded with on occasion.

"My hope is that these people will welcome us," said Lan.

Wet and slippery, moss covered stones left nothing to hold onto except for the tangle of low lying bushes that grew on their side of the falls. They kept slipping on the rocks, their legs getting scratched from thorns as they passed by. Halfway down, they could go no further. Lan searched from every angle, and although going back was an option, he felt sure there had to be a way down through here. After considering several different approaches, he walked out to the end of a ledge and looked over. A considerable distance below was a boulder. Smaller and narrower than the rock he was standing on, it had a downward slope to it that slanted toward the raging bottom. Covering the boulder was black and green algae, the flow of water, combing the slippery hair like threads straight. From there, a chain of rocks and ledges led vertically to the bottom of the falls, the only hand-holds, the bushes that were crammed into any crevice they could get their roots into.

Putting his lips to Ayashe's ear, he shouted over the thundering falls. "We have to jump."

She looked at him questioningly, not totally sure of his intentions or what the jimp word meant.

After handing her the spear, he sat at the edge and eased his hips over it. He held himself in that position for a brief moment, looked at the boulder below and without the least bit of hesitation, let go. He landed in the middle of it and immediately rolled to the side where he lay flat to keep from sliding off. Steadying himself, he carefully stood up.

"Give me the spear!"

Ayashe's face slowly appeared over the edge with a look that was a combination of fear, surprise and halting refusal.

"My spear!" Lan motioned as if to throw it. "Drop my spear down."

Holding the spear flat in front of her, she let go of it. The rolled up bear skin went over the edge next, and shortly after, everything else.

"Now jump!" He shouted.

The distance beyond the boulder to the bottom of the falls looked frightening, the space all around, vast and open. The loud and abrupt explosions from below filled her with diffidence.

Two birds, the male, bright red, the female, a tawny color with black stripes, glided on gossamer wings through the open space with material for a nest. They circled the front of the falls and then darted around to the back of it and out of sight. There, the chicks would be protected from predators like minks and owls.

This is a place for sky jumpers. Sisika live a happy life. They can go anywhere.

Above her, safe ground anchored with trees and level spaces was far more comforting. She had to think about this.

My people do not climb steep places like this. Never! This is not the way. I cannot…he does not really believe…

She leaned over just enough to see the top of his head.

"**JUMP!**" he yelled, cupping his mouth. "Do not wait! Jump now!"

"Jimp! Ha! Not Ayashe!"

She instantly stepped away with a smirk on her face.

I am not ready to do his jimp.

Another peek over the edge.

Look at him! He waits with his arms out as if to catch the wind. He thinks like the chtuktok (thunderfoot-mammoth). He cannot climb back and I will not be left here alone. If we fall, we will fall together.

Babbling softly, she paced back and forth before the edge. "I will go when I am ready to go, bg Bandu man, or any other name you wish to call yourself. Yes, your little one is going to jimp and then we will both be sky jumpers with broken wings, Mowachi man."

She stopped short and stood at the edge with horrible thoughts of instability and then falling through empty space. To fall freely through that open space with nothing to grab onto would be heart stopping. You suck in from panic and your mouth stretches to scream at the world, but despite those pleas, the animals do not care, and the only ones that do are waiting for you to come crashing to the bottom.

She looked over the edge with her toes hanging over the end of it. Breathing heavily, her brows stabbed at her nose as she hesitated with a thought.

No, it is too far and I am not ready.

"JUMP NOW!" He shouted.

She tried a few practice attempts, stepping back a dozen paces and running full tilt toward the edge, but always stopping short of the jump. In time, she finally convinced herself to get it over with. Retreating as far back as she could, she rocked back and forth for what she hoped would be the last time.

This was it. She was going to do it on the very next try---right now and not look away. She was going to run to the edge without thinking and…well…no…not exactly right now. The whole thing was making her shake uncontrollably. She squatted down to settle herself.

I must stop thinking about this and just do it.

After a long while of battling with herself, she became determined to finish the jump. She took a deep breath and with short, quick steps, ran to the edge. At the very end, she abruptly stopped. There, she stood teetering over it, her body, half bent with her arms making small circles in the air. Having changed her mind at the very last moment about jumping into nothingness, she could not stop the forward momentum.

She dropped into Lan's waiting arms with the both of them sliding down the slanted boulder and out into open space. Their bodies separated on the way down and fell for a seeming eternity until Ayashe felt herself suddenly splash into cold water. The deafening impact muffled her ears as well as her screams, followed by her body being sucked downward into the silence of a swirling current. Helpless and forced to flow with it, she was tossed and yanked about uncontrollably. Desperately, she fought to reach the surface, but the current was far too strong. Panic stricken, she kicked her legs and flailed her arms through the churning whirlpool. Rising upward, she bobbed to the surface where she struggle for a breath of air before swimming hard toward the outer edge of the swirling current. Gradually and with hard strokes, she was able to paddle into calmer water.

"Lan! She yelled, choking and gasping.

Standing on the rocky shore, Lan turned toward her voice, dove in and swam to her side. "It was in my head that I would not see you again."

Relieved, she held onto him and together, swam towards shore where she settled into his arms, shivering. Lan removed his vest and wrapped it around her shoulders.

"Wait for me here! Everything is up there on the rock we fell from."

The climb back was far easier to do alone. After his return, they walked out onto easy ground, made up of small rocks and pebbles on both sides of the river. It was now a fast flowing rapid that eventually would slow before cutting through the grasslands.

CHAPTER 6
OTAKTAY'S VILLAGE

Here began the flat place Lan heard so much about. Grass dominated the landscape for as far as the eye could see---a world unexplored by the Bandu or any tribe he knew of. They entered a game trail through grass that was taller than the height of a man.

How will I hunt the deer? There is no place that I can throw my arrows. I am like the cave bird that cannot see; only here the walls are made of grass.

Staying to a narrow game trail stamped flat by the passing herds that came down to drink was far easier than breaking through dense foliage. Wherever the trail branched off, they kept to the one that paralleled the river.

Mosquitoes and biting flies, stirred from their roost of grass blades, attacked Lan with persistent tenacity. Ayashe seemed to be untouched by them, as though she had an inherited resistance. She slapped at the ones that landed on his back.

Among the tall grasses, big bluestem, Indian grass and switch grass swayed in the incessant wind. Grains such as wild corn and barley grew in abundance. Alongside the now tranquil river, flowering red gladiolas and purple irises grew randomly along dryer ground. Field garlic of numerous varieties and colors flourished in small open areas where an occasional green and white butterfly orchid pushed out delicate petals. Saffron and day lilies were sporadic, as were daisy-like cat's ears. At infrequent intervals, lavender saw-worts, purple viper grass and orange goat's beard could be seen.

Underfoot, the trampled grass crawled with dice snakes. Beneath the stems to catch field mice, they had to be sidestepped constantly. From time to time Ayashe forgot to look, only to feel one slither underneath the flattened stems beneath her feet. It alerted her to keep her head down and to closely watch the darker places in Lan's shadow.

Ahead were the huts they had seen. Lan jumped up from time to time to look over the top of the grass. With no landmark to judge exactly where they were, it was like looking for a stick floating in a sea of waves.

The falls were far behind, the tops of the huts getting closer every time he jumped. Upon reaching the outer perimeter of huts, he motioned for Ayashe to remain quiet, though her focus remained on the ground lest she step on anything alive.

"We have to leave the trail," his voice, barely a whisper.

With as little disturbance as possible, they pushed through the last line of grass, careful to minimize the movements at the top of the stems. Just before the clearing that surrounded the huts, Lan parted the stems to the side and looked in.

One of many immensely tall posts, equal to the height of seven men, towered in front. Lined along the clearing with numerous others, it held fast from a footing dug deep in the ground. Half way up began a jumble of animal bones lashed to it in a haphazard fashion. Hides and antlers were dressed over them as if to recreate the animals as they were in real life.

On top of each posts sat a human skull, long deceased and chalked from exposure. There, they faced the outer vastness of open plains. In their settings they presented an image of lonely desolation, mold sticking to them like a ravaging disease. The green violation affixed itself to the few teeth left and to the insides of eye sockets.

Above Lan and blowing across one of the skull's cheeks, a thin tattering of long hair instilled in it an eerie life-like presence.

The death spirit still fights the life spirit that does not want to die.

Though human, these skulls were not human like he was. These were from men far bigger than anyone he knew of. Some had their long hair still intact, decorated with owl and condor feathers and strings of shell beads.

And huts were not what he had seen when they first looked from high up in the falls. These were tents of huge height and girth and like the skulls, lay in an air of desolation.

Winds that blew unbroken on the flats, whistled through the loose hides. The end of one of them had broken free and slapped continuously against the side of the tent. Out front, a swirl of wind-blown dust lifted into a twisting cloud. It drifted to the far end of the clearing, whirled around for a while and then dissipated into nothing. On that same side of the clearing, stacked higher than the tents, was something that held even more interest. It was so unbelievable; he could not discern what he was looking at.

"Duma…nu shatu…nu shatu duma!"

Before Ayashe could finish the loud welcome, Lan covered her mouth. He picked her up and carried her into the cover of grass with her protest muffled in his hand. She pulled away and tried to explain that these people were not in these covers. They were far from here, hunting where game was more plentiful. This was their place for the cold time and when they would eventually return.

I can see in your eyes, my Mowatchi, that you do not understand my words. Can you then understand them from the changes in the lines of my face?

His spear at the ready, Lan stepped into the clearing.

Does she think that I can fight them all?

As if expecting a hoard of charging men, he crept out onto hard gritty ground that was empty and abandoned. To his astonishment, Ayashe walked casually ahead of him, her arms swinging exaggeratedly.

"Duma…nu shatu…nu shatu duma!"

She went on to shout that they only wanted to use the tents and that they would then leave. Smiling back at him, she laughed and pulled on his arm. In the words of her people, she said, "See…it is only us!"

She dropped her bundle onto the ground and excitedly ran to the nearest tent. Walking under a pair of tusk that framed the entryway, she pushed the flap of hide that served as a door to the side and went in. The flap closed behind her, leaving everything inside dark despite the time of day. She grabbed the flap and yanked it loose to allow the outside light to stream in, scattering beetles the size of acorns into crevices.

Cold air, thick with mist, rolled up the steps like white smoke, lifting the skin on her arms into hair-raised bumps. Above her, the undersides of the mammoth and buffalo skins that covered the tent were old, yellow and stiff. Hairline cracks ran across the underlying surface of the skins in a complex grid. Hanging down were thin strips of sinew from the knots that secured the skins to one another and to the bone framing.

Tarnished steps that led into the black depths below ground were made of large rib bones. The first wobbled under her weight. She moved over to the corner where the step was more stable and pressed through a thick cobweb and onto something round that cracked and made a crispy sound, like the shell of a large egg. At first, the round thing had wriggled, but now that her full weight was on it, it did not move around anymore. Warm and sticky, she scraped the pasty innards off on the rib, held onto the wall of dried mud and imbedded skulls and carefully descended two more unstable steps.

CRASH!

The stairs buckled underneath her weight. She fell with it, sliding downward with the debris until splashing into a shallow, awful smelling puddle at the bottom. Dirt rained down everywhere, the splashing sound, echoing off the far walls as if those walls were a considerable distance away.

Beneath her feet, the ground felt damp and cold, the air, clammy with an aged smell of decomposition.

So dark...everything so dark...and cold.

With no way of climbing back, she wrapped her arms around herself. Shivering, she looked through the black emptiness and at the impression of a world-less night with a lack of dimensions. Remote and station less, its sole superfluous values seemed to be the cold and the rancid odors thick with the stench of rotting flesh. Although not readily apparent at the top of the steps, it was now nauseating. She had to pinch her nose shut and breathe through her opened mouth---so strong she could taste it.

Although it seemed pointless to go on any further, thoughts of her tribe in tents just like this, with children running about and women engaged in day to day activities, brought familiarity and fond memories back. So, there was no need to fear this one and other than the disarray and poor condition of it, it was a connection, nonetheless.

A steady dripping sound echoing off a far wall showed the tent to be cavernous.

Cautiously, and drawn with curiosity, she pressed down onto dirt that felt soft and moist. As she stepped fully into it, a light tickling sensation feathered across the top of her foot. She wanted to pull away from it, but decided that rather than to get stung by whatever it might be, it was better to let the thing finish crawling with its countless, tiny appendages. She cringed from the unpleasant feel of it and wished it would hurry, but the thing seemed endless and surprisingly heavy now that its hard body was fully on top of her foot. Finally, the last of the spiny legs pushed off.

"Rigbishka!"

She listened to the dripping sound and tried to determine its direction. **PLINK…PLINK…PLINK…PLINK…**

What is making that light? Could it be another way out?
PLINK…PLINK…PLINK…PLINK…

Waving her hands out front, she moved forward with a sense that she was nearing a post or support of some kind. Something just bumped her head and was left rattling continuously. She reached out to grab it.

Bones! A mas tet!

She pushed the bear skeleton, suspended from the ceiling, away from her and stepped toward the light. The bones continued to rattle behind as she edged toward the light that kept going in and out of view from the other things that were hanging from the ceiling.

PLINK…PLINK…PLINK…PLINK…

The texture of the floor started to change as well. It was wetter and colder with a downward slope to it, a gradual slope where the layer of air around her ankles got colder the more she descended into the darkness---as cold as ice.

Ahead, the light became clearer and now plain to see. It was nothing more than a narrow beam of dust filled sunlight streaming down from a wound in the skin overhead.

PLINK…PLINK…PLINK…PLINK…

Strange how after going for what seemed at least half way to the far wall through perpetual darkness, all she did was penetrate deeper into the unchanging nature of it and away from the bright outside with its glowing sun and fresh odors of spring. Here, the air was far colder than it had been by the steps.

This is like the big white the elders told us about when I was a child---snow for as far as the eye could see.

It covered the grassland in every direction and beyond where a man could walk in a lifetime---a hundred lifetimes. All the places that were now green were once white, although that was many generations before her time. Back then, there was no hot time. That was what her father's, father once said. "No green plants, only frozen ice across an empty place, a white place with few animals to hunt."

That tale was passed down through a voice from distant generations more numerous than all the fingers, all the toes of every man, women and child in her tribe---or of every tribe she ever heard of.

It was unbearably cold. Everyone covered themselves with the skins of animals and never took them off, unless they were in a tent like this with a fire raging strong from the biting cold outside.

PLINK...PLINK...PLINK...PLINK...

Flies, disturbed from their meal of festering tidbits were everywhere. No matter how much she waved at them, they would not go away. She had enough. She was going to get out of this gloomy place as soon as she figured out how.

A sudden growling noise from the back made her jump.

Nag boksta! It lives here. It found old meat and now it smells me.

Another growl

Somehow, she was going to have to find a way back to where the stairs were and try to climb out. She could not risk yelling for Lan. She had to do this alone or her loud voice could startle the animal, or whatever it was that was in the back corner growling. Getting to the steps was all she cared about, especially since that thing in the back still growled from time to time. She could hear it move, thought she heard it shuffle around, thought she heard it start to make its way toward the front where the stairs were; or where the stairs once were.

PLINK...PLINK...PLINK...PLINK...

If she was tall enough to get over one of the walls, she could then squeeze underneath the hide that made up the rest of the tent. Knowing how these tents were built and the walls that were at

least as high as the steps, she knew that would be near impossible without something to stand on.
CRASH!
She banged into the skeleton again and it made her jump.
Do not run. It will see my weakness.
She blindly stepped through the dark density out front while waving her arms.
Crunch! Crackle!
The wriggly thing!
The huge insect squirmed underneath her foot. She quickly hopped over what she guessed had to be a centipede the length of her arm.

Moving cautiously through inky blackness, she finally hit a pile of dirt and hard bone with her big toe. It had to be the debris from the steps, she thought.
Growl
She screamed.

Outside, in front of a mound of bones, Lan looked on in awe. He could not believe what he was seeing, yet, there it was—white---so huge—impossible---no animal could be this big.
Now, to get closer…just a little more…reach in and…
The immense tusk protruding from a pile of bones made no sense to him. It came from an animal he knew nothing about. Most of the bones in the pile were an accumulation from previous meals and were scorched from a fire. Others had been dragged into the village from the surrounding fields for tent building. The entire mound was huge and reached higher than the nearby tents.

Walking along the length of the tusk, Lan saw that it was wedged in among mandibles, leg bones and pelvises. He curled his hand over the tusk, looked up and saw an even longer one above it.

This is the long tooth the elders spoke of.

The tents themselves held interest. At the nearest one, he explosively slapped the hide at the entryway to the side. Startled by a swarm of beating leather wings, he stepped back for the bats that flew out and over the top of the tent like one great bird. He sighed with relief.

Seeing how dark it was inside, he left to make a few torches. Twisting grass stems tightly together for a slow burn, he started a fire and lit one of them. Holding it high, he stepped under supporting columns of tusks lashed together with thick ropes to support the entryway. Within the walls of the narrow passageway were mandibles and pelvises from mammoths, chosen for their size and strength. Caked together with mud and straw to form strong structural walls, the smaller spaces in-between were embedded with the human skulls of ancestors.

Firelight from the torch glowed across the animal bones, showing varying degrees of weathering, having been collected at random from the fields beyond the tents. Farther along, buffalo and antelope skulls were intermixed with more mammoth bones.

At the bottom of the steps he raised the torch to the cavernous interior where the full expanse of it could be readily seen. The walls of earth alone were twice as tall as he was with an overhead covering of skins that reached the height of five men standing on top of one another. An entire tribe of thirty individuals could easily fit inside.

To support the ceiling of heavy hides, four columns at the center of the large room were made up of mammoth pelvises interlocked together. Secured with a tight weave of thick ropes, the columns supported the suspension of mammoth hides which were sewn together to form a strong, wind resistant roof.

Across the open space of the upper tent, hung a huge mummified snake, large enough to swallow an elk. The color of umber, the head had missing eyes, the cavities left, black and sunken in. From the fangs, skeletons of small snakes, each the size of a man's arm, curled toward the floor as though ready to strike at anyone who neared.

Wolf skulls hung from ceiling supports. As Lan moved the torch around, their shadows chased one another around the walls. Propped up along a back wall in real life positions were a giant sloth and several grizzly bear skeletons.

He moved the torchlight towards another wall where a pile of broken rocks lay stacked. Discarded from tool making, the broken pieces were left there as if for some future use. Next to those and stacked high were well worn baskets discolored from the sun. Many of the reeds had split, making the baskets useless and left behind for repair. Broken spear shafts leaned against another wall, a few with blunted points, others with points missing.

Next to the four columns at the center lay a fire pit surrounded by blackened rocks and filled almost to the top with bits of broken bones and ash. Settled in the ashes lay a rotted buffalo head complete with fur.

In front of the pit, a row of seven mammoth skulls for sitting on, six with their tusk removed, spread halfway around it in a semicircle. The seventh and the largest retained its tusks, a massive, curling set of appendages that stretched farther than the height of a man.

This is where their leader sits. There will be a time when I will sit on one like this.

Leaving for the stairs, he climbed two thirds of the way to the top where he stopped to turn around. Torch light flickered inside, causing shadows of the wolf skulls to circle around the walls like flying black demons.

"Death Spirits!"

Pointing the torch at the entrance above him, he continued up the rest of the steps to the outside.

"Ayashe!"

Plink! Plink! Plink! Plink...

None of the steps were left intact. Ayashe reached as high as she could, only to pull down loose dirt. Clawing at what was left, she panicked in her effort to find a way out. She heard another growl and far louder than the rest.

"**Agh-h-h!**" she cried out.

She dug broken nails into the dirt wall that crumbled away like loose powder. Desperately, she felt for a buried root or anything to grab onto.

The growling continued.

She screamed.

At that instant, something grabbed her by the arm. She tried to pull away, but it held onto her firmly. She screamed again as loud as she could. Instead of pulling her down, the beast was pulling her upward, growling the entire time.

"Hold on to me," Lan shouted, straining to haul her up.

She kicked at the dirt for a foothold, but he was picking her up too fast. As soon as she was on the top landing, she pulled free and scrambled through the entryway on all fours to the outside. Coughing and stumbling, she fell to the ground where the smell of sweet grass and flowering plants filled her lungs. Her face burned in the bright sun and never felt so good. That was when she saw what had made all that noise. She started to laugh uncontrollably. Feeling foolish, she pointed at a large, loose flap of hide still vibrating in the wind. It was nothing more than a piece of skin---there at the bottom of the tent, down low and just above the ground, buzzing in the breeze like a trapped animal. It was nothing more than a piece of hide flapping back and forth.

"Iksta ki nag boksta?"

She shook her head at what she felt was stupidity on her part and how the darkness and awful odors played on her fears.

Lan helped her to her feet. "There is no two knife there!"

"Nah, twoniff?"

"Is that what made you scream? Is this your two knife? It is good then that I kill it for you." He ran up to the vibrating flap of skin and exaggeratedly jabbed it with the spear. "Now, it is no more."

"Ki nag boksta!" she said, shaking her head.

He put an arm around her. "Look up there…rain clouds. We can stay in the other cover. It is clean and will be a safe place to stay dry."

His words did not need any meaning. She could see the dark clouds he was looking at brewing in the sky. Following him, she let him lead her to the tent he had entered earlier and cautiously remained behind him. Once torches were set along the inside walls and lit, she went about cleaning and sweeping the floor of debris. Dung, the waste product of ungulates found stacked in neat piles outside, were brought in and placed next to the fire pit to burn later. Baskets and old spear shafts were thrown in to strengthen the fire she had started. In a short while, the enclosure became comfortably warm. With nothing left to do, she left for the river to bathe.

Smoke began to fill the tent. Lan searched the ceiling for the hole that would allow the smoke to escape. It was where he guessed it would be, in the middle and covered with a flap of hide. Tied to the flap at one end was a rope that led along the ceiling to a fixed overhead support. From there, the rope hung down the wall with the end secured to a stake. He untied it and pulled downward to uncover the hole. To close it, there was an opposing rope on the other side of the tent.

Billows of smoke immediately spilled through the opening to the outside. He returned to the fire and threw dung into the pit which burned much cleaner than the mildewed wood used to build the fire. Dung was also used to replace the torches, leaving the tent in a warming glow.

Entering the crystal clear shallows through a dense wall of reeds, Ayashe pushed her way through and waded into a slow moving current up to her thighs.

A pair of ducks dipped their heads below the surface, teaching hunting skills to a following of chicks. The newborns struggled to keep up as they bobbed over the wakes of their parents. Tiny orange feet paddled the water, pushing the ducklings along. They chased after the bugs that always seemed to be at least one beak length away.

One of the stragglers came within easy grasp. Ayashe reached for it, but it quickly paddled frantically towards the reeds. Another bumped from behind. She reached around and cupped the chick out of the water amidst a discord of protesting peeps. She snuggled it to her face with the duckling wriggling around to get free. It would not stop peeping. Smelling its feathers, she touched their softness with her lips.

"Is it your wish to leave me, little sisika?"

Still protesting, she carefully placed the baby bird on top of the water and watched it scurry away. It furiously pumped its tiny paddles while bobbing from side to side. The chick turned its head around to squeak back a profanity of peeps before disappearing inside the reeds to join its waiting family.

From the river's bottom, she brought up a handful of sand and scrubbed her armpits. She scooped more up and scrubbed her arms and legs. The gritty texture also loosened the embedded dust and grime from her skirt. It took a while to get it clean. When she finished, she scrubbed her feet and hands. Lastly, she dipped under and washed her hair as best she could.

On her way back to the tents, she almost missed the yellow and red puccoons and deep pink blazing stars growing at the side of the trail. She pulled them out in clumps along with red shooting stars before returning. The skirt, she left outside to dry before going inside.

Her face glowed as soon as she got halfway down the steps to look inside. Warm and inviting, the walls shook from reflecting fire. The dry floor smelled of freshly turned earth, the sweep marks left, running lengthy lines from one end to the other.

Lan turned to her from the bear skin he was sitting on and then quickly faced back around to the new netting he was making for the ax.

Radiant, naked and wet, Ayashe sashayed toward him with a planted smile. This was all so wonderful. She loved sharing their lives together like this and it seemed to please him as well. She put the flowers down and sat next to him on the fur. One by one, she separated them while leaning against his arm. A few were placed near the heat to permeate their scent. The pretty red and yellow ones, she spread out on the floor in rows of alternating colors.

Lan showed her the half-finished netting. "This is to carry my ax...eh!" feigning a blow as if he had an ax in his hand.

"Eh," she mocked, with a shy smile.

"There is nothing left to eat and my stomach is empty," he said.

Within the field of grasses grew natural grains such as wild corn. He left to gather armfuls of it. Familiar with its preparation, he picked out the ears, no bigger than a finger and shaved the kernels from them, leaving them to pile up on hide spread out on the ground. To this he added the eggs of wading birds nesting inside cattails along the river bank.

Like everything he did, Ayashe wanted to involve herself. She gathered the mix together, picking out bits of the tassles and husk the same way he did. When they finished and with no idea what it was going to be used for, she crossed her legs with her head resting on her fists to watch.

By now, the mix had grown into a sticky pile. A small trickle of water was added which surprised her, especially when Lan stuck his hands in to gather it all together. It looked like fun, so she stuck her hands in along with his. Once the batter began to thicken, she separated some of it into clumps and turned them over, pressing down on each one. The feel of it was that of thick clay and she quickly found she could form different shapes and make them stand up all by themselves.

I can make seed mud do things I think.

A sudden idea came to mind. She smashed down on the clumps and packed them all into one large mass. The pile in front of Lan, she added into the mix as well. She rolled it all together into one large ball then separated it into two pieces, one larger than the other. The smaller pieces were subdivided into four more, leaving a small amount on the side. The four, she then rolled into log-like shapes, leaving them for later. The large piece, she molded into an oblong spherical shape. By squeezing the front of it, a head and ears were formed. To the bottom, she attached the four log shapes and left the whole thing standing on them. With a tail added to the back end and finally a trunk and two tusks, the mammoth was complete, except for the tusk that kept falling off. After a few delicate fixes, she looked over at Lan.

"Is this your long tooth?" he asked.

Ayashe spread her arms wide. "Chtuktok! Hms bg, bg."

Lan picked up the mammoth sculpture. He turned it around, looked underneath and turned it right side up. He noted the way the back sloped downward toward the tail, the tusk that just fell off again and a fifth leg that seemed uselessly curled over its head.

What does this long tooth eat?

It certainly had a large stomach. He put his hand on his own and felt his hunger throbbing inside. He smashed the dough down, added more water to the batch and mixed it into one large, flat cake. Separated into smaller pieces, it was all put into two stacks.

Back inside the tent, the cakes were placed on hot rocks around the fire pit. After turning them over a few times until they turned dark and well cooked, he laid them on a mat of stems. Hot and smoking, he picked one up and blew on it. As soon as he bit off a piece and started chewing, Ayashe's lower lip widened downward in disgust.

Does he not know I only eat meat? I do not eat seed mud.

He looked like he enjoyed it, the way he kept making a happy face and swallowing mouthful after mouthful. Her brows lowered as she watched, then rose when he handed her what was left of the piece he was eating.

She took the unwanted piece from him, puzzled from the game they had played outside and why they were now eating it.

Maybe it tastes like meat?

"It is good," Lan encouraged, nodding for her to try it.

Her head shook with a no sign. "Me, jonga! Chtuktok! Bo bo! "Me…meat!"

Pointing at her mouth, she repeated the two words she had learned. "Meat…me meat!"

She tried to give it back to him, but Lan insisted.

Look at how he chews like a bondo gah. This looks like bondo gah waste. I do not eat bondo gah waste.

After another encouraging nod from him, she ventured to bite off a piece.

This has no taste.

As she chewed, it started to become bitter and too hard to swallow. She had enough of it. She spit it into the fire, wiped her lips and frowned.

Lan happily stuffed himself, dropping crumbs from his lips and smiling animatedly.

"Pbbt!" She blurted out, showing her disgust by making an ugly face.

Lan laughed. "We have nothing else. I will make a kill with the new sun. It is then that you will have a smile for me."

She slapped him on the arm for giving her such a horrible thing to eat. Leaving him to go outside, she climbed the mound of bones where she sat and looked across the flat, grassy expanse and crisp, pre-storm sky. The high vantage point sharpened a sweeping view across the flats along with a flash of light that lit up the horizon. It was followed by a thunderclap that rumbled and shook the twilight sky. Overhead, dark clouds, brimming with moisture, tumbled in towards her. In places, strobes of sunlight seared the edges of black clouds, leaving bright highlights along the ground. She was not there long before Lan climbed up and sat behind her.

"The sky spirits throw their kill sticks," he teased.

Ayashe giggled. She liked that he was there. She leaned her head against his chest to watch the grass run from the pursuing winds.

"It is like the big water," he said.

Seed full grass tops waved like surf-frothed white caps, so much like the sea and the storms on the coast. And no matter how many times they both had seen storms before, the buildup was enthralling. It seemed at odds that so much beauty could predispose so much turmoil.

The grouse hunt

The earth felt moldy and damp beneath their feet when they left at daybreak. Moisture left un-siphoned by the grass, sponged back to the clouds. The water soaked trail yielded under their weight, while above, a strong sun hinted toward another hot day

Grouse were among the many birds nesting in the grass. Their naive progenies scurried about, chasing insects in and out of the forest of stems with carefree abandonment. The camouflaged feathers of the males were beginning to change into the flamboyant colors of their fathers. Plump and tender and almost fully grown, they would be easy kills.

Ayashe followed close behind, unsure of the success of the hunt. Still full of doubts about whether the flimsy arrows could do anything, they were nice to look at nonetheless. Their artful design, and nearly as long as she was tall, along with the iridescent greens and pure white of the feathers, showed them to be different than any kill stick she knew of. Surely, they were too narrow and light to have any real power. She attentively watched as Lan notched one of the arrows into the end of the bow.

Now I know the use for the stick with the pretty rocks.

Ahead, a movement at the side of the trail caught Lan's attention. He drew his arm back, then disappointingly lowered it.

Ayashe scoffed and shook her head. *I knew it would not kill?*

Sitting in the middle of the trail, a rabbit froze in fear. Lan wanted plump birds, not rabbits. He waved the bow above his head. "Yah!"

The rabbit jumped into an irregular run and zig zagged down the trail for a while before abruptly darting left and into the brush.

As soon as they rounded the next bend, a sudden rush of feathers startled to the right. Laboring wings fought against the stiff stems as a grouse became airborne. The start was slow and not enough for the bird to catch the breeze above the grass line. Hit with an arrow, it fluttered down in a wake of loose feathers and squawking cries.

Excited, Ayashe jumped up and down. Impressed by the speed of the kill stick and Lan's proficiency for it, she shouted out while running through the grass to find the bird. "Na tu…sisika!"

Mastery of the bow was necessary for survival. Lan did not consider his skill to be anything out of the ordinary. He and his father were experts at using them. From an early age he hunted birds and frogs with an atlatl. By the time he reached adulthood, he was taught to use the bow instead.

Ayashe emerged from the brush, her lips touching the grouse while talking softly to it. She lifted the grouse up high, and as if it could hear, told the bird what a beautiful sky jumper it was. Petting it, she turned the dead bird's head toward her to get its attention.

"You have a good spirit. I will wear your colors and tell everyone who sees them that they come from a good little sky jumper."

Taking the bird from her, Lan held it up to the sky.

"Your spirit will fly to where I can no longer see you. There you will live again and thank me, as I now thank you for your gift."

The fire grew strong, the grouse gutted and most of the feathers removed. The rest would burn in the fire. From a makeshift framework, it hung over the fire pit to cook. Dripping fat sputtered and snapped in the flames, filling the tent with an appetizing aroma.

After traveling for so long without fresh meat, this would seem a feast. Game birds like grouse were rarely caught by Ayashe's people. She herself had never tasted one. With hungry anticipation, she watched it cook while Lan used the time to resume teaching her more of his words.

"Bird," he said.

"Bawd."

"Bird da," he corrected.

"Bawd da. Hms, sisika."

She reached in, tore off a leg and threw it into the air a few times to cool it off. Finishing that, she ripped out a piece from the breast.

"Bawd da. Me meat," she said, as she energetically rocked from side to side while smiling broadly.

After she finished eating, she licked her fingers and returned to the feathers she had lined up along the ground. Punching three rows of holes along the waistline of the skirt with a sharp bone splinter, she weaved the feathers in and out of them to form three color-filled bands. She put the skirt on and pulled it straight, fluffing out the feathers and straightening them until they looked just right.

Busily focusing on the last few knots in the netting, Lan had not noticed.

"Hm…humph!" she grunted.

He started to look up, or at least it seemed that way, and continued with…the dumb string thing.

"Mm! Mmm!…Cough! Cough!" Holding up a feather, she spun around with it.

"The feathers are more pretty on you than on the bird," he said, without looking back.

He liked what she did to the skirt, liked the way her hips leaned to the side. The netting finished, he reached up and slid his hand underneath the skirt and around to her perfectly round buttocks.

Ayashe reached for his braid. She lined it up next to a hand full of her own hair and with imploring eyes, said, "Me this."

Braiding Ayashe's hair was something Lan thought about doing before. If she was going to be part of the Bandu tribe, it was only fitting that she look like one.

After he finished her braid, he took the feather she still had in her hand and attached it to the end, leaving it hanging downward. Encircling her from behind, he palmed her belly, pulled the skirt up from both sides and held her mound.

"I like you this way," he gently said.

He turned her around by the hips, ran his hand down the strong line of her back and cupped her buttocks. At the same time, Ayashe grabbed his ready manhood through the deer skin and stroked it. She untied the sinew from his leg skins, squatted and pulled them to the floor. As soon as he stepped out of them, he laid back on the bear fur. Parting her lips, she held the skirt above her waist, lowered herself down and straddled him.

Amber light shined the walls while outside, the wind blew easy. Plumes of frail smoke drifted across a partial moon like an endless strip of black lace.

The remainder of the spring and summer spent at the tents proved productive, including learning one another's language. Ayashe struggled with many of Lan's words. It was far easier for him to learn hers and the gestures she used. He eventually only had trouble following her when she got carried away with something exciting she wanted to tell him and spoke too fast, or with too much enthusiasm. In time, he became quite fluent, pushing her for the right pronunciations. As the leader he knew he would one day be again, he did not want to be laughed at for miss-pronounced words.

Late summer
"It is good that we leave this place. I will wait for the coming sun. It is then that we will follow this river."

"Me pee poh hunts to river far that way," Ayashe said, waving in the direction of her village."

"Then that is what we will find."

She stroked the tattoo on his arm and wanted one of her own before they left. Its importance, along with the braid she wore, represented the image she wanted to present to her people. It meant everything to her. To accept that was to accept Lan.

Ayashe brightened. "You one time put snik to me?"

"Is that your wish?"

She tilted her head sidewise. "Yes! I ams bg wa tah pee poh. (Giggle) Mik snik to me," she begged.

Lan's lower lip lifted slightly as if he was considering that. He purposely took his time before finally answering her.

"You must first know why I wear the snake's spirit."

Lan's demeanor remained serious and it made Ayashe listen attentively. "Snakes carry the death spirit in their poison. Wear the snake and no one will harm you."

Remembering what his father once said, he recalled the exact words." *Snakes have a strong power that should not be overlooked. Wear that along with your other spirits, they all have a purpose.*

Back at the fire, Ayashe sat on one of the mammoth heads and looked on impatiently while Lan readied everything he would need; a sharp splinter of bone, charcoal for black, dried berries for color, and water to wash away the blood. The process took a while. It was not only painful for Ayashe, it was tedious. As he worked, he chanted under his breath, asking for the snake spirit to protect her.

He made the snake nearly exactly like his, wrapped around her arm and spitting at its own tail. Berries, dried and ground into a powder were mixed to produce red and blue dyes to make it appear lifelike. Unlike his, he filled in the eyes with red dye to represent fire to ward off not only death spirits, but sickness as well. Blue was used for the tail, the benign end of the snake left pointing downward.

"It is finished," he finally said.

He washed the snake clean and licked all around it to help coagulate the blood. The tattoo looked perfect.

Overjoyed, Ayashe aligned her arm alongside of Lan's and pulled on the skin to see the rest of it. It nearly matched his, although she liked hers even more.

"Now you are a Bandu."

In tears and at a loss for words for so wonderful gift, she ran out of the tent to the river to look at her reflection. Splashing in, she rubbed the tattoo and washed away the blood that kept obliterating the snake. She touched it over and over again, flushed with the same pride she had for the braid she wore since early spring. Back then it had given her the same rush. She loved the tight weave of the braid and the feather that had to be replaced from time to time. She brought it around to look at it and then to press it to her face as she imagined herself with Lan's tribe. It was as though she had been reborn. She also wanted to clarify in her mind what he had just said to her inside the tent. It was something she wanted and now knew it to be true.

Looking back at the tents, she crossed her arms and grabbed her shoulders with a thrill welling up inside. She took a deep breath and shook her head to feel the braid move from side to side while beaming with pride. What Lan said changed everything and now along with the tattoo, brought it all to completion.

She wanted to say that out loud to the world and in the same way---the very words of the Bandu. With so much joy inside, she looked at the sky and could hardly get the words out. After a following of tears, she shouted as loud as she could. **"I...Ayashe ... (sniff)...blong Bandu pee poh!"**

CHAPTER 7
ALEEKA

They left the village for good shortly after day break and walked the entire day. It brought them deep into the grasslands, the tents and mountains left farther and farther behind. Boundless herds, forever hungered by slow forage, grazed across the unending grasslands. Skittish, the animals ran off whenever they walked by. After a short distance, they would stop and look back without the fear of the slow moving humans ever catching them.

In places, the ground had been torn apart as though a strong wind uprooted trees and then slammed them back to earth. This, despite the fact that there were no trees growing here of any kind, nothing larger than a bush. Eying one of the dug out impressions, Lan puzzled over what could have made it.

"Chtucktok!" Ayashe bowed her arms with the thumbs pointing up to sign for a mammoth.

The print was wide. After putting both of his feet inside, there was still enough room for hers. The long stride of the animal took four of Lan's to reach the next foot print. The mammoth certainly must have been huge, he thought, as big as the bones back at the tents had shown them to be.

How do these men hunt this long tooth?

His fingers tightened around the spear, the quartz blade at the far end, reflecting the glint of the setting sun. Jostling it above his shoulder, he scanned both banks of the river.

By now fluent in Ayashe's simple language, he said, "We must move from this river...find a safe place to rest."

"We cannot make fire in the grass," she said. "Too much will burn, and the nag boksta...they come in the dark time. Soon there will be many, so we cannot sleep here." She pointed at the river bank. "We can only make our fires there."

Ayashe maintained a desire to learn his difficult language. "We mk fire plenty bg for keep twoniff that way."

"Two knife," he corrected.

After cooling off and washing in the river, she laid down a thick bed of grass. Surrounding themselves with piles of dung, they then lit them for a string of fires.

Lying on her back, Ayashe searched the skies where she followed a passing cloud. She thought of the many nights spent in places just like this where bon fires loomed and lit up the bank.

She drifted up to the sky where she waited weightlessly for a cumulous cloud to float by. Climbing on, she ran to the other side where she sat with her legs hanging over the edge to meet the sunset. There, the back of the world flushed brilliantly from the scorching flames. Orange light shined the mountains, shadowing the canyons from a sun that was slowly burning itself out.

Below, the grass roared at the late breeze. She rode the cloud until she saw a huge passing bird, powder white and owning the wind. She leaned forward from the edge of the cloud, let go and dropped onto its back as it flew by beneath her. She grabbed onto the feathers with her legs locked around its neck. Holding on tightly, she leaned to the side, her braid blowing behind as the great bird gently banked across the red sky.

As if they were one, they raised and lowered together from the bird's powerful wing beats, dipping and circling and then drifting on thermals. When the wind changed direction, they turned with it, then swooped and dove with breath taking drops. Stems flattened in their wake as they floated just above the sea of green.

Ahead, she could see the fires and Lan standing and looking their way. The bird soared up to him, hovered in place and gently tipped its wings. Ayashe *slid down as far as the upturned feathers at the end, where she jumped off and into his waiting arms.*

Away the bird flew, pumping giant wings and lifting graciously into the heights until it became a smaller and smaller speck in the sky, the white turning black as it burned into the sunset.

Dawn

"Long tooth," Lan shouted.

On a slight grade and looking to his right, Lan could barely see above the grass; the lumbering giants grazing a distance away. Downwind, he stood undetected, giving himself a less than clear sight of the Columbian mammoths. He stooped low for Ayashe and lifted her to his shoulders.

"O-o-o-o-h! Chtuktok!" She blurted out loud.

Adjusting herself on top, she almost fell and grabbed onto his face.

"I cannot see." Lan pulled her arms away, holding them out by the wrist to keep her from falling.

Like moving mounds of earth, the mammoths were an incredible sight. To Lan, they were overpowering and too hard to believe, yet, there they were right in front of him no matter how impossible that seemed.

"Look! The one with the two teeth that grows above his head and back toward the ground, it is bigger than the others."

"Sh-h! Hms Aleeka! Hms too bg to all chtuktok. No more bg to hms."

It was a humbling sight. The bull's head appeared massive, the back sloping down to a disproportionately low rear. Long, bristly hairs covered the animal completely and hung below its chest and stomach. The reddish-brown giant ambled along lethargically, plowing grass that only reached its knees. It grabbed huge clumps at a time, clearing the ground to the roots.

All of the mammoths grazed quietly. They seemed like peaceful giants, the silent feeding, disturbed only by the birds that were fluttering in and out of their legs to seek out disturbed insects.

Suddenly, the bull raised its trunk.

"Aaii...yi, yi, ayee."

A human cry shouted out from an unseen location. It was followed by another coming from the left, somewhere between the mammoths and where Lan and Ayashe were standing.

"Ai ai ai!"

More voices called out from the opposite end of the herd, and then a barrage of yodeling cries that now came from every direction. At first the herd seemed confused. They raised their heads and pointed trunks toward the shouting cries. A few started to run which panicked the rest. Trumpeting and dust filled the air from the driving limbs that battered the ground beneath Lan and Ayashe like earthquake tremors. The hunters shouted and raised spears. Along with the powerful tremors, it was a humbling sight.

"Why do these long tooth run from these men when they are so big?"

Ayashe had no answer to offer him.

Defiantly, Aleeka stood facing the threat until most of the herd ran past. After a last burst of ear splitting calls, the bull turned and ran off stiff legged to join the rest of the herd. Even Aleeka had long learned there was no hope against men. Although immune to their spears for its huge size, the fear was inborn and Aleeka too slow to crush the nimble hunters.

A trailing female stopped short to confront the hunter that ran alongside and kept stabbing her in the back of her ankle. The aim was to cripple, but the attempt failed. Another hunter she did not notice ran up and slashed into the same wound with a large bladed knife. It severed a tendon, a crippling injury that slowed her down enough so that others could rush in with spears.

Men attacked from all sides and stabbed her repeatedly with long pointed spears. A long haired hunter ran in closer than the others and thrust his deep into her belly. While struggling to remove it for another thrust, the female whirled around and curled her trunk around his waist. The man screamed and tried to pry himself loose from the mammoth that was raising him over her head. She blared triumphantly and threw him hard to the ground. While the man lay crumpled, she tried to stab him with her tusks. Other hunters closed in and thrust spears from every side, preventing her from aiming with accuracy.

The wounded hunter was bowled over and over from the mammoth's attempts to kill him. Tossed about into impossible positions, he tried to get up and fell backwards onto a broken leg. Overwhelmed, the female swung her trunk at the darting humans that deftly dodged her blows. She stamped the ground with one of her front limbs, twisted her great bulk around and made a last attempt at saving herself. The bloodletting spears were relentless and continued to weaken her. Falling onto her rear, she cried out with a terrifying scream. Her ears slapped against her face as her head swayed from side to side.

A lance, crafted long and thick for a devastating and final thrust was driven into a gaping wound in her stomach by two first hunters. It took the combined strength of both to drive a third of its length deep into the mammoth's gut, causing her to shriek out in pain.

Spurred on by this, other men tore into her with wounds that ripped her chest open. In an attempt to get to her feet, the mammoth propped herself up on wobbly front legs, unable to move

Hunters of the Columbian mammoth

the back ones. She lunged at a running hunter who ran across her field of vision in a distorted blur. Gallantly, she thrashed the ground with her trunk, her screeching calls going unheeded by the rest of the cowering herd, now resigned to her fate and the safety of their distance.

Second hunters that had waited just out of danger were now ordered in to bury their spears. Fighting back with the last of her strength, the mammoth's cries bellowed long and loud and solemnly wretched. Her trunk swung around wildly in a last futile try at hitting the hunter that kept sticking her in the side. With no strength left to fight, the front legs collapsed from underneath, sending her head crashing to the ground. Too weak to lift it back up again, her eyes rolled from the sickening feelings inside her gut. She shuddered from agony, screaming when Qaletaga (friend) and Sewati (curved bear claw) pulled the enormous lance out.

"Finish her," ordered Kuruk (bear), leader of the first hunters.

Qaletaga and Sewati pulled the huge lance out of her gut. Together, they drove it deep into her chest. The mammoth's legs straightened as she shrieked out a series of blood curdling cries. Along with the first two, Kuruk grabbed onto the spear and pushed it in as far as it would go.

Speaking softly, Ayashe said, "Matwua is from these men. Kuruk...he is strong to Nakoma (great spirit), the one who leads them."

Kuruk: Leader of First Hunters in standing
An elder and leader of first hunters, Kuruk was the biggest in the tribe. In fine condition, his scarred, thick veined arms were still muscular. For a man of his advanced age, his stomach still remained hard and narrow. Black-brown hair with a mix of grey streaks, hung freely over striating shoulders. The eagle feather he wore in his hair marked him as a first hunter and could not be worn by a lower rank.

Along with the stern projection he held about himself, Kuruk enjoyed a good tease now and then, although one would be hard pressed to realize he shared in it from the serious expression on his face. Rarely laughing, Kuruk felt comfortable in the company of men. Respect came easy, drawn from his physical prowess and confident manner. A deep and cavernous voice rolled his words without effort, commanding attention whenever he spoke.

"Chest is broken!" he shouted, the first to reach the wounded hunter. "Sewati! Come see!"

Running up out of breath, Sewati bent over and placed a hand on the wounded man's chest. "His chest is broken...as well as his leg!"

Ayashe ducked down. "That is Sewati. I do not like him."

Sewati shouted to the rest. "Come this way to Etu (sun). He can no longer stand on his feet."

A scruffy lot with dirt caked to body hairs and spears at their sides, the rest of the first hunters rattled in with animal bones banging against their chest. Wearing nothing but triangular patches over their groins, they collected into a semi-circle around their wounded tribesman. Behind them, second and third hunters ran in to glare along with them, the wounds that none of them could fix.

Sewati: First Hunter, second in standing
Tall and willowy, Sewati was not as thick muscled as the others. Second in command behind Kuruk, his hard face and character brought respect through intimidation. For the most part that was due to his dark sinister glare from beneath black wiry brows. The man had penetrating, hateful eyes, an evince that would cower most men. Besides his demeaning ways, Sewati was physically ugly as well. With cheeks and a hooked nose pocked and reddened, he was difficult to look at. His skin, prone to an acne condition, would often fester with new postulations. It conveyed, along with thin straying hair, the first hunter's poor luck at attaining favorable genes.

Aware of his looks, it contributed to making him a bitter man, causing an already compromised personality to deteriorate further. He was without a woman. Woman shunned him, so he stayed to himself. Besides Nakoma, Kuruk was the only other tribesman Sewati had respect for. As the best of the first hunters, the two excelled at tracking. They knew one another's moves without the need for hand cues; such as when to rush in or which direction to make their approach.

"There is nothing we can do for our wounded brother. Kajika… bring the red dirt," Sewati snapped.

Kajika: Carrier of the red dirt and shaman hopeful
A diminutive man with no rank as a hunter and nervous in his new role as carrier of the red dirt, Kajika (walks without sound) squeezed through the crowd of men. He leaned over Etu, two fingers thick with red ochre, to mark a double line on his forehead. A line also marked Etu's cheeks and all to release the pain and free his life spirit.

Rarely speaking, Kajika had always been shy and withdrawn, his small stature contributing to this. When the last ochre carrier, Wahanassatta (he who walks with his toes pointed outward) died, Nakoma, the tribe's leader, needed a responsible replacement for the prestigious position. There were plenty of capable men, Achak, Kuruk, even young Qaletaga could have all served well. However, those men were first hunters and needed in the field. The choice was not easy and it had been a long while that Nakoma tried to render a decision. Much had to be considered. The position would be life-long. The tribesman picked had to perform well and the way he did that would reflect on Nakoma as a leader.

He knew Kajika was not the right man to carry the red dirt, but he was motivated by something else. As a leader, he had to consider every man woman and child, not only to get the most from them, but also to enrich their individual lives as well, for the overall good of the clan. Alone and rejected, Kajika needed a higher status to give him the "shona" (acknowledgement for high achievement) that would make him strong in the minds of other men. What better way than to allow him to carry the red dirt and perhaps one day replace the tribe's shaman, Ohcumgache (wolf), who had grown old and feeble. Sure there would be jealousies, but time would remedy that, and in the end, the elders as well as the more sensible of the men would agree and respect Nakoma for it. Besides, Kajika was a terribly inept hunter.

The ochre carrier scooped another clump of red clay out of the skull cap and made a series of semi-circular lines across the wounded hunter's chest. Raising his arms for a chant, he began with the worry that he would not get it right the first time.

"I...ask for the nag boksta to...ah...to take our young brother. He comes to you without his kill sticks and will not fight you."

(Giggling and laughter)

Ignoring the two third hunter's antics, Kuruk nodded encouragingly at Kajika.

Kajika continued. "He waits with no one and is ready for his death."

(More giggling)

Kajika returned a prolonged stare at the two, Moki (deer), a grown man, and little Okhmhaka, (little wolf) a boy of ten.

"Take our brother fast to the clouds."

For, although Etu still lived, he would soon die from his wounds. Everyone there knew that. All that could save his life spirit then was for predators such as dire wolves or saber tooth tigers to consume him.

"Give him your gifts," ordered Kuruk.

Qaletaga handed Etu a chopping tool. Achak removed a personal ornament from around his neck and gave it to him. The chain of mole skulls had always been admired by Etu and he was glad the elder remembered. In the end, gifts were lined up on both sides of the wounded hunter and he thanked all of them.

"I welcome these gifts. Soon, I will watch you from the sky."

Unable to reach high enough to grip anyone's shoulder, as was customary, Etu nodded excessively to make up for it. Turning to Qaletaga, his good friend as well as fellow first hunter, he cheerfully said, "It is sad that you will not join me and become a sky spirit."

Thinking for a moment, Qaletaga smiled. "No, but I will eat this thunderfoot and take your woman for myself."

"That is good then," Etu replied, knowing he would take care of his children as well.

Akando (ambush), a young boy of fourteen and Achak's son, already stood taller than Kajika. He squatted before Etu and held his shoulder along with a head nod. "I miss Una (remember). Say the words to her that I miss her. It is my wish that one day I will join her. She was a good mother."

Wiping away his tears, he looked at the older first hunter with admiration. His desire was to be just as brave and if need be, as fearless when facing his own death. One of the last to run in to the kill, Akando had been held back by Nayati (he who wrestles), the leader of second hunters. Watching from the sidelines and only his third mammoth hunt in that rank, Akando had waited with frustration.

Etu nodded. "I will make the talk with Una and tell her your words."

He struggled to rise up on his elbows to see the faces of the men. As he paused to look at every hunter in the crowd, he thought of something he remembered about each one of them.

Achak...he is so wise. He always knows the truth and what to do. And there is Moki. It was a time when our life spirits faced the sun six hot times. It was then that we threw wet bondolo waste at each other. He cried when Nakoma took us to the fast water and pushed us in. It saddens me that Moki will never become a first hunter.

He searched the crowd for the leader of first hunters. He loved Kuruk and had always wished he was his real father. There were memories for every one of the men and most of them were good bonding ones. The sharp pain in his chest became unbearable, so he lay back down.

"Leave me and take this meat. Tell Nakoma I will look on him from the sky."

A resounding of good will and encouraging remarks were voiced by everyone there.

"Go…and be safe," Etu said.

Agreeing nods and comments passed among the men, having realized they lingered far too long. Akando stayed behind and poured water over the wounded man's chest. Standing alongside of him, Qaletaga ran stiffened fingers through his hair, the ragged edges of his nails, pulling annoyingly at the strands.

"I remember many hunts when we were second hunters like our little Akando here." He patted the boy on the head. "We learned much since then."

A slight smile on his lips, Akando nodded---too young to have shared in their past.

Looking down at Etu, Qaletaga said, "It was before many hot times like this when we were like Akando and wanted to be what we are now."

"That…that is the way…ugh…we will hunt again," Etu responded. "You…I…and all the rest of our hunters…and you as well, little Akando. There will be a time when we will all hunt together in the sky."

Qaletaga turned away from them and looked toward the sound of the loud voice he just heard. "Kuruk is calling for us to help carry the meat. Come, Akando, we can do no more for Etu."

Etu shouted after him. "My woman will please you. She has big legs."

Qaletaga: First Hunter, third in standing.
An impatient hunter, Qaletaga (guardian of the people) was quick to throw himself into a hunt with no regard for danger. Energetic

and rarely seen sitting, he often moved about as though occupied with some seemingly pressing task. Though young, his deeply tanned face was hard and beginning to show age lines around the eyes. He had a kind look about him and was regarded as handsome by the woman. More thickly built than the other men, his demeanor for the most part was calm and easy, 'though at times he could be forceful. Soft with his children, he was well liked by the children of others as well.

The mammoth had fallen on her belly with her forelimbs spread out from underneath. Kuruk barked instructions from the top of the animal's head. "Not there! Cut from the front," he ordered, yelling at a man cutting into the chest. He turned his attention to another. "That cut is too big! No man here can carry that. Cut it into two pieces."

Achak, Akando's father, assisted the best he could. The oldest of the hunters, he was exempt from any physical work. Instead, he made himself useful by guiding the younger boys in the butchering. Many were third hunters like Okhmhaka, Nakoma's adopted boy.

Born to the cold, this was the tenth time little Okhmhaka faced the heat of the hot time. It was his first hunt and up to now it had interested him. All of the hard work was far from finished, so he chose to play with Moki instead.

"Moki is thunderfoot waste," Okhmhaka badgered.

The two chased around the carcass a few times, until Sewati angrily grabbed the boy by the arm.

"Go stand with Achak. He will give you the piece you will carry." Scowling, he pushed the young boy away. "Useless!"

Achak had not noticed. Okhmhaka bumped into him playfully with an ever widening smile, his teeth as white as sunlit clouds.

"Are you ready to walk like a first hunter?" The elder asked.

Puffing up his chest, the boy patted Achak on the back side. "Yes…give me the biggest piece," he said, with as gruff a voice as he could make.

The elder returned a questioning stare. "So now you think you **are** a first hunter?" He affectionately brushed the boy's hair back. "Take that small piece…the walk is long."

Achak: First Hunter, fourth in standing.
Achak's (spirit) position was more out of respect and acknowledgement than for any ability as a hunter. Prone to forget things, he at times was unreliable. Always cautious, though some regarded that as cowardice, he never suffered the debilitating wounds that took so many of the hunters before achieving half his age. Despite that, his bravery had been tested on many occasions in the past and he had always proved worthy.

At one time, Achak's hair was silky black. Now, it had long changed to grey and reached his lower back. Average in build, his otherwise strong frame held a noticeable paunch. Achak's mouth crowded in a full set of teeth that pushed the front ones forward, leaving his mouth permanently opened when relaxing his jaws. Fatherly in mannerism, he was well liked by everyone.

Blood dripped down the backs of the hunters as one by one they single filed away from the kill and onto the game trail.

It was a while now that Etu eyed the empty trail, alone and thinking. He took in a light breeze and two white winged larks squabbling over a tuft of mammoth hair. Both switched and dove for the same rust colored strands even though shedded hair covered the ground.

Easing a slow breath into his aching chest, he lowered his head and the dust filled, matted curls to the ground to rest from the pain. It hurt where the thunderfoot had squeezed him, the redness swelling into wide welts. His head also hurt and now his vision was becoming blurred. He winced as soon as he touched his chin to his chest to look at the rib sticking up. Sweat ran down his forehead, distorting the ochre lines on his face into varnished rivers. Closing his eyes, he tried to hear the larks. Gone he presumed, gone on with their lives---only the wind now---the wind, the silence---little else. He forced a deep breath and let it out slow; and then the loneliness as he waited to die. Ready to embrace that death, he knew he would see it in the face of the saber tooth tigers and wolves that would soon come on the scent of the dead mammoth. He would then chant the words of greeting and offer his flesh in exchange for a journey to the world of all those who went before him. It was a world he prepared for since childhood; a place where he could renew friendships and watch from the great heights, his people on the grasslands below.

"Oh! He cried out, startled by the sight of two shadowy figures walking up. Stretching for his spear, sharp pain stabbed into his chest.

"Shatu duma! (welcome!) It is I, Ayashe, Matwua's woman."

Etu tried to focus, but her face was far from clear. "If you are Ayashe, then you come from Mantotohpa's people."

"Yes...they were once mine."

As soon as Lan's image became clear, it both surprised and frightened the first hunter. Noting the long braid, the deer skin leggings and body tattoos, he knew instantly that he had come down from the mountains.

"Mowatchi!" Etu reached for his spear.

Lan stepped on it, picked it up and tossed it out of reach. Like all of the other mammoth hunters, the man was huge.

The fallen hunter shouted. "You...you cannot kill me. I wait for the nag boksta."

Ayashe raised her hand up high and spoke sharply. "Lan has no wish to take your life spirit. Our walk is only to find my father's people."

"Then...where is your Matwua?" As he said that, Etu warily kept his focus on Lan.

"He stays in the high place," she lied.

The first hunter's jaw tightened. "And this...this Mowatchi...this is the man you now follow?"

She nodded quietly. "He is Mowatchi as is my mother, Alawa. This you know."

Lan squatted in front of him. He picked up a small stone and as he spoke, tossed it from hand to hand. "I can fix this bone in your leg."

"You speak my words?"

"With the good spirits, you will walk."

Ayashe found that incredulous, having never actually seen it done. "You can fix his leg so he can walk?"

"When it is finished, three moons must pass before he can walk again. Yes, it can be done."

Etu's head rolled to the side as he murmured in obvious delirium. Ayashe knew it would be hard to convince him of something she herself had never seen done before. However, her faith was with Lan.

She touched Etu's shoulder. "The Mowatchi is strong with me. He has a great shona and the power to fix many things."

"I am ...dead as we speak!" Etu moaned.

"Let him try," she pleaded.

"He cannot fix what is already dead. Leave me with the nag boksta. They...they and the nahgos have the power to send me to the sky."

"Is it not your wish to be with your people, your woman?"

"Yes...it is, but that is not our way. I will no longer listen to your words...or his words. I have chosen."

Lan tossed the stone to the side. "We will stay until the dark time comes. It is then that we must go."

The three turned to the sound of saber tooth tigers. They were far off and calling---too distant to be of immediate danger. There was no urgency, no running down of game that had to be fought over. Meat would be plentiful---fill their bellies to distended bliss. For now, the smell of man was strong and caution a safe option.

Lan motioned with his head toward the sound of the big cats. "The nag boksta will soon find you!"

Ayashe turned back from looking towards where the sound had come from. "You say it is your wish to be with your woman."

"Yes," Etu replied, his eyes wet from pain.

"When the dark time comes, there will be many of the nag boksta," she said.

"That is good then. I will wait for them."

As night neared, the roars became deafening. Soon, the saber tooth tigers would claim dominance over the kill. In the far distance, dire wolves were grouping in large numbers and beyond those, coyotes gathered to reap the spoils.

Far more assertive were the saber tooth tigers. The surrounding grass began to fill with them. They roared loudly to forewarn other predators of their rank as they directed order into the chaotic madness that was to follow.

Ayashe pressed to try and convince Etu. "The jonga watch the nag boksta and the nahgos. When the nag boksta go to the dead thunderfoot, do you not know that the jonga will have you in their eyes? It is then that your life spirit will be lost to them when they eat you."

The deep throated growl from a large saber tooth carried as though it lie only strides away. The pride had become more vocal. Hunger would soon embolden them as well as it would the coyotes that were fast becoming impatient with the order of things. Soon, the surrounding grass would be filled with them.

Etu, more than aware of that, could feel the tension. He did not want to end up in the jaws of a scavenger with his flesh stripped to the bone and his life spirit lost forever. He could easily imagine the faces of his ancestors looking down from the clouds and shaking their heads in remorse. Nor did he want to lose his present life to the unknown. This before him was real, something he could touch and smell and see. He really did want to love his woman again, to embrace his children---to hunt with his fellow tribesmen. With those realizations clear in mind, Etu weighed the out of norm option thrown at him.

Out there are the many jonga. It is true the nag boksta and nahgos will go to the thunderfoot and that would leave me here with the jonga.

The more Etu thought about that, the more it seemed that the coyotes were snickering back at him.

"This fix will give me great pain. I want something to bite on."

Ayashe hurriedly cut a piece from one of the straps and gave it to him.

"This is the way I will fix your leg," said Lan, drawing a stick figure in the dirt. "Ayashe, you leg sit."

Ayashe rephrased Lan's mixed up sentence so Etu could understand it. "Lan wants me to sit on your leg."

"My leg there," said Lan, pointing at Etu's groin. "I will pull this way."

While Ayashe sat on Etu's hips to hold him down, Lan would anchor his foot inside the man's groin for leverage while pulling his leg into place. Once set, he would use Etu's spear as a splint and bind it all together."

When Lan mentioned where his foot would be, Etu held onto his groin, but Lan reassured him he would be careful. After a lot of grunting and struggling, the bone was set and a splint completed. It did not take long at all, however, for the first hunter it felt like a timely, drawn out and agonizing ordeal. When it was over he let out a final sigh of relief. No longer did he feel the muscles tearing inside every time he moved. Both he and Ayashe were astounded that it could have ever been done.

"His pain will soon be many and then he will sleep," said Lan, eying Etu who appeared ready to pass out.

Whenever Etu breathed in, it pushed against his ribs and the pain of that was difficult to bare. Everything spun around as he fought to stay awake and then the outside turned black. He could not tell if the sky was spinning around anymore, only now realizing he could no longer hear the roars of the nag bokstas. He listened for the heckling jongas and the howls of the nahgos, but could not hear those, either. He could barely breath---could not hear---could not see.

Awakening to a vanishing sun, Etu lifted his head and flinched from the pain still there in his chest. Ayashe and the Mowatchi were standing on top of the mammoth, their backs to him while intensely watching something that was approaching from the distance.

Looking downward, Etu cocked his head. He could feel a subtle vibration beneath him.

Where are the nag bokstas?

He kept perfectly still and looked at the ground where the vibrations were getting stronger and then all of a sudden, stopped. He felt nothing more and waited quietly without moving. With intense concentration, he placed his hand on the ground.

The vibrations...they are still there.

Slight at first, he could feel them in his fingertips---hardly noticeable---easily confused with the feverish pulses racing up his arm; but no, these were tremors...and coming closer.

He put his ear to the ground and listened until the vibrations gradually increased in depth and density.

"Aleeka!"

Etu's face became ashen as blood drained from it.

He comes to this one.

Atop the carcass, the sight before Lan was horrifying. Out of a swirling haze of yellow dust came the ivory luster of slicing tusks. In full assault, the immense bull mammoth banged its crushing limbs down. Huge tusks hung below its knees, swept up and outwardly beyond its head where the ends twisted into upturning points.

The riotous fury stormed in, the raised trunk blasting the bull's supremacy. Earsplitting calls exploded across the flats as everything ahead of the monumental footfalls was threatened with crushing annihilation.

Turned toward the carcass, Etu watched with a held breath, Ayashe as she ran along the back of the dead mammoth in panic. Lan jumped off from the side and ran ahead of her in his direction.

The saber tooth tigers had long retreated from the tremors, as did the wolves and coyotes.

"Aleeka, …he comes!" Ayashe shouted.

"Run to the river," Lan shouted, back.

"Etu! We cannot leave Etu."

Lan worried for him as much as she did, but the pounding slams, Ayashe's screams, Etu's pleas, they all kept him from thinking.

"There is no place we can hide this man, no fire to protect us, no cave, no hole to…a hole! The thunderfoot! We can make a hole in the thunderfoot," he yelled.

"No time!" Ayashe screamed.

Running back to the carcass, he took out the ax and furiously began to chop into the stomach wound. Making little progress, he kept hacking at the opening despite the trumpeting and pounding steps.

Sure that he knew what Lan was trying to do, Etu held up a serrated blade used for just that purpose. "Here…this will make your cut faster."

Ayashe grabbed the large blade from him and rushed to Lan's side with it. Behind her, Etu crawled painfully toward them as fast as he was able to. In the far distance, the bull's head bounded high above the grass line, the ears flapping against the sides while trumpeting loudly.

"La-a-a-n! ...**Aleeka-a-a**!" Ayashe shrieked.

Lan paid no attention to the charging bull. He kept digging into the hide, pulling it back and cutting into it, then chopping and ripping frantically. The screams, the trumpeting, all of it became one, a conjoined madness he had to ignore if he was ever going to finish what he had begun in time to save them all.

(Bull mammoth trumpeting loudly)

Milky intestines spilled from the opening, the moving slime, spurting gas releasing bubbles and pouring onto the ground. It made popping and sucking noises as it spread out in an ever widening puddle. Lan kept cutting and slipping in the wet viscera, opening the incision as fast as the blade would allow.

The mammoth's footsteps and trumpeting were becoming deafening. It was almost there. The violent drops of its crushing legs quickened the exit of lagging intestines. In turn, it jerked the attached grass laden stomach from its resting place. The stomach moved, but just barely and then gained as it began to slide, gradually picking up speed on the lubrication of body fluids. The sack like organ slipped toward the opening where it braked against the lower half of cut skin. This caused the back end of the huge stomach to then roll forward and over itself and slither onto the ground. Still unbroken, the stomach landed on top of the open mouthed first hunter, pliably sliming over him before slapping onto the ground. Air trapped underneath sucked outward with groaning and sputtering and popping noises.

Dazed, Etu wiped the oily substance from his face. He reached for Lan who along with Ayashe, dragged him toward the cavernous opening.

(Aleeka trumpeting)

Slipping in slime, Ayashe fell to her knees, her legs splaying out to the sides before clumsily struggling to get to her feet. Lan's legs became tangled in intestines. He splashed sideways into the puddle. After spreading out on all fours, he carefully stood up, turned toward Etu and grabbed him by the arm. As soon as he did, both he and Ayashe went tumbling on top of him.

Etu screamed. Excruciating pain shot across his chest and leg. "Go!" (cough...cough) "Leave...leave me here!"

Trumpeting thundered through the air like an overhead storm. Ayashe scrambled to her feet. Lan braced himself by holding onto the edge of the opening he had made. He reached for Etu, but there was no way to lift him.

Filled with fear and unable to rise up on his one good leg, Etu fell onto his back to once again face death.

And then it all stopped; the noise, the slams, the mammoth's trumpeting. The three lifted their heads to the developing shadow that gradually blackened the ground out front. The dark image of the mammoth's tusks edged toward them like an ominous black cage, followed by the rest of the beast's shadow. Like an oozing black sludge, the elongated shadow crept up to the carcass and climbed its sides—a dark mass that leaned entirely to one side and then the other until it stretched enormously and endlessly wide, engulfing everything in its blackness. Ghostly and foreboding, no one dared look, afraid to even move, but stood paralyzed by the very size of Aleeka.

The immense, reddish brown body of the Columbian mammoth lurched forward, bringing with it a stench of the herd. Raising its trunk, the sound of its roar vibrated around them like boulders falling from the sky. Nothing other than the loudest crack of thunder was as loud as what Lan was now hearing from the beast. Its great size filled everything out front. It was there, an immensity where before there was nothing. A once barren space filled with an animal so big, Lan's mouth was left agape, taken in by the horrific size of it. Aleeka was tremendous.

The sun, low and brilliant across the horizon, cast a golden glow between the bull's monstrous limbs. Blinding to look at, they rose like burning columns as if to hold back the fire.

Aleeka moved forward and blocked the sun, made day turn to night and those beneath like insects out of their nest as they all began to scramble for the hole that would bury them.

Diving under shimmering muck, Etu draped intestines over himself. Paying no mind to the reeking odors, Ayashe struggled to pull herself over the lower fold of skin and into the vacated cavity where the stomach once was, but could not get her legs over the edge. It was just too high. She dug her nails into pink flesh, pulling and clawing until Lan pushed her in from behind. He rolled in after her and pushed her farther inside, as far from the opening as he could. Pitch black and swelteringly hot, they sucked in the smell of blood and viscera as each tried to catch their breaths. Ayashe's heart would not stop pounding.

"Lan...**Lan**!" Ayashe's voice, a hoarse whisper.

"I am here!" He grabbed her for reassurance.

Outside, the bull splashed through the slime. Curious, it nosed the double scent it found with confusion, the scent of man bathed in the scent of its mate. The flexible finger-like snout sniffed delicately over intestines and spillage, eventually hovering to a hump projecting from the middle. There, the trunk held itself suspended, the open nostrils facing the odd shaped thing with eyes that were looking back.

Sure this would be his end and not with dignity from a saber tooth tiger, Etu cringed under the slimy maze of intestines. Before him, he could clearly see into the two membrane lined tunnels, threatening to disclose his presence in the female's spoils.

The appendage snorted and swung to the severed belly and then back to the creamy paste clinging to Etu's face. Persisting for a desire to understand, the bull slanted its body forward to better play the sensitive organ that hovered only a stems thickness away. The end of the trunk circled around to the back of Etu's head where the nostrils stretched wide to test the odors. Whipping instantly back to the front, it began to sway back and forth like a pit viper. All of a sudden, it stopped and blew a short burst that cleared the slime away from Etu's face.

Horrified, Etu swallowed and could not keep from exhaling the deep breath he had been holding all that time. Aleeka had cleared most of the slime, leaving bubbly juices to drip down his chin like white foam.

Fully exposed, the female's scent was nevertheless still there, her dislodged flesh, the bafflement of it, too puzzling for the bull to comprehend. Exhaling forcefully, Aleeka backed away and lethargically circled to the other side of the carcass.

Seeing it leave, Etu pulled his bad leg in and covered it with intestines.

Lan poked his head out. "Etu?"

"I am here...under you."

Sticking her head out next to Lan's, Ayashe looked left and then right. "Where is Aleeka?"

"He is behind this dead one," Etu answered, in a shaky voice.

From the other side of the carcass, the back of the dead animal suddenly lifted then slammed down hard as the bull mammoth leaned into his mate to wake her from the deep sleep she was in. Unconvinced that she was anything but ill, the bull stayed throughout the night, relentlessly circling the carcass with a slow gait.

Touching clouds embraced the new sun, now searing its way through yesterday's night. The edges blazed brilliantly from the pressing rays---the chilled air, windless and silent.

Within the odor of digested grass stewing with fermentation, stood Aleeka, the bull's head low to the ground and weaving figure eights. At times, it shifted to relieve its limbs of their burdensome weight, flapping bitten ears at the flies it slept with. Then as it had the previous night, the bull lazily began to circle the female. It stopped now and then to push its weight into the carcass for a last try at waking her.

Ayashe poked her head outside and took in the morning air. All she could think about was the river so she could clean herself off.

"My need is to go to the river," she whispered hoarsely to Lan.

"Wait...Aleeka will soon go. He knows this thunderfoot is finished."

"My need is to go now," she insisted. She was tired and would wait no longer.

She stuck her leg out of the opening and just when she got her upper body through, a jolt from Aleeka hitting the backside of the carcass sent her slamming to the ground. Lying in entrails, she lay dazed and motionless. From the front of the carcass, Aleeka rounded the female's head and upon seeing her lying there, quickened its steps. It stopped short in front of Ayashe's still form, alert to the newness of her presence. He pushed at her side and rolled her onto her back, blew air through its trunk and pushed her body into a curl.

From the opening, Lan stared up at the huge mass before him. Two large folds of skin hung from the mammoth's jaws with streams of drool dripping down and mixing with the puddle of white slime. Hanging heavily from the jaws, tusks curled upwards and away from him, the dagger like points, looming out of view.

Etu grabbed Ayashe by the arm in an attempt to drag her towards him, but Aleeka already had her in his grasp.

Too painful to watch, Lan withdrew inside where he folded in sorrow, resigned to her loss. He felt helpless, covering his ears from the screams he knew he would soon hear. When none came, he picked his head up and listened; the only sound, body fluids dripping from up above.

Her voice is silenced by the long tooth. She is gone. She is no longer mine.

He squeezed his eyes shut and sighed deeply.

She was so beautiful, so perfect. When this is over, I will suffer her death all over again when I burn her body.

Aleeka tightened his trunk around Ayashe's leg and pulled her into the open with Etu's grip slipping from her trailing arm. Unable to hold onto her, he let go and remained perfectly still. Since childhood, he feared, "The Great One", and now felt helpless beneath it.

Dizzy and too afraid to move, Ayashe watched the live nightmare unfold before her. The bull tightened the curl around her waist and before she could think about what to do, the ground suddenly dropped from beneath her. With horrifying speed, she felt herself lift into the air and stop at a level where she could see into the bull's right eye. With no discernable white and encased in wrinkled skin, the eye stared blankly through a clear, black pupil. It gave little feel for the mind of the beast, but rather, was cold and still. Frightening to look at, she could not turn from the eye that was drawing her into its cold, dark depths. From deep within, a piercing light mirrored back, there to mimic the rising new sun. It had ascended as if from the animal's very own bowels; like an otherworldly sunrise, one that glared from beneath rust colored lashes.

The eye, devoid of movement for a clearer focus, lay motionless as if with an absence of life. In the moment of ethereal correlation, the two fixed for a time on one another, until Ayashe was suddenly jerked high above the bull's head.

"O-o-o-h!" she heard herself cry out, grabbing onto the rough, bark textured trunk.

From that reeling height, she could see the female lying in her spilled bowels and what she saw next made her stiffen. Immediately below, upturned tusks pointed at her like oversized spears. She sucked in when she was lurched further skyward and high above Aleeka's head, sure she was about to be dropped onto the impaling spikes.

Odd to look down at the back of a living, breathing, thunder-foot, the backbone that arched along the full length of it with sides that bulged in and out---the smell of manure---everywhere. Frightening, also, to feel vibrations rattle from a low pitched drone coming from deep inside the bull's powerful bulk. It became louder as it nasalized upward through the animal's trunk, shaking her body to the very core.

To Aleeka, the limp thing had been bathed in its mate's scent. It somehow belonged. He lowered Ayashe gently to the ground, curled its trunk into a ball and nudged her along until she slid into Etu.

From deep inside the bull mammoth's chest came a throbbing vibration that continued long and loud, rattling the ground until the pebbles and loose dirt at the surface shook for its duration. With no further show of interest, the mammoth turned and ambled away in the direction of the waiting herd. Its ears lay flat to the sides, the tail twitching across the back of its legs as the rest of his body swayed from side to side.

"Aleeka goes to find the others," Etu anxiously said.

Clambering out, Lan lifted Ayashe to her feet. He could not hug her enough. He thought she was gone. Instead, she was here with him, in his arms and alive. Still groggy and shaken, Ayashe, wide eyed, relaxed at the sight of him. Lifting her off the ground and petting her hair, Lan did not want to ever let her go.

"We can go to the river. Aleeka is gone."

"Aleeka,... (sniff) ...me many times afraid."

They both looked at Etu, draped in intestines. Ayashe did not know whether to laugh or cry.

Etu grinned---more out of a relief that the thunderfoot was no longer a threat. "Do not drag me. I will pull myself to the river."

The crawl was agonizing. Once there, he entered the shallows. The stinging pains in his chest he could deal with. It was his leg, red and swollen, that hurt badly.

Lan followed Ayashe into deeper water where he could not resist picking her up and throwing her in backwards. There, they splashed and chased until they grew tired of the game.

"If we go back now, before the two knife's return…," Lan said, loud and out of breath, "…we will find Etu's gifts and the things we left there."

Ayashe, pressing to learn his language, pointed to vultures circling aloft warm thermals. "Many twoniff, hms see death bawd."

"The two knifes will not look to us if we move fast. There is much meat waiting for them."

While Ayashe gathered Etu's gifts together, Lan climbed on top of the carcass. The height offered an unobstructed view of the grasslands where the monotony of greens spread to unseen reaches and so unlike the mountains he had climbed. Those same mountains appeared so narrow of height, sprawled along the horizon like low lying hills. It belied their true heights where the tall peaks knifed through the clouds.

And here, this flat, this green expanse with no observable end, its constant flow never changing. Like the sea, it pours sameness chased by the winds---lays reposed and embraced solely by the attending, cloud dropped shadows---there, where they drift across the forever golden, forever leaning, forever breathing grass.

Lan shaded his eyes to search for movement. Below, Ayashe finished stacking all of Etu's gifts and hunting tools into a pile.

"Nag boksta…he comes?" she asked.

"I see nothing," he answered, turning to scan the river.

Along the water's edge, a bull elk with a full rack raised its head. Off to the side, on the opposite bank, two buffalo were leaving a daily mud wallow.

Lan stabbed Etu's serrated knife downward and cut out a large piece from the mammoth's rear leg---as large as his own chest. Lifting it to his shoulder, he ran to the river with Ayashe already far ahead with the bear skin filled with their things.

Behind them, vultures floated down on rigid black wings and soon covered the carcass. They rushed to stuff themselves in the short time they had before the saber tooth's arrival.

Moving with urgency, and getting too dark to see anything, Lan pulled Etu into deeper water, using the current to float him towards a safer bank downriver.

Ayashe carried everything Etu left behind, tied securely inside the bear skin. The meat from the mammoth was held afloat, which she pulled behind her. It amused her to watch tiny fish fry darting about the crystal clear water to steal tidbits from it.

"We must talk to Etu that I will leave him in a safe place before we go to his people," said Lan.

Ayashe worried. *That is where Matwua was from. Sewati will know me from when I was traded to him. It is not my wish that I return and bring my Mowatchi instead.*

She told Lan of her concerns in Bandu, but none of that seemed to worry him. "Nakoma will be glad to see Etu still lives. For that, he will welcome us. We can tell him Matwua still keeps his fire in the high place."

Lan's words are true words. Matwua does not have the voice of his people. He can no longer go there. Would he not then stay in the high place if he still lived? Why would he take this walk and chance his death from Kuruk or Sewati? No one there could know he was already killed by Lan's ax."

"It is Lan's wish to leave you and take the walk to Nakoma," Ayashe said to Etu.

Disappointed at having to be left alone, he replied, "So I will then still see my death. Why did he make this fix and now he leaves me? It is all for nothing."

"We cannot carry you and you cannot walk. We will bring men to take you to Nakoma. There is no other way."

"I will say no more. If you must leave, this meat will not be enough. Your walk is the walk of three suns and three more for your return. I cannot hunt for myself."

"Lan will hunt for you. It is then that you will have enough."

She spoke to Lan in Bandu again. "You not go to Nakoma. Me afray. You stay, I go."

"Do not fear for me. I run with the spirits," he replied. Matwua hunts with my father and the two knife. You saw that in the sky and now they run with me."

Ayashe thought for a moment. *The three lights after he killed the nag boksta. I remember that well.* "Do your spirits run with Etu?" she asked, with genuine curiosity.

Lan nodded. "If they run with me, then they run with you, and now Etu."

Ignoring the both of them and their private talk, Etu remained in his own deep thoughts of regret.

Ahead, at a bend in the river lay a wide shoal. Lan pointed to it. "Up there! That is a good place to make a fire."

The shoal was bare of vegetation from the occasional floods that overran it. Osprey, ducks, herons and spoonbills were common to the shoals. Sandpipers skipped along its bank. Here, one could live on frogs alone. They were everywhere and of various species.

While Ayashe spread the fur out, Lan started a fire. Strips of mammoth meat soon cooked on the rocks placed around it. Etu could not eat, but Lan and Ayashe were famished.

"This meat is nothing like deer. It has its own taste," he said.

"Chtucktok…hms many times too good," she said, before stuffing another piece into her mouth.

The smell sickened Etu who painfully tried to find a better position to ease the pain in his leg. He was still not sure whether or not he had made the right choice. It could have all been over by now. He would have been venerated by the nag boksta.

While Ayashe and Etu rested by the fire, Lan took a short walk along the bank. He soon returned with the leg bone of a large wading bird, just the right size to make a flute. Naturally hollow, the inside of the leg bone was cleaned out with a stick and ten small holes drilled into it using the tip of an arrow. Leaning back and eying it with utmost scrutiny, he rechecked the finished flute, blowing into the holes as well as through both ends to clean it free of shavings.

After digging out a deep depression into the bank, he shaped it into a sitting hole so that he could sit in comfort with one side slanted to rest his back. As soon as he began to play, Ayashe lifted her head to the sound that carried like a lone wind whistling across the surface of the water.

Etu's head lifted as well. The musical tones were unlike anything he had ever heard before and far better than the rattling from Nakoma's saber tooth tiger skull, or Moki's drum beats on a hollow log---and something else; he could see again.

Three melodic tunes were played in order. The first sounded high pitched, the vibratos bunched together to welcome the new sun that ends the dark time.

The second, a full bodied sound, came from the flute's heart. The vibratos raised and lowered strongly to fill the hunting place with game; for it played for the hunter.

Like a mournful bird, the last played low with shallow vibratos. It lasted the longest and required a full breath to coax from the flute, the softest of the three melodies, for it wept for the loss of the brother sun and the end of day.

Daybreak

"The words of the Mowatchi are still in my head," said Etu. "I will stay and wait and I can now see where I look."

"Then that is good," Ayashe replied, glad that he got his vision back.

"Follow the water until you hear the sound on the thunder-foot," he said.

Ayashe knew exactly what Etu was referring to. It would come from the banging on a tusk in front of Nakoma's camp. Buried on top of a high mound to a third of its length, the reverberating tusk could be heard up to a half day's walk in any direction.

Concerned for Lan, Etu added a grave warning. "They will know you come. Make your talk only to Nakoma. Sewati will not welcome you."

Without responding, Lan left at a fast pace. With him was his bow and quiver of arrows.

"Your Mowatchi leaves us," a concerned Etu said.

Ayashe beamed with pride. "Lan goes to make a kill for you."

It was a while that Lan followed a game trail bordering the bank of the river. Finding fresh elk droppings, he followed the tracks. He soon heard them and their odor was telling. The sound of huffing was coming his way as the herd returned from quenching their thirst. With barely enough clearance to see, he hid behind a thickness of stems. A grooved, blood-letting arrow was already notched into the end of the bow. With another two between his teeth, he crouched low inside the brush where he waited for the last of the pounding hooves to pass by. The distinctive smell was there as one by one the elk crossed in front of him.

It would take at least three arrows thrown in rapid succession to guarantee a kill. After that he would have to remain hidden or the bull elk would run him down. Though the panicked herd would surely run off, the bull would be a threat if it remained with the fallen cow. And he could never kill a bull. As a leader, it was a brother and commanded respect.

The herd was only mildly startled when the cow fell, a tan affair with dark flanks. Her body lay across the trail, kicking at her neck to dislodge the arrow that blocked her breathing. In an effort to stand she fell back down, her lips vibrating and her teeth chattering until she lay still.

The bull elk trotted past the curious cows and calves with heads leaning to smell her sickness. Unfamiliar with the silence of the deadly arrows, nor where they had come from, the bull lowered its magnificent rack to press its velvety nose to hers. It sniffed gently and then casually inspected the rest of the run of her neck. He nudged her, pushed at her chest, pushed at the other arrows in her side and finally walked around the cow's body. Returning to her head, the bull lifted one of its front hooves and stomped the ground hard. Like ripples in a river, shoulder muscles quivered under its sorrel coat. It lifted its head and shook it to the sides, pawed at the dirt and touched the mare with a foreleg---the touch, clumsy and unnatural and too uncontrolled. After a final snorting breath, the Elk jerked its head around and then high stepped stiffly through the waiting herd.

Ayashe felt glad for Etu when she saw Lan floating the rear end of an elk down the river toward them. At first light, Etu was bid farewell and left there to wait for the men's return.

CHAPTER 8
NAKOMA'S TRIBE

Three days later

Slow drumbeats could be heard long before finding the well-worn trail that led to Nakoma's village. At its gateway by the river stood two tall posts, one on either side and each adorned from top to bottom with row upon row of human skulls. Trees uprooted from severe mountain storms often careened down the falls and through the grasslands on swollen rivers. It took the manpower of the entire tribe to drag and raise the posts into position over the deep holes that were dug for them.

Ahead, foot prints overlaid one another with the prints of the men dwarfing Lan's. "Come, we are losing the sun fast. I do not want to walk this trail in the dark."

They stepped between the posts to the sound of drumbeats. The closer they got to the village, the quicker the drumbeats became, as though their arrival was being timed.

"Etu's people know we walk this trail," Ayashe said, in a low voice.

"Do not change your steps, I have no fear for them."

"Lan...you must only talk to Nakoma and not any others."

(Drumbeats continue to sound from the distance)

She grabbed the arm he was holding the spear with and lowered it down. "They will not know your fear if your kill stick is carried at your side."

Lan knew that. He also knew not to stare or show any signs of aggression and to wait until spoken to.

By late afternoon, the tents came into view at a turn in the trail. At first sight, there did not appear to be anyone around other than the drummer who was sitting on a high mound made of rock and dirt. He stopped banging on the tusk as soon as he saw them. A narrow man, he lowered a thick leg bone, once owned by a living human and now his, to return their inquisitive expressions through a forced smile. Raising the leg bone, he resumed slamming it against the tusk. The aim was sent low to hit the thicker part for a lower pitch. As before, he continued without stopping, the eerie sound, vacantly hollow and very loud.

"That is the one that marked Etu with red dirt," said Lan.

Ayashe agreed with a silent head nod.

A boy ran out of a tent and just as quick, ran back in.

Along the full length of the clearing, a row of posts as tall as those at the abandoned tents, stretched to the extreme far end. And like those posts, precariously misplace antlers and horns stuck out of the tattered hides that blew and twisted from their skeletal bonds. Each post had a human skull on top, but at the very end, on the last two posts, was something different. The bark had been removed and the wood a lighter color than the rest, as if they had been recently put in place. And on top...

Passing through to the other side of the row, Lan looked back, but they were still too far to see clearly. He crossed the middle of the clearing where the dirt was packed hard and where a recently doused fire had been left smoking in the solitude. Next to it, a large leg bone, hollowed out to contain liquid, dripped the last of its contents onto the ground. Nearby, some sort of stick thing was tied together, a child's toy he thought, dropped in someone's haste.

Close enough now to see the two farthest posts and the skulls with their distinctive braids, it surprised and angered him. He instinctively grabbed his ax. "Those heads in the back are not from this tribe."

Ayashe pushed his hand away. "Look there!" her voice, just above a whisper. She motioned in the direction where she wanted him to look.

A final loud drumbeat left the camp steeping in resounding reverberation. Lan had not noticed. Angry at what he was looking at, his lips pressed together as he forced air through his nose. *Those are the heads of Bandu men!*

Ayashe nudged him in the side. "Bg mahn look to you." Clutching his hand, she jerked it to get his attention. "Look!"

Lan turned from the post to where she seemed to be indicating. The thin man was still there with the same pasted grin. Nudged again, Lan turned a little more and as soon as he did, he got a sudden start. While he had been eying the posts, a crowd of the most wild, unkempt men he could have ever have imagined had lined up along the tents. It was an intimidating sight. Like Etu and Matwua, all of these men stood much taller than he did, each one glaring back with annoyed expressions. A few started to talk among themselves when Lan looked their way, while others stood with arms hanging straight down alongside large oversized chests. Everything about the men was oversized, their heads, their hands, their shovel shaped feet with course growths of bristly hairs growing on top of widely splayed toes. Some rocked from one foot to the other, while all looked on with the same curious stares.

Heavy axes and bludgeoning leg bones filled their grips, though their combined strength, even without weapons, would have been overwhelming. And none came forward, each assessing the Mowatchi before them with the strange looking kill sticks.

Speaking out first, Sewati broke through the rambling comments. Filled with disdain, the rough edges of his words befit the image of his hard and worn appearance. His gravelly voice cracked with what he had to say. "Why does this Mowatchi come to the people of Nakoma?"

Along with his rant, he strutted arrogantly back and forth in front of Lan with long rigid steps while looking up and down at him through the corner of his eyes. His hands on his hips, he pushed out his chest and faced the men. Pointing stiffly at Lan, he spoke loud and authoritatively. "It is I, Sewati that will say my words on this Mowatchi."

"You cannot make his talk for me...or any of us, Sewati," interrupted Achak, stepping forward from a small group of elders. "We must first hear the words of Nakoma. He has the wise words to say to us."

A commotion along with finger pointing and quarreling broke out between the more at odds amongst them. It soon escalated into a near aggressive confrontation.

From behind the men, a commanding voice quieted everyone as Kuruk worked his way through the crowd. "I will hear no more of this. The Mowatchi's talk is with Nakoma...no one else!"

Trailing whispers and hidden hand gestures settled as the men listened to the voice that boomed louder and deeper than most. Turning his back to Sewati, Kuruk continued. "Achak knows the old ways. His words speak for me and it is the way they should speak for Sewati. We will wait for Nakoma and that is all I will say." He straightened to search the crowd for Nakoma's adopted son. "Okhmhaka! We are ready!"

The ten year old ran into the largest tent, along with a resounding of drum beats.

While Lan rechecked the posts, Sewati came up from behind and to the laughter of the men, grabbed his ax and pulled it out of the netting. Leaning over Ayashe, he put a hand on her shoulder while looking down at the Mowatchi to see if he had enraged him.

Lan immediately slapped Sewati's hand off of her, surprising the taller man when he grabbed the ax back at the same time.

Both eyed one another---hard and glaringly.

The men parted to make room for Nakoma. Though he led them, he claimed no title. He was simply called by his name, moving among them in reverence. No one spoke, the camp silent except for the heavy shuffle of mammoth soles crunching into pebbled soil. Held in place with strips of hide, the webbing crisscrossed his thick calves up to the knees.

(Drumming continues)

A triangular patch of hide protected his groin as it did all of the men---his chest, bare except for two, mummified wolf heads. These hung from his neck with pieces of ivory inserted into the eye sockets, making them appear as if they were in a hypnotic trance.

A ram horn headdress, ornamented with vulture feathers, thin strips of beaver fur and eagle talons hanging off the sides, sat heavily on top of the leader's head. It shaded a face painted in brilliant red ochre and rows of thin, black lines that ran vertically across his face from ear to ear. The redness contrasted strikingly with his black hair. In that hair was a dozen vulture skulls tied at random heights, completing his expression of the death spirits.

At the top of his personal mound, Nakoma seemed distant, sitting on a mammoth skull while looking down from a height as high as the top of the tents. Built to rid the tribe of generations of bone litter, it was consolidated with mud and grass to form a stable platform. There, he would hold court or quell the men's anger with words that could be heard.

As suddenly as the drumming began it ceased its monotone composition, leaving the camp in an expectant mood.

Nadie: Second wife in standing.
The most recent addition to Nakoma's tent, Nadie handed him a rattle made from a saber tooth tiger head. She became the leader's second wife when Wahanassatta, the last ochre carrier died from illness. No one had availed themselves to her, so Nakoma claimed

her, more out of her need for a man than for his need for another woman.

Nadie appeared to be a composite of a varietal mix of body parts, none of which seemed to fit. Long hair with a hint of grey, gave her the consistent look of someone who had recently emerged from a driving wind storm. Wild and frizzy, it gave her a frightening appearance, inflicted further by a longer that natural drooping face. Wide, indirect teeth missed their mark with the front row jutting from her jaws whenever her mouth was closed. Heavy brows dipped inwardly over eyes that were unusually close together. Even her nose appeared oddly shaped, looking like some sort of undefined, red animal that had decided to permanently roost there. Her back seemed to connect directly to the back of her head, if one could see past the complicated weave of matted hair. Shoulders that extended farther than most men, dropped sinuous arms to ape-like lengths. Her thick fingers would have better served those of a hulking male.

Sadly, Nadie's deformities did not end there. Her feet, like her hands, were large with globular toes, leaving footprints in the soil that appeared questionably human. Long toenails twisted and turned in upward spirals, the ends pointing at one another as if they were in an aggressive battle. Broken tips stabbed into twenty different directions as each clashed in a free for all in a war without end.

However, for Nadie, looks did not matter. She did not see herself as freakish or ugly. There were too many other important matters to deal with than to worry about ones looks. She never had to look at herself, anyway, except on those occasions when she washed someone's baby in the river. And those reflections in the water were merely fleeting reminders which only occurred during the best of times when laughing and playing with children.

She was strong and could carry as much as a man. She knew how to gut any animal, or make the ropes that constantly needed to be replaced. She was worthy of Nakoma. She knew she was.

The tribe's leader shook the rattle in the Mowatchi's direction. Handing it back to Nadie, he waved her away so he could sit alone on the mound.

As if on cue, Kajika began to bang on the tusk with audienced enthusiasm. He reached for the narrower part on top, hitting it harder to better resonate a high pitched sound. His dedication was whole as he banged away with heartfelt energy and long, full swings.

Nakoma watched with amazement at the ineptness of his new charge. He picked up a tibia from a wart hog, normally used as a gavel, and threw it at Kajika. "That is enough," he snapped.

The newly appointed carrier of the red dirt smiled shyly at the hushed crowd, embarrassed for having gotten so carried away. In the ensuing calm, Nakoma's relaxed expression returned. He took a first serious look at Ayashe, breaking for the moment, his reticent projection to slap at a horsefly on his neck. In a thick, strong voice, he said, "Shatu duma! I give you both many welcome. I will now hear the words of the Mowatchi."

As if to encourage Lan, he followed with a head nod, 'though not knowing exactly how he would sign back or how he himself would be understood.

Ayashe stepped forward. "Shatu duma! I will speak for my Mowatchi."

"You speak our words? Are you not Mowatchi like him?"

Ignoring the question, Ayashe began a long explanation of how they came to be there. "Lan is strong to his people in the high place. He came to me where…"

Lan tried to follow the rest of what she was saying along with the fast hand gestures, his only worry, the telling of Matwua's death. She finally finished with how they helped Etu and that he was waiting safely by the river with enough meat to last, as long as they went back within the next three days.

A man in the crowd loudly interrupted. "Etu is no longer with us. We left him to wait his death."

"Etu lost his life spirit to the nag boksta." Another called out.

Sewati stepped forward. "Her words are not mine. I looked to Etu. His chest was broken...his leg was broken. All our hunters were there. It was then that he waited for the nag boksta. He now looks from the sky."

An uproar of agreement spilled from the men that had been at the hunt. The disorder upset Nakoma who stood and looked past the crowd to the two elders that were trying to silence them. They were warning the loudest among the men to quiet down, both of them pacing back and forth and fuming with frustration.

"It was Kajika that gave Etu the red dirt," a man in front shouted, followed by agreeing voices.

"It pleased Etu to see his death from the nag boksta," said another.

A doubtful man in the crowd answered them. "None of you stayed to see. How do you know? What if he still lives like this little one tells us?"

"You were not there," a man next to him said.

The men would not stop arguing and Nakoma's patience had become strained. He wrapped his arms around the mammoth head and after taking a deep breath, lifted it to his chest. It startled the two men standing immediately below the mound into clumsily stepping backwards into the row behind them. Struggling with the heavy weight, Nakoma took two unstable steps to the edge and with a loud yell, heaved the huge skull into the crowd. It slammed onto the ground and rolled over once, forcing everyone in front to push those in back out of their way.

"No more talk. It is finished." Breathing heavily, Nakoma could still hear a few of the men at the rear still ranting back and forth.

"Kajika! Now is your time!"

Moki removed his thumb from the inside of his nostril to slap Kajika on the leg.

Engrossed in the commotion, Kajika had forgotten to watch for a cue. Jumping at the chance to hit the tusk, he picked up the leg bone and started hammering.

"Nakoma will hear only on the Mowatchi," he shouted, still banging on the tusk even though the camp had long grown quiet.

Red-faced, his voice softened with the last thing he said as he looked back at the sullen faces that were looking back at him. Inside that silence, he carefully placed the femur on the ground and feigned interest at something way off in the distance.

Ayashe held nervously onto Lan while staring up at Nakoma. She took a quick glance at everyone there, reading the doubts and contempt in their faces.

Stretching forward, the tribe's leader stared downward at Ayashe through the bottom of his eyes, "How did this Mowatchi fix on Etu something we cannot?"

"Lan has a strong power to heal. It is his way."

"Then it is true that Etu waits?"

"Etu waits by the fast water near where the thunderfoot was killed."

A questioning look came over the leader. "It is not the way of the Mowatchi to help one of us. That is what we know."

It was hard for Ayashe to continue to gaze up at Nakoma's frightening appearance and think at the same time. His expression was so stern, so directing---his demeanor, the whole brawny look about him put her on edge.

Their leader's power is strong. He is much like the death spirits he wears. When he looks to me, does he not see Matwua's death? Does he know what I know?

The ugly one…Sewati…does he not have me in his head from my trade to Matwua? When I tell them I belong to Mantotohpa's people, will they then remember me? Will I be welcomed?

She looked behind to the crowd of impatient men, bit her lip and blurted it all out. "I come from the people of Mantotohpa!"

Stunned, the men groaned in disbelief as another wave of doubts and accusations began to stir them. It took Nakoma by surprise as well. He rubbed his chin and gave what she just said serious thought. *She is too small to be from Mantotohpa. Is this how she knows the words we speak?*

Ayashe's attention was drawn to the back of the crowd where Sewati and Achak were talking to one another. She grew more concerned when Sewati then walked purposefully to the mound and climbed the steps. At the leader's side, he leaned over and spoke softly into his ear.

"Achak speaks that he was with Matwua when he took this little one for himself. She is from Mantotohpa. Achak knows this."

Nakoma, toying with the vulture skulls in his hair, responded, "Your words to me is as she speaks. So she is from Mantotohpa. Still, it is not inside my head that she would be so little?"

"It is Achak's words that say this."

"Where, then, is Matwua?"

Sewati mirrored the leader's questioning look, turned and glanced at Ayashe who was below the mound and staring at the ground between her feet. He remembered being there and some of the things about the trade, but that was a long time ago. That same day, he had shared dream drink with Mantotohpa. The results blocked out the rest of the memory. All he did remember was that besides Etu and Achak as well as Matwua and himself, Kuruk was at the trade as well.

From his distance from behind the men, Kuruk looked away from Achak to stare at Ayashe. Turning back to the elder, he said, "You say she is the one that was there? She has no power with me, that is why I did not have this in my head the way it is in yours. Now I see her in front of me like I did at the trade. She is the one that came with Mantotohpa. I walked with you and Sewati when we traded Matwua to them. It was Mantotohpa that took the many gifts from Matwua for this little one."

Achak shook his head. "Why then does she come with this Mowatchi and not Matwua?"

Folding his arms, Kuruk shook his head in kind. "It was then that we wanted to rid ourselves of Matwua. We could not wait any longer. I myself was glad he did not return with us; all of our men were."

Achak's memory was far clearer, better than Kuruk or Sewati's. "They did not know that it was Matwua who killed Una and the reason we gave him to Mantotohpa."

The corner of Kuruk's lips curled into a smirk. "No… Mantotohpa did not know this. For his own reasons, Mantotohpa did not want Matwua. It was after we left that trade, that Matwua took this little one to the high place."

Achak nodded, "If we did not want Matwua, and Mantotohpa did not want him, there was no other place for him to go."

Kuruk continued to shake his head. "Now she brings this…this Mowatchi. Does she not know we do not want the Mowatchi here with us?"

Still standing at the top of the mound with Nakoma, Sewati headed for the steps to join the rest of the men. It took four to return the mammoth scull back to the top.

Settled and much calmer, Nakoma sat, leaned forward on his elbows and glared intensely at Ayashe. Speaking sternly, he said, "Where is your Matwua?" Still glaring, he waited for the answer.

"The Mowatchi finished him," Sewati shouted, now pacing in front of Lan.

Nakoma held his hand up to silence him. With his attention back on Ayashe, his cavernous voice made her shudder.

"Matwua…where does he stand?"

Ayashe quickly responded with a ready answer, "He stands in the high place."

"The Mowatchi killed him," Sewati shouted, pointing at Lan and jabbing a finger in his direction. He repeated that, saying each word out loud while keeping his finger pointed at him.

"Mowatchi…killed…Matwua.

Mowatchi…killed…Matwua.
Mowatchi…killed…Matwua."

The men surrounding Sewati joined in, repeating the same words in unison.

"Mowatchi…killed…Matwua.
Mowatchi…killed…Matwua."

Ayashe did not dare look at Nakoma. Instead, she hung her head and stared at the dirt. She had to think. What could she say now? She turned momentarily to look at the men mouthing the words.

"Mowatchi…killed…Matwua.
Mowatchi…killed…Matwua."

Lan's gaze met hers. *If I was alone, I would kill this leader with my spear. I would then run from this place and they would never catch me… but I am not alone and she cannot run like I can.*

He squeezed her hand.

"Mowatchi…killed…Matwua.
Mowatchi…killed…Matwua."

Upon seeing Nakoma's cue, Kajika sprang into action. He banged on the tusk with feverish energy until the chanting quieted to a murmur and then silence.

The drumming stopped, the only noise left, a loud wind whistling through the tents. It seemed as if everyone had left, their exiting footsteps muffled behind Lan's deep thoughts. But the faces were still there, every one of them looking his way. He looked again at Ayashe with the kind expression she had grown to love.

I will give myself to them to do as they wish if they bring no harm to her and let her go to her people.

There did not seem to be any other way. His mouth parted, and when he was about to say the first word, he was interrupted by a boy's voice that came from behind the back row of men.

"It is in Sewati's words that tell us the little man from the high place killed Matwua. That is like a bo bo that bites the neck of a nag boksta."

It was Okhmhaka, Nakoma's son and what he just said caused an outburst of uncontrollable laughter to erupt from everyone there---everyone except Sewati. It set off a wave of hysterics and backslapping. No one could stop laughing. After all, how could such a large and belligerent man such as Matwua have been slain by so diminutive a person? Even Nakoma doubled over when he envisioned a rabbit biting the neck of saber tooth tiger in a deadly death grip.

Rarely seen smiling, let alone laughing, Kuruk let out a short chuckle. In his laid back, easy way, he shouted, "Sewati needs to eat the eyes of the great kitchka (eagle) so he can see better."

Along with everyone else, it was all Lan could do to keep from laughing as well.

Visibly humiliated, Sewati took a long, angry look at the Mowatchi and retreated behind the last row of men. Whenever their eyes met, Sewati would stare back, so Lan avoided looking at him altogether, but it did not stop him from laughing inside.

Nakoma paused with a thought. *I do not feel for a man who no longer hunts with us. It is this little one's words that Etu lives that holds my interest.*

Lifting the ram horns, he scratched his scalp and stood up with a glance at the mountains. He shook his head and then adjusted the crown, before waving for them both to follow him.

"Come…walk with me to my cover."

Embedded mammoth jaws cracked beneath his feet as he stepped down the mound. Without looking to see if they were behind him, he shuffled toward his tent.

With no intention of lagging behind, and certainly not with the hostile crowd standing there, Lan felt it was better to stay close to the tribe's leader. With each step, Nakoma's thick shoulders dipped to the sides, his strong gait, surprisingly easy and graceful for a man his size. Everything out front was blocked from view by the wideness of his back, his hair, dropping wavy hues to his waist like black corn silk. And like the rest of the men, his personal odor was strong.

Another odor, that of sour milk, became noticeable as soon as they rounded the first of a line of tents. Big like their men, women stood with plump newborns under their arms and dribbling milk running down their bloated breast. Children of various ages glared at the new people, two chasing one another in and out of their mother's legs.

Nakoma's odor marked the inside of his tent as well. It was seasoned and inescapable. Difficult to habituate to, it thankfully lessened with time.

Dispensing with his reluctance to breath, Lan took in the foul air from the tent floor. The enclosure appeared well lit and as large as the tents back at the abandoned village. Numerous human skull caps burned along the wall from mammoth oil. On a far wall, the usual array of skeletal parts and animal skins nearly covered its entirety. In front of it and stacked to the ceiling were baskets leaning precariously to one side.

The floor itself lay bare and swept clean, the fire pit, devoid of anything other than left over ashes. At the outside of the pit, a line of ten mammoth skulls were wrapped entirely around it. Sparse by tribal standards, Nakoma's tent held little else other than a large buffalo fur spread out in one of the corners for sleeping.

The leader took his seat on one of the skulls and it was toward these that he now directed. "Sit!" He clapped his hands and barked an order at Nadie. "Bring dream drink!"

Honovi: First wife in standing.
The more favored of his two wives, Honovi (strong deer) returned with a kind of beer made from wild barley. The fermentation, propagated from a salivated start was handed to Lan in a long, caribou femur spilling with foam.

A thick woman with a narrow waist complimenting small breast, Honovi had legs Nakoma often teased her about for looking like thunderfoot legs. She was pretty---to Nakoma, her eyes as clear as rainwater and unblemished skin any man would want to touch. Above all, it was her legs that were her best feature. Vein-less and covered with hair, they were big and strong with large calves. Nakoma lusted over her.

Removing the ram-horn headdress, the tribe's leader placed it on the floor next to his seat. "It is good that Etu waits." Belching loudly, he shook the hair away from his face and pushed it over his shoulders. "Many will go with Kuruk and Sewati."

"And I," said Lan.

"Yes, it is good that you go with them." Nakoma addressed Ayashe next. "And what of you…will you go with your Mowatchi?"

She glanced at Lan. "His wish is that I stay."

"You can sleep in Nadie's cover with the little ones."

She smiled at that.

Unfamiliar with dream drink, Lan liked its taste. Before he finished the little that remained in the femur, Honovi returned with a caribou stomach near bursting with more. She refilled the leg bone to overfilling which Lan sipped and then passed on to Nakoma.

Lifting it to his lips, Nakoma nearly drank all of it, wiped his mouth and belched again. He handed it back to Lan and continued, "You come to us from the other side of the high place…away from your people…alone?"

"My walk was long and with no one."

Nakoma stared at him. "Do all Mowatchi's speak our words?"

"I learned this from Ayashe."

"Why then did you not speak for yourself when you stood outside? Why let this one speak for you?"

"She is one with Mantotohpa. For this, her words are stronger than mine."

After a long pause and with a look of concern, the leader leaned forward and peered straight into his eyes. "Who is it that you run from?" His voice, soft and deeply resonant.

With pause, Lan returned the leader's steady stare. "Man Walking and his men…the Dinga."

As he spoke, Honovi filled the femur with every intention of lingering longer than it would take to fill the vessel. She did not notice when it began to flow over the top and onto the Mowatchi's legs.

"Go now, thunderfoot woman!" Nakoma barked.

Honovi huffed and turned her back to him.

Conveniently within range, the tribe's leader smacked her square on the right buttock; convinced her only purpose was to listen. Both embarrassed and enraged, she screamed and spun around, filling Nakoma's lap with dream drink.

The tribe's leader yanked the bag away from her and handed it to Lan. Grabbing her by the arm, he spun her around, placed his foot on her backside and pushed her towards the steps.

"Come back when I sleep."

Honovi stormed toward the steps, climbed half way up, stopped and gave him an ugly face. "Ooh!" She then ran the rest of the way, slapped the skin at the entrance to the side and rushed out of the tent.

As if nothing had happened, Nakoma addressed Ayashe. "There is much I do not know of your Mowatchi. It is my wish to learn more of the high place and his people."

Ayashe's lips were dry but she did not dare ask for any of the dream drink.

His attention back on Lan, Nakoma said, "Your people from the high place...why do they not follow you?"

Starting from the beginning, Lan explained how his tribe had been attacked, Sleeps by the Fire, and what he had told him he must do to find a new hunting place. He spoke about the big water, the size of which Nakoma could not even imagine, though he tried. His focus back on Ayashe, he asked, "And you, little one, what is it that you know?"

"Lan's wish is for his people."

She tilted her head with pouted lips to show sadness for him. Lying about Matwua, she explained that he was abusive and how she ran away, leaving him to live alone. To convince Nakoma of how she came to accept the Mowatchi, she told him about the nag boksta and the way Lan killed it with his spear. After she finished, she rattled the bracelets.

Clackety, clack...clackey, clack...clackety, clackety, clackety, clack!

Nakoma fingered the claws and gently grabbed both wrists to shake them for himself.

Clackety clackety...clackety clack!

When she told him about Aleeka and how they all tried to hide inside the dead thunderfoot, he laughed so hard he nearly fell off the mammoth skull. Spellbound and fascinated, he listened like a young boy about the unfamiliar world Lan came from and the surrounding tribes. He shared the Bandu's hatred for the Dinga and fear for the Manama and Wadu. He learned of their leaders, Man Walking, Sharp Knife, Wolf Spirit and Standing Tall; listened to everything Ayashe said about them.

With nothing left to add, she folded her hands.

"Why do you wear your hair like the Mowatchi?"

"I am Bandu."

"Bandu?"

She shook her head.

"So, you are not from Mantotohpa?"

"I was a child then and now I am grown. This is the man I walk with. For this I am Bandu."

"It will sadden Mantotohpa when he sees you this way."

Having waited quietly for them to finish, Lan had one final question to ask the tribe's leader. "The heads on the last two post with hair like mine. What of those men? They are from the high place, are they not?"

Slighted that he would be questioned, by no less, a Mowatchi, Nakoma studied him for a moment, pausing as if to get his facts together. Then calmly, he shook his head and began to relate a long tale of how he had come to possess the skulls.

"Do you not see that they look to the high place?"

Lan nodded.

"They look to the hunting place that they once called theirs. The same place that you now call yours. Hotuaekhaashtait (tall bull), a tribal elder we called Hotuaek, waited there with three young ones to show them the way to Wankan Tanka (Great Spirit). They go there to become men. It is a high place and close to our lost ones in the sky. They stayed for the time of three suns before we could call them men.

"When they began their long return, these young men found the old bones of two men very different from ours. They wanted to carry the heads back, but Hotuaek spoke to them to leave them where they lay.

"The three said to him that they were now men and not what they were before they first took their walk. For this, they did not listen to Hotuaek and decided to carry the skulls back.

"My words were mad words when they came to me. They brought to us the spirits of these men. I did not want to anger those spirits or ours, so now they sit and face the high place. You are a brother to them, Lan. It is good that they go with you when you return to your high place."

Lan nodded. "There will be a time when I will make that walk. It is then that I will do as you ask."

Nakoma appeared to be pleased. "When we are ready for that time we can once again share dream drink together."

Glad for the skulls to be finally out of his hands someday soon, he filled the femur. While handing it to Lan, he considered asking him directly if indeed he had killed Matwua, knowing full well that if he asked that question he would put both the Mowatchi and himself in an awkward position. Giving it more thought, he decided not to, 'though the more he became familiar with the ways of Lan and his people, the more he was convinced that that was exactly what had happened. For now he would dismiss it.

There is something here for me. This one has a power to heal and he knows others from the high place. It is good that I stay strong with him.
"Okhmhaka!"

The leader's son weaved his way down the steps, sidestepping the gathering of women and children that had collected there. He easily jumped over them and without so much as a head nod to any of them, ran to Nakoma's side.

"Bring Kuruk and Sewati, Moki, Qaletaga, Nayati and Achak. Hmm…bring little Akando, he should go with them."

The boy started to leave, then stopped short and waited until Nakoma nodded. He returned the head nod and ran up the steps while dodging the women and children sitting in his way.

"Okhmhaka!"

The boy immediately ran halfway down the steps, leaned over and looked in.

"Abooksigun (wildcat)…he must go with the rest…and, that…that…," Nakoma's thumb pointed to the side, "…thunderfoot waste."

"Kajika?" the boy blurted out.

"Yes, him!"

"Lan…come! We will talk to the men."

Fully inebriated, Lan could hardly stand.

Outside, most of the men had lined up before a communal fire as their leader barked orders.

"Nayati…Moki, when these men are ready to go, you bring the big skin. You will need it to carry Etu. Achak, Qaletaga…and you, Akando, you must also go with Kuruk."

Nakoma next spoke to his lead first hunter. "Your words are strong with these men. You will lead."

Kuruk felt slighted. Of course he would lead, like the way he led the hunts. He was a leader of first hunters. He was brave and skilled, fast and strong; strong enough to run a spear into a thunderfoot and not be afraid to pull it out and drive it back in. He commanded respect. Each and every first hunter obeyed him without question. Yes...of course he would lead.

—≼·≽—

Ayashe fit easily in the company of women. They all huddled around her and took turns fingering her bracelets.

Admiring the feathers in her skirt, one asked, "How did you catch that sky jumper?"

"Lan took it with his kill stick," Ayashe beamed.

"Did he scratch this on your arm?" Another asked, touching the image of the snake.

"Oh yes," she said, turning her way and nodding excessively.

"I would like one on my arm," the girl giggled.

"It looks pretty in my eyes," said another.

Ayashe twisted around to see who that was.

Someone else, an older woman, tapped her from behind while fumbling with her braid. "Is your Mowatchi a good hunter?"

"Yes!" she responded, turning to face her.

"Is he good to sleep with?" a young girl in front asked.

(More giggling)

Jerking her head around, Ayashe smiled at her without answering.

"Does he beat you and pull your hair?" another girl asked.

"Oh...no, never!"

"So, he is good to you!"

"Yes! Yes!" She assured, glancing at the girl who just said that.

A smiling, plump girl grabbed her by the waist, rubbed her belly and slid her hand downward. With a sexy tone in her voice, she said, "Does he touch you where it feels nice?"

The women all laughed.

Ayashe blushed while gently pushing the girl's hand away with a thumb and forefinger.

"Does he…does he?" the girl insisted.

"He…ah…y-y-yes."

The girl screamed, followed by the rest as they all jumped up and down while hysterically screaming.

Nakoma and Okhmhaka showed Lan the rest of the tents. Women talked in whispers as soon as they walked by, finding Lan's tribal appearance and manly good looks attractive. He glanced back and smiled, which only excited them further. Shying away, they turned from him to hide their embarrassment.

With a good command of their language, Lan said, "I smell thunderfoot," along with the appropriate hand sign.

"Come look to my Rama," said Okhmhaka.

Rounding the last of the tents, they made their way to where a year old mammoth stood tethered to the ground. It immediately raised its trunk in recognition for the boy, moaning deeply and rocking from side to side as soon as it saw him.

Okhmhaka ran the rest of the way. "This is my Rama. It is the word I talk for him. Look how I can sit on his back."

The boy shimmied up the mammoth's trunk and although he could not direct the animal in any particular direction, it was still fun to sit that high with the feel of a live animal below. Tethered with heavy ropes tied to mammoth pelvises buried underground, the juvenile bull could only sway back and forth. Okhmhaka patted the mammoth on the forehead with affection. "Lan, you come sit on Rama!" With that, he turned on his stomach and slid off the animal.

Reluctant to make a fool of himself, Lan hesitated.

"Go, Lan!" The boy encouraged, pushing him from behind.

Lan held back, but Okhmhaka kept pushing.

Amused, Nakoma tapped the Mowatchi on the shoulder and nodded encouragingly. "Sit on the thunderfoot. It cannot hurt you."

Lan leaned away from the inquisitive trunk and remained still while the young mammoth explored the circumference of his head. It seemed friendly enough. He let it nudge him until he had to step backward to keep from falling. Both Nakoma and Okhmhaka found that funny.

The clump of rust colored hair on top of the animal's dome shaped head was all Lan could find to grab onto. With one swift leap, he pulled himself up and straddled the juvenile's neck.

Okhmhaka already had one of the ropes undone. Nakoma undid another. Relieved of the tension, the young bull shifted its weight. Lan held on tightly while the last of the ropes were removed and left lying on the ground.

It seemed strange, to watch without effort, the ground moving below. It was disorienting, yet exhilarating at the same time. Lan's legs felt useless as the thunderfoot carried him around in a self-conditioned circle. That and a daily walk to the river was all Rama was accustomed to, the potential left unrealized since it was only a pet---a game to fill time.

A planted grin on his face, Nakoma looked on amused until a blank expression returned for a worrying thought.

This thunderfoot will one day be too big to obey my son. I will need to find a way...send him on a hunt with the others. He would like that. When he returns I will tell him the animal was sick and found his death.

Rama was a gift I could not stop myself from giving him. Why did I not kill this one when we killed its mother? I would now have no need to worry. Okhmhaka's feelings for this thunderfoot are much too strong...too strong for me to stop it now. He fed it well and look how much it has grown. His Rama must be killed...another time...another place...not now.

There was something else Nakoma wanted from Lan before he left the following morning with the men. Studying the details in the Mowatchi's tattoos, he said, "The spirits I wear give me a great shona. One like yours will only make them stronger."

"I can give you the power of the snake."

"The snake is your spirit. Give the death bird to me. It is good that I show this to all who see me."

With the necessary dyes in place, Lan took care to skillfully complete the tattoo. When finished, the leader admired the vulture so much; he could not stop looking at it. To celebrate, he shared more dream drink with him, until both fell asleep on the floor of Nakoma's tent.

Since Okhmhaka had taken what was left of spare rope, the women busied themselves with making more. Ayashe sat with them, twisting the dry stems together. Ropes could be made as strong as needed for any application by simply thickening them with more stems. To make them longer, each section could be weaved together so that they interlocked with one another, making the rope as long as needed.

Other women caught up with necessary duties. Loose hides from the tents had to be tied down and skins chewed to soften them to wear for the coming winter. And there was always the tedious task of collecting dung and bringing water in from the river. Between taking care of chores and watching children, the camp remained vibrant with activity.

Etu

The first hunter shuddered at the coming darkness. This would be his sixth night on the bank and the wolf pack was back to torment him like they had the night before. It was the black ones clan. He recognized the lead wolf by his large size.

With far too many saber tooth tigers---each cat three times the weight of a dire wolf---the mammoth kill was totally consumed. The wolves had no choice but to wait at a distance. When the huge cats finally left, there was nothing on the abandoned carcass except for cartilage and bone. After spending so much time waiting near a kill that produced very little, it was time to seek out their next prey.

The nahgos wound their way along the bank single file. Etu stretched for a better look. The pack seemed endless and had grown since the year before. Many were here that were not here then, like the juveniles that had survived a warmer than usual winter.

They come to take the rest of this meat.

Lying on his stomach, Etu pushed what was left of the elk carcass as far away from him as he could. He rechecked the tightly tied bundles of grass. The day had been spent making them and he hoped they would be enough.

I must light these now. Now, before they get closer.

He checked again. Traveling along the bank, a few of the nahgos were sniffing at the edge of thick growth. Others fruitlessly chased ducks into the water while the pack as a whole moved relentlessly forward.

They will not stop with this meat. They will soon have me in their eyes. I must light these now. It is not something I can do when they are here and I have kill sticks in my hands.

The fire! My fire is out!

Alarmed, Etu scattered the smoldering ashes to look for hidden embers. Pushing desperately through ash and dung, he searched, but the last of the embers had burned out.

Rama's bath

It was early morning when Ayashe accompanied Okhmhaka to the river with Rama. The mammoth entered the shallows on its own and happily bobbed its head back and forth while slapping its trunk across the surface.

Splashing water onto the mammoth's side, Ayashe said, "Rama likes sitting in the water."

"When Rama is happy, then I am happy," the boy said.

She cleaned the dirt from the mammoth's ears and dug out the yellow crusty stuff from deep inside. The ticks she found, she dropped into the river one at a time to see the bloated bodies sink to the bottom. It was revengeful and satisfying to watch them disappear into the depths; even more so whenever an opportunistic fish darted in to snap one up as soon as it was dropped in.

Sitting on Rama, Okhmhaka jumped off just in time as the young mammoth rolled onto its side, drenching Ayashe in a wave. She splashed back which Rama returned by slapping the water with its trunk. Joining in, Okhmhaka splashed the both of them until Ayashe grabbed and wrestled with him. With a final push, the boy fell backwards into the river with his hands high in the air.

"No more. You killed this ba ba yano (sturgeon)."

Rama continued slapping at the water.

"Your Rama is too pretty in my head," said Ayashe, throwing her arms around the juvenile mammoth's neck.

Rama raised his trunk and trumpeted loudly.

"He talks he wants flowers," said Okhmhaka.

Without any coaxing, Rama waded through the marshes to the cattails growing along the shore. He pulled them out by the trunk full, eating that and any other succulent that Ayashe and Okhmhaka brought to him.

"The inside of his nose is soft," she said, holding out a handful of flowers.

A tremendous appetite kept Rama feeding until late in the day. Ready for the return trip, the boy called out, "Come…he wants you to sit up here with me."

"No," Ayashe replied. "One day, not now. I want to walk here by his side."

Back at the tents, she went around to help anyone who needed anything. She loved playing with the babies and talking at length to the women.

The air inside the tents was stifling with humidity. Some of the women slept outside with infants between them and those that slept there, slept well.

Inside the women's communal tent, Ayashe joined Honovi with Okhmhaka trailing behind. Honovi found relief from Nakoma's constant demands by telling him she wanted to be with the new woman. Perhaps, Honovi had said, she could coax her for the real truth about what really had happened to Matwua. She commended herself for having thought of that ploy and that Nakoma believed her. In the end, all that mattered was that she got her way and she and the women along with their babies could enjoy the evening together.

With so much to talk about, Ayashe and Honovi stayed up late. Now tired with sleep laden eyes, they, like most everyone else, were on the verge of falling asleep themselves.

Having nestled between the two women, Okhmhaka would not stop talking. "It would be good if I make to my Rama to go where I want him to go. He knows the words I speak."

Bored with his rambling, the women politely listened. "Mm hm!"

"Rama is many times too big. He can make strong to carry our skins and meat on his back. Rama can carry all of it for us. I will make the talk to Nakoma. I know he…"

"Sh-h-h!" Honovi covered his mouth.

The boy pushed her hand away and in a softer tone, said, "I know my Rama can…"

This time Ayashe covered his mouth and whispered deep into his ear, though a little more hoarsely than Honovi just did. "No… more…**talk talk!**"

The boy giggled from the tickling sensation and demurely replied, "That is good! No more talk talk for Okhmhaka." Folding his arms abruptly over his chest, he nodded along with a stretched smile.

Ayashe wrapped her arms around him and held him tightly. Above them, the skins covering the tent flickered from the firelight below. She closed her eyes to it and led herself into a daydream, crossing to the other side from what was real to thoughts of her father, Akule and the rest of her tribe.

She stood alongside Lan before the tents with a son standing between them. The boy looked like Lan and had the bright eyes of her father. His hair shined like Nakoma's and she could see Alawa, her mother's face in his.

He will one day be strong and know many things, like Lan. I know this. With a hard body, like him...yes and brave and...oh... (yawn)...not afraid like me.

His hair...like...like...Nakoma's--shiny. Yes...very shiny and... and...(yawn).

Torn ear

Dawn; the chill of night lingered in the air. Other than a frequent breeze, the camp remained tranquil and still. As though weary of the winds, loose tent hides lay like spent, salient animals. They soon lifted, were whipped into submission by the returning winds and then lay reticently to wait for the next breeze.

Outside, one tribal member sat awake, listening to the moving grass and enjoying the solitude that only early morning could bring. Playing with bits of bone, the baby boy flung them into the air and pushed them into the dirt with graceless skill. He chuckled softly at his new found ability, stopping now and then to wipe the tickle from his nose with short stubby fingers.

A strong gust blew through the tents, carrying the scent of the tribe across the grassland. It passed over mostly barren and verdurous landscape and eventually to a lone coyote foraging through the underbrush. Unlucky with the success of its pack, it had only managed to snatch a sliver of meat from a kill while the carcass was being ravaged by the rest. Consumed in a melee of clashing fangs too vicious to compete with, the young coyote could only sit at the sidelines and watch. Low in rank, it ventured out on its own to find something to eat.

The Jonga lifted its head to sniff at a fresh odor, turning a torn ear in its direction. With new found eagerness, it followed the scent through a game trail until tents came into view. Poking its dog like head between the stems, Torn Ear picked out subtle movements next to the sleeping bodies. Without veering from it, he licked the moisture from his nose, his tail twitching with shallow innuendos of nervous hope. Moving forward with a rigid stalk, the scavenger-hunter's hind legs brushed by the last of the grass stems. With no thought of taking the long way around, it dared to enter the clearing. Boldly, it crossed the pebbled ground, low and silent as it paced itself. The coyote's head hung lower than its body as it moved forward unchallenged. Soft pads allowed the jonga to stalk quietly along the open space until it stood not a body length from the nearest sleeping form. It sniffed at a leg and slowly slunk away, stepping ever so cautiously toward the baby, now sitting and facing the opposite direction.

Toying with a stone, the baby pushed it along the ground. He tried to pick it up, but it slipped from his grasp and hit his thigh. Rolling along a crease in the flesh, the stone dropped to the ground. His outstretched palm patted the stone as the baby made try after try at grabbing it. His short fingers could close around part of it, but not enough to get a good hold on the smooth, flat surface.

He left it where it lay, tipped over onto his hands and knees and crawled toward the edge of the clearing. Ahead, the line of grass marking the boundary seemed like a promising objective. After a few knee scraping crawls, he sat up and leaned over his bent legs to pick up the short, interesting stick lying in his way. His wide eyes studied the rust colored appetizing thing, having already made a decision to eat it. With hungry anticipation, he brought the stick to his lips. Bubbling juices dribbled down the corners of his lips along with an accompanying gibberish as he aimed the stick at his mouth. The taste was disappointing and not what he had hoped for, so he slapped at it until it fell to the ground.

Ahead, and bending in the breeze, lay the thick growth that grew as tall as a man. With a clear path, he was not going to stop until he had some of that abundant green stuff in his hands.

Torn Ear stalked forward and then suddenly stopped to turn toward the sound of slapping skins coming from the tents behind him. His head snapped back to the front and weaved from left to right to test the odor from the baby.

In an instant, the jonga covered the open space between them, engulfing the child's head entirely within its jaws. The fangs dug deep into the baby's skull before the coyote lifted him high off the ground. The infant's arms and legs thrashed about for a brief moment and then hung limply at his sides as the coyote bounded off with his prize.

Awakening to her missing child, Ahmik (beaver) searched between the sleeping bodies with little worry. He often crawled off, only to fall asleep next to the others. Not finding him, she entered the nearest tent with the confidence that she would see him right away, carried there by a concerned tribe member. She strained her gaze into the dimly lit interior and was surprised and disappointed at not seeing him there like she thought she would. Becoming nervous, she went into the next tent and the next after that, until she covered every tent and bit of ground in between. Frantic, she hurried to the outer perimeter of grass where she ran along the edge. She spread the stems apart at close intervals to look for him crawling, but he was nowhere to be found.

"My baby!" She screamed. Crying uncontrollably, she screamed out again. "My baby is gone!"

And then the blood on the ground---her legs weakened and she fell to her knees along with a terrible feeling inside.

The entire tribe soon gathered around her, all with worried looks on their faces.

"Where is your baby?" Nadie asked.

"My baby...my baby is gone!" Hysterically crying, she got up and ran back to the grass line, slapping at the tall stems as she went along. She was followed by Nadie and Ayashe while others checked elsewhere in the dense foliage.

Carrying a spear, Nakoma and Okhmhaka, stood above the blood splattered ground and the prints of the jonga.

"Why do they look? This baby has found his death from the jonga,"

Okhmhaka understood exactly what his father was saying. "The baby's spirit is in the jonga. He can never go to the sky. He is no more."

Sighing, Nakoma put his arm around his son and waited for the woman to return.

Ayashe knew as did Nadie that the child's spirit was lost forever. Their only purpose for following Ahmik was to give her comfort.

Sixth night

Etu made a last try at finding glowing embers as he spread the ashes every which way. He slapped the smoldering bits of dung together and through the dim light, a spark briefly flashed and instantly went out. Breaking and blowing desperately on the end of the piece where it had come from, a grain sized ember began to glow red hot. Afraid to lose the only thing that could save him from the hungry wolves; he placed it on a bundle of grass and continued to blow on it. A sudden flash of light made him recoil from it and with a little coaxing; it spread into a glorious and bright fire.

For the hundredth time, he checked the advancing wolves.

The black one that leads sniffs the air at my wounds. He stands and waits to grow strong from my weakness.

Another bundle was lit and set aside. He did not want to chance the first one burning out.

They move again. They will soon surround me and see me from all sides.

After what seemed like half the night, the wolves finally began to embolden themselves. Inside the blackness, they surrounded Etu at a distance and in a variety of positions. Some sat, while others growled from time to time. A few, the more impatient among them, loped around in unending circles.

Etu tightened his grip around the spear. It had served well as a splint, but was now needed to save himself from the nahgos. He had sharpened a new point on it the night before, scorching it black in a fire to harden it. Squinting, he tried to look past the flicker of firelight and into the obsidian night. All around, a horde of yellow, gawking eyes floated inside the dark soup; blinking, moving, some disappearing, others reemerging only to stare back at him.

Concealed somewhere within that same darkness was the nahgo's leader, now facing the stars and howling into the cold night. More followed, howling with long drawn out calls that filled the void surrounding Etu. Fire was all he could think about. If what he had was not enough, then he would be in a fight to save his life. He could never kill them all, two or three, perhaps a few more than that, but certainly not their leader. He was far too strong, too determined, with a life time of wise decisions behind him and what had made him the pack's leader.

Etu clutched a fully enflamed bundle and threw it at the nearest one. He could hear the shuffle of paws as the running wolf dodged the fire ball.

His only salvation out of all of this would be that wolves were predators like he was. He would survive after all in the afterlife like he at first wanted to. And there was always the chance that the men were nearing. Surely they had to be close by. It was the sixth night, three to walk to the village and three to walk back.

If they heard the voices of these nahgos, their own voices would have reached me.

Conceding to the fact that he would have to fight the wolves alone, he listened to the shuffling paws as the predators tightened the circle around him.

They know I bleed like an opened bondo gah. Soon, the black one will fill the air in front of me.

Lighting another bundle, he threw it behind him where the fireball bounced along the ground and lit up the faces of scores of panting wolves. Their jaws, left agape with white fangs glistening, snapped in his direction.

More fire, he had more and would light them all if need be. He lit another bundle and sent it flying in a completely different direction. No matter where he threw them, all he could see was a mass of fur with no bare spaces in between.

They will soon be upon me and I only have three of these left.

The sound of panting and paws slapping in the muddy bank grew louder and faster as the rest of the pack got caught up in the increasing frenzy. Another bundle was thrown at the nahgos. Sparks shot through the air as soon as it hit the side of a passing wolf, its startled cry setting off another round of howling.

Etu threw the last two bundles. With a reliance on his good leg, he leaned on his knee, straightened to a half stance and fell back down. Rising on his side, he faced the brazen wolf that suddenly darted in. It snapped at the raised spear and backed away, followed by another that ran in behind it. The sharp point penetrated its rib cage, sending the wolf baying toward the rear of the pack. Another roar, followed by snarling, came from behind. Ignoring the pain in his leg, Etu struggled to twist far enough around to jab at a flash of fur as it ran past. He turned back around to the front just in time to see the outstretched paws of a large male in mid-air. As it came down, he quickly thrust the spear deep into its chest, the shaved point, stabbing past the ribs and into the animal's lungs. Holding onto the shaft, he leveraged the heavy wolf to the side and slammed it to the ground, snapping the spear in two. With the heavy ax all that was left to fight off the wolves, he held it out front and waited for the next to charge in.

This is my end. It is the black ones time.

Feigning blows with the ax, he swung at the wolves that ran by and jumped over the dying male. Everytime he did that, sharp pain stung across his chest from the broken ribs.

Another came from behind and sank its fangs deep into Etu's arm. With a powerful blow, he cracked the wolf's skull open. He never saw the black leader that came out of the darkness to slam him onto his back. Its frightening roar stormed into his face. He clutched it by the neck to keep the fangs from ripping out his throat.

Other wolves immediately joined in. Stabbing pains shot through his good leg, another pierced his arm, the teeth of both sets of jaws slicing apart the muscles inside.

A tearing sound coming from his right ear along with a prolonged growl shook loudly inside as the fangs of the animal raked the side of his face. The wolf peeled his ear completely away, stripping along with it a length of skin from Etu's skull. Snarling and growling ensued as the wolf fought with another to keep the piece for itself.

Holding the black wolf's head away, Etu tightened the grip he had around its neck...and then everything suddenly stopped---the chaos---the growling---the charging wolves. He no longer felt teeth ripping into his body. Completely still, the only thing he could feel was his own pulse throbbing inside the right side of his skull where his ear used to be. He could still think and believed he was there in the same place, but gradually was becoming unsure of that, too. Everything all around was quiet and empty, the presence of the nahgos seeming to have disappeared completely. His body felt as though it was spinning above ground in a slow circle at about the height of a grown man.

My body is weak. It is emptying of blood.

A sudden flash of light blinded him. One of his bundles caught on fire, he guessed.

"The black one!" He heard someone say.

In total disbelief, Etu stared at the face of the lead wolf in the fire light. It was still in his grasp and lying limp across his chest. He instantly let go and watched dumbfounded as it slid off his chest to the ground at his side. He could hear voices in the distance and the sound of splashing, and now the sweet sound of young Akando's voice. He thought he heard Kuruk. Yes…it was Kuruk… he was sure of it, and he could feel the heat of a blinding torch hot on his face.

Akando held the torch higher. "We killed many of the nahgos," he screamed, totally out of breath.

Etu could not believe what he just heard. He was sure it was Akando's voice and it was so close, it seemed as though the boy stood immediately over him---something about…nahgos. He looked through the blinding light and barely made out two shadowy figures on the other side of the glow---and then the faraway voice of Kuruk. "Etu killed this black one," he heard him say.

With a casual effort, Kuruk lifted the heavy wolf up. He had an angry look on his face as he slammed the pack's leader to the ground as if it was nothing more than a skinned fur. After examining the deep wounds in Etu, he knew the end was near for the fallen hunter, but said nothing to Akando.

Although Akando felt for Etu the horrible wounds he bore, death was not what the boy saw. The rage of the hunt was still pulsing through his veins. He was crazed from it.

"Kuruk killed this many nahgos," he excitedly said, with fast words and holding up four fingers.

Etu filled his lungs and could barely get the words out. "How many...did...you kill, little Akando?"

"I killed this," the boy answered, holding two fingers out for him to see. "I will wear the nahgo and own his spirit."

Taking hold of the boy's fingers, Etu brought them to his chest and held on to them tightly. He could not believe any of this. After all that had happened, here was little Akando holding out two blurry fingers to him. Nothing could have made him feel better than to see the boy's excitement.

"And I," Etu softly said. "I own this leader's spirit."

His grip loosened from the boy's fingers and then the three grew silent. It was a while that Kuruk waited there by Etu's side without saying anything.

Akando stood and stepped back when Kuruk reached over to place his hand flat on top of Etu's chest. In a deep voice and with resonance like the roar of a saber tooth, he bellowed, "Yes, Etu, you now own the black ones spirit. Run fast to the clouds my young brother."

Akando looked on with a beginning of tears as the leader of first hunters closed Etu's eyelids. Lowering his head, he shook with remorse and did not hear when Kuruk left quietly. It was a long while that Akando waited by Etu's side, before he joined the rest of the men gathering around Sewati.

Having encircled the wolf pack with torches, the rest of the hunters, by now, had run most of them into the river. Once there, it was easy to charge in after the slow swimming wolves and club them from behind as they struggled in the water.

Everyone there had at least one prize kill---everyone except for Kajika, Carrier of the Ochre. Lan had four---Sewati, five.

First and second hunters collected around Sewati, dragging their wolf carcasses behind. Left in a pile, they waited for the rest to join them while interrupting one another with stories of their kills.

Seeing Lan by the river with Qaletaga, Sewati said, "This Mowatchi stands with his little nahgos like a woman."

The men all laughed.

"He is many times too weak," he chided.

Dragging two wolves next to his other three, Sewati continued the snide remarks. "It is the women this Mowatchi should be with and not our first hunters."

Moki, a third hunter, joined in. "Sewati, you have no woman. You can take this Mowatchi for yourself."

More laughter.

Akando heard enough. He left his two wolves with the rest and spoke loud enough for all to hear. "The Mowatchi made his fix to Etu's leg. For that he is strong with me."

The men fell silent.

Sewati exhaled hot breath through clenched teeth. Pointing at Akando, he addressed the men, his voice cracking as he spoke. "This one talks of the Mowatchi like he is a brother. Etu is no more! No one can change that. Not you, not him and not the Mowatchi. It is the will of the death spirits."

Before Akando could answer, Sewati turned away to face the river, his hands clasped behind his back.

"No," Akando said, "We cannot change that. It is Lan's will that is with all of us," emphasizing his point by waving in the men's direction.

While keeping his focus on the river, Sewati retorted, "Humph! His will did nothing. Etu is no longer here."

"Yes…his power did nothing for Etu, but his will was strong."

Enraged, Sewati stomped over to the pile of wolf carcasses and kicked them hard. He then scanned the blank faces of the straight line of men who were standing behind their fiery torches and glared at them. "He is not a brother to me."

Remaining fast with his son, Achak returned Sewati's stern look. "The Mowatchi is strong with me as he is strong with Nakoma."

"The Mowatchi does not belong with us!" Sewati screamed.

Achak flinched and stepped away from the crazed man that was shouting into his face.

Akando kept his focus on Sewati, worried for his father.

Standing with his second hunters, Nayati smirked. Upon seeing that, Sewati rushed over to him swinging his hairy arms and looking directly at him. "The Mowatchi does not belong and his woman does not belong."

The leader of second hunters cowered and lowered his head. Every man there stood tight lipped and diverted their gaze lest they be next.

Akando left the men and returned to Etu's body.

Beyond the firelight and the men standing there, Kuruk paced quietly in the darkness. He was one with Sewati and had no desire to over shadow him with his higher status. He continued to pace at a distance, his arms folded across his chest.

Of the following of cringing underlings, a meek voice 'rose from the end of the group. "Th…the Mowatchi is strong with me." Kajika took in a shaky breath as he chose the words he wanted to say carefully. He even ventured to take a couple of bold steps forward of the row to spill out those words as fast as he could. "The Mowatchi is why we come to Etu."

Having emerged from the darkness, Kuruk stood behind Sewati with his arms still folded across his chest where he waited for them to finish what they had to say.

With all of the agreeing head nods shaking around him, Kajika thought surely Sewati would also agree with him. He checked, but he had turned his head to the side as though he could not believe what he was hearing.

Cautiously, he continued. "The Mowatchi is one with…"

Infuriated, Sewati would hear no more of it. "What is it that this man speaks? His words have no meaning to me."

He pushed the flinching Kajika back in line. "The Mowatchi is one only with the people he left in the high place. He cares nothing for us."

From behind Sewati, Kuruk lowered his head, stepped around him and casually strode in front of the line of men. "Enough! It is Nakoma who sends the Mowatchi to take this walk with us. There is nothing more."

Akando returned and stood alongside Kuruk with Etu's broken spear in his hands. "Etu would be with us as I speak to you. The Mowatchi did not know the black nahgo would take him as no one here did."

Even Sewati had to realize, as did every man there, that had it not been for the dire wolves, Etu would still be alive...and only because of Lan. They had no one to blame but themselves for not getting there in time.

Together as a group, the men joined Lan and Qaletaga by the river to assure the Mowatchi they harbored no resentment toward him. They patted him on the shoulders along with a lot of backslapping. When it was Kuruk's turn, he merely raised his lower lip and gave him a slow head nod, said nothing and walked away.

While Etu's body burned, wolf carcasses were skinned. Achak tended a fire rich with the smell of roasting wolf meat. None of the dried meat they carried in was eaten. Satisfied and full, nearly all of them helped to build up a pile of dung higher than themselves. The resulting bon fire lit up the entire bank.

There is something about fire that consoles those who reach out for its comfort---to join together---to exchange ideas. It was a time for men to be men, to taunt one another, to entertain; or just a time to be heard.

Lan sat with his elbows on his thighs and looked at the rest of the circle of sitting men, struck at how strange his relationship was with them. He was here among an entire tribe of much bigger men, alone and comparably safe from harm. Yet, he could never have ever foreseen any of this.

All around, the men stared simian-like into a fire that elongated their faces. Eye sockets became deeply shadowed, while cheek bones became more prominent. Teeth turned into surrealistic exaggerations of themselves, the toothy laughters, like those of a horrible dream. However, here all was well within the circle of men and Lan was well inside of it.

Eager to tell his story first, the third hunter, Moki, came to the forefront. "I remember a distant time before Kajika received his shona and became strong like he is now. He walked with us when the nag boksta were sleeping in the grass and we did not know."

"Kajika is sleeping in the grass right now," Kuruk teased, shaking the carrier of ochre as if to wake him.

Moki held his hands up to hold back the laughter that followed. "The nag boksta were many. We were all without words. We did not want to wake them, but their eyes were big like this."

Moki widened his excessively.

Another round of laughter ensued.

"We did not move. The nag boksta did not move. It was many times too long that we stood there looking at the nag boksta that were looking back at us. It was then that we saw one of them stand up and Kajika did this…

AAAhhhhheeeeeeeaaahhh!"

Moki's hellish impersonation of Kajika's scream got everyone roaring. Moki himself could not stop from doubling over while pointing at him.

"What did they do then," Nayati asked, though he already knew.

Moki could not contain himself. He could barely get the words out between his hysterical laughter. Exaggerating Kajika's fright, Moki's eyes widened while his whole body shivered, which got everyone laughing again. The topic soon turned to women and a debate over whose was best at love making.

Beyond the light of the bonfire, Sewati remained hidden with a steady and stern focus on the Mowatchi. Grumbling under his breath, he left to walk alone to the river.

With no one else coming forward, Achak stood with the fire to his back. "Lan…tell us about the high place you walked before this."

Other voices followed. "Say your words," Qaletaga encouraged. "I too would like to hear of the high place."

"And I," said Nayati.

"I also would like to hear of the high place," said Abooksigun.

Brushing the dirt off his legs, Lan stood and prepared to do the best he could to describe his people to them. For, he had an enthusiastic audience with a steady stream of interruptions and request to repeat what they did not understand. He told of short faced bears and cave lions, the rocky landscapes, the high cliffs, the water fall, the ocean and all of the tribes along the coast. Like mesmerized boys the men wanted to hear more, so he told them how he, along with Ayashe and Etu, were surrounded by saber tooth tigers, wolves and coyotes and finally about mighty Aleeka.

"The kill sticks you carry, how do you use them," said Kuruk, with genuine interest.

"I will show you my way to kill the nahgo."

Having killed the wolves in the darkness, no one had witnessed the power of the bow. Lan set the quiver on the ground and took out one of the longest arrows. All eyes followed his every move as grass was wound around the blade and secured to it. Immersed in the fat that had pooled beneath the cooked wolves, the blade was lit and the tail end of the arrow hooked into the bow. Like a comet streaking across the sky, the arrow flashed brightly in a long, high arc to the far side of the river. A trail of sparks and twisting white smoke followed behind.

Everyone there expressed their awe with gaping mouths followed by approving grunts. None of them saw anything like it. Other than an atlatl, there was a limit to how far a spear or rock could be thrown. The men excitedly talked over one another.

"His kill stick has a strong spirit."

"It can kill from a greater distance."

"It is more than I or any man here can throw it."

Kuruk removed one of the arrows from the quiver. "Where did you find the black rocks?"

Examining the spear, Moki was just as perplexed.

Achak had an important question to ask as well. "Nakoma tells us there are those from the high place that eat people."

A profusion of more questions and opinions followed.

"What is their taste?"

"Maybe it is like the Jonga."

"No! It is like the bo bo!"

"Is it true they eat the eyes of their enemies?"

Moki grabbed Akando's arm and acted as though he was about to bite it. "Will I be more strong if I eat this?"

Along with the others, Akando found that amusing. "If you eat my arm, your look will be like mine."

Questions and answers trickled down to a few, until one by one the men left to find places to sleep. Along the river, within beds of reeds, frogs croaked love songs to beautiful green maidens. And beyond the river, somewhere far out on the grasslands, a lone wolf howled companionless and distant.

So he could be alone with his thoughts of Ayashe and the way she smiled, Lan found a place off to the side to sleep.

She sat by the waterfall fingering strands of her hair, the evening light, softening her features. Behind her, the falling river cascaded over rocks on its way to chase the depths.

He went to her and caressed the pink rose of her breast, the feel of her hair brushing against his hand so real. Her sweet smell was remembered as though she was there before him, her long lashed, dark eyes dreamily looking back.

And then it all faded away. Something was wrong. He was suffocating. He could not move. He was being pulled out of his dream. Forcing his eyes open, he saw Sewati looking down at him while crushing his weight into his chest. Covering Lan's mouth with one hand, Sewati held a tight grip on his throat with the other.

The netting was empty when Lan reached for his ax. He gasped for air while the man's penetrating stare looked back with villainous intentions. The lead first hunter continued to lean into him, holding him down. Finally, in a softened voice, he spoke with relaxed words.

"Does this Mowatchi own his fear or does fear own this Mowatchi? Soon, my hunters will look to the thunderfoot. When the thunderfoot run, you and I will run with them. My hunters will only see the thunderfoot and that is all they will see. It is then that you will be in my eyes. It will not be in theirs to see me hunt you. No one will know that it is I, Sewati that will take away your life spirit."

Sewati kept his grip on him and waited for the words to be absorbed. He got up slowly, his focus still on Lan, grinned and calmly walked away.

For the rest of that night, Lan sat up with the ax in one hand and the spear in the other. In the early light, Akando awoke and was surprised to see him sitting there with his head hanging over in a half sleep. Moki had awoken also, leaning to shake Achak. Gradually, the camp stirred until everyone was standing.

"Sewati is no longer here," Qaletaga said to Moki.

Without so much as a raised brow, Moki pointed at the fresh tracks that were leading to the river. "Sewati goes to find your woman," he playfully teased. He slapped Qaletaga on the back, to which Qaletaga quickly wrestled him to the ground and tweaked his nose. Both helped one another up with Qaletaga disheveling Moki's hair.

Two and one half days later

The morning sun barely showed itself above the horizon when Okhmhaka's young mammoth began to feed in the shallows. Within a crowd of reeds, it happily took the stems Ayashe had collected.

As soon as Sewati saw them all together, he stopped short.

It was good that I took this long walk ahead of the others. She is there with Okhmhaka and not the women. She does not belong with us. When I am finished with her, I will look to the thunderfoot he calls *Rama. It must also be killed.*

Sitting on the mammoth, Okhmhaka turned back from looking at the trail. "Sewati is there. He looks to you."

Ayashe chose not to turn her head. "Are there no men with him?"

The boy stretched to see. "Only Sewati, he stands and says nothing."

"Do you not see Lan?"

He shook his head no.

"Do not look to him," she said.

"He walks this way, now," the boy said.

Refraining from scowling like he wanted to, Sewati forced a smile, his entire demeanor changing uncharacteristically. "Ayashe, it is to you that I wish to speak."

Ayashe worried for the boy. "You have a sad look for me, little one."

"He looks to you in a bad way. I do not feel good on this," he replied.

"I will talk to the ugly one and then I will go back with you and Rama. Stay and wait for me."

Fully naked, she waded onto the bank, turning her back to Sewati while putting on her skirt. Straightening it out, she brushed off the sand, brought her soaking wet braid around to the front and began to squeeze the water from it.

Sewati spoke loudly. "Your Mowatchi takes his walk with Qaletaga to Mantotohpa."

Her back still to him, she continued to fumble with the braid. "Do you not hear?"

She tilted her head slightly to the side. "I will wait here."

"He will not come! He goes to Mantotohpa!"

"It is not in my head that Lan would take that walk. It is I that has the need to go there...not Lan."

"That is why he sends me to you."

"No...I will wait with Nakoma."

Impatient, Sewati raised his voice even louder. "Your Mowatchi will not come. He took the walk with Qaletaga. He waits for you with Mantotohpa. I will take you...that is his words."

She folded her arms, still looking away from him and answered in a calm voice. "No, I will stay here and he will come to me...not to Mantotohpa."

"Then stay! I will leave you here and go to Mantotohpa alone. Your Mowatchi has no need to walk this way."

Ayashe spun around, looked him in the eye and blurted out loud. "Go then to Mantotohpa. It is many times good that you go."

Without another word, Sewati returned her long glare and left to follow the river in the direction of Mantotohpa's tribe. His strides were long and quick and heavy footed, while inside, he fumed with bitterness.

"He does go to Mantotohpa!" Okhmhaka stated, surprised.

Ayashe turned back to him while fixing her braid. "So...his words are true words." My only worry now is for Yahto. He will be mad when he sees a man from the high place...more than Mantotohpa. I must go to Mantotohpa before Lan gets there."

"I will go with your walk on my Rama," the boy said.

"That will never be Nakoma's wish. I will go with the ugly one alone. He will not touch me; and your Rama only walks from here to the covers. How would you make him follow to Mantotohpa?" She waited for a reply. When none came, she said, "See...it cannot be done."

Okhmhaka slipped off the side of the mammoth, leaving the animal in the river.

"Why do you worry," she said. Has this ugly one hurt any woman here?"

She leaned over and touched his face with her own, leaving a wet spot on his cheek. "He is a leader of first hunters. That is why Kuruk sends him."

Sulking, Okhmhaka glared back. "Why does your mouth touch my face?" He snapped, flicking the back of his hand across his cheek to brush off the wet spot.

Before he had the chance to say anything else, she patted him on the head and hurried to catch up with Sewati. She missed Akule and Alawa, as well as Mantotohpa. Mantotohpa had always been like a father to her. Kitchi, her best friend since childhood, would have her own children by now. Ayashe imagined her with arms outstretched to greet her. She could not wait.

In the hopes that Rama would follow her, the boy climbed onto the mammoth's back and kicked behind both ears. "Go Rama!"

As was his habit, Rama lifted out of the water and slowly ambled toward the tents.

"No! To Ayashe!" Okhmhaka barked.

He kicked the left side just behind the ear to make the animal turn that way. With no response he kicked again, but it only caused Rama to stand motionless and confused. After continually kicking left with his heel, the mammoth turned in a continuous circle to the left. Irritated, Okhmhaka kicked the right side, which only prompted it to circle right.

Frustrated, he jumped off. "Why do you not go where it is that I talk?"

Maybe it is best this way. It would not please Nakoma if I go to Mantotohpa. It is much too far. I will tell him that Sewati goes there with Ayashe.

By now, Sewati was far ahead. Ayashe had to run to catch up. "Your steps are many times too fast," she shouted.

Without answering, Sewati kept walking. Despite the heat, he distanced himself quickly from Nakoma's camp. Neither one spoke another word.

The only concern was if she changed her mind about following him. If she did, she would have to do it before nightfall. The way back would be treacherous alone, especially at night. The night was when the jongas and nahgos hunted these very same trails and she had no ax to protect herself or any way to make a fire.

Sewati's height stretched above the vegetation. At every curve she quickened her steps to keep up with his spindly legs. His long arms hung downward, paddling the palms behind like duck feet. As he walked, his head bobbed between drooping shoulders. From time to time, he pivoted it around to see if she was still there, his bristly brimmed stares, glaring intensely without breaking stride. His head would then pivot back to the front.

A narrow side trail, dense with growth, led away from the river. Ayashe was not sure about the new trail he was taking, since she could not remember the way she had come during the trade to Matwua. She never had a reason to concern herself with direction. She had always followed her tribe unquestioningly, occupying herself with conversation or watching animals in the surrounding landscape.

Why do I worry, he is a first hunter? It is six of the dark times that I am not with Lan and I will wait no longer. I must see him.

She snapped apart the sinew from the finger bone necklace and dropped it where it would be readily seen, at the entrance to the new trail.

Late afternoon; outside Nakoma's tent
"It is good that you returned with so many nahgos," said Nakoma, upon greeting the arrival of Kuruk and the men. "Where is Etu?"

"The nahgos took him," said Kuruk. "We put him in our fire where we found him."

"The Nahgos took him?" The tribe's leader looked away, shaking his head. "This saddens me, all this for nothing."

Eying Lan, he said, "Your Ayashe takes the walk with Sewati. His words to Ayashe were said to be your words. This is what Okhmhaka told me and now they go to Mantotohpa to find you. Why are you here with my men and not taking your walk to Mantotohpa?"

Surprised, Lan asked, "When did they leave?"

Okhmhaka pointed to where the morning sunrise had been at the time of Ayashe's departure. "Sun was there. It is long that they left to follow the river."

"I will find his path and when he is in my eyes I will finish…"

"Lan…wait!" said Nakoma.

Running off, Lan left before anyone could stop him.

The rest of the tribe first saw the Mowatchi when he ran past. They then saw their leader running after him with the wolf heads slapping against his chest. Nakoma tried to hold onto the ram horn headdress, but it slipped off and crashed to the ground behind him. Both wolf heads continued to dance about like unwilling riders, tortuously bouncing about until finally being thrown hard to ground.

At the river, Nakoma caught up with Lan. Running up out of breath, Kajika held out the headdress and wolf heads he picked up along the way.

"Lan! Leave my first hunter to me," Nakoma ordered.

In the Mowatchi, he saw the killing instinct that so obsessed his people. Everything he learned from him was there in his face. He clearly saw the difference between his own people and Lan's people, men who killed one another as a means to satisfy any wrong doings, whether true or not or only conjectured as true. In the Mowatchi was a will to kill for any reason or for no reason at all, a matter of course as easily dismissed as a hunt for meat.

"I will do what I must," said Lan.

"Then my men will go with you."

He looked hard at Nakoma. "I do not need your men. I will find this Sewati. If he does not touch Ayashe then he will live. If not…"

"I know the way to Mantotohpa." Having caught up to them, Akando spoke excitedly. "The trails are many and the way cannot be seen in the coming dark time. How will you know where it is that you walk?"

"I can no longer wait."

"Then I will take your walk with you," said Akando, looking at the tribe's leader for approval.

"It is good that you take him," Nakoma said.

"I can be your nahgo brother," said the boy.

Lan held him by the shoulders and looked directly into his eyes. "I do not want you to be my nahgo brother. If you would be my two knife brother, I will think on it."

"Twoniff? What is twoniff?"

"Nag boksta."

No longer willing to waste any more time, Lan turned from them and jogged up the bank.

Akando called after him. "Then I will be your twoniff brother." He ran to catch up.

Continuing at a steady pace, Lan removed the saber tooth tiger fang from around his neck and handed it to Akando as the boy ran alongside. "This is the spirit of the two knife. Wear this and he will run with you."

Left to stand alone on the bank with Kajika, Nakoma sharply snapped at him, "Give me that…and that."

He grabbed the wolf heads and headdress from a flinching Kajika. The two returned to the tents where the leader called for three of his best to join the search. Along with them he sent the third hunter, Moki. If for some reason they had to split up, no one would have to walk alone.

"You and Achak go with Kuruk and Qaletaga. I do not want to see Sewati's death from this Mowatchi."

<hr />

Reaching the side trail, Lan picked up Ayashe's finger bone necklace. "This is the way they walked. The string is broken…no blood. It is the finger she wears around her neck and now it is here."

Akando called out to Lan who was already ahead of him. "They are in the thunderfoot trail."

He placed his ax where they found the finger bone to mark it for the others and then hurried to catch up to Lan.

At the water's edge, Rama refused anything Okhmhaka tried to give him for the afternoon feeding. He even refused to go into the water.

"Why do you not eat, Rama?"

At any other time, the mammoth would have welcomed the trip to the river. Instead, it kept sniffing the ground while the rest of its bulk swayed from side to side.

"If you will not eat or drink, then we will go back and I will tie you to the ground."

The boy climbed on and kicked the animal behind the ear, but as before, the mammoth refused to move.

At that moment, Qaletaga and Kuruk ran past them. Achak followed at a slower pace along with Moki.

"They go to find Ayashe," Okhmhaka said to Rama. With no luck at getting his pet to comply, he got ready to jump to the ground. Just when he was about to, Rama bolted along the bank with both of the boy's legs hanging off the animal's right side. His body flopped up and down while hanging on to the long hairs on top of Rama's head. It took all of his strength to get a leg over its neck. "Rama! Where…?"

Holding on tightly, Okhmhaka's rear end bounced every time the mammoth took a step. Though the ride was exhilarating, it was also uncomfortable. With no choice but to hang on, he bounced along as the mammoth hurried stiff legged across the hard-packed mud.

"Okhmhaka!" Achak shouted, upon seeing the mammoth pass him by. The elder was beside himself. It was an exciting sight, even for him.

"My wish is to do that," said Moki, wide eyed and stretching to see. "I will get my own thunderfoot the next time we hunt them."

By the time the boy shot past Kuruk and Qaletaga, he learned to rise up on his knees to soften the ride.

Amazed, Kuruk's jaw dropped. "How did you…?"

His finger was left pointing down the bank at the fleeing mammoth. Never in the farthest reaches of his mind did he ever contemplate such a possibility.

Qaletaga, equally impressed, laughed out loud and along with Kuruk, patted one another over the boy's incredible feat.

For Okhmhaka, this was a whole new adventure. His smile stretched from ear to ear. "Rama, you give me a great shona." The boy could not stop laughing.

CHAPTER 9
THE THUNDERFOOT TRAIL

A late sun glowed brilliantly above the horizon. From his high vantage point on the mammoth, Okhmhaka noticed the back leg of the thunderfoot trail go by. He was well familiar with the trails inside, having been part of hunts that took place there since reaching his ninth summer. As soon as Rama got to the front leg of the thunderfoot trail, the animal slowed and nosed the ground, then suddenly veered away from the river.

"Good Rama!" He shouted, noticing Akando's ax lying there.

When Kuruk and Achak arrived at the same trail, Kuruk picked up the ax, his face, full of worry. "This is Akando's!" This is not the way to Mantotohpa. Sewati has no wish to go there."

"Okhmhaka and his thunderfoot…the Mowatchi and Akando, they all go the same way," said Achak, eying the mammoth tracks.

"Ayashe will see her death from Sewati," Kuruk worried. "Let us go to Kajika and Moki. We can take the back trail together and face this Sewati before this Mowatchi finds him."

Exhausted from walking all morning and part of that afternoon, Ayashe stopped to wipe sweat from her face. The trail they took after leaving the river and where she had left the finger bone had eventually widened and went straight with the sun on her left. At the time, their walk had seemed long and endless. They then turned to their left into a side trail where she stuck a few feathers from her skirt into the ground. At that point she remembered the sun shined in front of her on its journey toward the low horizon, but that was quite a while ago. The curve ahead would soon put the setting sun behind her. They were going around in a circle.

This will take me to the same place near where I left the feathers. Five fingers! It will soon be dark.

She brought her hand down and called out to Sewati. "This is not the way. All this walk and we go nowhere."

Sewati glanced at her, turned back to the front and grinned.

Ha! She knows nothing of this walk we call the thunderfoot trail.

In the form of a mammoth standing at the river and facing west, the trail cut through tall grass and took a full day to complete. It began by taking either one of two trails representing the front and back legs of the animal, both of which led away from the river in parallel. At this point, where the feet touched the river, the trails were close together.

Following the front leg at the west end, as Sewati had done, led to a large circular loop to the left of the main trail. Called the tusk trail, it was where they were now and soon about to approach its end. At the main trail just ahead, another loop in the shape of a raised trunk, curved to the left and around in a circle the same way. It led to the back trail or the top of the mammoth's body.

Continuing east; or along the back of the mammoth would lead to a short side trail representing the tail of the animal which ended at a pond. From the tail, a narrow path representing the hind quarters and back leg of the body, returned to the river. This allowed hunters exiting from both ends of the mammoth trail to join up.

Ayashe knew they were a long way from Mantotohpa's tents. *I do not want to sleep with this man. We must walk until we see their smoke.*

When she looked up again, Sewati was gone. Behind, lay the empty trail and a long way to the river---too far to walk alone. Without anything to defend herself from predators, she worried while searching the ground.

Not one rock in all this grass. My need is more for water and it is Sewati that carries it.

She ran to catch up and caught a glimpse of one of his legs just as he entered the trunk trail. There, his long strides kept him far ahead. Hurrying along, the trail seemed devoid of animal life of any kind. Tired, she took a quick check of the sun's position. It was now back on her left and seemed to be going down faster than she anticipated. Ahead, the curve continued in a gradual, almost undetectable circular direction toward the right. She ran until she was nearly out of breath, then slowed to a pace she could maintain for a while. Hearing something in the brush, she ran hard again until she had to stop to catch her breath. Bending over, she held onto her knees to brace herself from keeling over. She could go no further---not without a short rest and something to drink and eat.

I will ask Sewati for water. He carries meat. I will ask him for some.

Still panting, she looked up and saw Sewati standing there, having stepped out from behind a tight growth of stems. She froze at the sight of him, his groin patch in his hand. The freakish length of his manhood stood erect and it frightened her as soon as she saw it. She turned to run, taking only four steps before Sewati had her by the braid. He threw his spear to the ground and slapped her so hard; it sent her sprawling with her legs spread apart and her skirt above her hips.

"Oh!" she cried. Stunned and faint, she tried to stand, but immediately fell back down.

"Humph! So…it is your wish to go to Mantotohpa and in your head that I should take you to him?"

His chest lifted and fell from the sight of her full breast belling to the sides---so inviting to be fondled and bitten. He stared at her hirsute mound while untying slowly, the heavy ax from his waist. It dropped next to the spear with a loud thud.

Everything in front of Ayashe appeared blurry and spinning around her head. "If it is not your wish to go to Mantotohpa, we can go back to Nakoma...together."

Sewati said nothing. He stepped quietly between her legs, looked angrily down at her and reached around with a thumb to lift the water skin from his shoulder. It fell behind his back and exploded on the ground. Breathing heavily, he scowled. "There will be no more Nakoma...no more Mantotohpa and no more of your Mowatchi. I will finish you here."

Wiping blood from the corner of her mouth, Ayashe looked up at the blurry image of his body standing over her, tall and spinning around her with his legs spread apart. The spinning slowed with a repeat of his manhood drooping heavily to the side, thick with veins and a wide girth. She suddenly realized how far up her skirt was and how fully exposed she was to him.

Sewati's foot pressed into her stomach, holding her down.

She wiped off the semen drops that were dripping down with disgust. "Your look is like that of a jonga."

"Where is your Mowatchi...he does not come to you?"

"He will come and he will finish you," she said, shaking.

Overwhelmed by the thrill he felt for what he was about to do, Sewati dropped to his knees and pushed her shoulders to the ground. He snatched her by the throat and quickly guided his manhood deep inside.

Ayashe shrieked.

"I will make you feel pain. You are like the others," he yelled.

Ayashe started to cry. He was hurting her. She tried to push him away. "Lan will find you and take your life spirit," she screamed.

It pleasured Sewati to see the pain in her face every time he pushed into her. "Like...like Una. You are like her...so pretty. She had to be killed. When this is over, I will finish you the same way."

Ayashe made a try at grabbing the ax.

Reluctantly, he slipped out of her to kick the heavy stone away. He then grabbed her by the ankles and spread her legs over her shoulders. Entering her hard, he went in deep to her cry of resistance.

Grunting, he thrust his member into her again and again. "You are the kind I hate…so pretty."

Ayashe tried to lift her head high enough to sink her teeth into one of his nipples, but with her legs held over her shoulders, she could not reach it. She swiped at his eyes, managing only to scrape across his cheek. Sweat droplets dripped onto her face as she slashed at him again.

Withdrawing from her, Sewati caught both wrists. The back of his hand stung the side of her face, making everything out front turn white, melting her resistance.

Too frightened to do anything more, she cried as she lay back with submission. To live for Lan, she now knew she had to give herself over to Sewati. She tried to look as appealing as she could, though shook for the fear of him. She spread her legs out to the sides and lifted her mound high with her chest swelling in and out from the heavy breathing she could not control. She could not stop crying.

Her passiveness only encouraged Sewati's anger. He stood over her so she could see the violating part of him that caused her so much pain.

"Turn the other way!" He shouted.

Realizing this could be her last and only chance to save herself; she slowly got onto her knees and spread her legs apart. As Sewati lowered himself down, she suddenly darted for the ax on all fours.

"So…it is my ax you look for. It will not help you." He laughed.

Ayashe grabbed it, almost losing the huge rock when it tipped clumsily to the side. Up on her knees, she lifted it over her head where it wobbled uncontrollably to Sewati's snickering laughter.

He calmly walked over to her and stood with both hands on his hips. "So! This is your great power?"

Ayashe held the ax up while looking at his image through blurry tears. She squeezed her eyes shut and looked again, knowing she could not continue to hold the extremely heavy ax up much longer. It was shaking all over the place.

His lips touching her ear, Sewati spoke with soft, raspy words that sounded eerily kind. "Enough! There is nothing you can do. Soon, it will all be finished."

He reached for her braid, but the ax was already on the way down. Ayashe drove the heavy ax into his foot with all of her strength. Sewati's earsplitting cry sounded dreadful. The sharp stone had cracked heavily into bone, caving in the crown and splintering everything inside. Sharp pieces stabbed through the skin.

With no regard for direction, Ayashe jumped to her feet and ran. Whichever way the trail took her, she was willing to go. She was lost, so what did it matter which way she went as long as it was far from him. She ran knowing Sewati was right behind her. Afraid to look, she desperately followed the trail until coming to a fork. Turning left along the backbone of the mammoth trail, she kept on running, then walking, then running again. Her lungs filled with hot musty air as she listened for the running steps she knew she would soon hear. Finally stopping to turn around, she checked down the trail while gasping to get her breath back. The grass on both sides swayed in the incessant wind with no sign of the first hunter. She strained to listen, but other than the wind, there was nothing else. It was too hard to believe---almost laughable.

He gave me no choice. He hurt me and would have killed me, and now I must find the river.

Facing the light of the setting sun, no longer visible behind the growth, she guessed at its location somewhere below the brightness. She turned from it to check the trail ahead.

If this takes me to the river, I can find my way in the dark.

With a hope that the predator packs were hunting elsewhere, she stayed with her choice until seeing a large clearing to the side of the trail. She warily crept up to it and peered inside. At its center, the ground appeared trampled and mottled with clumps of uprooted brush and grass. Expansive, the clearing was enclosed with thick walls of tall grass.

The *thunderfoot know of this place!*

She stood in the middle and checked along the edge where the unbroken walls circled back to the trail. Deep red clouds enflamed the skies, while all around, grass leaned from the blowing wind. High above, a lone hawk soared in its daily vigil for rats. Circling with wing tips pointed skyward, it used the last bit of daylight in its effort to beat the night. For in that coming darkness would secret the leaning grass, as it would secret the tragedies that would unfold within them.

If he could walk, he would be here to finish me.

While standing perfectly still, she searched the line of growth for movement. The thought of spending a night out here was not something she wanted to think about as long as there was some light left. She took in the steamy air and let out a powerless resolve. It was all so terrifying, though the fear was no longer for Sewati. The real danger was for the coming dark time---here, where nag bokstas and nahgos ran these very same trails, predators that would certainly come on her scent and the easy kill she would make. She returned to the trail where the dark and narrow walls lost all of the familiarity they had when there was more sunlight. Thankfully, it appeared empty. Encouraged, she went back to the middle of the darkening clearing where there was still a little light left and where she was sure she would be alone.

Then the scraping of shuffling paws sounded from the trail. She held her breath. A young coyote with a torn ear and certain the night was his, turned a wet pulsing nose around the last of the stems to peer inside.

Startled at first, Ayashe had no need to worry. She only had to remain calm. If it persisted, she could risk yelling out. That and a few clumps of hard dirt thrown in its direction should frighten it enough to send it away.

Torn Ear raised and lowered its head, gaging her size as if considering the possibility of bringing down so sizable a prey all by itself. It stealthily neared, stopping after a few short steps to examine the human's odor, disbelieving the good fortune it had stumbled upon.

Backing up from the middle, Ayashe scanned the ground for something of use, something to throw, but it was bare and the thunder foot waste too soft to be of any use. She swelled her chest and spread her arms boldly outward.

"Go little jonga! You cannot eat me. My life spirit is not for you to take."

The coyote remained at the entrance, quietly pointing its nose at whichever body part she moved. When it appeared as if the coyote was about to leave, it turned its head rearward to look down the trail. As if waiting for something, the scavenger stayed in that same position without turning back.

More rustling could be heard. Birds she hoped. She listened for the calls, but there was no other sound except the rustling noise and now the soft steps of fifteen more coyotes as the rest of the pack silently entered the clearing in a long file, one behind the other. No longer lifeless and barren, the once empty space began to fill with the bodies of the entire pack.

She tripped over a hole in the ground just when the pack started to circle around her. Curious gazes fixed on her as the rest of the continuous line of scavengers single filed inside. The ones in front were pushed in from behind until Ayashe was completely surrounded by the pack and their musky odor. It became so strong it started to irritate the inside of her nose.

Lastly, a large alpha female rounded in from the trail, her tail raised high with authority. The pack's leader suddenly lashed out at a subordinate male, forcing it to the outside.

The rest stood by patiently, some sitting on their rumps. Tongues pulsated from open jaws while a few nervously paced about. The wait frustrated many of the others as they started up with a resurgence of loud calls.

Ayashe held her stomach from the quivering inside with shaking hands. *This is where the jonga will come first. They will begin to eat me while I still live. I will soon see my own death and the end of my life spirit with no chance to go to the sky.*

She closed her eyes and could still hear shuffling and snickering as the coyotes settled disputes among themselves. She was not going to look.

"Eat fast. I do not want to feel your teeth."

And then all was silent. When nothing happened, she dared to open her eyes. Something was making the coyotes slink to the very back of the clearing. Familiar with their cowering ways, she turned to stare at the trail.

A new and louder set of shuffling paws was coming from the game trail. Although frightened before, the beast that was yet to come sent searing hot chills up her spine. She kept staring and listening, backing up as the shuffling grew louder---closer, and then they were there, causing the coyotes to scatter at the back and pace about nervously.

The head of the beast was all she could see, having stopped to peer into the clearing. It took another step inside and now she could see its entirety, a male saber tooth tiger, an animal six times her size. To further insure its dominance over the kill, the huge cat's eyes went shallow and then it roared, its jaws gaping immensely wide with incisors that were as long as its head. Within the clearing, the sound of it was so loud it scattered the jonga. Ayashe, on the verge of fainting, continued to breathe heavily with the hope that her heart would stop beating.

The nag boksta follow the jonga. It is there way.

Coyote's had a keen sense of smell, far greater than a saber tooth tiger's. They had a symbiotic relationship with each other.

The saber tooth relied on them to sniff out large prey while in turn, the coyotes were left the spoils.

The male fully entered the clearing along with his mate, an animal that was nearly as big as him. Ayashe now knew what she must do. She would chant for the nag boksta to take her life spirit. It was the way of her people and salvation from the jonga that would deny her access to her ancestors in the sky.

Still frightened beyond anything she ever experienced in her life, she stood tall, raised her arms to the sky and began her chant.

It was late in the day when Rama passed by the tusk trail and much later still when Ayashe's fresh scent drew him into the trunk. As soon as Okhmhaka saw Sewati, he tried to stop Rama, but the mammoth was steadfast on finding her.

To keep the broken pieces together, Sewati held onto his foot with both hands. He glared up at the boy and sneered. It was all he could do but to look on in disbelief at the sight of him riding by on top of the mammoth.

"Rama will not stop," Okhmhaka yelled. "Where is Ayashe?"

In obvious pain, the first hunter muttered to himself and was not understood. Puzzled, Okhmhaka stared at all the blood as he was carried along. The trail ahead lay in shadow and he worried for the coming dark time. Arriving at the back trail, Rama veered left and broke into a charge along with a series of trumpeting. When they arrived at the clearing, the juvenile bull ran in and slammed the first of the saber tooth tiger's out of the way. Startled, both cats bolted for the opening and away from the crazed mammoth.

Rama quickly drove his tusk into the chest of one of the scattering coyotes, killing it instantly. Without stopping, he targeted another one and sliced a tusk deep inside the animal's gut. With the dead coyote hanging off the end of it, Rama swooped his head downward and swept a cowering female off the ground. He lifted the two of them high into the air and then dropped them back down. Still alive, the second coyote squirmed around to try and stand. Rama stepped on it and slowly pressed his foot down hard. One by one, the ribs cracked until the animal's entire rib cage suddenly caved in.

It was the saber tooth's experience that wherever there was one mammoth there would soon be others. The male did not want to tangle with an entire herd, no less Aleeka, especially since the herd's stench was still strong inside the clearing. The rest of the coyotes followed until the runaway pack settled into a slow lope.

As they ran through the trail, the saber tooth cat's nosed the ground for the fresh scent stewing inside the hot dank air. The male stopped to assess it and was soon joined by its mate, their nostrils flexing in and out for the odor of blood coming from the trunk trail. The leader ran ahead of the others with hunger pains rumbling inside his belly. Without slowing, he followed the trail for a kill that would soon feed them all.

Back at the clearing, Rama affectionately curled his trunk around Ayashe as Okhmhaka jumped off and ran to her side. Amazed, happy and surprised, all at the same time, she sat on the ground wide eyed. Hovering over her was Okhmhaka and his ever widening smile.

"How…how did you do this?" she blurted out.

"Rama! He looked to find you and now we are here."

She scrambled to her feet and pasted herself to the mammoth's trunk. Still in surprise for the wonder of it all, she climbed onto Rama's back assisted by the boy who pushed from behind. Climbing on, he sat up front. Ayashe wrapped her arms around his waist and pressed her face into his, leaving a wet spot on his cheek. Okhmhaka thought to wipe it off, but decided to leave it there. They both laughed at that.

"It is I that now has shona," he said. "It is as strong as Kuruk's."

Drenching herself from his water skin, Ayashe satisfied a long thirst and gasped out loud. "Your shona is a great one, Okhmhaka! No one has ever done this."

The boy felt proud. This truly was a strong power and one day his thunderfoot would make him known everywhere with a power that only he would have.

Rama exited the clearing where Okhmhaka kicked behind the left side of the mammoth's ear. To Ayashe's surprise, as well as the boy's, Rama turned on command. She hugged him with sibling endearment, the mammoth's gentle gait, as comforting as a mother's embrace. Cool breezes blew through the dampness from across the grassland, while behind them, red clouds marbled into the sunset. The night was beautiful.

Okhmhaka kicked both sides, lurching the animal forward. His fist raised into the air as he energetically shouted. "Go, Rama! Go fast!"

The boy was on top of his world and nothing else could compare to it. Nothing!

CHAPTER 10

THE SCAVENGER'S WRATH

The sky absorbed the setting sun's fire, broiling the clouds like a suspension of red hot coals. Sizzling and frothing in that voluminous height, they burned like a necromantic inferno, sealing the grasslands in a grip of fiery damnation.

Within the depths of that satanic like caldron, bubbled a potent mix, one that swirled with the hooked beaks of vulture and the tailings of coyote. For, soon would unleash a malice of these devoted scavenger minions, now racing within the waves of their contentions.

Tipping on its axis, the caldron poured scalding hot acid as if from the Death Spirits very own lips. There it boiled forth a pour of snickering beasts that dropped into the thunderfoot trail below. Blood lust splashed along the bends and curves and then 'rose to an undulation as the scavenger minions chased between the whipping walls of blades. With each lash, the punishing grass tips dipped into the red molten sky and then beat down with unrelenting blows to spur them on.

Tongues hung from gaping jaws, the coyote's pants, hissing like nightmarish whispers. Trailing at a distance were the circling vultures, low and just above the grass line.

The saber tooth tiger's strides stretched to a full run while the pack of coyotes followed at a safe distance. Not far from the unseen prey, their leader slowed to a stop. Ahead, the trail curved left and funneled out of view---there, where the prey lay hidden, out of sight and silently waiting for them. Uncertain of the dangers that lie there, the male crept forward. Within the blood's odor was lent a trace of telling torment. The prey lay in agony. He could smell it. He tasted the air, lapped the drool from his jaws and then checked the pack following nervously behind.

Sewati leaned heavily onto the knee of his good leg while reaching for his spear. He smelled the stench of nag bokstas and jongas and it only maddened him further. If he killed one or two, the rest would leave---otherwise…he would kill them all.

Alternating his fingers up and down the shaft, he pierced the trail for the first to stick its heads out. His grip tightened around the wood while welcoming the coming conflict, slighted by the pack's choice of prey. He was a strong man of the tribe, a first hunter with many hunts behind him. He had shona. How dare they.

Edging around the curve, the male straightened with ears raised high and the wet nose of his mate bumping into his flank. The anticipation unnerved her, so she squatted to urinate. Behind them, where the curve ended, two more heads moved up as the first of the coyote's eyed the human with the stick in his hand.

With his spear jerked back, Sewati shouted, "Come, so I can run this kill stick into your chests. I have no fear for any of you."

Excited snickers emboldened the rest of the pack of coyotes that were waiting at the back. Despite both cat's possessing powerful bites, neither one came forward.

The male strained through the grayness to appraise the man's size and pointed stick. Blood trickling from an opened wound was a sure sign of weakness. Still, the prey had to be tested.

Despite a mangled foot, Sewati jabbed the spear at the first to run in, forcing the male to retreat. The female took her turn, only to back away from stabbing wounds to shoulders and chests.

Sewati laughed. "Is it in your heads that you will take my life spirit so easily?"

Once again, the male rushed in and just as quickly retreated. Seizing the opportunity, the female, having learned to charge underneath the spear, bit fiercely into Sewati's wounded foot. Her head shook viciously as she drove the enormous fangs as far they would go. The bottom fangs sliced through the sole and pierced through the shattered bones inside, reemerging through the skin of the crown. One of the top two fangs, both longer than the lower ones, sliced through Sewati's ankle bone, nearly shearing it in half.

The first hunter snapped his head back along with a scream of pain. He grabbed the thick hide of the female's neck, wrinkling it in his grip as both fell to the ground. Holding onto the fur, he stabbed the spear deep into her throat. By leveraging himself on his good leg, he was able to pull the spear out and stab her again.

"Mph!" he grunted.

Sewati glared at the nag boksta lying nearly dead at his feet. With a final lunge, he hatefully rammed the spear through her heart.

The pack of coyotes nervously stepped back, bobbing their heads and sniffing the air.

She is finished. With her dead, the rest will soon leave.

Still kneeling, he lowered the spear to the ground and slowly lifted his head high with an air of satisfaction. The scowl was replaced with a calm grin as he eyed the recoiling pack. The pain in his foot was there in all of its unmerciful torture, tempered solely by the self-control of a first hunter.

The male saber tooth, having slunk behind him in the scuffle, continued to quietly wait there and evaluated the prey. No longer threatened by the forward striking spear, the saber tooth charged the inattentive human, stood on his hind legs and slapped front paws onto the first hunter's shoulders. With tremendous pressure and speed, it dug its fangs into the back of Sewati's neck, driving them deep into muscle and bone. Instantly, the coyote's ran in, filling the open space before Sewati. He screamed just before another bite ripped out the soft tissue of his throat. Now paralyzed from the savage attacks to his neck, he choked and fell silent as he dropped to the ground with no resistance to the male that continued to chew through the vertebrae.

Sewati's dismembered head rolled down his chest and bounced off of Torn Ear. The young coyote merely glanced at it before it pulled and yanked at an opening in the stomach, hungry for the prized intestines inside.

From behind Sewati's carcass came a roar that panicked the pack. The coyotes backed away as the male stepped toward his mate's side. For a time, the lamenting saber tooth tiger continued to sniff various parts of her, licking the wounds free of blood. No longer famished or interested in the prey, the big cat left the what remained of Sewati to the pack and calmly vanished into the night.

Ahead, Lan saw feathers sticking up out of the ground. "These are from Ayashe, she left them for us to find. This is the way they walked."

"That is the trunk trail," said Akando.

Both entered it, hot, damp and filled with the fresh fragrances of flowering plants and young grass shoots---nothing that would give a clue as to what lie ahead. As they neared Sewati's carcass, Akando ran up to the small patch of trampled ground. A pair of coyotes exploded from it with the one behind running off with a sliver of dirt encrusted skin in its jaws.

"Run spirit stealers." Akando threw his ax at them, but missed. He ducked the vultures that beat enormous wings in a furious effort to escape. Debris and clouds of black flies filled the air as the bird's scrambled for room to fly.

"It is a nag boksta and it is dead!" Akando shouted, waving the flies away from his face.

Exposed bones and trailing innards from Sewati as well as the female's carcass were left exposed, along with a carpet of white maggot eggs sticking to them. Pooling blood spread outwardly, bordered at the edge by sucking ants.

Amidst the drifting debris, a tuft of black hair floated slowly downward. It eventually landed on Sewati's dismembered head.

Akando shook from the sight of it. "It is Sewati! The jonga ate him!"

Matted with blood, Sewati's face looked back with a sinister glare. To both Akando's and Lan's astonishment, one of the eyes slowly moved to the right and stared at Lan.

Akando backed away. "Sewati's spirit still lives?"

Out of the corner of the eye, a rust colored centipede emerged from inside the head, humped its back and then reentered the eye in the same place, forcing the eye to turn the other way.

The boy breathed in a sigh of relief. "It is only a rigbishka! Sewati could not fight the jonga that were many."

With his instep under the jaw, he turned the head over to face the other way, scattering roaches the size of acorns back into the brush.

"Sewati no longer has a spirit. I cannot take him to Nakoma."

"I see nothing of Ayashe," said Lan.

Akando felt his relief. "Then that is good. She still walks this trail and we will find her. When we make our fires, they must be small. Everything here is dry. If our fire is carried by the wind it will kill our hunting animals."

He picked up Sewati's spear and studied it as if to appraise its worth. Frowning, he sent it flying deep into the brush. Both men looked at one another and nodded without saying anything. Akando then turned and jogged off to find Ayashe.

Sewati's ax lay nearby. Lan picked it up and tossed it from hand to hand. He brought it back and with an underhand swing, threw it in the same direction as the spear. Removing his own ax, he took it out of the netting and looked down at the female saber tooth.

"You killed Sewati and now he is no more. For this I will keep your spirit."

Removing both fangs, he wiped off Sewati's blood from them and stuck them into the netting along with the ax. Turning to Sewati's head, he spat on it and softly mumbled, "Our hunt for one another ends here."

Kuruk and Achak waited in the dark outside the trail leading to the pond. It had been a while since Qaletaga and Moki left to search for signs of Ayashe.

Achak lifted a torch over his head and peered into the dark trail. "Why are they not back? It is long that we wait."

Without answering, Kuruk sat quietly chewing the end of a long stem.

At the pond, Qaletaga stood before white water lilies blanketing the surface and the green pads that dipped in wind-born ripples. Dragonflies flitted about in the torchlight, skimming just above the surface for prey. Beneath blossoming swamp milkweed, butterflies slept in the hidden darkness---the bank, thick with reeds.

Letting out a deep sigh for a denied sleep, Qaletaga yawned and boringly pushed the small patch of hide to the side to let his curled up manhood drop straight down. He shook his head from the stiffness and aimed at a water beetle negotiating the uneven litter between his feet. A strong yellow stream knocked the insect over and onto its back where the beetle became trapped by its round bowl design. Unable to keep from drinking the salty soup, it kicked tiny legs at the yellow flood coming down, to Qaletaga's delight.

"Ugly rigbishka!"

After filling all of the water skins, he left to join up with Moki.

"I hear them," said Achak. "Moki walks like the thunder foot."

"Kuruk stood and stretched. "He could empty our hunting place with that walk."

Upon seeing Moki, Achak called to him, "Why do you walk so hard?"

"It is the ground that walks hard," returned Moki, used to the elder's quips.

To the men's startled surprise, Ayashe and Okhmhaka approached from the opposite direction.

"You found her!" said Kuruk.

"The jonga tried to eat her and Rama killed them all," the boy energetically replied.

Ayashe laughed. "Not all of them…only three."

"Where is Sewati?" Achak asked, straining his neck to look up at them.

"I saw him in the trunk trail. His foot was bleeding," said Okhmhaka.

"And what of Lan and Akando, did you not pass them on your way here?"

Ayashe's face brightened. "No, we did not see them. Were they looking for us?"

Kuruk gently placed his hand on the mammoth's trunk. "Then, they are still on the other side of the Thunderfoot Trail. Go to Nakoma. Tell him we will soon return with Sewati. I will find your Lan and tell him of our words to one another."

A shudder went through her. She could never tell Kuruk that it was she who broke his foot. If she told anyone, it would have to be either Lan or Nakoma.

Still on the back trail, Lan entered the clearing. He immediately noticed the three dead coyotes and studied the confusion of tracks along the ground. "Ayashe was here!"

Lowering the torch, Akando crouched down next to him. "There are many of the jonga and two nag boksta prints here... and look at this one, the foot print with Ayashe. This is from one of us and not a full man."

"Okhmhaka?"

"Okhmhaka!" Akando agreed, studying them closely.

At that moment, Kuruk and the rest entered the clearing.

"What did you find there?" Kuruk boomed.

Akando looked up from the prints. "Ayashe's foot tracks and those of little Okhmhaka."

Kuruk pointed his thumb backwards. "They passed us sitting on Rama. I sent them to Nakoma."

Lan looked at him hopefully. "Is she...?"

"She has no wounds," he replied.

Lan lowered his head with relief just as Akando put his hand on his shoulder.

"Okhmhaka, he..." Before Kuruk could finish, he grinned and took a deep breath. "Okhmhaka sits on Rama with your Ayashe. His shona is a great one."

Qaletaga could not contain his excitement. "Rama knows the words Okhmhaka speaks."

Just as proud, Achak smiled while shaking his head. In a soft voice, he said, "This is a great shona."

"Okhmhaka ...Ayashe? On Rama's back?" Akando only now realized the full meaning of what they were saying.

"Ayashe was sitting on top of Rama with Okhmhaka," Qaletaga repeated.

Like the rest, Lan's thoughts were also on the boy. *When I am one with Okhmhaka, I will give him the gift of the two knife.*

"What of Sewati? Did you not pass him on the trail?" Kuruk asked.

"The jonga took him," said Akando.

Looking crushed, Kuruk's eyes closed. "There is nothing else for us here. Let us all return to Nakoma. He waits by the river."

As the men began the long walk back, Kuruk followed behind Lan with a troubling thought.

Could it be that this Mowatchi killed Sewati? Akando looks to him. Is he with him on this?

He thought to go back and check, but that would discredit Akando and he did not want to do that in front of the men. Sewati was dead, killed by the jonga. His life spirit no longer existed and that was the way he would leave it...for now. As he listened to the young second hunter carry on about Sewati's dismembered head, he raised his own with another thought.

If it is true that the Mowatchi did kill Sewati...and Matwua... then who will be the next to fall to his ax? After our return to Nakoma, I will make this walk again...alone. It is then that I will know what happened to Sewati.

The reunion dance

Kajika stopped the dance that kept evil spirits from harming the men on the Thunderfoot Trail. After a few more shakes of a rattle, made from an ancestors skull filled with finger and toe bones, he spread a handful of herbs into a fire.

The entire tribe had stayed up the whole night waiting and worried. Now, along with an early sunrise, Nakoma sat with Nadie and Honovi to hear from Ayashe about her ordeal.

"Kuruk will soon bring Sewati," said a beaming Nakoma.

"He cannot walk. I broke his foot with his ax. He wanted to kill me," Ayashe replied.

"That was the worry of your Mowatchi."

"Yes, and your Sewati would kill me like he killed Una. He spoke that he..."

"Una?"

Ayashe nodded. "He spoke that he killed Una and wanted to kill me the same way. He did this to me." Her hand gestures showed how she was raped.

Uninterested, Nakoma shrugged that off. He was more interested in Una. "So…it was not Matwua that killed Una?"

"Matwua?" Ayashe leaned back, confused.

"You did not know? It is Matwua that we all spoke that killed Una. This is why we sent him to Mantotohpa for your trade. Mantotohpa did not know of this kill and we did not tell him.

In total surprise, Ayashe said, "Matwua never spoke this to me or to Mantotohpa, only that he was no longer a first hunter with you."

The tribe's leader leaned forward, fingering the vulture skulls in his hair as he stared at her with sympathy and genuine concern.

"Matwua found no peace with our men and Mantotohpa knew that. We no longer wanted him here with us. And now you say it was Sewati that killed Una." Nakoma nibbled his lower lip while slowly rising to his feet. "So…it was **not** Matwua." He clapped his hands. "Nadie…bring dream drink!"

When she returned with it, he handed the femur immediately to Ayashe. Both surprised and honored, she grinned and took a long and deserving drink.

"These men will soon return with Sewati," he said. "If your words are true words, he will no longer be one with us. I will send a runner to Otaktay when Sewati's foot is fixed. My wish is that Otaktay's people will take him."

Unaware of Kuruk's meeting up with Lan on the trail or Sewati's death, Ayashe believed as well that they would soon return with him. She said nothing more about it. She would deal with Sewati's return when she had to, not now.

Even Lan cannot fix that foot.

In the center of the temporary camp, a bon fire lit up the bank. To celebrate the reunion, a femur overflowing with dream drink was passed to Qaletaga and then to Kajika, then Nayati and Ayashe, and finally back to Nakoma, with more interceptions from Kajika then the rest. Before long, the carrier of red dirt stumbled around the fire incoherently mumbling chants, none of which celebrated the reunion. He chanted for marriage, new births and plentiful game. Even the manhood ritual was included. And somehow, in his head-spinning delirium, Kajika remembered the women and their milk supply, giving them a fair representation. He soon passed out; his careless stumbling no longer a threat to the women whose turn it was to dance.

Oversized hips shook and swayed. Breast flopped about in all directions as women held hands and chased around the fire to the stamp of the men's feet.

Ready for the dance with her favorite shell necklace, headdress of flowers and a skirt so short, her pubic hairs were showing, Nadie joined the ring of women. Her strange bumps and grinds seemed erratic and out of step to the rhythmical slapping of rib bones from Nayati and little Okhmhaka. Along with them, Nakoma shook his rattle with systematic fervor. Their incredulous looks at one another did little to discourage what Nadie perceived to be an artful mating dance.

Her thin arms slapped at her sides while tubular legs miraculously kept the wriggling excesses from toppling over from inebriation. Her huge head leaned forward and bobbed from side to side. At any suspense giving moment, her jutting knees would rise up for the awkward leaps she made. It cleared the ground of competition, leaving Nadie all the more convinced her sexual lure proved irresistible.

She was unstoppable and only had gotten started. Her head stuck out beyond her chest where it kept pace with the rhythmical timing. Flapping arms and hands dangled loosely at the sides, keeping rhythm with the tribal drumming. Weighty eyebrows flicked frequently at Nakoma as she worked herself into a romantic obsession. It drenched her in an odorous sweat that dripped from her breast and hairy armpits.

Worried for the horrible foreplay, Nakoma recoiled at the thought that his every tolerance for her flesh would be called upon that night. He groaned woefully and turned to continue rattling the saber tooth skull in a different direction, while shaking his own in self-pity.

The celebration ended when the dream drink sedated the enthusiasm of the tribe, including that of Nadie's. Thanking the spirits for their divine intervention, Nakoma rested from the romantic pursuit. He got up and stood over Okhmhaka while the boy slept. Rama towered behind, his trunk curled next to the boy. Touching the rough feel of it, Nakoma instinctively pulled away.

"Humph! Rama! He even has a name for it."

The end of the trunk played over the boy's chest. It touched, then hovered and on occasion lay flat, then lifted and started all over again.

It was surprising to Nakoma how fast the ivory had extended a full arm's length downward where it began an upward growth that would one day send it into a grand curve of virile armament. Loose wrinkles, fully apparent when the animal was first brought there, were already filling out with the thunder foot doubling in weight. It performed the boy's every bidding, bonded to him like a father's son. It pleased him to command such an imposing beast and because of his love for it, Nakoma could not bring himself to butcher the animal. And certainly not after what he saw that night. Yet...despite all of that, he could not help but think of the day when the thunderfoot would grow into an overpowering bull with a temperament to match. The bull in musk would be unmanageable no matter how well a command the boy had for it.

The thunderfoot so far was harmless enough. There would be no danger in keeping it. For now he would wait, and then he would see. He would make a decision then.

"She is here," said Nadie, grabbing Lan by the arm as soon as he returned with the men. "She stands by the river and waits."

Lan took out one of the fangs and handed it to her. "This is for Okhmhaka. Tell him he is now my nag boksta brother. It is the same way I gave this power to Akando."

Leaving her, he ran to the bank to find Ayashe. When he got there, she was nowhere around. Standing in the silence, he soon heard her soft voice coming from behind.

"You are here and now I am with you." As she said that, she undid her braid, brushing it out with trembling fingers. Her eyes were wet, a bloated sunrise, scarlet and framing her from behind like a cameo. Her thick hair blew across the face of it like long, black flames.

"You are prettier than spring flower," he said, wiping the tears from her cheeks. "Now you stand before me." He held her by the waist with Ayashe holding onto his shoulders and leaning her head back.

"Yes…I am here, bg Bandu man. Jonga…he try to eat me. I, so…ah…matay, so…"

"Afraid!"

"Afray…I many times too plenty afray and I say to jonga, eat to me plenty fast…and Okhmhaka, he come on Rama and…and… jonga and nag boksta, they many times run this…and I go this."

Left with her arms crossed and pointing in two different directions, Lan continued to wipe her tears and rock her back and forth. "There is no more worry. No more jonga and no more nag boksta."

"No more jonga! No more nag boksta!" She affirmed.

She went on to talk about Sewati and how she used his ax to crush his foot.

Lan framed her face with his hands and looked kindly into her eyes. "The jonga took Sewati's life spirit. He is no more."

"Sewati…is no more?"

"He is finished and now I am ready to leave Nakoma for your Mantotohpa."

She embraced him, squeezing him tightly. Breathlessly, she asked, "When do we go to Mantotohpa?"

"I asked Nakoma to send Qaletaga on our walk. His wish is to also send Kajika with us. It will be four that will go to Mantotohpa with the first light.

CHAPTER 11
MANTOTOHPA'S TRIBE

It was exciting for Ayashe to be nearing Mantotohpa's tents. She had so looked forward to reuniting with her parents, Akule and Alawa. She missed Kitchi (brave) and Paco (eagle); little baby, Sisika, (bird) and the rest. As she held onto Lan, she swallowed at the sight of the thick cloud of dust that was coming from the trail ahead. Qaletaga and Kajika followed behind.

At the sound of voices and shuffling feet, Lan stopped and held his hand up in alarm. "They come! Stand with me!"

All four stood fast as the dust cloud lengthened in their direction. Lan and Qaletaga held their spears pointing up in friendship.

The dust cloud grew ever larger, the sound of shuffling steps getting nearer before the approaching men could be seen. Every step moved like one, their bodies held stiffly with chest thrust forward as the men whispered loudly.

"Huh hah huh hah huh hah huh hah huh hah!"

Poles carrying human heads waved above the grass line, the combined whispers, to emulate the breathing of the long deceased. The sound from so many was loud.

"Huh hah huh hah huh hah huh hah huh hah!"

It continued until the high pitched voice of their shaman shouted a chant---each time, answered by the men.

"Hunna hunna, hanna hanna!"
"Yah!"
"Hunna hunna, hanna hanna!"
"Yah!"
"Hunna, hunna, Wyah, wyah!"
"Yahhh"!
"Wyah, wyah!"
"Wy yah, wy yah!"
"Kimonobokamay-y-y-y!"
"OOOO! OOOO!"
"Hunna hunna, whyamay-y-y-y!"
"OOOOOOOooo!"

Rounding a curve, the front line of men suddenly came into view. All of them wore high headdresses framed with wood. They were adorned with the brilliant colors of mandarin wood ducks; blue, iridescent purple, red, orange and green. As they straightened out of the curve, the shaman, wearing a red, wooden mask with a frowning face carved into it, raised his hand up to stop them. In the other he carried a pole with prairie dog skins hanging off of it and on top, the skull of the previous shaman in reverence to his once high status. The rest stood in place with poles and axes held over their heads. On cue, they slapped them together after each of the shaman's chants.

"Hunna hunna bockama-a-a-y?"
Crack! Crack! **"OOOOoo!"**
"Wyah wyah wyah!"
Crack! Crack! **"OOOOoo!"**

With this, they all took three steps forward and stopped, leaned at the waist, then straightened back up and shouted, **"OOOOOOoooo."** *Crack! Crack!*

The chant over, the tight group shuffled forward with skulls bobbing overhead. Every step was timed together while all had about them the purposeful mindset when facing an enemy. The rhythmic scraping sound of so many feet coming their way frightened Kajika.

"It is many that come," he squeaked.

"Stand straight and show them no fear," said Lan.

A decorative spirit stick was all Kajika carried, held limply at his side. Made of a collection of leg bones from wading birds tied together so that they rattled, they were dyed green and adorned with strips of fur.

The men coming toward them were powerfully built, their heads shaved around the sides. The rest of their hair grew long, including a crescent shaped patch above each ear. The ear lobes themselves stretched from the weight of human vertebrae. Bones pierced noses, grossly distorting them, and all of the men wore red-orange ochre. It covered their heads and necks.

At the forefront, the biggest of the lot waved for the rest to break stride.

"That is the one that is called Yahto," Kajika meekly said. "They look to Ayashe."

Qaletaga worried for Lan "They know of Ayashe and Kajika and they know of me. My worry is for you."

His focus steadily on Mantotohpa's men, Lan ignored what he just heard, pushed his chest out and held his head high.

Sprinting ahead of the others, Yahto ran with an assortment of small animal skulls clattering noisily against his chest. Alone, he continued the harrowing and loud whisper. **"Huh hah huh hah huh hah!"**

Behind him, the men waited while energetically pounding the end of their poles into the ground along with their chants.

"Kimonobokamay! Kimonobokamay! Kimonobokamay! Kimonobokamay! Kimonobokamay! Kimonobokamay! Kimonobokamay!"

Qaletaga held onto Kajika, although he appeared to be fading fast. Lan grabbed him by the arm and together, lifted him to his feet. Pale and managing the slightest of head nods, Kajika left the spirit stick where it fell.

Yahto: Lead First Hunter in standing
A full height reached by his twenty second summer, Yahto was the tallest in the tribe by two heads, and far taller than any man from any of the neighboring tribes. Arrogant and boastful, this was tempered solely by the bond he had with Mantotohpa. As well, he was accustomed to the cowering responses to his intimidating size, which he enjoyed immensely.

Yahto's calves were as wide as his thighs, his shoulders as thick as the heavy ax he carried. A handsome, strong-faced man, his stern discipline befit the overpowering image the sight of him instilled. Long, slack hair bounced against his back from the crushing leaps across large patches of ground. Screaming and waving his ax, the huge man was a terrifying sight.

Yahto knew that and charged in with his spear held high and a reliance that if the three men held any evil spirits, they would panic and run from him---take their evil spirits back where they came from. Yahto was having a great time.

"Huh hah huh hah huh hah!"

As each step brought him closer, an urge to run became an even stronger option for Kajika, now on the verge of burying his head in his arms.

"Huh hah huh hah huh hah!"

Dust settled over the four as Yahto stormed in to an abrupt halt, the only sound, the bone necklace knocking against his chest and his heavy breathing. Black glossy hair blew behind him, the vertebrae in his ear lobes, settled and no longer swinging back and forth.

Showing no sign of cowardice, Lan held instead a gaze without falter from the moment Yahto first started to run at him, to this very instant.

Wild eyed and his arms outstretched, the giant of a man lowered his head and screamed so loud, so resonantly deep, it shivered down Lan's spine. It was so deeply basso, one could almost count the vibrations.

"Why do you bring this Mowatchi?" He shouted.

Lan straightened as tall as he could. *This one could be different from the rest. Why did he run at me?*

As persistent as was the man's intimidation, Lan deceptively masked his fear. It was a while that both men stood and looked at one another---Yahto looking down and Lan looking up. And chilling for him to return that stare, knowing full well those huge arms could snap his bones with little effort.

The rest of Mantotohpa's men filled the open space around them, followed by a stench of sweat and unwashed bodies. Stepping out from the center, Mantotohpa, the leader of the tribe, stood next to his prime, first hunter.

"Yahto…enough!"

He turned to look with difficulty at Ayashe's welcoming smile through milky-grey cataracts. "Shatu duma, Ayashe!"

"Shatu duma, Mantotohpa!" she readily answered, as she stepped around Lan to the front.

Mantotohpa immediately wrapped his arms around her, stroking her hair as if she was of his own blood.

"We missed this little one," he said.

"I look to see Alawa and Akule. It is too long that we have not spoken our words together," she said.

All around Mantotohpa, his men lit up at the sight of her.

"It is the one that belongs to Akule!"

"The little one is back!"

Yahto's cavernous voice reverberated loudly. **"Why do you bring this Mowatchi?"**

"Enough, Yahto," Mantotohpa grimaced. "They will have their talk when it is time."

Frustrated, the huge first hunter retreated to stand with the rest of the men.

"I belong to Lan," said Ayashe, searching Mantotohpa's face for the smallest sign of acceptance. "He leads the Bandu people on the other side of the high place."

"Is that why you wear this." Mantotohpa flicked her braid with no show of emotion, his gray eyes, seemingly without pupils. In consideration for her, he nodded at Lan while firmly gripping both of the Mowatchi's shoulders. With the disinclined greeting, he shook them firmly which Lan returned.

What will Akule say when this little one brings her Mowatchi to his cover?

And, yet...the more Mantotohpa focused through poor vision at Lan, the more he sensed a hidden strength, one he could feel inside---a strength that went beyond the pretension and what he physically could see.

There is more to this one than size. He is a leader of men like I am. He must have a power I do not see.

"What is it that you carry in that cover," he said, pointing to the quiver of arrows.

The arrow Lan took out to hand to Mantotohpa was as long as Ayashe stood tall. Mantotohpa examined it closely and wanted to burst out with laughter, especially from the way in which it was presented in such a serious manner. Too flimsy and thin for its length, it puzzled him. Composing himself, he asked with feigned sincerity, "What can this kill?"

"It kills the jonga and the nahgo..." Lan responded, "...and the thunderfoot."

Yahto stepped forward. Scoffing at what the Mowatchi just said, his thick voice amplified within the confines of men. "Humph! The Mowatchi speaks our words!" Turning away from him, he stared at the arrows. "His kill sticks are many times too weak. I see no power in them."

Other voices alternated around Yahto.

"It cannot kill the thunderfoot."

"His kill sticks are not like ours."

"They cannot kill anything."

The arrow passed to Yahto, who grabbed it and turned it around to study it. The first hunter merely shook his head and gave it back to Lan.

Next, someone put the bow that had been passed to him in the leader's hands. Mantotohpa eyed it with the same scrutiny, assessing it for a purpose he could only guess at. He liked the etching and colorful stones. It was the sinew string connecting the ends that puzzled him.

"What can this kill, it has no weight?"

The rest of the men quietly closed in with their own doubts. Remaining confident, Lan welcomed the chance to show them a real power, one that would undermine anything they had.

"Ayashe, bring back an animal head from out there." Holding his hands out, he showed her the appropriate size skull he wanted.

Following Ayashe, Mantotohpa's men eagerly assisted in looking for a large animal skull as they fanned out in all directions. Some checked the brush in the immediate area while others searched distant fields. Accumulated down through the centuries, it was a long while before the men returned with the largest ones they could find like buffalo, deer and pronghorn, some cracked with age, others too small and rejected.

In a helpful gesture, kajika presented that of a coyote, sure Lan's kill stick would go through it.

"No, Kajika. My need is to show them my strength. Let them find one."

"And if it does not go through?"

"It will," Lan reassured him.

The collection became sizable and all of it rejected for being too small.

"Enough of this," said Yahto, slamming the skull of a large buffalo into the middle of the trail.

"Good, then," said Lan.

Sun bleached, the bone's density and size was just what he had hoped for. He stood over it and raised the bow above his head along with one of the thicker, bloodletting arrows. Waving them both in the air, he shouted, "This is how I will kill the thunderfoot." He put the two together with the arrow notched in the sinew.

Another round of doubts voiced from Mantotohpa's men.

"It cannot kill."

"The Mowatchi does not know the strength of the thunderfoot."

"It is only in his head and not in his kill sticks."

"Many times too weak."

"This one is not a first hunter."

Lan, speaking to Ayashe, pointed down the trail. "Take this and walk until I tell you to stop."

Kajika followed along as she carried the buffalo skull under her arm. On the way, they passed the row of smirking faces, continued for a few more steps and turned around even though Lan had said nothing.

"Go farther!"

Twenty paces---Ayashe slowed and looked back.

"Keep taking your steps!"

Twenty more steps, Lan continued to wave them on.

Kajika worried. "His kill stick will never come this far."

"You have yet to see my Mowatchi's power," she said, turning again toward Lan. "Here?"

"More!" he answered.

They went another ten, stopped and turned around. Tilting her head to the side, she leaned and looked back as though tired of it all.

"There!" He shouted.

Not one to take chances, Kajika muttered quietly to Ayashe, "I have my own power." He dug into one of the pouches he carried. "The brown seeds. No! The dark ones will work better."

Curious, Ayashe looked over his shoulder.

"This will make Lan's kill stick go where he looks," he said, as he sprinkled the seeds over the skull.

Qaletaga took the long walk to where Ayashe and Kajika were standing. As he passed by a man at the end of the line, he could hear what he was saying.

"I cannot throw my ax half that far."

Others next to him shook their heads and agreed.

Standing alongside Lan and Mantotohpa, Yahto frowned. "This cannot be done. It is too far."

At the other end, between Kajika and Ayashe, Qaletaga ignored the elbow digging into his ribs.

"Qaletaga!" Kajika muttered, between stiffened lips.

"Not now!" Qaletaga snapped.

Paying him no mind, it was better to ignore the carrier of the red dirt than to be part of whatever new nonsense he had concocted. Instead, he scanned the troubled faces of the men looking their way.

Not all of these men from Mantotohpa have a wish like their Yahto to see Lan's kill stick break inside the tatanka. I know as well as he must that it will never go through. When it is over, I will stand by Lan when he picks up the broken pieces.

"Qa...le...ta...ga!"

He continued to ignore Kajika.

"The dark seeds." Kajika looked around before continuing, "I gave the dark seeds to the head of the tatanka. I must now leave the rest of the seeds where our mowatchi stands or his power will not be strong enough."

Sighing deeply, Qaletaga said, "It is good that you try. We have nothing more."

Nodding, Kajika slipped behind the men and gradually worked his way towards the other end of the trail until he was standing behind Yahto and Mantotohpa. His head lowered as he checked through the corner of his eyes for a chance to approach Lan without being seen.

Tensions mounted along with the arguments that broke out; while inside the quiver, Lan fumbled around for the one special arrow he would need---the one with a red line around the shaft. Finding it, he straightened the tail feathers and inspected the blade.

This is the arrow Sleeps by the Fire said his words to.

"This kill stick is the strongest. I said the hunting words for it alone. The stone was sharp and the wood dry when it was made. Save it for a time when you must use it. When that time is now, use it with much thought. It can only be used once. It is then that you must break the arrow and bury it under a stone so that no one can ever use it again."

"It can only be used once," Lan mumbled, under his breath. The arrow notched, he looked across to the far end of the trail.

Alongside him, Yahto grinned as he looked on with Mantotopa, his arms folded across his chest.

Lan put the bow momentarily on the ground. *This arrow looks no different than the others. My hope is that its spirit is strong.*

He grabbed his father's molars in one hand, the special arrow in the other, leaned his head back, closed his eyes and spoke to the arrow's spirit.

"Fly with the wind! Only you can finish where all others will fail. It is now that you must fly strong for me."

This was all too much for Yahto. He had enough of the stalling. "Do it now, Mowatchi. Your kill stick will not get any stronger." He slid his groin patch to the side, grabbed his penis and shook it at Lan. "Is it also your wish to blow on your kill stick, or should I wet it for you."

The uproarious laughter that followed did not stop until Mantotohpa's arms lifted to silence them. "Let him finish. It has no power and my wish is to go back when it is done."

It was the opportunity Kajika was waiting for. He quickly stepped forward and sprinkled the seeds over Lan's bow, still laying on the ground while repeating a chant of his own.

Yahto grabbed him by the arm and pushed him to the ground. "What is it that you do there?"

Clambering to his feet and bent over in subjugation, Kajika smiled deviously, keeping his gaze on the huge man as he slipped away sideways until hidden behind the men.

The look on Lan remained stern while holding his breath and drawing his arm back. He became one with the arrow, focusing on the skull and nothing else. He would ride the brother wind; fly with his father and the feathers to his back. Together they would break through the buffalo skull as if it was made of nothing more than thin egg shell.

Everyone remained focused---the air, tense---the breezes, light---the silence, filled with expectancy. Like the sound of a raging wildcat, the arrow hissed past the startled men, forcing many into the foliage behind them.

CRACK

The buffalo skull exploded. Every one of Mantotohpa's men stood in awe.

"His kill stick flies faster than the sisika?"

"This cannot be."

"I wish to make one for my hunts."

"The Mowatchi has a great shona."

Nothing flew faster, not even the eagle. It was wonderful, intense; the potential so great. From his distance it brought no harm to the barer.

Staring at the broken pieces, Yahto could not believe what he had just seen, yet, it happened right there before him. The arrow went clean through. If it could do that to a bondolo skull, he did not want to think of what it could do to his own.

As soon as Qaletaga caught up with Kajika, he lifted him off his feet. He could hardly contain himself. "Your fix was a good one. I will tell Nakoma."

Ayashe proudly ran up to Lan. "They now know you have a strong shona. It is the same way that it is in my head."

Among the crowd of men, Mantotohpa quietly stole away so he could be alone. There, he looked west towards the mountains and at the cols nestled between them. Although he could not see them clearly, he knew they were there. He no longer heard the excited voices that had drowned behind a troubling thought.

Out there is the place that touches the sky. It is the place of the Mowatchi. If this one did not fear Yahto, his spirits cannot be weak. My worry is that they are stronger than Wankan Tanka (Great Spirit).

Mantotohpa's Village

Akule held his arm out to Waquini (hook nose). "What do they find there that makes them so happy?"

Waquini grabbed onto the elders arm. "Mantotohpa returns with the others."

"Come! Take me to them."

With the boy's help, the elder squeezed through the confusion of jostling bodies from other tribal members. Amidst the shrieks and laughter, names were shouted as children ran in and out of the crowd chasing one another. To see above their heads, Akule had to stretch and with arthritis acting up like it was, it was painful to do so. He let go of Waquini as soon as he saw his daughter walking alongside Mantotohpa.

"My Ayashe!"

Their eyes met for an instant. When Ayashe tried to get through, the children enthusiastically surrounded her.

"Move from her," Alawa scolded.

More than anyone else there, she wanted to get close to her daughter. She pushed her way through the crowd until at last she got close enough to wrap her arms around her. "Shatu duma! It is too long that I do not see you."

"Shatu duma! Too long!" Ayashe loudly replied, over the chaos of the welcoming crowd.

Alawa gazed adoringly at her, surprised at how much she had matured. Her daughter left a young girl and now returned a beautiful woman. "You are not in the high place with one of Nakoma's?"

"Matwua? No...I no longer belong to him. I walked from the high place with Lan."

"Your hair...why do you wear your hair that way?"

"I am Bandu, like Lan. He is the one I now follow."

"Bandu? Here? Where is this one you call Lan?"

Ayashe turned to find him in the crowd just as Akule broke through.

"Ha, ha-a! Ayashe, Ayashe," he cried. "Your look is different... older...pretty inside my head."

The crushing crowd proved to be too much for Akule. His daughter was suddenly driven away from him and toward the women's communal tent. Alawa tried to hold onto her as best she could, but the crowd pushed her to the side as well, separating her from Ayashe for the moment.

Akule would go no further. *"This is no place for me. I will have my talk with Ayashe by my fire when the women are finished with her."*

Inside the well-lit tent, Wawawetska (pretty woman) giggled loudly. "Your Mowatchi is pretty in my eyes."

"Your eyes should not look to my man," Ayashe said, pushing her, to which Wawawetska playfully pushed back.

In what sounded like a scolding voice, Ayashe's mother said, "So...you are Bandu now!"

"Lan make kill to twoniff." Ayashe showed her the claw bracelets. Hms take to me from high place. Mak gd fix to Etu."

"You talk the words of my old people, the Wadu...how did you learn this?"

"Lan show to me this woads. They blong same to Bandu."

Alawa held onto her daughter's hands. "Then I will talk to you the same way. It is long that I used these words. They are not with me the same way."

"I spik old woads so no one here know things I talk."

Her mother reached out for her necklace. "You still wear the finger bone I gave you."

Ayashe nodded.

Alawa's worn hands gently outlined her daughter's face. "I missed you and so did Akule. Will you stay here with us?"

"Lan, hms wish is to take hms pee poh bock from Dinga pee poh."

"The Dinga? The Bandu were never strong. Their people are not many. Your Lan will never take them back alone. Stay with us. Mantotohpa leads well. Lan can become one with us."

Someone tapped Ayashe lightly on the knee, but she was too immersed in thought to pay it any mind. *Where Lan goes I must follow. Does Alawa not understand this? It was the same for her. How could she not...*

"I will speak those words to Akule," Alawa continued. "He will make the talk to Mantotohpa."

Quanah (fragrant), a boy of five that Ayashe had no previous knowledge of, kept tapping her on the leg.

"Is it your wish that I should pick you up?" she said, smiling at the boy. She sat him on her knee. "What are you called?"

"Quanah. The words you speak to Alawa...they do not belong to me," the boy said.

She cradled him in her arms, looked into his large brown eyes and affectionately brushed her face against his. "Does little Quanah want me to stay?"

Embarrassed, the child looked sheepishly at the floor and wrinkled his cheeks into a wide grin. Checking around at everyone sitting there, he pushed the middle of his lips into his nose.

Wheeze…sniff, sniff

The children laughed at the noises he was making, which made him laugh, too.

"I like you little Quanah. Do you want me to stay?" Ayashe asked again.

Quanah slunk his head between his shoulders and puckered his lips into a bird's beak. "Quanah like many good," he squeaked.

The boy's laughter joined the rest of the children who were shoving one another and hysterically laughing along with him.

"He has no one," Alawa said, stroking the boy's long, wavy hair.

"Where does he sleep?"

"With Talmelapachme (dull knife) and his little ones…or one of the elders; Chancoowashtay (good road), Kwatoko (bird with big beak)…never with Mantotohpa."

"Why do you not take him?"

"We are too old, Ayashe. He is wild like the nahgo. He already runs like one."

"That is sad." Ayashe looked at Quanah. "Are you wild like the Nahgo?"

"I am not a nahgo?" The boy said, aloud.

Ayashe tickled him in the ribs. "Yes, you are a naah…go!"

Shaman's tent

Mantotohpa bounced off of Yahto's shoulder, slapping his hands together while trying to regain his composure from the hilarious account he just heard from the Mowatchi.

"Did Aleeka leave you?"

The entire confrontation with the bull mammoth was told in glorious detail. Lan finished by telling them how the jonga had killed Sewati."

"Nakoma's meat will not last," said Mantotohpa. "He will need to hunt again soon and now he has lost two of his best first hunters. I will send him what I have with you on your return. He would do this for me the same way."

The tent had filled with every man in the tribe. Elders sat in front while the rest found places in back. Taking his usual seat between Yahto and Odakotah, Mantotohpa stretched his legs toward the glowing fire pit. On the other side, Qaletaga, Kajika and Lan sat cross-legged on the floor.

The elders closest to Akule leaned out of his way as he stepped toward the front of the fire with dream drink spilling on everyone sitting there. He stumbled on the legs sprawled out toward the pit and with a heavy thud, fell to the floor.

"Thunderfoot waste!"

He tried to save the dream drink, but it splashed across the hard packed dirt floor. One of the younger men got up to help him to his feet.

"I do not need you," Akule snapped, wiping foam from his legs. He continued to mumble under his breath as he snatched the walking stick away from the man.

Across the entire wall before everyone that was sitting there, a shrine of skulls was stacked from floor to ceiling. Inside each, burning mammoth oil lit up the faces of the elders sitting in the front row, leaving those at the rear in total darkness. Peering at the faces he could see, Akule gathered himself together and stood before them to address Mantotohpa.

"This Mowatchi that sits with us is now the one my Ayashe follows. It is my cover where he will sleep."

"Do you not know that if the Mowatchi stays here with us it will anger Wankan Tanka?" Mantotohpa barked."

"I stand with the Mowatchi called Lan and the two men that took the walk with him," Akule sharply responded.

An elder, Dichali (speaks a lot), left his reserved place to be heard. A hideously pale, wrinkled old man, his narrow body was covered with body piercings and an array of animal bones. A headdress of green, freshly picked ferns held in place by a strip of human skin, was adorned with strips of beaver fur that hung down both sides of his face. Tufts of white downy feathers outlined the entire lower portion of the headdress as well as the eagle feathers that were stuck inside at random intervals.

"The Mowatchi that Ayashe walks with must go from us. Send him back to Nakoma. He must know this man's spirits are not welcomed."

Finished with what he felt he had held in for too long, the elder returned to his place with the agreeing faces around him nodding their approval.

Yahto agreed fully. He made his way with heavy steps to the front of the fire pit where he held an ax above his head. "I stand with Wankan Tanka. Send this Mowatchi back to the high place. We do not want him here with us."

"My woman, Alawa, is a Mowatchi," Akule screamed. "Is it no longer in your heads that she is also from that same high place? It is long that she sleeps with me. Our little one, Ayashe, belongs to all of us. She is one with our people and one with Mantotohpa. Do you not welcome her?"

Mantotohpa sprang to his feet and pushed Yahto's arm down, silently gesturing for him to stand back. He then stared at each and every blank face visible in the fire light. "The Mowatchi will stay and only until the passing of two suns. That is when he will return to Nakoma. Not before! That is all…it is as I said and I will hear no more."

He then addressed Yahto with a stern order. "When they take this walk, you will go with them. I send you so no harm comes to the Mowatchi. If death finds him, you will never be welcomed here again."

Next morning

The path leading to the river from Mantotohpa's tents stretched emptily except for two women huddled in conversation. Lan could hear the excited voices of two boys playing in the river.

"Waquini!" Quanah yelled. "Kill the water ba ba…fast…now, do it now. There look! Fast! Kill it!"

Stabbing a pointed stick at a racing shadow just below the surface, Waquini, the older of the two boys, missed the fish as it flexed its tail and darted into the reeds.

"Give me my stick back," Quanah yelled, doing his best to yank it away from the older boy's grasp.

Holding onto it firmly, Waquini said, "Quanah…look! More water ba ba."

Quanah snapped his head around, but saw nothing where he was pointing. At that instant, the older boy held the stick high above his head and well out of reach.

His arms folding in frustration, Quanah said, "No! I will not look at no more water ba ba. You look!"

At the water's edge, Lan waded in to bathe.

Approaching him, Quanah, asked, "Can you make me a kill stick? We are first hunters and want to kill the ba ba yano?" (sturgeon)

Lan was instantly drawn to the boy, his smiling face, bright eyes and eager expectations. "Find the top of a bondo, then wait for me here."

Shortly, strips of sinew were laid out on the muddy bank, as well as the stick the boys were using and the sharp flint blades Lan would need. The boys soon returned from the direction of the tents with a shedded deer horn and set them on the ground.

"Put these in the water," Lan said, handing them the sinew.

As soon as Quanah made a grab for it, Waquini already had the string like strips in his hand. Missing the opportunity, Quanah wiped his nose and folded his arms out front.

Lan said, "This kill stick is for you Quanah. You were the one who asked me to make it."

He wedged the deer horn between two large boulders and split it in two. Only one of the spikes would be needed. Whittled down to form a barbed hook, he fluted the end of it to fit onto the stick.

Quanah spread himself out on the ground, his head resting on his fist and his cheeks pushing into his eyes as he watched through the narrowed slits. Stating with an air of authority, he said, "This will be my kill stick. It is not for Waquini."

The sinew that Waquini soaked in the river was now used to wrap around the barb, securing it to the end of the stick. To form a solid handle, Lan wound more sinew around the middle of the shaft and tied it off. When it was finished, he left the kill stick out in the sun. As the strips of sinew dried they would contract, further tightening the knots.

"This is not your time to touch the kill stick. If you do, its spirit will not be strong."

Quanah nodded, his arms still folded across his chest.

Lan said, "When it is dry, wait for me. We will soon return with baskets to put the fish in."

"Mm hmm." The boy kept a steadfast focus on the barbed spear.

I am strong with my people. I have to watch the kill stick. I will soon hunt the fast water and everyone will come to eat my ba ba yano. They will walk from the high place to give me gifts. Many will come and know me… Quanah, first hunter of the ba ba yano.

It was a while now that he watched and waited with no sign of either one of them returning. Impatient, he checked the kill stick.

It is almost dry.

Lan's words remained strong in his thoughts. *"This is not your time to touch the kill stick. If you do, its spirit will not be strong."*

Disregarding that, the boy gave the handle a light tap with the tip of a finger…and then another. After some thought, he convinced himself it needed a good feel with two fingers. It was hard to contain his excitement.

This will be my kill stick…, not Waquini's!

Continuing his vigil, he checked the knots progress from time to time, now lying on his belly, his head propped up as he reached in to grab and hold the…

"Lan look! Quanah touched the kill stick!" Waquini yelled.

Quanah jerked. "No…I…I…was not going to…"

Dropping the baskets on the ground, Lan gave the boy a long, hard look. "It is I that must now have the talk with the Great Spirit of the water ba ba and I know he will be mad at you."

He gave Quanah a shame face before looking up at the sky. "Great Spirit of the water ba ba, do not take this little one. He does not know of your power."

He snuck a quick glance at Quanah who was standing wide eyed with his arms stiffly at his sides.

"Great Spirit of the water ba ba, the one that blows fire from his tongue and has teeth like the nag boksta."

At this, Quanah's mouth opened wide in horror, his eyes as big as goose eggs.

Maintaining a serious demeanor, Lan held his laughter inside while keeping a focus on the sky. "This little one speaks that he will not take the first fish...," another sideways glance, "...that he will give that one to me."

Both astonished and amazed, Quanah looked on in disbelief. The Mowatchi was actually talking to the great and powerful spirit of the water ba ba. It was incredible. And here he had no idea a spirit of the water ba ba even existed.

As if he was carrying on a conversation, Lan animatedly continued. "Yes...yes...that is many good. Yes...I will say your words to him. I hear you Great Spirit of the water ba ba. Then it is done."

Nodding at the sky, he folded his arms as he faced around toward Quanah. "The spirits were not pleased."

Open mouthed, Waquini, the older of the two boys, raised his brows along with an agreeing nod, although, not totally sure if what he had just witnessed was real or not.

Lan picked up the kill stick with Quanah at his heels. "Let us go to the water."

"They will not touch me will they?" the boy asked, his voice shaking. Hurrying along on short, stubby legs, he tried to keep up.

"No...not now and when I talk to Quanah he must listen."

"I will," the boy answered with all the sincerity he could give. With that seeming finalized, he ran ahead and waited on the bank for the two to catch up.

Fish filled the shallows, the dark shapes streaking by beneath the surface.

"There is the ba ba! He is there…and there…and there!" Quanah spoke as if surprised at seeing so many, even though he knew the calm tributary to the fast flowing river always teemed with fish. It was part of the reason for positioning the camp nearby.

"I see them," said Lan, standing at the edge.

Pike and perch, catfish and smaller sticklebacks, bullheads, large eyed silver breams and sturgeon fry were among the many swimming in the shallows. Frogs and salamanders were also plentiful. Snails of different sizes, colors and shapes, climbed the reeds and water ferns where both pink and white oleanders expanded in full bloom. Predator insects, such as whirligigs and water beetles chased after dragonfly larvae and fish fry. The river teemed with life.

To the boy's high expectancy, Lan waded in with the barbed spear and aimed at a small catfish. Stabbing it, he grabbed it by the gills and flung it onto the bank.

Quanah laughed. "A ba ba shu."

The boys scrambled for it at the same time. The oily fish slipped from their hands and flopped along the slick ground. Every time they tried to grab it, the fish slid closer to the water's edge. With the slope favoring the fish, it slipped back into the water. Quanah made a final grab for it, but at the last moment it wriggled into deeper water where it disappeared into the dark currents farther out.

He stamped both feet and shouted at Waquini. "You lost the ba ba shu."

"It is Quanah that lost the ba ba shu," Waquini shouted back.

A rabbit sized carp sailed over their heads. Shortly, a perch landed alongside, then another small catfish and then two more.

One by one, the boys scrambled to snap the fish up and put them into a basket.

A frog came sailing over their heads.

"What is your word for that," Lan asked.

"Ba ba bo bo," Waquini answered.

It was the same word for rabbit, except that the word for fish had to be added first.

Next, a squirming eel slapped into the mud.

"And that?"

"Ba ba nooey," Quanah shouted, giggling.

While Lan moved farther out into the shallows, Quanah, with a disgusted look, coaxed the huge no leg back into the river with a stiffened toe.

Something much bigger was on Lan's mind. Seeing the white of a young sturgeon the size of an otter slowly drift through the reeds, he speared it. It was a struggle to grab onto the gills while it thrashed about. The water frothed and splashed until he forced it closer to shore. The boys ran in to help and grabbed wherever they could. As soon as they got it onto the bank, they both shouted at the same time, "ba ba yanoooo!"

Outside Akule's cover, Alawa's fire burned high. The smaller fish, she placed on rocks around the pit. Waquini dragged the sturgeon behind him to feed the rest of the tribe and then returned to join Lan at the fire pit.

"I like ba ba lo," Waquini said.

Impatient to eat his, Quanah replied, "I will eat the ba ba shu."

Before the boys could get their hands on the ba ba doe, Akule grabbed it. Similar to catfish in looks, the white flesh of a bitterling tasted sweeter. Frogs were more to Alawa's liking.

Akule nodded approvingly. "You are a good hunter, Lan. Why did Nakoma not make you a first hunter like Yahto?"

"It is those words that I have said many times inside my head," said Lan.

Alawa flipped her frog over and left it to finish cooking in the flames. "It would give you a great shona."

"Their words are mine," said Ayashe. "Your power is strong. You can be a leader of first hunters…like Kuruk."

The frog now ready, Alawa picked it out of the fire and tossed it into the air several times before biting off the crunchy head. Well-cooked and stiff, the arms and legs stuck straight out; the fingers and toes, burned black and spread wide.

Akule said, "You must make this talk to Nakoma. He is the one that can make you a first hunter." With a matter of fact tone in his voice, he explained the ritual. "You must first hang from the post. Your body will be dry, but you cannot drink. The shotzus will eat your flesh and when they bring you down, the first hunters will put you inside a small cover with hot rocks. It is only then that you will see the spirits that will walk with you."

"That is when you will have your shona," Alawa followed, a sparkle in her eyes.

"That is my wish," said Lan, looking down at Quanah, overstuffed and sleeping against his leg. He cupped the boys shoulder. "Even little first hunters need their dream time."

"Dreams are where a man's wishes lie," said Alawa. "What are your wishes, Lan? Is Ayashe in them or will she stay here with us?"

"Ayashe is part of me. That will never change. She will go where I go."

The two men looked at one another for a long silence. Then, at the same time, both pointed at one another and together said the same thing. "Dream drink!"

Last day

Saddened, Ayashe took a final look at the tribe. Beside her stood Lan. Ahead, Yahto and two of his tribesmen, Tohopka (wild beast) and Sahkyo (mink), carried cooked meat on their backs. Following behind with their own burdens were Qaletaga and Kajika.

Amidst the sad faces of the tribe, Ayashe could see Odakotah (friendship) and Pannoowau (he lies) out front. Zoi held his woman along with his little ones. To the side stood Mantotohpa… and there…Akule…kind old Akule. Next to Alawa she could see Quanah, holding onto his kill stick and looking back, miserably.

"Oh…little Quanah. His look is so sad."

Ahead, Lan walked onward, quickening his steps. Ayashe did the same. She did not want to look at the boy, either. It was too hard, but then she had to.

Unsure of himself and pleading, Quanah ran toward them with hesitation in his steps. **"La-a-a-a-n!"**

Lan kept walking at a fast pace, but Ayashe could not help from turning around to see the boy now running as fast as his little legs could carry him. No one said anything. No one had to.

"Lan…wait!" Quanah cried.

Halfway there, he saw Lan turn around. Tears flooded down his cheeks along with the same old doubts and rejections from the past. Nothing in his short life had ever been sure or stable. Alone and with no one to call his own for what had been far too long, he knew now where he wanted to be. And the only way to fix that was to run and hope that he would not be refused again. He had to try, keep running and not stop, because if he lost this time, he was always going to be alone.

Just before he jumped up, Lan dropped the meat he was carrying. He caught the boy, still holding onto his kill stick while sniffing and rambling. "I do not want to stay he…he…here." *(Sniff)* "My wish is to go with you-oo-oo-ooo." *(Sniff)*

Lan leaned away to say something, but the boy held on so tightly, he had to peel his short arms away from his neck.

"So! My little hunter brother has it in his head that I should take him with me?"

Quanah could not stop the new surge of tears from streaming down his face as he braced for yet another rejection.

"It cannot be done," said Lan.

"N-n-no?"

Quanah could not deal with what he just heard. It was not what he hoped Lan would say.

"There is no way that I can do this," Lan said.

"I will not eat what you kill. I will use this," the boy said, holding out his new kill stick.

Feigning deep thought, Lan replied, "There is only one way."

The boy looked at him wide eyed. "There is?"

"I must first make you my little nag boksta brother."

"You…you will?"

Only then can you follow me. I have said my words."

Quanah burst with joy. He was finally going to belong to someone. He crushed his face into Lan's and laughed and cried until he fell asleep in his arms.

CHAPTER 12
THE PATH TO FIRST HUNTER

Meat bore heavily on the file of men, except for Yahto. He carried his with little effort. Despite a steady drizzle that persisted throughout the day, they made good time.

By nightfall, a pack of wolves showed themselves often. Torches kept them away until they entered the night fires of Nakoma's camp.

Loud drumming

In the confusion of welcoming voices, women eyed Yahto, impressed by the size of him. Holding onto one another, they shouted out bold, teasing proposals even though they had men of their own.

"Here is one for you," a young woman said, pushing her best friend in front of the handsome giant.

Drumming continues

"He wants you, not me," the woman being pushed teased. The two stepped out of the way as the huge man passed without a second glance.

A motion to end the banging from Nakoma, along with a few shakes of the rattle, brought Moki's drumming to a stop. Realigning the ram horn headdress, the leader waited on the mound for the tribe to settle down. Mothers escorted children out of the clearing while Nadie hastily filled in the few places on Nakoma's cheeks she had missed with red ochre. Finishing that, she clacked her way down the bone steps and slipped into the nearest tent.

The dried meat the men carried lay stacked into a neat pile at the foot of Nakoma's mound. Towering above those that stood there, Yahto's great size impressed Nakoma. He ignored him for the moment and pointed at Quanah. "Is this little one a first hunter?"

Ayashe reached for Quanah as he scooted behind her legs. "He is Quanah, the little one who has no one."

"I do have someone!" Quanah blurted out loud, wrapping an arm around her leg. He hooked the other around Lan's and returned Nakoma's wide grin.

"That is the kill stick of a first hunter, is it not?" Nakoma asked.

Shyly nodding, Quanah looked away from the glaring man sitting on top of the mound.

"Would you like to stand up here and show it to me? It is a high place."

"No!"

Nakoma stood and stretched as if he could see into the night.

"There are many of the bondo out there…and…and thunderfoot. And…what is that big animal by the fast water…Aleeka?"

A few of the men turned their heads.

Realizing it was only a ploy to get him to climb the mound, Quanah nervously laughed along with everyone else.

"If you come up here, I will let you hold this," said Nakoma, shaking the rattle, his brows fluttering like butterfly wings.

The boy looked on with mild interest, committed to staying where he was.

"And this one? You are the one that is called Yahto?"

"Shatu duma!" Yahto replied.

Nakoma raised his hand up high and returned the greeting.

Yahto chose his words carefully. "It is good that I see once again the one that is called Nakoma. Mantotohpa sends me to bring these gifts. This man is Sahkyo and that one is Tohopka. It is with the Mowatchi that we walk and what Mantotohpa wants for him."

Coming to the point at the beginning was viewed as proper and not the insult it could have been if it had been said over dream drink, especially, if it was not agreed upon. That would be viewed as deception hidden behind the welcoming veil of trust.

Stroking the wolf heads, Nakoma asked, "And what is it that Mantotohpa wants?"

"It is Mantotohpa and I, Yahto, that say it is you that must make the Mowatchi a first hunter."

"The Mowatchi! A first hunter?" Nakoma smirked. "Why would I anger our spirits in this way?"

Ayashe whispered to Lan. "Akule spoke his words to Mantotohpa. It was Akule who asked him to give you the gift of first hunter and he would not."

Nakoma's men started arguing.

"The Mowatchi's wish is to be a first hunter with us."

"First hunter, it cannot be done!"

"No Mowatchi has ever done this!"

Drum beats resume banging and then abruptly stop.

Nakoma exploded. "I will not anger Wankan Tanka in this way. If it is Mantotohpa who talks for this man, then it is Mantotohpa who must make him a first hunter."

Yahto angrily responded. "Mantotohpa fears this one's spirits. That is why he…"

"As I do mine!" Nakoma looked over at Lan. "Is this your wish?"

"Yes…it is my wish."

"Then go back to Mantotohpa."

Annoyed, Yahto sharply retorted, "It is **you** that first welcomed him. It is **you** that showed him the way to our people. So it is **you** who must give the Mowatchi this power."

Enraged, Nakoma stood up and shouted back, "I did this for his woman. She comes from your people, does she not?"

The huge man below folded his arms and looked steadily at Nakoma. With a voluminous voice, he said, "Mantotohpa has spoken his words…**and they are mine.** We will **not** call on our great spirits. **It is you…you who must make this Mowatchi a first hunter. It is you who must take that chance.** If that is not your wish, then you must send him back to the high place."

Concerned for their leader, Nakoma's men moved forward. At the forefront stood Kuruk, sure he would be heard from the long bond he had with Nakoma. While making his way up to the top of the mound, not a word was spoken.

Too soft for anyone else to hear, Kuruk said, "We could kill this Mowatchi and not have this worry."

Showing no reaction, Nakoma put his finger tips together and listened intently.

"Or…we can give him the power of first hunter."

Nakoma waited to hear more, but Kuruk said nothing else.

Why does Kuruk, the best of my first hunters…does he not know it will anger our hunting spirits? This shona is for our men…not for one from the high place.

Kuruk continued. "It is good that we keep him strong with us. He has many there that follow him."

Nakoma leaned away from him. *Kuruk is right, with the Mowatchi one with us we will have his words if more of his kind come in great numbers? We cannot stop so many without someone to speak for us.*

The leader motioned with a wave of a finger for Kuruk to lower himself down. "Our spirits will not say those same words."

"How do you know this? We never gave anyone from the high place this power."

Nakoma fidgeted in his seat. "It cannot be done. No one has ever…"

"You have already saddened Wankan Tanka." Karuk's voice sounded as scolding as a disappointed father's, his gaze lowering to the vulture tattooed on the leader's arm.

The sudden realization took hold of Nakoma.

I may have already angered our spirits. Or is this death bird from the Mowatchi only on my arm to stop his death spirits?

That alone would vindicate him, although it was too late to change any of that now. And Nakoma did not want to wait for the next hunt to find out that his people were going to be starved by wronged spirits.

Kuruk did nothing to hide his anger. "It is you who must speak to our spirits...not me."

Frowning, Nakoma gritted his teeth and replied, "It is not in my head that this Mowatchi is worthy of our spirits. He did nothing!"

Kuruk stood straight, leaned his head back and stared down at the tribe's leader. "If it is done the same way for the Mowatchi as it is done for our men, it cannot be looked at any other way."

"Then that is not enough." Nakoma scowled, banging his fist on his thigh. "He did not go with our elders to the high place to become a man. He did nothing. He cannot..."

Kuruk head lowered until his lips touched the leader's ear. "Then let us give something of the Mowatchi to our spirits."

Nakoma grimaced and whispered back. "Kill him?"

Kuruk continued. "Let us give our spirits..."

After he finished what he had to say, he stood back, pressed his lips together and waited for the leaders answer. The two men grew silent for a while---a very long while. Finally, Nakoma reluctantly nodded his approval. Before Kuruk reached the top step to go down, Nakoma stood at the edge of the mound. "All of you first hunters...and you Lan...follow me to Ohcumgache's cover."

As soon as everyone quieted inside the shaman's tent, Nakoma took his place before the altar. Behind him, stacked from floor to ceiling were skulls from the tribe's ancestors.

"Hurry with the fire!"

Lighting up the inside of the tent, Nadie rushed to finish the last line of oil filled skull caps on her side of the wall. On the other, Honovi finished with the last of hers.

"Kajika! The spirit fire," Nakoma snapped.

An immediate response from the men voiced from the back. None had ever seen the spirit fire lit before, not even Nakoma himself, only the elders and that was a long time ago. The tribe's leader was to pay homage to the ancient ones, acquaint Lan's spirits with theirs. Just the thought, the mere mention of mixing spirits like this required appeasement.

The leader clapped his hands. "Nadie! Honovi! Go!"

"I have more to…," Nadie started.

"Go now!"

Other than their rushed steps toward the entranceway, all remained quiet inside. Conferring with Ohcumgache and a group of elders, the tribe's leader nodded continuously as he and kajika were told the order of the ritual. Finally, all but one of the elders and the old shaman took their places.

Ohcumgache, wearing a black, bear skin robe, assisted by the elder, covered Kajika's face, neck and hands with a glistening green, pasty substance made from pulverized grass and animal fat. All the while, the shaman recited chants under his breath. Another, dark, almost black, bear skin robe was draped over Kajika's shoulders, the hood pulled over his head.

Indicating he was ready, Kajika, a shaman hopeful, unraveled the end of a thin rope from a deer horn on the wall, pulling it down to open a large venting hole in the ceiling. Disturbed debris drifted downward in the stream of sunlight, along with a whirlwind that twisted his robe around him. His arms rose up to it, because he knew, like everyone else there knew, this was not without risk. The Wankan Tankas (Great Spirits) were stronger than anything and none of it could be taken lightly. It was only the first step, the beginning and once started, had to be finished.

With considerable effort, Kajika, along with assistance from Moki, slid aside a heavy stone slab. It revealed a deep pit that had not been opened since before Kajika's lifetime. They both stepped back from the foul smell of rotted mammoth oil comparable to flatulence.

Two canes held Ohcumgache steady as he yelled out in a worn, quivering voice, "Push the outside skin to the side."

A first hunter, sitting nearest the steps, ran up and spread the heavy buffalo skin at the entrance open and tied it off. Highly combustible, gas drifted upwards towards the vent at the top of the tent, aided by the draft coming from the opened entryway. Once it dissipated, Kajika dropped a torch into the pit. A fire ball quickly consumed the rest of the rising gases that burned black toward the ceiling along with an acrid odor. It billowed through the vent until the fire below turned blue.

At the same time, a raven outside screamed in a high pitched screech. No longer did Lan feel he would be alone with the coming ritual.

The black bird has followed me to this place and now it is here to watch over me.

Turning to the altar, the old shaman, his elderly assistant and Kajika, lit each of the skulls filled with mammoth oil. It left the altar aglow in yellow, flickering light. Ohcumgache next gave Kajika a handful of ashes from the bodies of those very same skulls.

After conferring one last time with the shaman, he faced the pit and tossed in a small amount of the ashes along with a chant. "Hayolahanahana!"

The first hunters immediately answered.

"Hayo...hayo!"

More ashes were thrown in.

"Hayolahanahana!"

"Hayo...hayo!"

Another handful was given to the carrier of the ochre from Ohcumgache, which was then thrown into the pit followed by the same chants until all of the past leaders were given homage. When it was over, the two elders separated from Kajika and took their places before those that were seated.

After a last and final talk with the shaman, Nakoma joined Kajika at the altar. Behind the tribe's leader, fire roared from the pit. It was hot on his face when he had turned there to look; hot on the back of his legs, but it was not the heat he was thinking about. If he chose wrong, he would have to answer to these very same ancestors.

The way to Wankan Tanka is not something we can give so easily.

"Lan…if we give to you the power of first hunter, what is it that you will give to us?"

"My power to heal," Lan replied. "I know the plants that will end your people's sickness. Some of your men are without women. I have women that will follow me from the high place."

"The black rocks, will you also bring that with your women?"

"More than all of your hunters need."

Seeming pleased, Nakoma rubbed the back of his neck and appeared to be thinking hard. He approached Lan, stood before him and stared straight into his eyes. "Then that will not be enough. There is something of yours that we must take."

"I have nothing else that I can give."

Nakoma's glance met Kuruk's, who quietly nodded from the back row, his hands folded out front.

Behind Nakoma, Ohcumgache made his way to the altar in preparation for what was to come.

"There **is** something," Nakoma added, the compassion in his voice, deceiving and eerily soft.

All around, men closed a circle around the Mowatchi.

Lan blurted out loud, "I will bring you women and black rocks. I will bring kill sticks. It is my hunting spirits that I cannot give…"

"It is not your hunting spirits that we want." Nakoma continued, still glaring. "It is something else of yours that we must take from you. Your life spirit!"

Visibly shaken, Lan reached for his ax. Two men immediately grabbed his arms and took him to the ground.

"Take his hunting things," shouted Kuruk.

Someone took the quiver of arrows. Another removed the ax from the netting. His spear went next.

"And this!" said Kuruk, removing the bandana.

"What of the spirits scratched in his skin," said Kajika.

"Those are his spirits. They cannot help him here," Kuruk snapped.

Two more men held Lan's legs down while another pressed the Mowatchi's face sideways to the floor. Above Lan, Kuruk straddled him with a sharp ax in his grip.

"Kajika! Start the words!" Nakoma ordered.

Kuruk held the ax firmly in his grip; a flint ax honed as razor sharp as the knife he carried.

Kajika began the chant. "Hoonawanawhamay."

The first hunters repeated that.

"Hoonay, Hoonay! Hah!"

"Hoonawanawhamay."

"Wha may! Wha may! Hah!"

Kajika's voice quivered nervously. He was sweating profusely---as much as Lan.

"Hoonawanawhamay."

"Hoonay! Hoonay! Hah!"

"Hoonawanawhamay."

"Hoonay! hoonay! Hah!"

Twelve times, they repeated the chant and then there was silence. Kuruk raised the ax high above his head, hesitated for a brief moment and then slammed the ax straight down. The lead first hunter could not falter. He could never falter, having swung an ax too many times for that.

Just before severing Lan's head, Yahto grabbed his arm and pushed Kuruk to the side. With words that were loud and deeply basso, he said. "This Mowatchi must live. It is Mantotohpa's wish that I stand with this one."

"He cannot live. It will anger our spirits!" Kuruk shouted.

Yahto shouted back. "Killing the Mowatchi will anger Mantotohpa. Many of your first hunters will die. Is this what you want?"

Kuruk glared intensely up at Yahto. For a quiet moment, neither man said anything else. Finally, Nakoma, in a softer voice, asked, "What is Mantotohpa's interest in this Mowatchi?"

"His woman! It is Mantotohpa that would not be pleased to see Ayashe lose this man."

"Then take him back with you and make him your first hunter."

"This cannot be done," Yahto replied. "It was you who welcomed him, so it is you who must talk to the spirits."

Armed with knives or axes, Qaletaga, Moki and four others edged closer to Kuruk.

At Yahto's side, Sahkyo and Tohopka raised their axes high.

Quietly, Nakoma glanced at Kuruk, closed his eyes and with reluctance, nodded in his direction.

Kuruk, ignoring him, quickly snatched the ax back from Yahto. Before the bigger man could react, he suddenly spun around and slammed it straight down.

"Hoonawanawhamay."

"Whamayyy…whamayyy…whamayy…whamayyyy!"
Crack

It was almost too quick to see before troubled sighs gasped from everyone there.

"It is done! Shouted Kuruk.

Lan's eyes remained tightly closed. As soon as he opened them, he saw what Kuruk had in his hand.

Holding up Lan's braid, Kuruk pointedly stated, "We must give something of yours if you are to be a first hunter with us. This then will be your gift to our great spirits."

Possession of the braid was immediately taken by Kajika, unraveled on the way to the altar and handed to Ohcumgache. Rolled around the point of a stick, the shaman ignited the hair into a ball of flames. He shook it continuously, releasing a trail of singed remnants that lifted toward the ceiling in a continuous black line along with the smoke. Standing next to the shaman, Nakoma looked on as the singed hairs lifted toward the ceiling vent.

The rest of the men crowded in to follow the blackened remnants that were now moving to the outside of the plume, where they swirled around underneath the overhead hides.

"It must go through the hole," one of the men said.

Lingering there, the singed hairs continued to drift in a circle underneath the ceiling.

Men shook their heads and commented.

"It goes nowhere."

"Our spirits do not want this Mowatchi."

Lan lowered his head in dismay. *If it does not go to the outside, I will have nothing left to prove myself. They will then send me back to the high place...or finish me here.*

"Look!" Someone shouted.

Lan held his breath.

Picked up by an upward draft, the hairs spiraled and suddenly sucked out of the hole to the outside.

The raven screamed at the exact moment when the hairs exited the hole. It was timely and a good sign. Although not final, Lan's spirit, so far, seemed to have been accepted.

As everyone returned to their places, Kajika removed a hollowed out bone from its place on the altar. With one end in the eye socket of a burning skull, he used it like a funnel to gently pour a small trickle of water inside. It caused steam and a rush of flames to instantly shoot from the eye. He continued until he treated each skull the same way, along with the ritualistic chants that he said under his breath.

Nodding and satisfied for the moment, Nakoma replaced him and stood in front of the altar to address the Mowatchi.

"Soon, your time will come to meet our great spirits. It is our wish that they welcome you as a first hunter. Only then will you be a brother to all other first hunters everywhere and they will be brothers to you. It is only then that we will call you a first hunter."

He motioned for Lan to rise to his feet. Grabbing his shoulders, the tribe's leader firmly shook them. "Your shona will only follow you when you finish your path to first hunter. I know you will be that first hunter, because I feel it here." Nakoma banged on his chest with his fist. "Here is my gift." He untied a pair of eagle claws from his waistline and gave it to him.

After the roar of approvals that followed, the rest lined up to offer gifts of their own. Akando was first in line, smiling from ear to ear. He handed Lan a groin patch to the laughter of the men.

Next, came his father, Achak. "I carried these for too long and now I give them to you."

Lan tied the string of bear teeth he gave him around his neck. Wolf hides followed and soon filled his arms from the same men who went with him on the long walk to Etu. Skull caps and a vessel of mammoth oil, plus an assortment of shells, were given to him from Kajika. Even Yahto gave him a gift, ripping off a necklace of a small mix of animal skulls and handing it to him.

With a stern look, he said, "This path you wish to follow to first hunter will give you a great power and shona. It is only then that you and I will walk side by side…not before."

Standing in the dark by the back wall next to the stairs, Kuruk silently looked on with doubt showing in the hard lines of his face, his arms still folded across his chest. Before anyone else made a move to leave, he climbed his way out of Ohcumgache's tent to contemplate alone.

Daybreak

The entire tribe gathered at first light in front of the row of tall post, the third and fourth of which was reserved for Akando. Aynga would hang between the fourth and fifth. Between the last two, capped with Bandu skulls, Lan would hang like the others for two days and two nights.

Naked and ready, the three stood before Kuruk and Kajika. Waiting at the side stood three elders holding grass mats dense with shotzus held fast within a tight weave of grass matting. Helpless, the ants remained immobile except for the jaws that emerged on the other side---jaws that were as long as a man's thumbnail and filled with toxin. Each mat held over fifty ants each and would serve to weaken the promising first hunters with stings so painful and powerful; one bite took days to heal.

"Drink more water," Nayati's woman said to her man.

"My stomach feels like that of a fat thunderfoot. I can not drink anymore." he replied.

Next to them stood Qaletaga, the first hunter assigned to him. "We must now begin the marking with red dirt. There will be no water when they raise you."

Nayati grabbed it, his hands shaking while drinking to near bursting. As he waited for the rest of the preparations, he walked around in aimless circles. To calm his nerves, he softly recited chants under his breath.

At the neighboring posts, Nadie assisted Achak with his son Akando. Looking over his shoulder at Nayati, Akando said, "I am ready. Give me the red dirt."

Each sense used in a hunt had to be lined so that the spirits would know where to enter. Starting from the middle of Akando's forehead, Nadie drew two straight lines across both eyelids to aid the hunter to see. She dipped back into the ochre and connected those lines with a line that ran down the top of his nose.

"Wait...I have to rub it," he said.

"I will rub it for you. Is that enough?"

"Yes...finish the marks."

The red line was continued over his lips and chin. Parallel lines were drawn around both cheeks and down alongside his ears.

"His neck," said his father, "the marks must go straight." After it was done, he pointed to the boy's lower ribs. "When you get to this bone, the red dirt goes this way and that way to make his breathing strong.

"And here also?" Nadie asked, drawing two wide even bands around each bicep.

Both stooped down for the lines that went around each calf and where Achak interrupted again. "Higher…they must go higher."

"And here?" she asked, pointing at Akando's feet where she remembered they had to fan out to the sides.

Taima, Qaletaga's little girl of seven, sauntered up smiling and proud. Wearing Akando's wolf skin like an oversized cloak, she held out a basket nearly filled to the top with ornamental treasures.

"Here is Akando's hunting spirits," she said, full of confidence and purpose.

"The men stand and wait," said Achak. "We must hurry."

Nadie checked to see how far along Nayati was with his markings. "His woman is slow with the marks and Qaletaga has done no others."

"Kuruk is finished with Lan's," said Akando.

"He has done many," Achak replied.

Nadie said, "The big one, Yahto, stands with them. I see Lan's little woman sits and waits by his side."

Lowering for the necklace of otter claws that Nadie put over his head, Akando remained still as she followed with colorful shell ornaments that she affixed to both ears. The attached tassels of red mammoth hair hung nearly to his neck. Around both upper arms and calves were wrapped bracelets, also made of spotted snail shells.

Finger rings with the claws and beaks of small birds attached, were slipped onto each of Akando's fingers. His father tied a necklace of large, black and white osprey feathers just below the otter claws so that they lay flat across his chest, covering his pectorals.

"My nahgo is pretty," said the promising first hunter.

Nadie affixed the wolf skin around his shoulders. Pure white with black tips, the underside of the fur had been chewed until it was as soft as baby skin. The head of the wolf was left attached and the lower jaw removed so that the black nose and pure white upper canines hung over Akando's forehead. The rest of the fur and tail draped down his back.

Admiring him with love in her eyes, Nadie said, "You have shona already."

Akando grinned.

"Will you still meet me in the grass when you become a first hunter?"

"I will," he said, his eyes as bright as sunlit orchids.

With his father shuddering from what was just said, and his back to them for the moment, Nadie teasingly reached under Akando's groin patch. He had always been there for her, as she had for him; ever since he was old enough to mate with. Their meeting place was special, out in the grass where Nadie would wait. Most times, but not restricted to, during the late evening around sunset, she would be there, naked and waiting. As soon as he arrived, she would lay back and spread her arms out to receive him, her hips lifted high to love him, to bring pleasure, to relish in those fiery feelings she desired and could no longer wait for.

Theirs was a romance of opportunity, a love of want rather than a love for one another. To Nadie, Akando was still a boy, 'though a handsome one at that and without Nakoma's attentions, there were no other choices. She was young, she had needs, and Akando the only one besides Nakoma she desired enough to fulfill her. Before Akando there was Takoda, but that ended long ago. His woman saw to that.

For Akando there was no one else, no one of his age or older that had not been taken already. His choice was to either share his feelings with Nadie or stay alone with the lustful urges that overwhelmed him from time to time. With no one else to compare her to, she became a partner of need---a first physical love---a love of release and partial fulfillment; for sadly, it was not a complete love. Nakoma knew, everyone knew, it was accepted---understood. Besides, the tribe's leader was relieved for it.

"Let us begin," Kuruk shouted.

Thick ropes hung down from the top of the posts, swaying in the wind like waiting serpents. Yahto braced Lan from the front, holding him firmly so he would not fall forward from the shotzu stings to follow.

An elder handed Kuruk a mat of shotzus which he immediately pressed against Lan's back. The ensuing pain was immediate and heart stopping, the only reaction from Lan, the grimace on his face as he held back an urge to scream out loud. A low whimper from either Akando or Nayati could be heard and then all went silent.

Yahto pulled the mat off, ripping shotzus from their jaws and leaving most of the sharp pincers imbedded in Lan's skin. He held the Mowatchi up from dropping to the ground. As well, both Nayati and Akando were also helped as they waited half bent from the effects of their own poisons.

A fire started, Kajika, wearing an array of striped shells and wrist rattles, threw off the hooded robe. Except for the dark green dye on his arms, neck and face, his entire naked body had been covered with red ochre,

Excitement filled him as he added a log to the fire. Cinders were moved around as he poked and coaxed it from underneath. More twigs were then added and stuck between the logs, then more logs thrown on top until the fire grew into a virtual inferno. Flames soared upwards in a surge of billowing smoke---thick plumes that smoldered with fiery insides---the core, a deep red—so furiously red; like molten magma, the logs turning white and splitting in the intense heat. Sap blistered and exploded in every direction.

While Kajika chanted, Kuruk faced the future first hunters, raising his voice over the thundering of the enormous fire. "Now is your time to be strong. Do not look to the hunts behind you, but to the first hunter you will be. Look there and you will see our great hunting spirits. It is they who will walk with you."

Beginning with East, Ohcumgache, wearing the bear skin robe, threw ashes into the four directions. Following a check of the sun's position, the shaman's hand slowly lifted and pointed to the sky for Kuruk to begin the raising.

Like the newborn he was meant to emulate, Lan stood naked and ready to emerge into that world of first hunter. With toxins burning inside, he held himself rigid for the four pieces of flat bone Kuruk held in his hands. Each was the length of a forefinger and honed to sharp points at both ends.

While Yahto held Lan firmly in his grip, Kuruk pinched a thick fold of skin and muscle in Lan's back between two of his fingers. Lan gritted his teeth as soon as he pushed the bone through, twisting the point deep into muscle.

Ayashe turned away and covered her eyes.

Having forced the bone through to the other side, Kuruk left both ends sticking out of the skin. The three remaining bones were inserted the same way so that all four formed a square in the middle of Lan's upper back. To this, they tied a webbed harness and finally, the ropes that would be attached to it to lift him higher than the tents.

"You will be last," Kuruk said.

For a brief moment, he held Lan's shoulder in a firm grip before moving on to Nayati.

A slight grin on his face, Yahto took a long look at the Mowatchi's limp body and shook his head slowly from side to side. "You will not make it to first hunter. Not everyone does. Some have seen their death on the ropes." Yahto glanced at the sky and then back at Lan. "If the spirits welcome you, I will stand at your side. It is only then that I will be a brother to you. Those were the words of Kuruk and now they are mine."

Unable to stand on his own from the stinging shotzus, Nayati hung limply in Qaletaga's arms.

"Raise him," shouted Kuruk, pointing to the top of the posts.

Nayati's cry sounded pitiful and with a lack of control as soon as he was raised. He could take no more. "Enough! Bring me down!"

"Stay there!" Kuruk encouraged.

"Ugh! No! Bring me down. My wish is to end this."

Lowered to the ground, the leader of second hunters collapsed and had to be carried unconscious to the river to soak his wounds.

Refraining from that same shameful exhibition, Akando threw off the wolf skin and ripped away the groin patch. He cringed from the burning poison when his father pressed the mat of shotzus against his back. Dropping to his knees, he gradually stood back up, but had to lean against him to keep from falling.

Achak inserted the four bones into his back, followed by the netting and finally the ropes.

"I am ready," said Akando, in a weak sounding voice.

"Raise him!"

To Akando, Kuruk's command sounded so pitiless and uncaring, although he knew that not to be true. He clenched his teeth before suddenly being pulled away from the ground. The excruciating pain of that took everything he had left inside to keep from crying out, but it was too much to hold in. Before reaching the top, he let out a blood curdling scream heard by everyone.

For Nadie, seeing him high in the air with his head hanging over his chest was too much to bare. She ran from the horrible scene and into the leader's tent.

Kuruk wasted no time in moving over to Lan. "Raise him... now!"

Pulled off his feet, Lan in an instant lifted higher than Nakoma's mound---higher than the top level of the tents, the skin on his back, stretching like those very same tents. He threw his head back from the intense pain that shot through every part of him, breathed in deeply and forced the words he now shouted at the sky.

"I am Man That Runs Too Fast! I lead the Bandu and I will show you no fear. I will eat this fire that burns inside me."

The clouds, serene and crisp in their heights, soon paled into an ever darkening sky.

"Wolf hunter...if I die...I...I am ready to run with you. Take me...so we can hunt the elk together."

Although the burning stings felt hot in his back, it was not yet the gut wrenching pain that ripped and belched blood. It was not yet the pain that strangled the throat of torturous outcries. This would be bearable pain, a pain defused behind spiritual beliefs, thereby moved from body to soul---moved to the imaginary world of abstract reality.

Sweat poured from him, and then the sky, although clear, turned completely black. Lan was there in unconscious detachment, rising upwards into its harboring dream. He now lived in the non-living world of fleshless thought and cataleptic salvation. There was no more pain, only euphoria and a sense of well-being.

In the length of one breath, the wind brother lifted him high into the murky haze of a cloud. It was exhilarating to fly so high and to feel the evanescent moisture on his skin. It felt cool and wet, but did not cling to him. He emerged from the other side and out into the empty depths of an embracing sky. before him flew the black raven, its wings spread black against the blueness.

From that reeling height it was breathtaking to look down at his green valley, his forest, his winding river—his vermilion cliffs. Like no more than grass blades, trees rippled across the foothills with a stream no wider than a spider's line. In the far distance, elk chased the descending radiance of the sun.

All around were the greeting hands of loved ones as they cheered and surrounded him. Each shouted his name and rode the wind brother along with him through the clear, copen sky. It was a joyful reunion and when the greetings were over, they parted to the sides to clear the way for Wolf Hunter.

> *Tall and regally adorned in a full robe of white furs and white feathers, Lan's father approached with a spear in his hand. He held it out to his son, the hawk feathers blowing in the wind. Smiling, he put a hand on his son's shoulder and spoke with a voice full of compassion. "The forest keeps count of **ALL** of her children."*

For the entire day, ropes creaked under the weight of the two promising first hunters. Now began the long wait, for here it would all begin or here it would all end. Weakened and dehydrated, a ritual would soon follow of arduous sweating in a small tent, the herbs and hot rocks inside, sizzling with steam. The two would see their demons, for here would be born the power of first hunter. To endure this, was to endure the most trying of hunts. Respect as a first hunter was to have a shona of the highest order; one to be honored across the farthest reaches of the grasslands by every man who hunted there.

As he did every evening, Kajika found solace from loneliness at the bachelor fire---a place, too, for troubled husbands to seek relief from pestering wives.

"Will you go with us when the tatanka come?" asked Qaletaga.

"My eyes do not see the tatanka, Kajika answered, playing his tongue into a space between his teeth.

"Your look is sad. This is a good time. Soon we will have two more first hunters."

"That is not what saddens me."

"What is it then?"

"It is something I cannot…" Kajika reached down and dug his nails into dirt as he tried his best to hold back his emotions. Sighing deeply, he looked at Qaletaga and then at Achak as he searched for the excuse that would mask the insecurities he felt.

"When it was the time that Nadie lost her man, Wahanassatta, It was I, Kajika, that wanted her. It was then that I did not have my shona, so it was Nakoma that took her."

Both men exchanged surprised glances at one another. They waited, but heard nothing else from him.

Speaking first, Achak had a ready answer. "If it is your wish to own Nadie, you must first make your talk to Nakoma."

Kajika shook his head and stumbled on what he said next. "I...I have said this...in...in my head many times, but, it is Nadie that gives me worry. She...she does not look to me the way I look at her. It would not please her to be with me."

Achak felt Kajika's pain. Widowed and alone himself, he replied, "You carry the red dirt. For this you have a great shona. It is gifts that you need to give to Nakoma. With gifts, Nakoma will give you Nadie."

"I have thought on this. The gifts I have are many, but not enough."

"Then we will give you more," said Qalatega.

Moki, having awakened from a late nap, groggily scuffed his way to the bachelor fire. Although the men were in conversation, he had not, yet, focused on what was being said. He scratched his rear, yawned and aimed his backside at the fire while popping the dirt globules clinging to the hairs on his chest. A prolonged yawn was followed by silently unloading the long volume of gas he had been holding up to now.

Whooosh

Consumed in a bright flash of light, the fire ball singed his back side.

"**Eeee!**" he yelled, jumping out of the way. He rubbed both cheeks and fanned his rear while everyone else laughed.

"I have the nahgo I killed. I can give that to you," said Achak.

"What is it that you will give," Qalatega asked Moki?

"Give? What?"

"It is Kajika that needs gifts for Nakoma."

"Gifts? Why would I give gifts to Nakoma? Moki asked, with as much interest in that as he had for Ohcumgache's shriveled up old woman.

"It is Kajika that has a wish to own Nadie," said Qalatega.

Still rubbing his backside, Moki looked at them as if their minds had floated off in the fast water. "Gifts! Ha! Yes…gifts. I have a gift. I will give this. He moved aside the triangular patch to shake his manhood at them. He knew they would laugh at that and laughed along with them. Inside, he was glad for Kajika and nothing would please him more than to offer gifts of his own.

Dawn

As the camp enlivened with normal everyday activities, Kajika waited for Nadie to emerge from Nakoma's tent. In time, he saw her walk to the edge of the clearing carrying baskets for the edible roots she wanted to dig up. With Akando hanging from the posts, he knew they would be alone.

Nadie was truly beautiful---to Kajika. She walked with grace and an air of femininity that to some may have seemed awkward, but to his knowing eye, they were the ungainly strides of strength. In Nadie, he saw the son that would one day be bigger and stronger than he was---a son who would become the man he was not---the first hunter he could never be. Through that son he would relive his own youth---the life he wished he had---the life that should have been.

A duck with a broken wing hid beneath a corner of one of the tents where the children that were playing there had not noticed. Emboldened by hunger, the duck cautiously emerged to the joy of the children.

"Look there!" Mahpee (sky) shouted, "sisika."

Quanah felt sadness for the duck and the way it flopped around. "We can find food for it."

"Kill it," screamed Taima, Takoda's littlest girl.

Quanah hurried to catch up with Mahpee. Taima passed him and it was all he could do to keep up. Staying well ahead, the duck settled a distance away only to rise just above the ground and well out of arms reach.

Through the clearing and around the tents, the chase for the elusive duck continued on, darting and changing directions. Knowing the children were close behind, the duck circled behind Rama's forelegs. Under the mammoth's body they ran; the duck, Taima, Mahpee and finally little Quanah. Behind him and only a hair's length away from the boy's short, scurrying legs was the tip of Rama's trunk. His body was left twisted precariously, the trunk underneath his belly and stretched toward the other side.

The chase ended when all three children could go no further. Taima held back the rest from entering the brush. She knew the risks. "We do not go there," she said, the excitement of the chase in her voice.

"Why," said Quanah, disappointed and out of breath.

Taima shouted at him with a scolding look. "That is where the jonga hunt. Do you not know this?"

Quanah flinched and meekly asked, "Are they there now?"

"Yes!" she stamped, fuming with a mad face to reaffirm herself.

The best of the edible roots were farther out which Nadie knew very well. She ventured beyond where the others dared go. There, the biggest and sweetest of tubers lie just below ground. She began to dig into the hard soil with a wedged stone, fully aware of the chance she was taking. It put her on edge just to be there. She would linger no more than she had to, digging as fast as she could to collect enough to last.

It was then that she saw the saber tooth. She trembled as soon as she did, too afraid to even scream. Nothing could be more frightening than to stand before a large saber tooth tiger with its focus on you. To her horror it crouched low and started to slink in her direction. She tried to remain calm and think of an option. She could throw the basket at the nag boksta with the hopes of startling it long enough to run to the tents, but those were a long way off. Holding the basket out front, she slowly got to her feet and began to creep backwards from the glaring beast.

A low rumble, heard by no one except Nadie, made her shake from it. She dropped the basket, too afraid to reach down to pick it back up. She continued to back away from the most terrifying thing that had ever happened to her.

The saber tooth lowered its rear, roared and suddenly bolted toward her. Nadie covered her eyes and waited for the impact that she knew would soon knock her to the ground and immediately after, the tearing sounds from her flesh being ripped from her body.

Kajika let out a blood curdling scream.

Nadie's eyes opened in time to see him standing rigid and screaming at the top of his lungs, and then as he fell backwards into the brush like a stiff, falling tree.

Running passed her at full stride was the returning saber tooth tiger with the duck in its jaws, racing away from the terrible high pitched sound it just heard. All Nadie saw was the passing predator and not what it had in its jaws. Relieved, she turned to the welcoming site of first hunters running up and carrying spears.

"Nag boksta! Nag boksta!" she shouted, while pointing to where she last saw the huge cat. "Kajika saved me from the nag boksta."

Two men shook him awake and lifted him to his feet.

"You saved me," she repeated.

Kajika groggily responded. "Huh!…I did? Ah…y…yes, I did!"

"Kajika sent the Nag Boksta away," said Qaletaga, surprised.

An elder, eager to give his own version, said, "The nag boksta pushed Kajika down and ran from him."

A man at the back repeated what he thought he heard to those who could not. "Kajika wounded the nag boksta and it ran from him."

Nakoma, doubtful and frowning, appeared annoyed at the interruption. "Take him to his cover!"

Running ahead, Nadie entered the tent before the men. At the bottom of the steps, she pointed to a buffalo skin spread into a corner. "Put him there," she said.

She sat next to him and listened to the various versions from the men of how Kajika had saved her. In time, they all left, leaving Nadie alone to comfort him.

"I can get you water if that is what you want." She continued to lightly stroke the side of his face while returning his amorous gaze.

"I have no need for water. Resting here with you is enough."

"I have to go." She rubbed his chest.

"No…stay with me."

"My need is to fix the roots."

"Stay."

"No…I can not."

"Leave it to the others. I want you here with me."

She covered his lips with a forefinger. "I will come back…soon."

He watched her go up the steps and smiling back the whole time until reaching the top landing. Bending over, she looked in. "Soon, I will walk this way. It is then that I will give myself to you."

"I will wait."

"My eyes will see you then."

"And mine."

"See you then."

"See you then."

"I go."

"I know."

"See you."

"Come back."

"No!"

"Yes!"

"I can not."

"Then go!"
"I will!" *Giggle*

"Bring him down," shouted Kuruk.

Lowered to a sitting position, Lan was given enough water to wet his lips and then left to recover. He felt nauseous and weak. It seemed he was lowered only moments before when he felt himself being lifted and dragged through the dark and into a small tent set up in the middle of the clearing. Inside, there was hardly enough room for one person and the small fire pit before the entrance. Eased to the floor, he sat with his head hanging down and his arms at his sides. It was a while that he sat there, alone and thinking until finally looking around.

The inside was confining, the tent walls, little wider than his shoulders. If he could make himself stand, he would have to bend over. Although dark, light from an outside fire penetrated through a few of the cuts in the hides and where sinew was woven through them to secure the skins to the wood framing. The skins themselves flickered yellow from the fire outside.

A green hand pushed a flat wooden board between the entry flaps to drop hot rocks into the small pit. It was Ohcumgache's hand, green and thin and before long another set of scorched rocks dropped inside. More followed, until the fire pit filled and the tent became stifling hot.

His arms across his thighs, Lan took in a deep breath.

When the spirits come, I will not fear them no matter how many there are.

His back burned from the shotzu stings and inserted bones still in place. Worn, exhausted and mentally drained, it was everything he could do to keep from calling out to end it all. Kuruk would then yank him from his misery. He could have all the water he wanted. He could eat and rest. And then he would have to live with that---a failed first hunter ordered to the back of the hunts along with Nayati, Moki and the younger boys.

The flap spread open. A handful of chopped lophophora, a hard to find cacti, was dropped onto the rocks. White smoke suddenly spread throughout the tent, the ensuing mescaline euphoria---immediate and totally encompassing. Imperfections in the hide soon metamorphosed into living, moving animal parts, like horns and digging hooves and mad, snorting nostrils.

From across a grassy plain, thundered in a great horde of charging buffalo. Naked and holding his spear, Lan stood in wait before the ground that kicked up before him. Like a rumbling, raging storm, the heavy footed beast enlarged as they closed in. When they reached him, he raised his spear and one by one killed them all, casting them off to the side into dissipating apparitions.

More came and more fell and as each vanished into nothing, he felt his arms and legs grow. His body soon dwarfed the monstrous beasts until none dared challenge him anymore.

Through the yellow haze came a brilliant thunder clap, followed by the white slicing tusk of a charging mammoth. Lan stood tall, raised his spear and pointed it skyward. There, he held fast and defiant to face the great Aleeka. Instead of running him down, the bull slowed from a full charge and halted before him---Man That Runs Too Fast, a first hunter whose height now towered high above the bull. Snorting heavily, Aleeka lowered his trunk and succumbed to the greater power.

"Take him to my cover," Nakoma ordered.

Carried down the steps of Nakoma's tent with his feet dragging behind, Yahto and Kuruk brought Lan to the row of mammoth skulls and sat him down.

Before Lan, Kuruk stood holding out a femur filled with dream drink. "Drink this. I want to know your dream?"

Nothing tasted so good. With his body so depleted, it did not take long for the room to spin around. Within that dizzying blur, he saw Kuruk looking back with a repeating worried look. He was saying something, but his voice seemed far away.

"What is it that you saw in the cover?"

Nakoma asked the same thing. "Your dream, what was it that you saw."

Smiling back, Lan tried to focus. *I never noticed Kuruk's teeth were so perfect…and so white.*

He felt someone else shaking his shoulders. He looked up to see Yahto standing over him, his basso voice, resonating inside the tent. "Tell us what you saw! We must know your dream!"

Lan made every effort to keep his head from weaving all over the place. "I saw the hunting animals. It was their wish to kill me."

"Did you kill any of them?" asked Kuruk.

"I stabbed them with my kill stick and they left me like the smoke in my fire."

"Is that all you saw?" Kuruk asked, wide eyed and wanting to hear more.

A slight smile curled into a proud grin as Lan searched their faces. "It was Aleeka that ran at me next."

"Aleeka? Did he kill you…in your dream?"

"No…he asked that I would own him."

Kuruk straightened. "No one here has ever seen the great Aleeka in this way. You have a great shona. I feel good on this."

The heavy hand of Yahto slapped down on Lan's shoulder. "It is a good shona. It would please me to hunt with you at my side."

"And I," said Kuruk. He and Yahto grabbed one another's shoulders for the success of the ritual.

Nakoma reached for Lan's. "It is good that I look to our new first hunter. Take this wanbli wiyaka (eagle feather) and put it in your hair. It will mark you as a first hunter so all can see you for your shona."

The following morning

"He waits," said Nadie to Kajika, holding the front hide to Nakoma's cover open. A basket of neatly arranged gifts lay on the ground outside the entryway; a coyote tail, hawk talons, an assortment of shell necklaces, a wolf fur and lastly a prized bear skin.

"Go now," she stamped, parting the opening wide.

Kajika peered into the gloomy darkness, took two short daring steps and then slowly backed out of the tent. "Do I give him these gifts, now?" He whispered.

Frustrated, Nadie sharply replied, "Tell him first the words that I told you to say. When he asks for gifts, come back to me."

Pushed in by her, he stumbled inside with the hide abruptly closing behind him. From the top of the steps, he called into the darkness with a shaking voice. "Na…Na…Nakoma?"

"What is it that you speak?" the leader snapped from below.

"I…I have…g-g-gifts."

"Gifts? Come, speak to me!"

Working his way cautiously to the bottom of the steps, Kajika crossed the floor through the dim light of two skull caps. He waited to adjust to it, opening his eyes wide until seeing Hanovi lying on a fur. Naked after a recent steamy interlude with Nakoma, Honovi's legs were spread wide to cool herself, her large thighs pressed to the floor and seeming wider than they actually were. Her prominent mound, thick with hair, lay so very inviting. He could not stop himself from staring. She sure was beautiful to look at. Any man would want to…

"Kajika! Here! Now! Sit!" Nakoma growled.

Kajika flexed.

"This way!"

"I…I…"

"Sit!"

Quickening his last few steps, the tribe's ochre carrier scrambled for a seat two mammoth heads away from the leader's naked body and froze.

His back to him, Nakoma faced the opposite wall. "Speak!"

"Speak? Uh…yes…speak. I have mm…mm…gifts, many gifts. I…I have mm…many gifts."

"Gifts?" Nakoma appeared indifferent. A pause and then he waved his hand in a circle to speed things along. "Gifts and…"

"Y-Yes, yes, many gifts…gifts to give to…to…to you. I have many gifts."

Drenched in sweat, Kajika dug deep for the right words to say. He took a quick glance at Honovi.

"Many…ah-h-h…gifts…to…to…"

"To?" Nakoma encouraged, still waving and looking at the far wall.

"To…to…"

The leader spun around and leered at him. "Why?"

"Kajika jerked in his seat. "W-w-why?"

"Why do you give gifts to me?"

Mad at himself, Kajika could not control the nervousness or his own heavy breathing. He thought carefully, took hold of his emotions, then finally, and as fast as he could blurt it all out, said, "It is my wish that I own N-N-Nadie."

"Nadie? Your wish is to own Nadie?"

Slunk low on the mammoth head, he braced himself for the leader's next response, meekly voicing his cautious reply, "Y-y-yes. I have…m…many gifts."

"Gifts! Gifts! Then show me your gifts!"

Kajika sprang from the seat and rushed up the steps to the outside.

"He is like a hunting nag boksta."

"Did he say yes?"

"He asked that I bring the gifts to him."

"Then that means yes!" She embraced him, nearly choking him unconscious.

She reached into the basket for a necklace of rat skulls which she looped over his head. "When you give these gifts to Nakoma, tell him that it is you that feels many good to give him these gifts."

Still shaking, Kajika raspily repeated that through the lump in his throat. She laid the wolf and bear furs across his extended arms and put the basket filled with shells, fangs, coyote tail and talons on top of that. These were followed with freshly picked flowers. With everything ready, she held him firmly by the shoulders.

"He **will** say yes."

"He will?"

She leaned back and folded her arms, tilted her head sideways and gave him a long look with raised brows. She followed that with a lengthy sigh, a kind and knowing gaze and finally, smiling eyes. "Yes…he will!"

"He will!" he pointedly repeated, nodding back assuredly.

She pressed her cheek to his, which caused some of the flowers to fall off. "Here…now go!" she said, balancing them carefully on top.

With everything ready, he again felt his way through the dark to the bottom of the steps. Across the floor he gingerly stepped, half way there and he had not lost a thing; on toward the mammoth heads, past the voluptuous Hanovi and her thick, flattened thighs and gloriously matted mound.

"My gifts!" he blurted out loud just as the coyote tail slipped off. He leaned the other way, but could not stop the flowers from falling. He made a valiant try at catching the talons, but that caused the basket of shells to turn over and explode across the floor.

Still holding onto the furs, he looked down helplessly at the gifts lying scattered everywhere. Disappointed in himself, he dejectedly dropped the furs on top of everything else and sighed.

A wide smile on his face, Nakoma turned away to laugh silently in the direction of the far wall. "Leave it! Go! She is yours!"

"Mine? Nadie is mine?"

"Go…go…go!"

Kajika backed away from the leader while nodding excessively. "Ah-h-h…many good. I am many glad to gifts…to give…to gifts you, too."

"Yes! Yes! Go! Wait…and what of those?"

Perplexed, there was nothing else left that Kajika could think of. He checked himself, looked along the floor and felt all around his chest where Nakoma seemed to be looking. "Ah, these!" Removing the rat skulls, he handed them to Nakoma. "I am many glad to gifts to you. Uh, no…gifts give you…"

"Go!"

Having quietly waited on the buffalo skin, Honovi's pulse quickened as she lay back with anticipation.

After a quick stretch, Nakoma pushed out his chest along with an erect manhood, heavy like a mammoth's trunk. "Thunderfoot woman…Aleeka is ready."

CHAPTER 13
OTAKTAY'S TRIBE

Nestled in the foothills of the mountains, Otaktay's tents spread along the shores of a lake. To protect from the occasional floods, the tents were built above ground on platforms supported by posts.

At the center of the village with a frontal view of the lake, stood the tallest and largest of the platforms. At the rear, the typical mammoth head served as a base for Otaktay's throne. Covering the tall and sturdy poles that formed the back of the throne, hung a large bear skin, the head and sneering jaws facing downwards. Above that, a dozen fully mature elk racks were stacked one on top of the other. Overhead, reed mats, supported by a surrounding wall of mammoth tusks, sheltered the throne from sun and rain. At the outer edge of the platform, four posts towered high above the rest. Stacked around each of the poles, from top to bottom, were a variety of animal skulls with few spaces between.

Panting heavily from his great weight, Otaktay made his way to the throne. To his left, four wives waited to serve his every need. To the other crouched Subu, a gelded saber tooth tiger he raised from a cub. Sprawled out and overly fat, the tethered nag boksta never went hungry. Meat of all kinds was thrown into his pit, a deep hole in the ground with a ramp that lowered from overhead ropes. Ravenous at night, Subu especially enjoyed the flesh of humans, his reward for those who slighted the tribe.

"You...come sit with me!" Otaktay ordered.

Newly acquired and the more favored of his wives, Quiet Spring was more than a pretty face. She had a body to match with an easy temperament. Mute since birth, she shyly 'rose to her feet and squatted in front of Otaktay, her head leaning in subjugation.

Her long braid in his hand, Otaktay said, "You have no feelings for me. One day you will carry my child. It is then that you will see me in a different way."

Unique among the big men camps, Otaktay's women originated from different tribes. Unbeknownst to Nakoma and the other tribes in the grasslands, his new wealth had derived from a journey across the high place. After traversing the mountains before the last cold time in search of women, his men found themselves in the hunting grounds of the Dinga, the same tribe that had annihilated the Bandu. Surprised and surrounded, Otaktay's men were captured. During the ensuing interrogation, Man Walking, the leader of the Dinga, realized Otaktay could provide him with what he needed most---meat and skins. Since his lands had become depleted of large game and unwilling to cross the tabooed lands himself, Man Walking made peace with Otaktay for concessions. As part of that settlement, Otaktay agreed to supply him with a steady stock of dried meat from many sources; deer, buffalo and mammoths among others. In exchange, Man Walking gave him obsidian and captured women stolen from his surrounding tribes. To keep Otaktay loyal, the Dinga kept his lead first hunter hostage.

From the last trade, Otaktay acquired Quiet Spring and because of her beauty, kept her for himself. Back then, he was in fine physical condition. Now, after the enrichment of so many trades, he remained in camp and grew fat on the spoils while Hachi and the rest of his men continued the arduous journeys.

At his throne, Otaktay stood up to look at the dark cloud of honking geese that were migrating south from across the grasslands. Alongside, his three other wives pointed at the sky.

"They come!" said one.

None of the women could contain their excitement. Below the platform, the rest of the tribe gathered along the foot of it. Children screamed and laughed at the sight. The amount of geese filling the air seemed unending. The front of the massive flock drifted down and alighted onto the surface of the lake. There, the flocks would feed and replenish themselves for the long journey south. Along with fledged juveniles, the birds soon covered the lake in its entirety and more were still filling the skies from a far off distance.

It was an exciting event for all and one that had been highly anticipated. As the last of the geese settled in, the tribe finished gathering small rocks.

"We are now ready to kill the sisika," Hachi said to Otaktay.

Every available man, woman and child lined up before the platform, anyone who was not either sick or otherwise unable to participate. The last of them finally stepped into the irregular line to await orders from Hachi. After a short briefing, he assigned each one to a place around the lake where they were to wait for a signal from him. Learned from the Dinga, the method proved highly fruitful.

His arms slowly rose up and when he was sure he had everyone's attention, he dropped them down.

"Throw your rocks!"

Like a hail storm, rocks rained down on the geese. Water splashed all around the birds as blows from the rocks killed or stunned a large number of them.

"In the water! Now!" Hachi ordered.

The entire tribe ran in to retrieve the geese, grabbing as many as they could before the birds could recover. Carried back to shore, those that were fitfully flapping their wings were slammed to the ground and piled in with the rest.

Next began the task of removing the feathers. The birds that were not eaten at that night's feast would be smoked over fires to preserve them. Nothing would be wasted. Feathers, bones, and beaks would all be used for decorations, the innards, highly prized and eaten as well.

The feast began with everyone surrounding the fires and engorging themselves. Tearing off a thigh from a second bird, Otaktay stuffed himself along with his four wives.

"Hachi, we have many of the sisika to take to Man Walking. You will soon have more women for yourself."

Otaktay's hardened leader of first hunters rammed the side of his fist into the nearest post. "Man Walking does not have us in his eyes, he does not stand with me."

Otaktay disagreed. "He needs what we bring. He is one that kills his own. He will kill us the same way and take what is ours."

Scoffing, Otaktay gave Hachi new orders. "He fears the long walk to our hunting place. Go with the men and take the sisika to him. He will soon look to you the way I do. When you return with more women, I will give you the first three."

The following morning, Hachi, along with most of the first hunters, burdened themselves with sacks of cooked geese as they made their way up a worn path toward the mountains.

Turning to one of his wives, Otaktay said, "Man Walking gives me a great shona. It will give him much pleasure to see so many of the sisika."

The Dinga camp

Inside the Dinga leader's massive longhouse of timber planks, Man Walking's warriors finished trickling in and sat to one side. In front sat the elders, taking places beneath human skeletons hanging from the rafters, many with braids attached to their skulls. All along the walls hung a variety of game animals. Too hot for a fire, the only smoke inside came from the shaman's herbs---light and lifting in the stench-filled air. Daylight seeped through the cracks in the walls, leaving the interior dim and gloomy.

Man Walking, black from a coating of charcoal mixed with animal fat, paced about naked for war to emphasize what he was about to say.

Scar-drawn animals embellished his skin. On both large toes he wore rings with owl beaks sticking out like claws. White and black eagle feathers were tied at the elbows with their tips pointed toward his wrist. The back of his hands had wolverine claws fastened to them, strapped in tightly with the sharp ends extending beyond the knuckles. Tipped with poison during raids, they were there to rake deep, festering wounds into the enemy's skin, or preferably, to render them blind.

Before the men that were sitting in anticipation, Man Walking anxiously kept pacing in an oblong circle. He finally stopped short and snapped his arm in the direction of the mountains, causing ten thumb sized snake skulls tied to the ends of his shoulder length hair to sway back and forth.

"I have no more wish to give Otaktay any more of our gifts. When his men come with theirs, we will welcome them and give them ours. That will be our time to silently follow their tracks to Otaktay and kill him. It is then that we..."

A troubled elder, standing up before the front row, alarmingly spoke out. "If we kill Otaktay, there will be no one to bring us meat."

"Then, I will make his people our people. Those that do not follow our wishes I will kill and eat their eyes."

The same elder quickly replied. "They walk the sacred high place, the spirits that live there are too strong. Everyone here knows it is a place we do not go."

The rest added to his protest, shaking their heads in agreement.

"Yes...those were once my words," replied Man Walking. These men from Otaktay walk this path and no harm comes to them. We can learn that walk and follow their tracks to their hunting place. Every man that goes with me will own what they find there. Our spirits will protect us."

In a low drone, the men repeated the last thing he said. "Our spirits will protect us."

Another elder stood up. "If you make your fire in the high place, the giant wolves that travel in great numbers will eat you."

Man Walking sharply answered him. "Those wolves do not touch these men from Otaktay. If they do not touch them, they will not touch us. We have more power than these big men. Wait... and when they leave us that will be our time to dress for war. I will say nothing else on this."

The elder, pointing at a human skeleton overhead, said, "If you must go with our men, then bring us Otaktay so that we can all feast."

The men laughed.

The elder continued, "We have the best of Otaktay's first hunters with us. He must be killed or he will run to lead them."

"I have thought on this. I had that first hunter killed as we made our talk."

Man Walking sternly looked back at his warriors. "It is done. Our spirits will protect us."

Low voices answered in unison. "Our spirits will protect us."

Late evening: Nakoma's tents

Women adorned with large snail shell necklaces and anklets made of bone beads danced around a bon fire before Nakoma's tent. Celebrating the acceptance of the two new first hunters and Nadie's marriage to Kajika, a variety of fruit and berries lay on furs. Odors of cooked fish and meat of many varieties filled the camp. Swaying hips and sexy grinding by the women, enticed many of the grinning husbands to grab their mates and lead them away for quiet interludes.

To add to the rattle shaking, Moki joined Nakoma and Okhmhaka where he commenced to bang on a hollowed out log. Along with them, the lively tones of Lan's flute were welcomed by all. It turned heads, especially from the children that circled around to listen.

The joy, however, was not shared by everyone there. A new worry kept Kuruk at the rear of the firelight.

Sewati is where I found him, in the trunk trail. It is as Akando said. I saw the dead nag boksta there, myself. It was before that when little Okhmhaka saw Sewati alive with his wound so I know their words are true words.

It is the words of my runner that I must now say to our Mowatchi and it weakens me where I stand. For now, our talk will have to wait. When he makes his fire...that will be my time.

Before long, the celebration ended. Fires soon lit the front of every tent as tribal members quietly rested from the excitement of the day.

Approaching Lan, Kuruk said, "It is my need to speak to you that I come to your fire." Motioning for him to follow, Kuruk turned his back to him and left for the river. Alone, with the sound of ripples lapping the shore, he clasped his hands together and stared at the moon's reflection in the shimmering river's flow---waited for Lan's footsteps to grow silent behind him.

"Word comes from the people of Otaktay. They look to the high place, a place where our young ones become men. It is the place we stand to find our spirits and now others like you have found us."

Surprised by what he just heard, Lan remained silent, keen on learning more.

"Otaktay trades gifts with the one he calls Man Walking."

At this, Lan was taken aback. Fear gripped him, but the fear was not for him. The last thing he wanted was to bring warring tribes to these bands.

Kuruk continued. "Many of the Mowatchi women are now owned by Otaktay. Some are from your people and call themselves Bandu."

Lan fumed, "If it is in this Otaktay's head that he should own my people, then it is in mine that I must kill him."

"And I," said Kuruk. "You are a first hunter with a great shona. For this we will follow you as you have followed us."

"Then it is done. We all go to Otaktay."

"It is done," said Kuruk.

Both men gripped one another's shoulders to lock in the bonding agreement. As first hunters an obligation had been formed. Lan's new status ensured the loyalty of every first hunter in the tribe.

Kuruk immediately formulated a plan. "We will tell Otaktay we want to trade. He will welcome this and when they drink their dream drink that is when you will kill the nag boksta he calls Subu with your many arrows. I will go with Yahto and kill Otaktay and Hachi. Hakan (fire) must also be killed. You will then have your people. The rest will follow you."

Lan searched Kuruk's face for hidden meanings, but saw nothing but sincerity. "It is then that I will protect you from all those that come from the high place."

Kuruk's jaw tightened. *Yes…that is what I see in my eyes, Mowatchi. You will soon be the one that Otaktay's people will follow as well as the one that sees our enemies before Nakoma's people will.*

At first light, Yahto, eager for excitement, joined the waiting men. He had made a pact with Lan and was determined to keep it, despite the fact that this was not his tribe and he held no obligation if he decided to leave.

"My wish is to go," Akando said to Lan.

"Stay here, Nakoma needs you."

"You gave me the power of the twoniff. Now we are first hunters. We did this together. The way I stood with you to find Ayashe, that is the way I will stand with you now."

Nakoma reluctantly nodded. "It is no longer in my hands. He is a first hunter. He makes his own choice."

"Then, it is finished, my two knife brother," said Lan. "Go with the rest."

Filing behind Kuruk was Yahto and his two men, Sahkyo and Tohopka. Behind them, Takoda, Qalatega and a dozen others waited for Akando and Lan to join them. Akando took his place at the back of the line while Lan took his alongside Kuruk.

"Go with the spirits," Nakoma shouted.

Jogging off, the men recited a war chant.

Tears ran down Ayashe's cheeks. She cried out to Okhmhaka. "He goes and leaves me."

Along with her, Quanah cried, so she lifted the boy up to comfort him.

Slighted, Okhmhaka had hoped he would have been picked to go as well. Although far from a first hunter, his shona remained strong. "I will go with Rama. No one will see me leave if they sleep."

"Then l will go with you," said Ayashe.

"And me," said Quanah, an eager look on his face.

"Can Rama carry us all?" Ayashe asked.

"Rama is many times too strong."

"Then let us go to Rama and fix him for the long walk."

It excited the three to ready the mammoth for the journey to Otaktay's tents. Having been there before, Okhmhaka knew the way.

Two wide straps were thrown over the animals back to hold down the layers of buffalo furs for sitting on. Secured to the top rear strap was tied baskets of food. Ayashe adorned the front one with bright yellow puccoons strung over the sides like large buttercups. It encouraged Okhmhaka to add decorations of his own. He drew wide circles around Rama's eyes with brilliant red-orange ochre. Quanah stole duck feathers from one of the tents which Ayashe secured to the tail.

It was still dark the following morning when Ayashe arrived with Quanah sleeping in her arms. Okhmhaka already had Rama untied and was impatient to leave. The sun barely broke the horizon when they left the village, leaving the tribe in slumber.

The human sacrifice

Along the ground below the front of Otaktay's platform, the entire tribe spread themselves before him, both curious and guarded as to the reason for the council.

"Come sit by me," Otaktay said to Quiet Spring, reaching over to pet Subu lightly on the head.

The saber tooth wrinkled the top of its nose and licked the air. As always, Quiet Spring took her place, sitting subserviently on the other side of him.

Otaktay's demeanor instantly changed. "Hakan gives me words I have no wish to hear. He speaks of you that you sleep with Uluma.

Quiet Spring's head jerked upwards. Realizing her love for Uluma had been exposed, she tried to back away, but Otaktay quickly grabbed her by the braid. He then stood and looked for Hakan among the crowd. "Bring Uluma to me."

Hakan, Hachi's temporary replacement, along with another man, seized the rebuffing lover by the arms and half carried, half dragged him to the top of the platform.

"Are these words, true words?" Otaktay barked.

Pushing his chest out, Uluma attempted to look brave and defiant. Inside, he feared for his life. "Let me take Quiet Spring to the high place. It is there that we will stay and never return."

"She is not yours to take. You did not give me gifts for her. We made no talk on this. Is it in your head that you can take what is mine?"

"I...I have no words..."

"Enough of this! Take them both to the pit and tie them there."

Looping a noose over Quiet Spring's head, Hakan lifted her off her feet and dragged her towards Subu's pit. Along with them, the tribe's shaman followed behind, shaking a human skull rattle and covered from head to foot with a full garment of straw. As he swayed from side to side, he mumbled chants to death spirits. In place of eyes, large red gourds, cut to the shape of wide glaring eyes, covered half of his face like an overgrown fly. Along with the rattling, it frightened the children that ran away at the sight him.

To lower the ramp, Hakan gave the waiting men that stood there a signal. After untying two ropes from a pole, the heavy ramp dropped suddenly. It slammed to the bottom where pieces of scattered bones and dust shot outwardly from the sides.

In the same way as Quiet Spring, the men dragged Uluma into the pit, stripped and left him tied to a huge log lying on the ground. With no further attention, they were both left to await their fate with Subu.

Collecting around the top edge of the pit, tribal members glared while pushing and shoving one another for the best positions. Women held onto their children lest they fall inside. Even Otaktay would be unable to stop Subu's eating frenzy once it started.

Drumbeats

"Bring Subu," a woman shouted.

"It is time," a child called out.

His dream drink finished, Otaktay set the vessel down and loosened the rope securing Subu to a post. None of his wives walked on the same side as the saber tooth. Only Otaktay had command of the oversized beast and by this time of day the big cat had become agitated with the long wait. Led to the ramp, the impatient Subu alternately marched its front paws in place, lifted his head high and sniffed the air.

Otaktay slipped the rope from around the predator's neck. Wooden planks creaked under the weight of Subu as he carefully paced himself to the bottom of the pit. There it circled a much anticipated meal, sniffing at the new odors mixed in with the old—air that reeked with the stench of bowel waste; the waste of digested humans.

Stepping back from the rising ramp, Otaktay shouted. "Let it begin!"

Along the edge, eager, smiling faces leaned forward.

Subu roared

Children gasped. Some of the mothers hid their eyes, but most did not bother.

The nag boksta inside its pit below jumped on top of the thick log and roared again.

Uluma screamed, lifting his head to see the roaring beast standing where his feet were tied. If she could, Quiet Spring would have screamed along with him. Instead, all that came out was hoarse breath.

The saber tooth ripped into Uluma's body with its long fangs as though an entire pride was there fighting it for the meat. The man's wretched screams were exceedingly loud, even heartfelt for some of those watching. Others laughed nervously. There were no silent moments between Uluma's screams as his bowels and urine released and flowed yellow down the sides of the log.

The torture Quiet Spring's lover was suffering left many of those watching cringing in horror. Others stayed to the end, laughing and raising arms to point and make gruesome comments.

"He will eat inside the chest next," said a first hunter.

"The other leg will be next," the man next to him said. "If that is what he does, you must give me your ax."

"If he eats the chest first, it will be your ax that you will give to me," the first replied.

Otaktay laughed. "Do you see my woman in your eyes, now… Uluma?"

Subu quickly devoured the rest of the soft innards of Uluma's stomach cavity, finally killing the unconscious first hunter when his jaws snapped the spine in two. The entire log shook as the body was torn free of its bindings. The saber tooth clawed the corpse until it fell to the ground and where it ripped into the muscular buttocks. It did not take long before there was nothing left but a head and bones scattered along the ground.

"Finish the woman," someone called out.

Her chest, lifting and falling, Quiet Spring raised her head and forced out what sounded more like a choke than a scream. Uluma's death terrified her and now it was time for her to die the same way.

Subu slowly turned to face her and roared.

Proud of his nag boksta, Otaktay looked away from the pit to address his three remaining wives. "There is no other man here that will take any of you from me again.

From the platform the following morning, Otaktay waited with Hakan for their runner to reach them.

"Why does he return so fast?"

"He has something of worry," said Hakan.

Upon getting there and gasping to catch his breath, the runner relayed what he had seen. "A Mowatchi is with them. Nakoma's men are many."

"Mowatchi? Nakoma's men? Why do they come? Is that man not Dinga?"

"What he wears is from the high place and also that of Nakoma's men. He is a first hunter."

"A first hunter?" Looking puzzled, Otaktay sat with Hakan to wait from the platform. The rest of the men soon lined up before the trail.

The chant, very different from the one Nakoma's men used when they first left the tents was a deceitful chant of welcome and friendship. Despite that, the Mowatchi that Otaktay and Hakan saw with them left them both curious and guarded at the same time.

"Why do they come when most of our men are not back from their long walk?" Otaktay worried.

"I sent another runner to the high place to find Hachi," Hakan said. "He and his men will soon be here." He then stepped to the edge of the platform. "Stand front! First hunters...stand front!"

Otaktay turned from him and ordered the ramp to Subu's pit to be lowered into position. He then stepped heavily onto the wooden planks where halfway down an astonishing surprise awaited him.

"Subu did not finish you?"

Still lying helplessly tied to the log, Quiet Spring had endured the entire night waiting her fate.

"When these men leave, my Subu will return. He will then finish you and you will be no more."

Bloated and lazily sprawled out, the saber tooth tiger turned away in a futile attempt to keep Otaktay's rope from looping over its head. Having been disturbed from a deep sleep, Subu lethargically followed the tribe's leader up the series of ramps to the main platform. There, Otaktay waited, wheezing out of breath. Beside him, the saber tooth tiger sat up lazily to one side with a keen interest for the sight of approaching men. Entering between outlying posts, the file of men spread themselves before Otaktay's platform with Kuruk and Lan stepping forward.

Captured women from the Bandu tribe covered their mouths in surprise. None dared speak, lest they dangerously expose Lan, biding their time instead to save Quiet Spring. Ignorant of Lan's success and whether or not he was a captive himself, they remained silent. For his own reasons, Lan did likewise and without a hint of recognition.

Kuruk raised his hand up high and was the first to speak. "Shatu duma!"

Otaktay stepped to the front of the platform to greet Kuruk as he and the Mowatchi approached from below. "Shatu duma, Kuruk. It is always good for me to see so great a leader of first hunters."

"And I, to see the strength of your great power, Otaktay."

"Why do you come, now, when there are so many of the tatanka to hunt?" Otaktay asked.

"It is I, Kuruk and the words of Nakoma that ask that we trade with you for the black rocks."

Otaktay laughed. "So...the power I have with the Dinga has reached you."

"Your shona is a great one, Otaktay. You own Subu and now the way to the Mowatchi."

"And many women," Otaktay followed with another laugh. "Who is this Mowatchi?"

"He is Lan. We gave him the power of first hunter."

"First hunter? No one will fear him!"

Laughter from Otaktay's men followed.

"You laugh at what your eyes do not see. His spirits are strong. In his vision, the great Aleeka asked that he would own him...and his woman is from Mantotohpa."

Eying Kuruk with suspicion, Otaktay sharply snapped back. "Is he Dinga?"

"No...he walked alone and now walks with us."

In deep thought and seeing that the Mowatchi had no braid, unlike his recently captured women, Otaktay nodded subtly. After a long silence, he asked, "Are any of my women from his people?"

Searching for an answer Otaktay would accept, Kuruk said, "he knows no one here."

At that moment, the runner sent to Hachi was returning and racing down the hill toward them. Reaching the platform, he spoke loud and fast. "They come with more women and many of the black rocks. They bring skins…many taken from the bodies of men."

"When will they reach us?" said Otaktay.

"They come now."

"Then let us have dream drink!"

A special event, each journey to the Dinga camp brought new wealth to Otaktay. The return of the hunters excited everyone in the tribe. New faces would be welcomed and to some of the women standing there, familiar ones bonded from a shared past.

Loud drumming

Single file, the returning men dropped their loads of skins. Four women, pushed by Hachi to the top of the platform, lined up in front of Otaktay. The lead first hunter untied their hands, leaving them shaking and dripping with sweat before the leader. Next, he ripped the sinew from each of their skirts and yanked them off one at time, leaving them naked and trembling.

Lan tightened his grip around his spear and spit on the ground. *Wadu! These women are not mine.*

"The three you will take, which ones will they be?" Otaktay asked.

"Hachi pushed a pregnant woman forward of the remaining three. "This one is yours."

"Yi yi…caw caw caw…eee yi yi…caw caw!"

Everyone there turned heads toward the hills and to the heavily wooded forest where a mass of screaming voices and war whoops called out to one another. Every man, woman and child stood in fear as they all looked towards the madness unfolding in the hills just out of sight.

Beyond the hill before them and deep within the trees, stunned Dinga warriors fought for their lives. Unawares to them, while secretly following Hachi and his men, they in turn were being followed by the more numerous and hostile Wadu.

Hidden from view, Dinga warriors died in large numbers, their eyes plucked out and eaten where they fell. Bodies were beheaded and skulls lifted on spears. Wadu warriors rejoiced even before the carnage ended, the straggling enemies chased down and captured for a coming feast.

Running from the slaughter was Man Walking and two of his closest warriors. Clubbed from behind, the two warrior's cries were ignored by the Dinga leader as he outran them all. All too soon, he lost the trail in the unfamiliar terrain. He ran up steep embankments, across streambeds and overgrown thickets heavy with thorns. He paused to recover, looked back and felt relieved to see that no one had followed him. Furious at the loss of his men, he pressed on to leave as much ground between him and the Wadu as he could. He continued running until he stumbled and fell down a steep slope from a maze of roots crisscrossing the ground. Exhausted and out of breath, he got onto his hands and knees while choking for air. Breathing in deeply, his eyes widened with terror at what he saw next. Two pairs of black feet, the toes armed with bear claws, stood before him. Shaking, he slowly followed the legs, black with charcoal, upward toward two grinning faces. Both Wadu warriors quietly blinked back, their eyes encircled with white ashes. Finger bones hung from their necks, the skin on their chest and stomachs, covered by scar drawn animals.

In an instant, everything in front of Man Walking flashed brilliantly white. It then vanished into nothing as the strike of an ax finished separating his skull nearly in half.

Sharing the Dinga leader's plucked eye balls, the warriors sawed off Man Walking's head, ran a spear through the ears to keep it all together in one piece and raced out of the forest to show off their prize.

Amidst the celebrating calls from the victorious Wadu going on behind him, Wolf Spirit, the tribe's leader, looked to the new threat from below. His face, scarred from battle, his lip and nose torn, the Wadu chief relaxed with a pleased grin. His fingers ran lazily across two rings of tightly packed finger bones as he assessed the value of attacking the camp. Hanging off the side of his hip, a string of five more fingers waited to be boiled and the bones added to the rest.

With nearly as many, Standing Tall, his second in command, approached him from the hills. "They finished Man Walking. They now bring his head."

"That is good. It is long that we follow him and the women he stole from us."

Pointing his spear at Otaktay's camp, Wolf Spirit stated. "I stand here and see many of the big men at the bottom of this hill. They stand and look at us where we stand and look at them."

Standing Tall grinned. "We have the strength to finish them like we did the Dinga."

"Yes…that would be easy. They do not have many. Bring ten of our men. My wish is to sign to them first. If they give us enough gifts we can leave that for another time. My men need their rest and the way back is the walk of many suns. Besides, I see nothing else here other than our women that I want."

Standing Tall's face wrinkled into a sneer. "It is as you say and one of them carries my child."

From the platform below, Otaktay looked away from the hills and the small group of Mowatchi men that were walking towards him. He shouted to Hachi. "They come to make their talk. "You and Hakan go with me.

Kuruk called out to Otaktay. "Lan knows their words."

"Then send him."

Behind Otaktay, eight women from the Wadu tribe, including the recent captives, pushed to the front, some with babies in their arms.

"Hide them with the others," said Otaktay. "They must not be seen."

He returned Subu to the pit and ordered the ramp raised, locking the saber tooth tiger in with Quiet Spring. The four then made their way up the hill to meet the small party halfway between the line of trees and Otaktay's village behind them.

On both sides of Wolf Spirit, the few men he had with him said nothing. Instead, they appraised the strength and boldness of the group that were assertively approaching them.

His finger pointing at Lan, Wolf Spirit said, "You are not one of these men."

"I am Man That Runs Too Fast. My People are Bandu. Some were taken by this man who calls himself Otaktay."

Wolf Spirit motioned for the warrior holding the Dinga leader's head on a pole to raise it higher. "Before the cold time, words were spoken that your tribe was finished. I now have Man Walking's head and they have no leader."

"He had many that followed him," said Lan. "It was then that my need was to find a new hunting place and now I am here. Otaktay is the one that leads these people."

Hearing his name mentioned twice and still huffing from the climb, Otaktay shouted at him. "This Mowatchi does not have many with him. Tell him he must now leave and never return."

What Otaktay just said worried Lan. Otaktay was outrageously underestimating the Wadu's strength and it would put all of them in danger.

Many of the Wadu are still with the trees. Otaktay does not know this or the great power of the Wadu.

"Why do you wait?" Otaktay barked.

"I cannot tell him your words. He has many that follow and wait for him."

"Tell him!" Otaktay insisted.

For Lan, a sudden realization came to mind that he knew could lead to an answer to everything.

This Otaktay will soon find his death from his own words. I will say no more to him. There will soon be something here for me.

Lan casually turned to Wolf Spirit. "It is Otaktay's wish that you take what you will of the Dinga and not return."

Wolf Spirit stared hard at Otaktay. "Tell this man we can take what is his as well. Does he not know how many of my men stand with the trees behind me?"

As soon as Lan repeated that, Otaktay lost control. He waved for the rest of his men to join him on the hill and then stepped back and pulled out his ax. In a loud, authoritive voice, he shouted, "All that you see here is mine. I will hear no more…"

Before Otaktay could finish the sentence, three axes brought Hachi to the ground. At the same time, Hakan, who jumped in front of Otaktay, was axed as well, crushing his skull. Otaktay, despite a spear rammed into his side, shouted out loud in a harrowing call while defiantly swinging his ax.

Surrounded and held down by Wadu warriors, he was silenced by Standing Tall's spear to the heart. The Wadu tribe's second in command quickly separated Otaktay's head from his body. He rammed a spear underneath it and raised the skull high for Otaktay's men to see, eyeless, as Standing Tall finished chewing on one. The other was enjoyed by Wolf Spirit. He swallowed the warm liquid that oozed from inside the well chewed eyeball followed by the rest while looking back and nodding with a wide grin.

"His life spirit is no more. Without eyes to see, he can no longer fight us."

From where he stood boastful and full of life merely moments ago, Otaktay's head hung from a pole in little more than the time it would have taken for a man to take ten breaths.

"Grab this one," Standing Tall ordered.

Lan's spear and ax were taken from him.

"If you live with them, then you must die like them."

By this time the rest of Otaktay's men had climbed halfway up the hill where they stopped short. Emerging from the surrounding hills, the entire band of Wadu came running in response. The huge mass of men stood shoulder to shoulder for as far as the eye could see. Many held the heads of their kills which startled Otaktay's men into slowly backing away.

Yahto and Kuruk formed a defense line in front of the platform. They were joined by the rest of Otaktay's men, ready to defend their lives and those of the women and children.

Standing Tall welcomed the coming conflict. "Kill this Bandu!" He screamed.

Wolf Spirit waved for his men to remain where they were. "His words only speak for these people. The Bandu never took from us."

Suddenly, Wolf Spirit looked away from him. Below, on the same outlying trail where Nakoma's men had first arrived from, something huge was approaching the village. Along with him, everyone on the hill looked down with curiosity.

"There is a large animal there...what is that?" Wolf Spirit asked Lan.

Those in Otaktay's camp were not as startled. All of them had seen mammoths before. The only surprise was that the mammoth was there and not out on the grassland with its herd and that there were three people sitting on top and seemingly in command of it.

"What animal is that?" Wolf Spirit repeated.

"It is the long tooth," said Lan. And the one that sits there is my Ayashe."

"Look!" shouted Standing Tall. "She wears a finger bone, a sign she is one of ours."

With no fear of being attacked by so few, Wolf Spirit and Standing Tall, along with the ten tribesmen, went down to question Ayashe. Lan followed behind.

Upon nearing the mammoth and impressed by its great size, Wolf Spirit carefully approached, looked up at Ayashe and sharply asked, "Why do you wear the sign of the Wadu?"

"I blong Alawa," she answered.

"Who is this Alawa?"

Lan said, "She is Alawa's little one. Alawa belongs to your leader, Fire Walker."

Taken aback, Wolf Spirit faced him with a questioning look. "Fire Walker?"

Standing Tall appeared just as incredulous.

Lan pointed toward the west. "Alawa was taken from Fire Walker's hunting place by the big men to a place far that way. It is the new place Alawa now calls hers."

Annoyed, Standing Tall said, "Why does she not speak for herself."

"She knows little of our words."

"Come...come to me," said Wolf Spirit.

Sliding off of Rama, Ayashe nervously approached the Wadu leader.

So this is the great Wadu my Alawa belonged to and now they are here in my eyes. For too long, this is what I waited for.

Reaching out for her necklace, Wolf Spirit examined it thoroughly. The finger bone appeared properly aged. "Fire Walker is in the sky. His strength still lives with us. He was one of our great ones," Admiring Ayashe's beauty, he said, "I see Fire Walker in the lines of your face. You are one of us, but you are also one of them."

After some thought, he motioned for Standing Tall to follow him to where they would not be heard. "Let us leave them. It is not my wish to dishonor Fire Walker."

The solemn look on Wolf Spirit's face also spoke for Standing Tall as well. "No...that cannot be done. Fire Walker still lives here in my chest."

"I still may have a need for these people..." Wolf Spirit said to him, "...trade."

Returning to Ayashe's side, he asked, "Who is it that you now follow?"

"Lan! Hms Bandu pee poh, my pee poh."

"Then...who will lead?"

Lan stepped forward. "I will. Many of the women here are Bandu. There are others that stand with you." He turned and waved for the Wadu women to come forward, shouting with words Otaktay's men would understand, "Let their women come to the front."

"EEEE, ai, ai, ai!" shouted the Wadu women as soon as they were freed to run to their leader's side.

Overjoyed, it quelled for the moment any lingering hostility left in Wolf Spirit as well as Standing Tall. His attention back on Lan, the Wadu Chief remained quiet as he looked deep into Lan's eyes for the slightest sign of weakness. Instead, he saw the same returning, studying gaze and assuredness that could only have been honed through confident leadership. He leaned over Otaktay's headless body and picked up his ax. Holding it out to Lan with both hands, he calmly and in a low voice, said, "That is good. It will be you who will lead. I cannot lead in two places with so much distance between them."

Lan took the ax from him, emotionless and silent.

"My time will be for the Dinga," Wolf Spirit continued. "I now own those people. We sleep in the hills and in the early light we will leave this place. There will be another time that will come when you and I will have our talk."

"What of my people that live with the Dinga?" Lan asked.

"I will send them to you with many of the young ones. We cannot hunt for so many."

With peace made between the tribes, the Wadu prepared to eat well. Geese would soon fill the bellies of many, while Dinga flesh, roasting on open fires would fill the rest.

On Lan's return from the hill, Bandu women, their braids swinging behind, immediately ran up to him. In the excitement, their shrieks at first were not understood.

"Come quick!"

"The two knife, hurry!"

"Quiet spring…she is with the two knife!"

They grabbed Lan by the wrist and pulled him along with them to the top of Subu's pit. Still laying on its side, bloated and spread out, Subu drowsily raised his head up. Uninterested in all that was going on at the top of the pit, he lay back down.

Seeing her tribe's leader looking down from the top of the pit, Quiet Spring slowly returned a recognizing nod. Filled with emotion and renewed hope, she remained frozen less she startle the saber tooth.

A thick arrow, pulled from the quiver was notched into the bow. Lan quickly aimed for the animal's juggler vein. No longer lethargic, Subu jumped up and twisted from the stabbing pain in its neck. Another arrow followed and then another. It took a total of six to silence the beast, to which Kuruk and the rest shouted admiration.

"He is one of our first hunters," said a proud Kuruk to Otaktay's men."

Yahto, just as proud, added, "His shona is a great one. He is one with Aleeka."

"He killed a nag boksta with only his spear and now look how quickly he killed this one," said Akando.

The ramp lowered. Lan, Akando and Yahto ran down to Quiet Spring's side. Untying her, Lan lifted her off the log and cradled her in his arms. Delicate in demeanor, she immediately embraced him with love in her eyes.

Carrying her up the ramp, Lan left the awful smell behind. "She is from my people. Look how much she has grown. It is good for me to look at you Quiet Spring. These are now our people and where we will stay."

Quiet Spring tightened her embrace, sighed deeply and gently smiled at everyone there.

"My wish is to follow you," said Yahto to Lan, his focus on Quiet Spring who was shyly returning his smile. "I will follow you like I followed Mantotohpa if your wish is the same."

A slight grin on his face, the tribe's new leader replied, "It is done. My first words to you as a Bandu are for you to take Quiet Spring to the water and rest there with her."

Without hesitation, the huge man eagerly took the girl into his arms and left for the shore of the lake. There, he made a fire with a cooked goose warming in the flames.

Lan laughed inside at what he knew would come next.

Akando chose his words carefully. "It is my wish to stay as a Bandu. We are twoniff brothers. It cannot be any other way."

"Yes, I need my two knife brother here with me. How else will I find my Ayashe the next time she loses her finger bone?"

At a bon fire on the bank, while sharing dream drink, Nakoma's men became reacquainted with Otaktay's. Staying up late and with a hope for a good future, the men that once followed Otaktay, now embraced the new leadership.

Awakening with the sunrise, Ayashe and Quanah climbed the platform to be with Lan. With the Wadu long gone as well as Kuruk and his men, there was much that was needed to be done, like the pit that would have to be filled in.

Ohkmhaka had left with Kuruk during the night; proudly wearing the saber tooth fang and riding Rama with a promise to one day join the Bandu tribe. Kuruk sat behind him, thrilled at the new and enjoyable experience of the ride.

Qaletaga decided he also wanted to join the Bandu tribe. He left with the assurance that he could return with his wife and two daughters as well as Etu's family that he had promised to take care of. All that would remain from Nakoma was the return of the two Bandu skulls and Qaletaga would see to that. The skulls would then be mounted on posts above the main platform.

Before the throne, Lan faced the lake along with Ayashe and Quanah at his side. All that once belonged to Otaktay was now his. Behind them and above the throne, the bear skin had been removed. As a gift to their new leader, Otaktay's men stayed up half the night skinning the saber tooth and drying the hide. It hung in the bear's place, the fangs left intact and the head leaning downward. The claws were fastened to a flat piece of bone and made into a necklace so that it would lay with the dagger like points resting against Lan's chest.

Ayashe patted the back of his head. "Your hair is growing and will one day be as long as mine."

Odors of smoked geese still filled the air. Out front, the lake's waters lay still and mistful. Beyond it, beneath a blue and unhampered sky, laid the endless grassland. Behind the village were the foothills that led to mountain peaks that soared through the clouds.

Lan picked up Quanah and wrapped his arm around Ayashe. She was holding the end of her braid to her breast while toying with the feather at the end.

"So, now, everyone here is Bandu," she said, still looking at the feather.

"Yes, we are all Bandu and this is ours. Soon, the cold time will come. It is then that we will leave for the place that belonged to Matwua until the cold time passes."

At the far end of the platform a raven and its mate alighted on two posts. The male spread its wings, stretched its neck and screeched at the new sun.

Pronghorn Plateau, Wyoming
Paleoanthropological dig site

Fumbling with the fossil finger bone between two of her own, Dr. Anderson interrupted the long silence. "I wonder if they had children."

"They may have been the ones who buried them here," said Singh.

"How many would you guess they had?" she asked.

Chuckling, Halstrom, said "With a body like she must have had, he probably chased her every chance he got."

"No, seriously, take a guess."

"Don't forget, primitive societies have a high infant mortality rate," he said.

Barbara pouted. "You're no fun. Well, my guess is that they had...oh-h...ten, maybe?"

"Ten? Why ten?"

"Survival, more children would have insured a more stable population. Throw in disease and predators into the mix and you would need the extra births to sustain that number."

"That's exactly right," said Halstrom. "We see that in the current primitive tribes of today, like the Toulambis of Papua New Guinea or the Tupiniquim and Carijo tribes of the Amazon."

Singh said, "It amazes me that we still have people living in the Stone Age in our present time. In some ways, I really envy them."

Halstrom's hands folded together, his long look at the two skeletons lying side by side, heartwarming. "Geneticists have already proven that there are Neanderthal genes in the European and Asian populations to this day."

"Why do I feel relieved?" said Singh, with a laugh in his voice.

"There's Asian and European blood in your Pakastani genes, too, Singh. So don't feel so relieved."

Doctor Petak Singh sighed. "Yes, your right, I momentarily forgot about that. Too bad they weren't from Denisovan. I would have preferred to be a lot taller."

Dr. Halstrom looked back from staring at the two skeletons. "I'm sending these two off to the museum in New York only because I have to satisfy our biggest sponsors. When they're done with poking holes in the bones and presenting them to the scientific world, I want them back. I plan to approach every political influence I have available to me in the state government, here in

Wyoming. I'm going to do my very best to have these two wonderful specimens displayed together at the nearby Center in Thermopolis outside of Casper. I was thinking somewhere on grounds with their own memorial.

"I don't believe they will let you do that, Doctor Halstrom."

"Why not, Singh? Once castes of the bones are made, the museum could return the originals."

"Still...I don't think..."

"I believe he's right," said Barbara. Once the skeletons are in their hands, you'll never get them back."

"Not if I get it in writing first. Otherwise, we won't release them...pretty simple, right? If not we can always play the Sacred Indian burial card."

"I don't understand, Doctor," said Singh.

"The N...A...G...P...R...A!"

Petak eyed Dr. Halstrom questioningly. "The Native American... um...Great...eh...Gathering...Geromino, I give up, what?"

Barbara Anderson interrupted. "The Native American Graves Protection and Repatriation Act. It protects American Indian burial sites from destruction."

"I don't get it," said Doctor Petak. We already did that."

"You mean by digging them up? Yes, we did, but we had permission for that from the private ranch owner. It's the bodies themselves that we're talking about. We're right next door to the Wind River Reservation. They could claim burial rights to the bodies. If New York gives us a problem, all we have to do is hold a little meeting and leave it up to the Arapaho and Shoshone to settle it. I'm sure they'll see it our way even if we have to build the memorial on the reservation.

This will be a gift to the people of Wyoming and the world. May they rest in peace, together and forever.

The End

APPENDIX

Characters
(In order of importance)

Oregon Coast

<u>Bandu Tribe</u>

Man That Runs Too Fast (Lan)	Tribe Leader
Sleeps by the Fire	Shaman
Quiet Spring	Deaf Mute

<u>Dinga Tribe</u>

Man Walking	Tribe Leader

<u>Manama Tribe</u>

Sharp Knife	Tribe Leader

Wadu Tribe

Wolf Spirit	Tribe Leader
Standing Tall	War Lord
Fire Walker	Revered Warrior

Wyoming
(All names below are authentically Native American)

Nakoma's Tribe

Nakoma (brave warrior)	Tribe leader
Kuruk (bear) Pawnee	Lead First Hunter
Sewati (curved bear claw) Miwok	First Hunter
Qaletaga (guardian of the people) Hopi	First Hunter
Achak (spirit) Algonquian	First Hunter
Matwua (enemy) Algonquian	Banished hunter
Akando (ambush)	Achak's son
Kajika (walks without sound)	Ochre Carrier
Ohcumgache (little wolf) Cheyenne	Old shaman
Nayati (he who wrestles)	Second Hunter
Ahmik (beaver)	Nayati's wife
Moki (deer) Hopi	Third Hunter
Ohkmhaka (same as Ohcumgache)	Nakoma's son
Honovi (strong deer) Hopi	Nakoma's wife
Nadie (wise) Algonquian	Nakoma's wife
Una (remember) Hopi	Akando's mother
Wachiwi (dancing girl) Sioux	Qaletega's wife
Taima (thunder)	Qaletega's Daughter

Mantotohpa's Tribe

Mantotohpa (four bears) Cheyenne	Tribe Leader
Yahto (blue) Sioux	Lead First Hunter
Ayashe (little one) Chippewa	Akule's daughter
Akule (looks Up)	Ayashe's Father
Alawa (pea) Algonquian	Ayashe's Mother
Quanah (fragrant) Comanche	Orphaned boy
Waquini (hook nose) Cheyenne	Quanah's friend
Odakotah (friendship) Sioux	First Hunter
Pannoowau (he lies) Algonquian	First Hunter

Otaktay's Tribe

Otaktay (kills many) Sioux	Tribe Leader
Hachi (stream) Seminole	Lead First Hunter
Hakan (fire)	First Hunter

WYOMING PALEO INDIAN GLOSSARY
(Mostly fabrication)

Ba Ba (fish)
Ba ba bo bo (frog-fish jumper)
Bawna (Spear)
Bo Bo (rabbit-jumper)
Bock tu (squirrel-tree runner)
Bondo gah (elk, deer)
Chtuktok (mammoth-thunderfoot)
Jonga (coyote)
Keya (turtle)
Ki (no)
Kitchka (eagle)
Matay (afraid)
Mowatchi (man from the high place)
Nag Boksta (saber tooth tiger)
Nahgo (wolf)
Rigbishka (many leg-insects)

Saban (nightfall-dark time)
Shatu duma (welcome)
Shona (high achievement
Shotzus (poisonous ants)
Sisika (bird-sky jumper)
Taka or tok (yes)
Tatanka (buffalo)
Wankan Tanka (great spirit)

Printed in Great Britain
by Amazon